MAKE THE DARK NIGHT SHINE

Koge,
Not knowing is
most intimate.

Dimitri · [illegible]

[illegible]

[illegible]

MAKE THE DARK NIGHT SHINE

A ZEN NOVEL BY

ALAN LESSIK

REBEL SATORI PRESS
New Orleans & New York

Published in the United States of America by
Rebel Satori Press
www.rebelsatoripress.com

Book design: Sven Davisson

Paperback ISBN: 978-1-60864-286-1

Library of Congress Control Number: 2023945002

To Nina:
Your love and activism
reside deep in my bones

Dizang asked Fayan, "Where are you going?"
Fayan said, "Around on a Pilgrimage."
Dizang asked, "What is the purpose of the pilgrimage?"
Fayan replied, "I don't know."
Dizang said, "Not-knowing is most-intimate."

—A Zen Kōan, from the ancient Chinese
Book of Serenity, Case 20

1. WHEN YOU RETURN TO WHERE YOU ARE, IT WILL BE CLEAR

Another long night begins, and again my thoughts turn to you, my daughter, my dear Nina. Not that you know I am here and with little likelihood that you know much about me. While unknowingness has stopped me before, I am compelled by urgency to share my story before it disappears into the plumes of smoke enveloping London. For that reason, I have decided to write what I can remember, what I imagine remembering and what sometimes I would have liked to remember.

Five nights ago, as the German bombs pummeled this block, I thought it might be my last night on earth. The adjacent building, in which I used to glimpse families through the bars of my window, was destroyed in an explosion preceded by the high-pitched squeal of a bomb descending, our only warning of impending destruction. My walls shook from the impact as plaster and dust fell everywhere. With the flames rising next door, I was still locked in my room. My guards were gone for the evening; I had no possible escape. Fortunately for me, the fire burned itself out rather than spreading. In time, the cries and noise of blazing timbers and collapsing walls subsided.

Given what I have just experienced, my life most likely will end far from my home, if I still believe in such a notion as home. The details are unclear, yet with utter certainty I acknowledge that my life will end, as does all human life. My best guess is that the bombs reverberating through these walls with increasing ferocity will finally reach me. Here in Clapham, the hail of bombs instantly reduces buildings to their original components—stone, wood, iron, plaster — while fires burn out of control, until in the morning light fire squads can safely emerge to put out the last embers.

I remain curious about how death will feel when it comes. Having already accepted this human fate fifteen years ago when I entered Eiheiji Monastery, I don't hang onto the delusion of life evermore. If there is something to know about what follows death, the secret will be revealed then, just as each breath we take presents the next.

Yet, my dear, this perspective does not prevent fear from rising up, especially worrying that death in these circumstances will be painful. I witnessed the torment of the earth heaving in Japan and the subsequent destruction of the place where I was born and spent my childhood. However, those memories do not prepare me for my extinction by these bombs. Even with the global war that is raining terror on cities and the countryside, most people still hold the belief that their lives will end peacefully, and surrounded by those that love them. Perhaps writing to you will aid me in preparing for the unpreparable.

We make up stories, which we call our life. I have spent years accumulating stories before letting them go. My many teachers along the way have encouraged me in such a practice. I preciously hold onto memories, yet I have learned that even the most important events are ultimately inconsequential. Right now, your story, our story, is the last one I have left to tell; the one to which I still cling, containing both hope and regret, sitting deep within my bones, waiting for a joyful resolution that appears more remote than ever. I can only let myself picture a future time and venue when you will read these words. This hope pushes fear aside, allowing me a presence and purpose in life.

So, my Nina, the daughter who I have never embraced, the daughter whose voice exists in my imagination, the daughter whose presence has been a dream, I hope to give you my last story. If you receive this letter once the war is finished, you will certainly be older than your current seventeen years.

For this reason, I am addressing this letter to an adult Nina, who like the child Nina will remain an enigma to me.

On their last day, Zen monks customarily write a verse to voice their final thoughts about living life in the midst of death. My verse will exceed the customary length, describing your beginnings, my wanderings, and what I have learned on the way. The mystery for me is that I will not know what I have to say to you until I finish writing, which I consider an appropriate result amidst all that has transpired. I will write you a kōan, a paradoxical Zen teaching story. My advice, after decades of study, is to approach a kōan through the heart and not the mind. Let these words flow over you as an expression of my love.

My foremost desire is for my writings to help fill in the blank space called father for you. What could you possibly have said, when your schoolteachers asked about me: 'he abandoned us, and I know nothing about him?' Yet a quick peek in the mirror should remind you of my absent influence in the shape of your eyes and the color of your hair. You must have wondered, when visiting classmates living with grandparents, aunts and uncles, who your ancestors were, what they were like and why they also abandoned you?

As you will discover, I, too, harbored some of the same feelings and questions that resulted in my lifelong search for family. I know what it feels like to endure the looks of pity from well-meaning adults which also caused me to ask, 'what did I do wrong?' Had we lived together, I would have been there to guide you. But as that was not meant to be, I hope my words here can make up for what we have missed together.

At the same time, I recognize this goal is unachievable, a paradox itself. Please forgive me if at times I sound too much like a teacher. Moreover, please forgive me if what I write about may not fit your idea of a father. As impossible as this request sounds, I hope you can suspend judgment until you read the chronicle fully.

Beginning a tale is its own kōan. A beginning creates its own particular direction; the act of committing words to paper eliminates other possibilities. I could start at my birth, or the birth of my father or his father. My early time in Japan, our family circumstances, the growing military presence, foreign influences, my schooling ... all are beginnings; all are essential; all will be addressed by the end.

But as I dream about you, one corner of the world comes forward. In the summer of Taishō 8 (what you would call 1919), I arrived in Constantinople, distant from everything I thought certain. A place so foreign its name no longer exists.

ON A PILGRIMAGE

2. WHEN YOU FIRST SEEK DHARMA, YOU IMAGINE YOU ARE FAR AWAY FROM ITS ENVIRONS

As the wooden piers announce our entry, we are thrown from side to side as men wrestle our steamship into submission after 26 days at sea. The engines shudder to a stop, and the chugging of the turbines that accompanied us since we left Yokohama is replaced by the shouts of the stevedores loading and unloading cargo, the blast of whistles blowing as ships leave and enter the Golden Horn, and the murmur of excited passengers maneuvering through its narrow galley-ways. Safely in harbor, our lonely ship joins dozens of others emptying their flotsam of passengers onto the narrow docks below.

From our perch high above the deck on the captain's bridge, Mitsu was gazing ahead, his eyes partially closed, with a cockeyed smile on his face as he sniffed the air.

"Can you sense the difference, Kenzo?"

"What difference?"

"The air. I was so accustomed to the open and endless salty sea that I forgot what land smells like." He takes in a deep breath. "I can smell foods being prepared on kitchen fires with pungent spices I don't recognize. And even that aroma is suffused with the dusty, dry land and its ancient buildings erected on even older ones. We are far, far away from what we call home."

"You are so right, Mitsu," I responded. "Nothing is as I imagined it in my dreams. Are you sure we made the right decision to come here?"

"Of course we did. Your doubts always travel with you despite better intentions. As a young boy questioning my village priest about the realm beyond the visible, I already knew I would leave, never to come back. Now that we are here, can you even recollect the breezes from Tōkyō which we knew so well?"

Captain Watanabe, overhearing our conversation, simply said, "How does the wind permeate everywhere?"

Despite our weeks of travel, the captain's utterances still challenged me—his questions and statements making little sense to me. Of course, Mitsu always understood him. He had an intuitive, poetic sense of the world around us, whereas I was invariably searching for facts to guide my way.

"Kenzo, the wind of life is telling me that everything will be different from this point on. And together, the two of us will have experiences we can't imagine."

Although I was not sure how to respond to him, as per his usual he expressed what I could not yet put into words. That was another of his talents.

"Your beginner's mind will serve you both well as you discover the many treasures here," said the captain, pointing across the hazy harbor. "The largest mosque on earth, originally built as a Christian temple, lies on the other side of the large hill. Such is the nature of change over the centuries. What you will not find are Buddhist temples or Shinto shrines. While our spirits never ventured to these regions, please remember that you are now carrying them along as you explore these new lands.

"It has been my pleasure to serve you on this voyage. I have been honored to have diplomats aboard that will represent our great country well."

With these words, he bowed and turned to direct his crew in securing the ship. We hustled down the stairs to plunge into the stream of humanity and our new lives in Constantinople.

You may already be surprised, my daughter, by the turn of the events.

While stories can begin anywhere, I also should have warned you that they can travel in myriad directions. How could I not have immediately introduced Mitsu? Without him what I call my life would not exist. From the moment we met, he brought out qualities in me that I doubted I had and emotions that were buried deep in pain and denial. And without him, you would not exist either. Human stories are about interconnectedness; soon you will understand your own relationship to him. Despite everything that happened later, and the long interval since, Mitsu continues to remain at the center of my thoughts.

Meeting Mitsu was not preordained, yet the conditions were right to unfurl a path for us both. Our third-year economics professor sat us in the traditional *i-ro-ha* order, so that Mitsu was ahead to the left of me. In our first class together, I found myself staring at the back of his head and arms. I can still picture the shape of his head, how his hair fell on his neck, the size of his ears and the movements of his arms and shoulders. Occasionally, when he twisted back to listen to another student's response, I glimpsed his beautiful, gentle face. That is the moment our lives changed.

Answering the professor's queries, he spoke clearly and confidently as someone who had already mastered the subject matter. His deep and resonant voice delighted my ears and made me want to hear more. Men are able to fantasize based on less information than this. From what your mother taught me, women do that also, so I expect that you might know what I am talking about.

After class, I introduced myself. Our type of men can identify each other by signs, without speaking exact words. Proximity, the look in one's eyes, the words we use, and, most of all, an intuition. We receive no formal training for this; life presents the lessons over time. A lingering stare, a smile equally met, an invitation for companionship answered unequivocally, and a suggestion to meet at public places of special significance, such as a seemingly chance reference to a tucked-away teahouse in Yoshiwara, can all point toward what we desire to know.

In our case, we made an appointment to meet in front of the *ochaya*. In my excitement, I had not paid attention and did not remember anything about the day's lesson. I made a mental note to ask Mitsu about class notes. The day crawled by as I attended to my studies and completed some chores. I changed clothes several times prior to deciding what to wear for our meeting. Finally dressed, I caught the tram to Minowabashi, the closest stop to the bar on Edomachi Dori.

He was already standing on the street. "I am sorry I am late. I hope you have not waited long."

"Kenzo, you are not late—in fact, you are precisely on time. I always try to arrive early, in case there is a delay along the way, which was the case today. As I was entering the Willow Gate, I witnessed a heated conversation between one of the professors from the school of philosophy and his 'date' for the evening. Although I tried to sneak past, he called me over and asked me to take her with me. I politely refused, telling him I had plans for the evening. 'I hope your evening goes better than mine,' were his closing words."

"Well, we won't know until we go in," I said as we ducked under the *noren* in the doorway.

Men were lounging at tables, eating and drinking and talking animatedly. Attendants, young men about our age, were obviously chosen for their enviable demeanor. One of them led us to a table near a corner where our conversation would be more private. Even the three singers playing the *shamisen* and drum were men dressed as beautiful courtesans.

I took full stock of this man sitting across from me - clean-shaven and fair-skinned with beautiful, manicured black hair cut short in a modern style accentuating his dark, penetrating eyes, slender face, and full, smiling lips. Although we talked for hours, Mitsu's eyes are what I remember foremost from this cold night so far away in time and distance. They were dark, yet full of light and cheer. He was not shy, and whenever I peeked up, his face was lit up with excitement. As I gazed back at him, his soulfulness pulled me in and washed over me. Instantly, I felt we were one, inseparable, and that somehow

Mitsu would complete the missing parts of my life. Little did I know how true that prescient thought was.

In the excitement I forgot all about the class notes, and fortunately I was not called upon the next day. We began to study together daily and fell into each other's life naturally, easily. Soon enough we graduated. Mitsu had pulled me along, making me study harder than I would have done on my own. Despite his lack of social standing, he made me a better person.

You see, I had been accepted by Tōdai, Tōkyō University in the traditional way via family connections; Mitsu entered using the new system based on his qualifications and testing. His family still farms in the Kanto region to this day. The reforms enacted at the end of the last century permitted him to be the first from his village to receive a full education, making him eligible to take the exams for the university.

A government service job was waiting for me as my father was a member of the legislature, or, whenever his party was in favor, a cabinet minister. Despite Mitsu's high scores on the government entrance exam, he did not have the political backing needed for such an appointment. I prevailed on my father to pull strings so Mitsu could enter the Foreign Service at the same time I did. My debt to Mitsu was thus partially repaid.

We rented a six-*tatami* room near Asakusa, not far from the Ministry; two young men, reveling in the possibilities of having a hand in forging a better future for our society. We saw ourselves as the vanguard of a new generation of Japanese that would create and further the democratic and modern growth of our country on the world stage. During the long days as new Ministry trainees, we were instructed by senior diplomats in the intricacies of diplomacy and trade, as well as partaking in discussion groups to talk about economics, and political and social development. Those discussions often continued as we roamed the streets of Yoshiwara and Ginza at night, popping into cheap bars and restaurants, arguing until late at night with our colleagues about politics, the arts and our futures.

Outwardly, we appeared no different than other men our age. However,

Mitsu and I considered ourselves modern practitioners of *shudō*, a sacred intimacy between men, which my *samurai* ancestors had passed from generation to generation.

Shudō was not merely about sex. Adhering to high standards of ethical behavior, we practiced pure-heartedness toward each other and all living beings. Its precepts encouraged us to excel in whatever we did, including the arts, poetry, martial arts, sport and work. By sharing our strengths and learning from each other we became a unit able to overcome adversity, better than each of us could on his own.

Like many of Japan's cultural ways of being, *shudō* lost its public expressions following the introduction of the backward ideas of Christian morality by Western missionaries. Privately, a minority of men continued its practices of intimacy and trust. Others, like my father, were oblivious to its modern-day incarnation. We saw ourselves as the holders of the flame of Japanese culture while we also embraced modern ways.

When I received my appointment as the Consul General to Turkey, my joy was tempered by the heaviness of responsibility. Every posting is a stepping stone to other positions throughout the world. Appointees were normally much older than my twenty-eight years, so my posting was a sure sign of my father's influence. Despite the challenging relationship between us, the appointment provided the possibility of escape from the inevitable for at least a decade. If I stayed in Japan, over time the pressure on me would grow to accumulate a wife and children. Odd term, 'accumulate,' but most men, my father included, viewed families as little more than possessions.

As I had great latitude, I appointed Mitsu as Deputy Consul, ensuring we would jointly explore this unfolding adventure. To prepare, we engaged French and English language tutors. French, the traditional language of diplomacy, was Mitsu's specialty. Japan's historical ties with Great Britain, and the emergence of the U.S. as a global power, made learning English essential for both of us.

Miss Bowers was a British tutor, assertive and formal in her demeanor while often exhibiting a strange sense of humor—a characteristic we thought unusual for a woman. After many weeks of study, she invited us to stay for tea. While we prided ourselves on being capable students, keeping abreast of the complicated grammar drills, we were nervous about an unstructured conversation with her.

As she filled our cups full of green tea and set a plate of tasteless British biscuits in front of us, she casually inquired, "Have you gentlemen been friends for very long?"

"We met at the university, Miss Bowers," I answered.

"Oh, how nice. Why did you become friends?"

Mitsu glanced at me quizzically. "I am sorry. I don't follow. My English is still not very skilled. What do you mean, 'become friends'?"

"It's a silly question—pardon my asking. I am always curious about how friendships get established, maybe because I have been happily living on my own. I moved across the globe without any family or close friends. You two seem to have a special bond. Is that unusual, or are all friendships between men similar here?"

I ventured an answer, speaking as I stared at the floor. "In our ancient *samurai* culture, men bonded with other men to protect each other. Sometimes they formed life-long relationships. As you know, *samurai* don't exist any longer, yet Mitsu and I have chosen to live by these principles. Does what I say sound strange to you?"

"All men are silly, of course, and your lives are strange. We women do the identical thing; we stick closely to each other as best we can. The biggest mistake a woman can make is allowing a man to run her life. I am aware it's a man's world, but frankly that does not mean that men do the job well. Sometimes men find the right men to assist them, just as women find the right women. I once had such a close friend for over twenty years. Her untimely death meant I no longer had any ties keeping me in England. I hope this fate never befalls the two of you. Even in this remote place, she remains in my heart and lives in my memory."

Her words were confusing, and I was eager to hear Mitsu's thoughts on what she said. As soon as we finished our tea, we politely bade our farewells. The evening stream of businessmen and officials on the streets swallowed us until we stepped into a food stall for a quick bite prior to returning to our flat.

"What do you think she meant by her questions?" I asked as soon as we were in our flat. "I felt insulted by her chatter of what men do wrong."

"Her questions were very odd, Kenzo, although based on her overall disposition, I don't believe she intended to be hurtful. But it was curious of her to ask why we had become friends." He paused. "Such a personal question made me uncomfortable. We have never spoken about our friendship as if it were independent of us. Our friendship is who we are. What else is there to acknowledge?"

"We confide in each other about everything, and share our thoughts about politics, food, work, theater, the arts. Everything that interests us we share. That's what friends do."

"And *shudō*, of course," he added quietly. "*Shudō* is our life, and our lives are *shudō*. It's how we act that is most important, not just the words we use."

"You are right. The first time you gazed at me after economics class, a bolt of desire zigzagged through my body. How could I not want to discover more about you?"

"I felt it, too. I would never want to be alone like Miss Bowers. Does *shudō* exist for women? She seemed quite wistful as she spoke about her friend. As long as we stay together, we won't have that worry."

I pulled him close and kissed his neck. That evening so long ago still floods my memories. We were so young; an endless future stretched ahead of us. Neither of us foresaw the life we would soon lead.

3. MYRIAD THINGS COME FORTH AND ILLUMINATE THE SELF

On a pilgrimage, each step is important and opens the way for the next. Within an hour of our arrival, we were exchanging bows with a consular official who came aboard to welcome us.

From our first glance, he fascinated me, as I had never seen such a hairy man. He had dark brown, curly hair and an elongated thick beard of a matching color that came to a point under his chin. His sparkling dark eyes and bushy eyebrows danced on his large forehead when he talked. His face was rounded out with a formidable, bulbous nose and large mouth. He placed his arm across his chest as he bowed.

"Welcome, Sir Consul. I hope your trip was excellent. Let me introduce myself. My name is Gül."

Perhaps it was the surprised look on my face, as I took him in, that fortunately caused him to misconstrue what I was thinking.

"Ottomans only have one name, so please call me Gül." His wide grin showed his large, almost animal-like teeth. "Please come this way. The rest of the staff are waiting for your arrival at the consulate."

He guided us down the swaying gangway onto the equally shaky pier laden with cargo. On the ground, we saw hundreds of passengers waiting impatiently to pass border control.

"Why are there so many people here?" Mitsu inquired. "Where are they coming from?"

"They are mainly Ukrainians and White Russians fleeing the civil war tearing apart Russia. With the Red Army's impending capture of Odessa across the Black Sea, more than 100,000 refugees have made the journey here. Some with their riches packed in trucks and suitcases, others with just a tattered bag. As conditions get more desperate, more and more are taking flight."

"We knew the Red Army had already reached Vladivostok, seizing control of most of the East," I said. "But we did not have much information about what was happening on the European front."

"The French and the British have pretty much abandoned Ukraine and Crimea, so the fighting may not last much longer. The shipping lanes on the Black Sea are still open, but once Odessa falls, that will be it, as the risk of attack will be too high. I will brief you on the political and economic situation once you are settled."

He directed us to the diplomatic section, bypassing the lines of refugees amidst the large piles of luggage and household items they carried. Gül seemed to know everyone who worked there, from men sweeping the floors to the head of immigration who stamped our papers and waved us through. Outside the building, a horse-drawn carriage was waiting.

Our carriage bumped along a narrow, winding street on a steep hill. "On your steamer," Gül explained, "you passed the Golden Horn, entering Europe. Galata, which contains the diplomatic district of Pera, is about a ten-minute ride on the other side of this hill. The old city, Stambul, is on the opposite side of the Horn. The buildings you saw as you docked are simply a few of the mosques, palaces and markets filling its packed streets."

Our driver carefully maneuvered around the crowds of people and carts brimming with fruits, vegetables, and other goods. Comparable to our ports, muscular men strode alongside their comrades, although the men here struck me as taller and heftier, their dark hair and thick beards making the contrast with home greater. Like Gül, most were wearing colorful embroidered vests over light-colored shirts. Their pants were tight; brightly colored boots encased their feet. Even though we had many foreigners in Tōkyō, the men here were unlike anyone I had ever glimpsed there. From the smile on Mitsu's face, he was obviously enjoying the sights as I was.

As the sun set, darkness shrouded the increasingly mysterious streets as a lamplighter ignited the gas in the street lamps one by one. Up ahead, the bright fires burning in the passing taverns illuminated scenes of men carrying hefty platters of food. These glimpses made my stomach growl, as we had not eaten for hours.

The carriage abruptly halted, throwing us forward.

"Excuse me, Sir Consul, we have arrived at the consulate."

We jumped off the carriage to face a large three-story stone building built in the previous century as a mansion for an official of the Ottoman Empire. The broad, heavy doorway of glass and metal led to the marble entryway, where the consulate staff was lined up, waiting for us.

"I never imagined living in a place as grand as this," I whispered to Mitsu, the staff bowing as we mounted the large stairway.

"I know. In Japan, only the most powerful would reside in a building similar to this one. This stairway alone is of a size I had only beheld in the Imperial Palace."

Upstairs, we were ushered into a large western-style dining room that could accommodate twenty guests around a huge table with ornately cushioned chairs. I was shown to a spot at the head of the table.

Despite the preparations for my career, I never gave a thought to how I would live overseas. Normally, we call where we live, 'home.' Yet 'home' was where I lived in Japan, not in such a strange place as this. Home must mean something else— this was merely a house, a dwelling, or maybe a residence. Yes, here we would reside—short-term, without connections of culture and family. People live differently when they merely reside; they treat their lives differently as well. Just as doors, windows, floors and ceilings can be arranged in unlimited ways, our attachments to where we live are equally varied.

The little I know of your story, Nina, makes me assume that you understand this. I know your mother moved you from place to place, as funds ran out or new men appeared in her life. Did you ever feel 'at home?' I wish I knew what that meant to you. I know its significance is complicated for me. There is so much that we could have talked about in person, so much that we have in common despite the distance that separates us.

Completing the shock of entry into this new and extravagant world, for the next several hours we were treated to a celebratory dinner. Consuming plates of Japanese and Turkish food, we drained one of the barrels of sake we brought with us. In a short time, my head was aching from the multiple toasts, buzzing from strangers coming up to meet me, and the tastes of the familiar and unfamiliar food.

Quick enough, our first evening in Constantinople was over as the last visitor headed out into the dark night. We were shown to our sleeping room; exhausted, the two of us tumbled into bed.

4. YOU ARE FAR AWAY FROM ITS ENVIRONS

A rap at the door woke us from our deep slumber, and although my mind was groggy the brilliant rays of the sun indicated that it must be morning.

"Sir, you should arise soon as we have much to do today."

I was not even sure who was calling me, but jumped up nonetheless.

"I will be ready shortly."

"Sir, your clothes have been set out for you."

"Thank you."

I must have had a strange look on my face as I tried to identify who was talking on the other side of the door, and Mitsu smiled at my confusion. "I made the preliminary arrangements with Gül last night. He's worked here from day one and has vast connections throughout the region, which were useful in arranging the lease of this building. He suggested showing us the old city today, then tomorrow he will commence with our diplomatic introductions."

"Honestly, last night is just a blur. What would I do without you taking charge of things all the time?"

"Don't worry, I feel Gül will watch out for us as well. My initial impression is he's quite competent and amiable."

In the anteroom our clothes were not only neatly laid out, but Gül had also correctly identified all of the pieces required for formal Japanese wear. As we dressed in our kimonos, I wondered who this man was.

Nina, can you remember the first time that you took up something new?

Can you still feel the sensations or your emotions? These moments have a preciousness to them, no matter how ordinary the situation. Our first months in Constantinople were like this. With all that I have experienced in life, as I write to you the smoky aroma of my first taste of coffee still comes back to me. I was entranced by the thick, bittersweet taste compacted into such a tiny cup, lingering on my tongue long afterward. That one cup introduced a new way of beginning the day.

Satisfied and wakened, we were hustled out. The city appeared less mysterious in the sharp light of the day, yet it was completely unlike any Japanese city. The buildings, made of wood or stone, were two or three stories high, each smashed against the other. The cobblestone streets reduced the dirt in the air, but horse hooves and wagon wheels clambering alongside of us as we roamed created an incessant din.

In the morning heat, men and women chatted as they ambled from one shop to another, loading up their purchases. Gül identified the origins of the passersby from various parts of Anatolia and other countries, distinguished by their own local clothing: the Russians in their furs, even on this hot day; Ukrainian men and women in fancifully embroidered tunics and red boots; the suited, waistcoated and cravatted British appearing quite constipated in their outfits; and the Arabs, attired more leisurely in their flowing white robes and headdresses. More types of humanity were assembled here on one block than existed in the entirety of Japan.

At the quay, our ship was still moored near the Galata Bridge. Recently built, the bridge was its own little city of fishermen, who used thin poles the height of two men to cast into the green waters, the lucky ones hauling in substantial-sized fish to be put in baskets. Back and forth along the length of the bridge vendors loudly announced their presence, trying to attract the attention of well-dressed men and parasol-carrying women who were meandering across to the old city, Stambul, on the far side.

A man's voice emanated from the heavens and sprang into song as we were about to cross the Golden Horn. Like a flock of birds responding to a stimulus only they perceive, all of the men around us turned in the same direction and threw themselves to the ground in prostration. In Japan, only our priests perform prostrations at temples but here every man was bent over, their foreheads on cloths, chanting. Their eyes half shuttered, they reverently repeated this behavior over and over, in unison. One last time, they stood up, glanced one way, then the other. The singing man's voice finished; life returned to normal.

"Muslims pray five times each day," Gül explained, "reciting different verses each time. At the end, the person peers over his right shoulder to view the angel writing his virtues, then to the left for the one writing his faults. The *muezzin* calls us from the top of those minarets," he said as he pointed across the water at the slender towers of the building I had noticed as the ship docked.

During my time in Constantinople, whenever I heard the *muezzin's* call, all thoughts stopped—I became aware of the air entering my lungs, the heat of the day on my skin, the beating of my heart. Later, I learned much more about such experiences, yet even then I was in awe of these magical sensations.

Gül led our trio across the bridge. The mosques were even bigger than I had thought—circular, several stories high, topped with a dome. He invited us inside the one nearest to the bridge, through a doorway covered in ornate Arabic script.

"Please remove your shoes," he told us. "This is the custom."

"We understand, we do the same upon entering temples at home," Mitsu responded.

A soft light emanating from the windows encircling the blue-and-white-tiled dome filtered to every corner. I felt both humbled and lifted up by the grandeur of the hall.

"This is as empty as a Shinto shrine," I whispered to Gül, "which also doesn't have seats, ornamentation, or statues. The enormity of the chamber makes me feel insignificant."

"During prayer," he explained, "the floor pulsates from hundreds of men with wave after wave of bodies chanting, prostrating and moving, dropping their individuality."

Leaving our own thoughts behind inside this quiet temple, we entered a maelstrom of activity in the narrow lanes of the old city. Merchants were unloading foodstuffs, metal wares, rugs, clothing and furniture into tiny shops. Young children ran underfoot, stopping to stare at us before running off, giggling. Displays of cut pastries stacked into towers a meter high lured us into cafes to snack and drink cups of coffee while we talked and watched the movements outside.

We abandoned the street to enter a vast, crowded market hall. Oh my dear Nina, your own imagination could not invent what greeted us as we ventured in - the musical chants of vendors announcing their wares mixed with the screeching of wild birds for sale and the yells of tradesmen as they pushed their way among the throngs of people. Our noses were enticed by aromas of unusual spices and strange fruit, while disgusted by the odor of so many unwashed bodies tightly packed in. Our eyes feasted on the myriad bright colors of weavings and clothing displayed for sale.

We dove headlong into the tumult. Although attired in our formal kimonos, we were pushed and nudged by the crowd without apology. As I was reaching my limits of being bumped and bruised by men trudging by with larges boxes on their backs, a shop owner took pity on us by inviting us into his little stall.

He served us mint tea as we reclined on silk-covered cushions atop elegant carpets protecting us from the dirt floor. What a refuge this was in such a chaotic quarter. Gül translated for us.

"Welcome, gentlemen. From your dress, I can assume you are from Japan."

"Yes, you are very observant," replied Mitsu.

"Your country is not far from us. Asia is right across the strait," he joked. "The silk I sell originated from your homeland. Turks are connected by history and culture to Asia. Our forefathers created the trade between our side of the globe and yours. The designs are our own, but they are produced by your threads. Our two countries are connected by the appreciation of beauty."

He began rolling out bolts of the finest silk woven into unfamiliar designs, not stopping until the floor was covered. While we had no intention of purchasing anything, out of politeness we could not stop him from showing his wares.

The contrasts we experienced that day, loud and quiet, rough and smooth, pleasant and unpleasant, are the very epitome of existence itself. As we watched the hubbub in the aisles, the merchant and Gül chatted privately. Mitsu and I found ourselves mesmerized by the men striding by, intently talking, their arms around each other, whispering in one another's ear, occasionally touching their partner's face or hair. Sometimes one would hold the other's arm, or even entwine their arms. Glancing at us, the merchant nudged Gül, and they both laughed.

Gül spoke up, "By the way, my friend here suggested I bring you to the *hammam*."

"*Hammam*, what is that?" inquired Mitsu.

"*Hammam* is a public bath. I think the Japanese name is *onsen*."

"*Onsen*," I exclaimed. "We have not bathed properly for weeks since we entered the ship. Let's go this instant."

"The *hammam* for men is on the other side of the market. We can go forthwith if you would like."

We bade the silk merchant farewell, promising him we would return to drink more tea and peruse his fabrics. As we reentered the crowds, I brashly put my arm around Mitsu's shoulder, although he instinctively brushed it off.

"It's okay. No one will care. It's an opportunity we've never had."

He shyly nodded in agreement. Despite our cultural expectations of not touching each other in public, we quickly warmed to it. Gül noticed but kept any thoughts he might have had to himself. Guiding us past innumerable stalls containing everything from dry goods to carcasses covered in flies at the butchery, past the fish market, then by the fruits and vegetables, we finally found the far exit. The crowds thinned as we strolled farther down a dusty street, shaded by low, brown buildings on either side. Gül entered a nondescript building and we followed him in.

A wizened man with a dark black beard and graying hair kissed Gül's cheeks and embraced him as a long-lost friend. He gave each of us a towel and directed us to changing cabins, where we disrobed. Emerging from the cabins, Gül led us into the *hammam* itself. Our first stop was the washing stations where we would clean ourselves.

"Kenzo, how can this be almost identical to our *onsen*? I can't wait to clean off the dirt from these weeks of travel."

We each sat facing a spigot, using towels to wash our bodies. Mitsu came over and washed my back as was our habit. Gül invited me to do the same for him. He had hair everywhere, including on his back. His rough dark skin and his strong muscles mesmerized me as I washed him, the warm water sinuously followed the musculature of his back.

Finished, I washed Mitsu's smooth back. Delicateness versus roughness, I thought. Bodies are different, each one entrancing.

We raised warm buckets of water over our heads to rinse, then, partially cleansed, proceeded to the adjoining area. Wafts of steam emanating from the walls filled the room, allowing for glimpses of the ornately tiled dome above us. Slowly the steam seeped into every pore of our bodies, releasing the dirt even the soap could not reach. I relaxed, intoxicated by the steam and heat. Shortly, Gül indicated we should go back to rinse again. Following another session of steam, he led us into the third room, where three towels were laid out on a giant round slab of stone. The heat emanating from the stone dried us as we relaxed further, talking quietly.

I thought we were done when an attendant entered carrying a wooden bucket of sudsy water and a large sponge. He covered Gül in the warm, soapy water until he almost disappeared under the foamy suds, after which he roughly washed him from head to toe. He directed him to turn over and repeated his efforts.

It was my turn. Despite what I judged minutes ago, the sponge and suds were soothing to the touch as he rubbed and caressed me as one would a baby. A cool pail of water thrown on me ended my reverie. I might even have screamed since the others laughed heartily. I joined them as I admitted the humor of the situation. When he finished massaging Mitsu, we rested. Soon, the towel underneath me was dry again, and my body was clean and warm.

The moon peered over the rooftops, watching our departure amidst hugs and kisses for each of us from the proprietor. As we were famished, the piquant aroma of fish being grilled caught our noses at a small nearby stall. We cemented our friendship with our comrade Gül with mugfuls of beers.

5. UNDERSTAND ONLY WHAT YOUR EYE OF PRACTICE CAN REACH

Someday, dear one, I am sure you too will travel. Of course, that is near impossible now as war consumes nations on both sides of the Pacific and Atlantic. No one realized how the problems of a few nations would veer out of control, plunging the entire world into warfare. Never in history has war been fought simultaneously around the globe. The interconnectedness of our reality has become obvious. Fighting will hopefully end soon enough; however, its legacy will have untold effects, creating unforeseen instability down the line. The cycle of cause and effect is endless.

The western nations believed World War I to be 'the war to end all wars'. Although Japan was not actively involved as a belligerent nation, we became rich as a munitions supplier. On the other side of the earth from Europe, we were busy feeding the bloodlust by supplying silk and cotton to clothe the troops, ships to transport them, and weapons to kill them. As the saying goes, one does not have to bloody his hands to be part of a fight. The growth of our infrastructure and economy fed the dreams of our politicians who believed that we would take our deserved place on the international stage where we would right the wrongs that were committed against us.

Regretfully, you have suffered greatly from the ancestry you gained from me. From the moment of your birth, you were called a half-breed, among other indignities. I have witnessed what atrocities humans can commit against each other, but it is unfathomable to me why anyone would treat a child—a beautiful, intelligent child—this way. Sadly, even while writing this, I have already witnessed such cruelty in my lifetime, in addition to the harm that can come from words alone.

Living far from Japan demonstrated to us a multitude of possible lives. We were fascinated by even the most ordinary of details. One can read about what others eat, yet until you taste these foodstuffs directly, no point of comparison exists. Foods that are alien to our tastebuds are common to others; vice versa, foods that others revile such as kelp and raw fish are delicious to us. If the sense of taste is common to every human, how can others eat foods we regard as strange? I can't envisage a gull flying above Constantinople refusing a fish offered from Japan.

Meetings were the lifeblood of being Consul General. Even though Mitsu and I represented the government on trade matters, we were not particularly busy. Turkish government officials, other foreign delegations, and/or local merchants would contact us for possible business arrangements and the purchase of military or civilian products. Since Japan had not established a full embassy yet, we also carried out basic diplomatic functions. As a consequence of the fall of the Austro-Hungarian Empire, British, French and Italian troops divided up control of various areas of the city. Rumors of subterfuge, cells of Turkish nationalists, and movements of military troops swirled through the populace. The Sultan, who had no power as the titular head of state, answered to the British.

The political confusion in Turkey was somewhat matched by the confusion in Tōkyō. Japan had sided with the Allies in the Great War and was thus a signatory to the Treaty of Versailles ending the war. Our meager reward was the annexation of Germany's small territories in Asia. The Treaty also allowed us to send consular delegations throughout Europe, including Turkey. The political frontier was constantly changing as various parties fought for control over Parliament. In the preceding ten years, Japan had six prime ministers. My father was the foreign minister for several governments.

Whenever he was out of office, he was plotting to get back in. Neither his desire for power nor his skills to promote himself were passed on to me.

Essential to my job was the maintenance of close relationships with the three major powers. We had regular meetings, where I negotiated an occasional minor contract for silk and cotton needed by the occupying armies for clothes, bedding and towels. While we met the Sultan at a large ceremonial gathering, the British ambassador was the de facto political head in Constantinople. Thus, creating connections at the civilian staff level of the delegation was key. We were very fortunate to have Gül as our confidant, as he seemed to have friends everywhere in the diplomatic community and the Turkish government. We quickly learned that building relationships was more likely to occur in the clubs and official residences, where parties and dances were celebrated frequently, rather than in formal meetings in consulates and embassies.

One by one, we were taken to the offices clustered near Pera to meet the main diplomatic officials from Britain, France, Germany, the U.S., Russia and Italy. Each consulate was its own venture into a foreign country, resplendent in different customs, dress and attitudes.

Regretfully, I cannot say we were equally attended to, even though we were all diplomats. The French, who enjoyed our exoticness, were won over by Mitsu's fluency in the language. At the Italian Embassy, the Ambassador effusively kissed and embraced us as he set us at ease. The Americans and Russians had limited delegations, so our meetings there were perfunctory. We easily forged the many relationships key to carrying out our job. Only at the British Embassy did we find an air of moral superiority attached to virtually every conversation.

During our second visit to the British delegation, the Deputy Ambassador, Edmund Kinver, warmed up a bit, surprising me by inviting us for an evening out on the town.

"A nightclub called Maxim's, run by a black man formerly from the U.S. South, recently opened in Taksim Square. I heard from a reliable source of his very successful club in Moscow in the days preceding the Revolution. He introduced Negro jazz musicians to Russia."

"I am exposing my naiveté, but what does one do at a nightclub?"

"Chap, you certainly have lots to learn. It's where men can go to drink, smoke cigars, banter and watch a show. The private salons allow for conversations and enjoyment we cannot have elsewhere. I insist on your joining our group."

"I appreciate the invitation. May I assume my deputy and our liaison are also welcome?"

"Of course. Gül is well-known, trusted and enjoyed among us. From our previous encounter, I recognize that your deputy is not only indispensable, but also appears to be your constant companion. Yes, our men will enjoy meeting you both. Please join us on Friday at 8:30. Tell the maître d'hôtel you are joining my party."

"Thank you for including us. We look forward to a delightful evening."

"Oh, so do we, so do we!"

As we retreated, Gül whispered, "Excellent, sir. Kinver has clearly warmed up to you, as few outsiders get invited by the British to their private salons. Constantinople has not seen a place such as Maxim's. It opened quietly last month and is just now getting attention."

"If we are going to such exclusive environments, we should have European clothes made for us. Honestly, they appear uncomfortable, but I suspect we would blend in better. What do you think, Mitsu?"

"At home, I would never wear such clothes even if they are becoming accepted in government and business. I prefer holding on to our unique and traditional ways. Just look at the variety of dress we have seen here. But that said, the standards for the diplomatic community are different. Gül, can you arrange for a tailor to take our measurements?"

"I anticipated your needs—an excellent bespoke tailor will come by in the afternoon. He works quickly, so your suits will be ready by Friday."

True to his word, our suits were completed on time. Trying on these costumes was a curious sensation. I say costumes as these clothes camouflaged our customary identities. The pants, shirt, waistcoat and jacket fit much more snugly than our kimonos, taking away the freedom of movement of my arms and legs that I had previously taken for granted. While I was not sure how I felt about the fit, I did enjoy examining how Mitsu's suit nicely accented his body, showing his trim torso.

Tying the cravat was a special problem. We recognized its position was around the neck but were unable to ascertain how to properly create a knot. We called Gül for help. He faced me inches apart, concentrating those big furry eyebrows of his on the task, pulling my collar up against my cheeks as he draped the cravat around my neck, twisting, turning and pulling until he had firmly yanked the knot into shape. We were so close that I could inhale his scent. Perhaps you have noticed, my daughter, how every person has their own particular scent. If you close your eyes, you can differentiate one person from the other. I last saw Mitsu almost two decades ago, yet his memory still brings the cinnamon spiciness of his musk to my nose.

Mitsu enjoyed watching me being dressed. I wish this carried fond memories of my father dressing me as a child, but, sadly, those memories were few and far between as he frequently disappeared on government business, rarely even noticing me during the times he was present. I could not envisage him delicately tying a cravat or helping to fit one on me. Frankly, I knew little about him. I must confess, one of the reasons I am writing you is the admittedly vain hope that you will be able to develop an appreciation of your distant father from words alone.

Mitsu, being a quick study, mastered this cravat-tying. We donned our waistcoats, which made our torsos even more defined, buttoned them up, and slipped on our jackets. Dressed in this outfit, I tried walking. Bound up as we were, I could not determine how my arms should move. Gül laughed heartily at our attempts at a task which European boys do naturally. He showed me how to swing my arms slightly as I lumbered about, not too high yet not holding them straight down without movement. Reminded of the exacting movements of *kabuki* and my *jujitsu* training as a youth, I tried to feel where movement was natural within these garments. Gradually, I adjusted to where they allowed for easy movement and where they did not.

Before I continue my recitation, I am guessing you have a number of questions. One of them will be answered very soon: Where in my story is the woman who gave birth to you? I hope you are also a little curious about me. I don't know what your mother may have told you, but her negative feelings toward me likely have shaped whatever she said. Surely, she told you I was a diplomat, but did she even mention Mitsu and how much he meant to me?

We had no confusion about our relationship, although we quickly learned that the West held different attitudes. I suspect your mother raised you thinking that deeply loving relationships are strictly between men and women. She knows better.

Simply put, other types of relationships, including those between men themselves and women themselves, flourish in all societies. I have already mentioned the ancient tradition among my *samurai* descendants of *shudō*, referring to men who had loving lives alongside other men exclusively. Until Westerners forced their way into Japan during my grandfather's days not so long ago, men jointly creating lives together was not necessarily considered the norm—yet it was seen as one of many ways of living.

Westerners were shocked by certain aspects of our culture. With my ancestors' desire to emulate the West, these parts of life and history, including *shudō*, became hidden or died off. We have struggled since then to determine the right balance of modernity within our traditional cultural heritage. Desire and attraction cannot be eliminated by decrees or laws. In our culture, open displays of affection were frowned upon, so certain practices continued as before.

To be clear, Mitsu and I loved each other. We planned our future together; we coordinated our daily schedules; we thought of each other as our primary. As men, we also had interactions with other men. The precepts of *shudō* demanded respect in any connection. I am relating this to you because events will soon become more complicated, just as life itself is complicated.

Walking the short distance from the consulate to Taksim Square, dressed as English gentlemen, seemed to change the very streets we were on. Passersby barely noticed three well-dressed men ambling the streets of Pera, quite a change from the stares that had normally greeted us wherever we went. At the same time, we were both aware that through donning these clothes we dropped an influential part of our Japanese identity. We had more than a little trepidation, anticipating that these strange garments were transforming us in unforeseen ways.

Without Gül, Maxim's unprepossessing façade would have eluded us. He led us to a small lane near the main square, where a line of carriages stretched down the block, waiting to drop off well-coiffed men and women at the entrance. I waved to a group of my colleagues from the French Embassy. Their inquiring stares shifted to surprise as they recognized us. As we guessed, our new attire was already changing expectations of us.

At the door, the maître d' bowed, his arm across his chest, and escorted us to the British delegation. Striding down a narrow hallway, we were invited into a room framed by a doorway with plush, red velvet curtains. A haze of cigar smoke blocked a clear view of the men drinking and laughing as they lounged on thick, brown leather chairs. As Edmund greeted us, the men paused their conversation to identify what new guests were joining the party.

"My, how you chaps have dressed up. You put away your dresses and are indistinguishable from proper Englishmen. Who was your tailor?"

Gül answered for us, "Mr. Hammersmith. I believe you are acquainted with his work."

"Acquainted, my man, he is one of our best. I am surprised and delighted. He doesn't work for just anyone."

"Don't worry, sir. He works for none other than the best. He had no hesitation when I called upon him. Our delegation leaders already have a positive reputation within the diplomatic community."

"Hmm, there may be more to you chaps than I fancied. Please, gentlemen, have a seat. May I offer you a drink?"

As we sat, the rest of the group resumed their boisterous conversations. Edmund brought us glasses containing a rust-colored liquid.

"Ah, here's our best whiskey for you. Is this your inaugural post?"

"Yes, for both of us. We launched our careers at the Foreign Ministry after our graduation from Tōkyō University. Our commission is to prepare for a full embassy to follow," Mitsu responded.

"Ah, university chums. That's the best means to get underway—alongside a companion you can trust. Amongst us all, only Christopher over there did not go to Oxford; he's a Cambridge man. If you and your mate have been through the forms, you get to appreciate how you will work and, more importantly, enjoy fun times. English universities are known for the latter."

"Honestly?" I interjected, "to us, a British education is the highest form of scholarship. You have the best professors and lectors."

"Naturally. Few of the lot here succeeded at university because of their brains. For most of us, the key was our wit and beauty. Well, that, plus our fathers' bank accounts. We had occasion for study but spent more time assessing the right chums for future endeavors. The wrong ones lead you to a boring career as a bureaucrat, hidden in the back hall of an obscure ministry of the king. I prefer to be among the gayest ones, the ones who can discriminate between good and bad Champagne and know how to throw the best parties. Without any women in our lives to bother us, we make do." He grinned at us like he was sharing a secret.

"Our university is based on merit," I replied. "Even someone without a family pedigree can be successful, if they are able to prove themselves. Even though I came from a former *samurai* family, I took the same entrance exam as Mitsu, whose family were farmers. We progressed through the ranks together."

"How fortunate for you both. Is what they say true about *samurai* men?"

"Um, what do you mean? *Samurai* don't exist any longer. My grandfather was one, though."

"They say *samurai*s believed that sex with women depleted their vital bodily fluids. Therefore, they preferred to have sex with men to stimulate and strengthen their own masculine energy. Am I correct in this?"

I glanced at Mitsu, not sure how to acknowledge his line of thought.

Mitsu on the other hand had no hesitation. "It appears that you have studied traditional Japanese culture. Most Westerners know little about what we call *shudō*. Do British men have comparable practices?" I admired Mitsu for his ability to respond directly and appropriately.

"Our training begins at British boys' boarding schools. Just imagine dormitories of young men discovering puberty with each other. Such early training sets the future for many of us. The British diplomatic corps is renowned for the large number of its men glad to be far removed from Victorian England, in exotic locales such as Constantinople, where the mores are, how should I say, less restrictive. I hope I don't offend you, but I sense more than a business relationship between the two of you. Let me be frank, Mr. Gül usually seems to identify our type of men and makes sure to introduce them to us."

I was flummoxed. This was not a conversation we had ever had with anyone. My assumption was that our form of masculinity was unique to our culture alone. I had not expected to meet any men outside Japan harboring attractions akin to the two of us. Could whole other worlds exist of men identical to us? As much as I was annoyed by how Edmund peered down on us, there was another side of him I found intriguing. I turned to Gül to ascertain what he made of the turn of events. He nodded at me knowingly.

Mitsu continued the conversation. "You are a very astute gentleman, my friend, if I may call you that. What of your colleagues here?"

Edmund pointed up with the second finger extended. "We are all just so. Truly, we are considered poofs or homosexuals."

"Poofs, homosexuals…these are not English words our teacher, Miss

Bowers, taught us."

"I am sure Miss Bowers, whoever she is, would not have a lesson where you repeated, 'I am a poof. I revel in men.'" He noticed that we were confused so he continued. "These are words to describe men who are attracted to other men which generally are not used by polite company. 'Poof' is a derogatory word for homosexual, a more clinical word describing the men that behave like us."

Mitsu laughed louder than I had ever heard him laugh, causing heads to turn to discover what was going on. "Yes, you are right. Miss Bowers did not prepare us well at all. We will need more conversations to expand our English vocabulary."

"Come join the rest of the men for a drink where we can continue talking."

As Edmund introduced us, each man thrust out his hand toward us. I was still getting used to this greeting over our bows of respect. The conversation flowed from one topic to another among much laughter. We thought our conversational English was improving, but we found most of what was being said incomprehensible.

Edmund noticed our ongoing confusion. "Eventually, you will follow us better. Among ourselves we speak a different language—Polari—which contains many euphemisms, a code for what is not being said directly. If outsiders are listening, they will not catch what we genuinely mean."

"Thank you for the explanation. That's why parts of the conversation sounded unintelligible," I responded. "I have heard that in ancient times the *samurai* had a similar secret language. Sadly, it has been lost."

"I do wish to find out more about the *samurai* sometime, and since we are talking about such matters let me give you a piece of unsolicited advice. You will thank me for it one day. You will need one more thing to live as a diplomat in Europe. You will need a beard."

"A beard?" I was confused. "Everyone here is clean-shaven except for the mustachioed among you."

"A beard, my dear consul, hides your face—that which you honestly are. To hide your true desires for men, you will need a woman as a consort. With a woman at your side, you will not stand out or expose yourself to questioning. Certain among us here are in fact married, but that is too extreme for me. I myself call upon a friend whose company I enjoy for those public events where a feminine partner is expected."

"This sounds very complicated; I will require much more study to thoroughly comprehend your ways. In Japan, even asking personal questions is considered rude. Unmarried younger men are considered marriage-ready only when they have gained career success. Any close contact between us and a European female would be considered scandalous. Therefore, no one would ever expect either of us to marry until we return."

"All I can say is you are not in Japan any longer. Rumors fly quickly in our circle of society. The sooner you make such a decision to protect yourself, the better. Your friend Mr. Mitsu will not be scrutinized as much as you will be as Consul General."

I pondered what this might mean for me. Why should I hide behind someone else, especially a woman? Functioning in this part of the world was more complicated than I thought.

Several minutes later, your mother appeared.

6. FOR A BIRD, SKY IS LIFE

A young woman entered, carrying a large box strapped around her shoulders. Her short yellow dress trimmed with fringe on her shoulders and arms was sewn with hundreds of tiny jewels that reflected the light, a sunburst in this otherwise dark room. Her blond hair, cut short in the modern style, framed her thin face, dainty nose and rosy, make-up brushed cheeks. Her deep green eyes highlighted by her darkly painted eyelids astonished me as I had never witnessed eyes of that color previously. She looked like she had emerged from a magazine.

"Cigars, cigarettes, gentlemen?" were her opening words. She spoke English with a Slavic accent. From our few brief weeks in Constantinople, I was already capable of identifying her as one of the thousands of refugees from the Russian civil war.

Edmund spoke to her directly. "Please give these gentlemen cigars. They are recent arrivals to this country, as I assume you are. Where are you from, my beauty?"

She blushed slightly but did not appear intimidated by our friend. I noticed that about your mother: not much intimidated her and neither was she deferential in her tone.

"I am Ukrainian, originally from Kharkiv. On the most exciting day of my life, my boyfriend, a White Army captain, and I fled to Odessa as the Red Army approached my city. Of course, I had no idea even more exciting or terrifying days were ahead of me. Odessa is the most glamorous city in Ukraine. Dmitri and I would promenade along the boulevard to the famous steps into the Black Sea. As we strolled arm in arm, we stopped at shops where he bought me jewelry or a handkerchief. I admired what a handsome couple we were in the reflections of the store windows. At the sea, I would sit on a marble bench gazing at the children playing on the shore, as he would fetch me ice cream from the cute little wooden kiosk on the corner. Oh, I should not be boring you gentlemen. I can jabber all night. You wanted cigars, didn't you?"

I had already recognized Edmund as a mischievous fellow; his response confirmed my observation.

"Your anecdote is fascinating. We are hanging on every word. You have such a command of the language; you must be an actress."

"Sir, I am quite respectable, not some sort of fallen woman. I would have delighted in living in Odessa forever. Kharkiv was such a boring provincial town. As a young girl, I hungered to escape and discover the world, but my family laughed at what they called my pretensions. My father planned my marriage to Schmul, his business partner's third son, but that was not the future I dreamed of. At school, I studied French and English. Even then I knew Ukrainian or Russian would not get me far. But it did get me Dmitri. The first time I saw him dressed in his uniform, festooned with ribbons, badges and epaulets…my heart swooned."

With a quick smile to his compatriots, Edmund encouraged her on. "My dear, please continue—my companion here, Mr. Uchida, is enraptured by your tale. Aren't you, Kenzo?"

"Kenzo, what type of name is that? Are you Mongolian? All Ukrainians have Mongolian blood in them from the days of the Cossacks; you can see by the shape of our eyes." Her fingers outlined her eyes as she talked.

"My lady, you have not mentioned your name, so I am not sure how to address you except as perhaps Mrs. *Kyaputen*."

"Oh, I am not Mrs. Anyone, sir. My name is Elisabeth, Elisabeth Dobrovska. You can call me Elisa."

"I am pleased to meet you, Miss Elisa. I am Kenzo Uchida, the Consul General of Japan to Constantinople. This is my deputy, Mitsu Katayama."

"A general," she murmured excitedly, "so you would outrank my captain if he were around anymore. But he's gone."

Edmund jumped in, "Why would anyone drop a darling like you? He must have been a scoundrel to desert such a delightful young woman."

"As I said, I enjoyed our time in Odessa. Dmitri promised to marry me once the war ended. Suddenly, everything took a turn for the worse. The Red Army broke through the ranks at the outskirts of the city, and Odessa was surrounded. Chaos spread as everyone tried to escape. The British abandoned us; overnight their ships were gone. Dmitri disappeared as life got more desperate. Shops closed, and food was scarce. No one had any news, just rumors."

The men in the room were quiet, taken in by this brash woman who seemed to have few boundaries. Even Edmund, who had started her off, was following her story closely.

"Then one morning he returned to our flat and said we had one hour to pack our belongings. I did not own very much, just the dresses, jewelry and the little presents he bought me, which we could pack in one trunk. As I packed, he handed me a heavy package with something metallic wrapped in paper to hide among my tchotchkes. He also had me sew my jewels and money into the seams of my coat. We had very little time, but I am an expert seamstress, taught by my dear mother. I had scarcely completed my work when we heard a knock on the door. Our driver arrived; he took our trunk as we rushed off.

"Outside, pandemonium reigned as the streets were filled with crying and screaming people running toward the harbor. Dmitri took the reins while the driver pushed ahead, guiding his horses through the melee. Occasionally someone would try to jump on the wagon, but Dmitri would push them off. Honestly, although I was afraid, I also found it thrilling, like I was in an adventure story."

She paused for a moment as she recalled the events of that day.

"Those few blocks to the harbor seemed an eternity, but we finally got to the pier where the French ship *Fraternité* was docked a short distance from the shore. Dmitri shoved a piece of paper into my hand, shouting above the unruly crowd, 'get on that before it goes!' I forced through the maddened throngs, clutching this paper. Ahead of me, the driver, our trunk on his shoulder, mowed everyone down in his path. The horror is frozen in my memories. My complete focus was on the boat. A force took hold of me as I shoved and battled my way forward; nothing else mattered.

"Upon finally reaching the pier, a large officious man blocked my way and said that no one but ticket holders were allowed. Only then did I glance at the wadded-up paper—a passage for one to Constantinople. He waved me in, directing the driver to put the trunk on a barge tied to the boat. I scanned the crowds for my Dmitri but could not find him anywhere. I screamed Dimitri's name as they lifted me on the boat, but he was gone."

The room fell silent as we were entranced by the drama of her tale. One of the men offered her a seat, relieving her from the box of wares. Someone else poured her a whiskey, which she downed in one gulp.

Mitsu broke the silence. "It must have been horrific to be alone and scared, having no way of knowing what was next, while losing the man taking care of you. What did you do?"

"Man taking care of me, what man has ever done that?" she snorted. This particular group of men nodded sympathetically.

"Dmitri did not care about me. He only wished to be seen alongside an intelligent, beautiful woman. He was a peasant. Though he dressed well, he had a peasant's mentality. He knew nothing of the fine arts—music, opera, and poetry. He would chide me if I longed to go out on the town at night. So, I went by myself or sometimes even was escorted by another man.

"I do owe my survival to him. Yet on the ship, I began to anticipate what was next. I never looked back."

As she continued talking, I puzzled over such an unusual person. She exhibited an independence I had noticed in Miss Bowers, but whereas Miss Bowers seemed overcome by disappointment, Elisa was full of energy and determination. She was sure of herself and appeared unintimidated by anyone. She clearly had won over the men, who were peppering her with questions. They brought her into their conversation in a good-natured way, similar to how they had done with the two of us. She intrigued me; I liked her, not exactly quite knowing why.

"Continue, please," I implored. "What happened on your trip to Constantinople? Most of all, how did you arrive at Maxim's to entertain us all?"

"You are the unusual one, aren't you? Normally the trip from Odessa via the Bosporus would take two days. But the ship carried triple the normal passengers, each bringing large trunks of valuables. The French, fortunately, are much more civilized than the British."

"How can you insult us? Don't you say another word." Edmund's face was stern, his pride evidently hurt.

"Oh, you sophisticated gentlemen understand exactly what I mean. Your ships deserted us without warning. So much for the might of the British Empire. More to the point, every one of you appreciate that the best of foods, the Champagne and wine you are drinking, are French. I won't ask who has not had a French paramour here, because as a cigarette girl we eavesdrop on all sorts of conversations. Except for our Japanese general, you each have your own secrets. Please don't curse me for telling the truth, or else, Mr. Edmund, I might have to have a word with one of your fellows in the neighboring salon."

The men roared at this retort as Edmund turned a shade of red, which I had not thought possible. Yes, she was extraordinary, a talented European geisha.

"As I was saying, the French did their best to treat us respectfully. Ours was one of the last boats to leave, and we wasted no time in shoving off. In the distance, smoke and fires showed the advance of the Reds. Over the following day, occasional gunfire was aimed toward us, but we were far enough from shore to be safe as we chugged through the choppy waters of the Black Sea.

"By the time I got on board, no staterooms were available. I was not in a place to make a big fuss, so I slept on the deck among others in the identical situation. Lying down, I watched the stars go by as they rotated in their constellations. So many stars are visible at sea. I remembered the stories my father told of the Greek sailors who plied their way by these very shores, searching for the Golden Fleece. I identified the various animals, including the eagle, Aguila. Embedded in Aguila is the constellation of Antinous, consecrated by his lover. Accompanied by the distant fellow travelers above us, I felt secure. Gazing at the limitless universe is exhilarating, don't you think, Mr. General? Can birds distinguish where they are in the sky? Do they measure distances, or do they simply exist in the spacious air?"

Before I could answer, she continued.

"Eventually we entered the Bosporus, passing the cliffs and the roving rocks that threatened Jason's Argonauts. We were forced to stop at a garrison to delouse the ship before we entered the city. Our conditions were crowded, yet we were fine people—not some villagers without hot water and baths. The truth of the matter is the officials glanced at our papers only to demand bribes from each of us. They took our trunks and put them through steam to kill any bugs, which ruined every piece of clothing. My fine dresses were shriveled, forever stained by the odor of insecticide in every seam. Fortunately, they did not search the contents of the trunks or the clothes we wore. I wore my coat with its sewn-in secrets day and night as the weather was cool."

At that second, a very large woman entered. Although she was in a dress, everything else about her seemed masculine, from her muscular arms to the shadow of a beard on her face. Her voice was low and gruff; there was nothing delicate about her. "What are you doing, Elisa? I have been searching for you for the past 30 minutes. I am sorry, gentlemen, this one talks so much that her work is a secondary priority. She does not seem to realize that for every cigarette girl inside this club, five women outside are lining up for her job."

Oddly, I felt a protective urge. "Madam, Miss Elisa sat momentarily while we perused her items for sale. We are having a party here and have bought every cigar she carried. I just requested some more. I am the one you should blame for detaining her. I am new, posing too many questions."

Edmund gave me a queer look, and grinned. "Yes, our friend only recently arrived, but he is catching on quite rapidly. Anyway, Frau Helga, you have yourself spent many an hour among us at the old club. Are you jealous of our little bird here?"

"Hardly, I'm the cock in charge and she's but one in the flock."

For the second time tonight, uproarious laughter ensued in appreciation of such a witty retort.

"Miss Elisa, here are two gold *lira* for the cigars including a tip for yourself. Please bring us more, and perhaps some food."

As I handed her the money, she stared straight into my eyes. No Japanese woman had ever done that. She gave me a long wink and a smile as she took the money and disappeared.

Frau Helga turned to me. "You might prefer to be careful, Mr. Consul. I am told Miss Elisa is on the lookout for a husband. Supposedly the last man of hers dumped her as soon as she arrived here. I told her it was impossible that these White Russians would ever marry a Jewess."

"But she told us he stayed behind," I responded, unsure if I had been following the conversation correctly.

"Oh, she did? Well, I won't contradict her. Beware of that one. She is a bit big for her britches, expecting her fancy education to suffice. The school of hard knocks teaches you a lot more. She has grown up quite a bit in the weeks she has been here."

7. WHEN ONE SIDE IS ILLUMINATED, THE OTHER SIDE IS DARK

Over our morning coffee with Gül, we reviewed the events of our previous evening.

"What a fabulous time. We lingered at Maxim's far later than I had expected, drinking and enjoying ourselves. I hope we made a good impression on our British hosts. But Gül, I have a question, 'Who is Frau Helga?'"

"She has been a fixture at other clubs since before the war. She has an exceptional reputation, so Maxim's hired her immediately. No one knows her complete history, except that she is a German man who enjoys dressing as a woman. The British call it 'drag.'"

"A man! Now I understand how she, or do I say he—"

"We use she; Helga won't have it any other way. Some of us have met her male persona, but most of her fans would never recognize her on the street. She dresses up nightly at the club, manages the personnel, and functions as the bouncer if trouble arises. I once watched her physically carry out two men, one in each arm, without smudging her makeup or knocking a single lock of hair out of place. She is aware of everyone's secrets yet can be completely trusted. It's no surprise she was hired to run almost everything at Maxim's. She visits all the salons but seems to enjoy the British, for obvious reasons."

Mitsu seemed to be lost in thought until he finally said, "There was one conversation we should continue."

"What conversation, Mitsu?"

"The one about you needing a beard. Initially, I thought it odd, but as I pondered what they told us, it more or less began to make sense. We don't yet understand the ways of Europeans, but I heard enough from the other men there to gather that the life of a homosexual in the West can be nightmarish. They told me about a famous British writer, Oscar Wilde, who was admired by so many but was convicted for what was called 'gross indecency', apparently for having sexual relations with another man. He was sent to prison for two years."

"Gül, what do you think about that?" I asked. "Is it true? *Samurai* men have had a venerable history of male friendships and sexual relationships, even if such ways are currently somewhat expressed underground. Woodblock prints depicting sex among men are a revered part of our culture. For us, the unspoken is one's own business."

"Life is different here," he answered. "These men are fearful of someone exposing their lives. Far away from home, they can be relatively safe, but I have observed how differently everyone behaves when the British Foreign Minister comes to visit. Overnight, every man you met at Maxim's produces a girlfriend or wife. It surprises people to hear, but the Ottomans decriminalized homosexuality more than six decades ago. Maybe we are akin to your *samurai*—you have glimpsed how on the street men swagger closely, their arm around the other's shoulder. We can blend in easily. Most of those men are married. However, their male friends are much closer to them than their wives."

Mitsu jumped back in. "Let's return to the beard, Kenzo. It seems crucial to find you a female consort. Someone who can travel as we move on from this post. You will be the one commanding attention—I'm no more than your deputy, no one will notice me."

"This seems a very drastic move. I cannot pretend to care about a woman while I am separated from you."

"Kenzo, I must say Mitsu is correct," Gül responded. "Here, I can keep watch for you, but once you leave the country, you will have to be careful. You will receive lots of scrutiny since you are not European, unable to hide from stares and gossip. Having a woman by your side during public events will be useful. European customs and laws are not very favorable to men of our demeanor."

"And how am I supposed to go about finding such a person? I cannot just interview her, 'Excuse me, would you care to front for a homosexual Japanese man?'"

"Here is why I brought it up. I would say, dear Kenzo, the answer appeared at Maxim's. Remember how Miss Elisa was gazing at you? She was not only comfortable with the men, she also positively sparkled around them. She's the type of person you need."

"Miss Elisa…hmm, an interesting idea. She has a number of positive attributes — she is strong and not easily intimidated by situations, well-educated, and speaks a number of languages. Sophisticated men seem to appreciate her style and comportment. Her obvious enjoyment of the spotlight would deflect any attention. Gül, I trust your opinion. What do you say?"

His eyes lit up and his substantial eyebrows twitched around as he pondered the idea. "Of the women at Maxim's, she is one of the few who might be a good fit. She seems independent and confident. Frau Helga told me more about her. She is definitely not interested in getting married. However, Helga also told me that each time Elisa has shared her narrative, the details appear to change, making it difficult to know what is real and what is not. Despite that, she said Elisa can keep secrets, as apparently, she has a number of her own. If you are interested, I will contact Helga."

With that conversation, your mother entered my life. Gül and Helga made the arrangements for Elisa to join us at the consulate. We met in our salon where large, overstuffed chairs were arranged in clusters around lacquered tables. After an assistant served tea and departed, I turned to Elisa.

"Miss Elisa. Thank you for coming here today. I have a delicate situation, and you might be the right person to assist me."

"I can't imagine what I might be able to do for you, but I am all ears, as we say."

"I will try to be direct, although this is complicated. My deputy Mitsu and I have both a professional connection and an intimate one. You may have noticed that the other night when we met you. You certainly have a sense of the type of men who come to the British salon."

"Oh, don't be concerned, Mister General, Elisa has seen much in her time. She knows how to keep a secret."

"Excellent, which leads me to discuss a related topic. To keep the relationship between Mitsu and me private, I would be best served to have a woman as part of my public life. You might have heard the term 'beard' used by some of the men."

She nodded affirmatively.

"I would propose that you become my public consort at parties, social events, and even certain diplomatic ones. To be blunt, I need someone I would enjoy bringing to those events. There would be no intimacy at all, if you understand my meaning. I know this is much to ask of you and I expect you will need to reflect on my proposal—"

Before I even finished, she interrupted, "Even as a child, I've dreamed of such a sophisticated, carefree life. With so much to discover, so much culture to explore, so many countries to see, I was not made to be some man's wife taking care of him and a passel of children. I ditched that notion long ago. Dmitri gave me the means to do what I want. Since you won't want control over me, this sounds ideal. Yes, yes. Thank you for your offer. We shall become the best of friends."

I was taken aback by her enthusiasm, but given our previous encounter, I was not surprised. Maybe surprise is the wrong word. I was ready to be surprised by this woman, who seemed unique as anyone I had met. I was curious about how she became so independent and sure of herself. I must admit I was a bit envious of how your mother was continuously open to new ideas and experiences. She longed for something beyond her reach, and she was motivated by that desire. Her yearnings would generally keep her buoyant, even during the hardest of times. I was won over by her, enough so to only later realize that I missed the warning signs. Beguiling others was also one of her talents.

"Mr. Uchida—that sounds so formal. May I address you as Kenzo? Your first name is light and more inviting. Initially, when Frau Helga broached our meeting, I was suspicious. I asked her, 'What does this yellow man require of me?' I don't mean to offend you; I didn't know any better. Frau chastised me for being so rude. I have no familiarity with your culture and have heard whispers of the mysterious ways of the East. I will need to learn a lot more if we are to become a team. I wouldn't trust any man, no matter where he came from. But Frau Helga explained how you are one of very special types of men that women can trust and who will treat me as an equal. I am intrigued by that possibility most of all."

"Your honesty can overcome your lack of knowledge of me, my background, and culture. I can tell you right off, you are as mysterious to us as we are to you. We will need a special bond of honesty. Mitsu once told me a Buddhist saying, 'When one side is illuminated, the other side is dark.' What we perceive about each other is equal to what we are unaware of and do not perceive. Both sides make the whole person. Also, you must consider Mitsu. He is as much part of me as the air I breathe. You must be willing to also accept him. I am hoping you can do this."

"I understand. Jealousy is not a trait I have. I am not possessive. I enjoy luxury yet have lived with pittances. I wish to be cared for yet will fight for my independence. Most of all, I desire to be appreciated for who I am. Whomever you treasure and care about is part of you, and I will respect him equally. However, we must have separate lives. I must insist similar respect is given to me. As long as I am discreet, I must be free to have my own friendships, especially with regards to men."

"Agreed. Let's have a toast to our 'business' relationship." I rang for my assistant, and he returned, carrying a bottle of sake. He poured cups for each of us, which Helga handed out. "Mitsu, are there other logistics we should address?"

"I have confidence in Miss Elisa. There is one issue we have not discussed. On your salary as the Consul General, Kenzo, you do not earn enough money to maintain a lavish lifestyle. I don't want Miss Elisa to think you will be able to extravagantly support her. I am sorry to bring this up. I hope you are not offended by my words."

Elisa was quiet and peered over the room as if she had just noticed the ornate vases in the walls and the large candelabra on the main table. "Gentlemen, only a prostitute would introduce the topic of money. The money I earn at Maxim's is mere pocket change. I could not afford to live as I do currently, based solely on what I earn there. In addition to the jewels sewn into my coat, Dmitri stashed a heavy metallic package inside my trunk. Those four bars of gold shall allow me to live quite comfortably."

"Gold," exclaimed Frau Helga. "Four bars of gold, a fortune. Where did he get such a thing?"

"Frankly, he told me little about his soldiering. I suspect they were the spoils of war from one of the banks in a city they overran. He was always very generous—the jewelry he gave me was genuine, not fake costume trinkets. Since I arrived, I have had to sell a couple of the jewels, but I still have more in addition to the gold. So, Mr. Mitsu, don't worry about supporting me. While I would never reject a gift from an admirer, I am an independent woman, not beholden to anyone."

She gave us contented smile and raised her cup. "*Na starovya!*" she exclaimed, clinking her cup.

"*Kanpai*! is how we toast, Miss…"

"Will you please stop calling me Miss? My name is Elisa, not Miss or Mrs. You may refer to me as Mademoiselle, if you wish not to use my name."

Even Frau Helga was impressed. "I might have misjudged you, Elisa. You have more gumption than most women. So many of the White Russian women who are down to their last fur cling to the pretensions of their previous social status. I assumed you were one of them, but now it all makes sense. A woman not born into riches understands the value of money. You will go far in life. I am not sure what might possibly stop you, but be careful - none of us can foresee the future."

"Another matter is left to attend to," said the ever-practical Mitsu. "Kenzo has never escorted a woman on his arm. While it sounds simple, it's not our custom. We cannot have ..." he paused for a second. "We cannot have Mademoiselle trailing three feet behind Kenzo as if she were a Japanese wife."

Frau Helga took charge. She moved a few overstuffed chairs to the side with a quick swipe of her hand and pulled me close to her. She raised my arm up. "Kenzo, stick out your elbow, no, not like you are knocking someone to the side, but extend your arm across your body. That's better. Elisa, come over here, slip your hand in. Now, Kenzo, don't be so nervous. Take a breath and look directly at Elisa. You can even smile, pretend it's your Mitsu holding onto your arm. Now the two of you take a step."

I felt uneasy having her so close. My nose was assaulted by a flowery perfume, mixed with a light smell of her body and hair pomade. The hand holding my arm was diminutive, almost without substance. We were about equal height, so her face was inches from mine. I saw the pores of her skin, the dark makeup on her eyelids and what appeared to be a mole on her chin.

All of this was disconcerting. Taking our first step, I tripped and lurched forward. Even dear Mitsu was laughing, though I knew he was concerned. He came behind me to put his arm on my shoulder. The three of us inched around until I got the hang of it. He stepped back, letting the two of us manage by ourselves. Of course, Elisa knew what she was doing and assisted. I got brave and guided her to the large main staircase. We glided up to the landing, where we turned to our little crew of admirers, who cheered as I gently and smoothly escorted her to the bottom of the stairs.

Frau Helga clapped her hands in delight.

"Kenzo, you are an excellent student. Of course, three of us had to intercede to teach you how to walk! You need to enjoy yourself and show off your attractive partner. Once you do that, you will be fine.

"We have one final lesson, Kenzo. You must practice kissing Elisa's hand."

Elisa extended her hand. I had witnessed men greeting women by kissing their hands, but I just stared at her in a confused manner. One more time, Frau Helga stepped in to gently extend my hand to meet Elisa's, then elevate hers close to my lips. I peered at her hand as if it were a foreign object. I turned to Mitsu for reassurance, who was also getting emotional. Frau Helga nodded, and I kissed her hand.

My brain froze while recording the moment, which is coming back to me as I write. How odd, I thought, my lips can sense the slim shape of her fingers as well as the roughness of her knuckles. The smells I had noticed earlier were much fuller, almost overwhelming in their intensity. In my hand, her hand seemed strangely petite, nothing like Mitsu's. She had a smile on her face, as she closed her eyes briefly when my lips touched her skin. There was nothing else in the room, nothing else in the vast eternity for me at this juncture. I was aware of my body standing on the rug, my stomach taut. I felt a slight breeze, which I realized was my breath, releasing the air from my lungs.

I let her hand go and stepped back.

"Bravo, you both look magnificent. I expect that the two of you will be the talk of the town soon enough. My work here is done." Frau Helga took a little bow, which was incongruous for a person of her size.

Gül came over and kissed Elisa on the cheeks. Mitsu bowed to her, chatting softly for a minute before she and the others exited. Alone, Mitsu lifted my hand to his mouth and gave me a kiss that shook me to my toes. He squeezed me closer, peered into my eyes, and kissed me again.

"Kenzo, I hope we are together forever."

With pride filling my chest, we walked hand-in-hand to our bedroom, not needing to say a word, fully enveloped as one without boundaries.

8. THE MOON DOES NOT MAKE A HOLE IN THE WATER

The *Ballo Italiano,* held in the Ambassador's residence on the Asian side of the city, was the most sought-after event in the social calendar, to which only the highest-ranking members of the international community were invited. Our invitation included a note from the ambassador stating he was personally looking forward to seeing Mitsu and I. Upon mentioning this to Edmund, he pointed his finger in the air and assured us that we had much in common with the ambassador, despite the presence of his beautiful wife.

Since he already had our measurements, our tailor prepared formal eveningwear for us. Another costume, another way of being. As I was tying Mitsu's bow tie and arranging his waistcoat, Gül entered to inform us of Elisa's arrival.

"I believe you may be pleasantly surprised," he said, betraying little else.

"Thank you, Gül. Please escort her to the waiting room, as we are almost finished here."

I turned back to Mitsu. "Tonight will be special. We are ready to premier new roles on a *kabuki* stage—our costumes are fit, masks are on."

"Kenzo, during our university days we used to fantasize about going to formal diplomatic parties. How quickly those dreams have turned into reality! The best part for me is accompanying the most handsome man in Constantinople."

We kissed, did a final straightening of our ties and inspected each other.

I gave Mitsu a playful slap as we stepped out.

Standing by the large ceramic fireplace was a radiant woman wearing a blue silk dress, exposing her lower leg. A sash somewhat resembling an *obi* was tied to the side of her waist rather than her back. The dress hung from her bare shoulders on thin jeweled straps that glittered in the light. Her powder-blue, high-heeled shoes matched the color of the dress. Elisa, our little ingénue, had become a cosmopolitan woman.

"What do you think? The dress came from one of the most fabulous French designers here in the city. He said it is what everyone is wearing in Paris these days. I am terribly excited about tonight."

She twirled, the skirt billowing around her.

"You will be the most beautiful woman at the ball as you make your debut. I am honored to be your escort for the evening. The carriage is waiting—let's go."

She put her arm in mine as we entered the carriage. Mitsu followed behind, making sure she was comfortably in. The carriage driver took us to the Galata ferry landing, where we caught a boat for the short trip to Kadiköy. Clearly, most of the passengers were headed to the same affair. A number of men eyed Elisa, trying to discern our pairing. At the station, waiting carriages whisked us to the Italian Residence, a large four-story stone building. At the entrance, the doorman took our invitations and announced our names.

A few steps inside, Elisa was ecstatic.

"Look around. There are flowers everywhere, and their scent is glorious, making me dizzy. I have finally arrived in society. All the guests are so elegantly dressed! How marvelous, Kenzo, a waiter is offering me Champagne. Less than a month ago, I was the one doing the serving."

We each took a glass from the tuxedo-clad waiter. "*Kanpai,* here's to our first party."

We clinked our glasses and sipped what was to be one of many drinks. Shortly, we espied Edmund among the crowd and waved him over.

"Well, my chums, I am glad you are here. The Italians consistently throw the finest parties. The best drink and food, in addition to the most handsome men and beautiful ladies." Turning to Elisa, he extended his hand. "And whom do we have here, accompanying the Japanese delegation?"

"I do believe we have met, Sir. You may call me Mademoiselle Elisa. I have recently arrived on the arm of my dear Kenzo."

It took Edmund a minute to identify her. "You have been transformed, my darling, simply transformed. Although my eyes turned to you as soon as you entered the hall, I honestly did not recognize you. Kenzo has heeded my suggestion. Your secret is mine. I won't tell a soul, well, maybe except for the boys."

"Please let them make their own conclusions, but know from this point on, Miss, um, Mademoiselle Elisa is my consort. I wish my words to be respected."

"Rightly so, old chum, rightly so. A pleasure to meet you, Mademoiselle. I expect you will be the belle of the ball. Kenzo, may I have the pleasure of dancing with your consort this evening?"

"Please do," I replied. "I have not yet learned how to dance. It is something that Japanese men do not do."

"Kenzo, when in Constantinople, do what Constantinopolitans do! Watch me later on. By the next party I will have taught you some steps. You will have to learn—dancing is a requirement at these affairs. During the wasted time we spent at university studying international politics, no one ever suggested how important such social graces were needed for success."

The evening whirled by—more so for Elisa than for Mitsu and me. The Italian ambassador and his wife were making their rounds and greeted Elisa with a kiss on her hand.

"Signorina, you are a vision of beauty, a shining star diminishing all others in the firmament above. I am pleased you are fortunate to have the arm of Consul Uchida. He is one of my most trusted companions here. You might have much in common with my charming wife, Sofia. The two of you must get to know each other better. Don't you agree, my darling? She gets lonesome whenever I have to attend to my frequent late-night work meetings." At this, he winked at me.

"Please enjoy yourself, my dear. I would enjoy the pleasure of a dance, if your companion does not mind."

For the second and not the last time during the evening, I gladly assented.

As we mingled arm-in-arm among the crowd (where I managed not to stumble), quite a number of couples introduced themselves. Elisa engaged them in lively conversation, which often ended with, 'We must have supper one evening soon.' As Edmund intuited, she was a hit. If any of the men did recall her from Maxim's, they were silent, not revealing her secret. A few men indiscreetly inquired where I found such a delightful young consort.

We moved into the ballroom where a band was tuning up. As promised, Edmund invited Elisa onto the dance floor, where they moved beautifully synchronized across the floor. I did not know the difference between a waltz and mazurka, but I admired how the couples gracefully slid about the room. Mitsu and I watched intently as we commented about the athleticism and beauty of the men.

True to his word, the ambassador monopolized Elisa for quite a stretch. I sensed he danced for several reasons—one of which was for the crowd to notice this mysterious woman and, by reflection, the man who brought her. I was glad she was happy. As for me, my reputation was improving by the minute. Some of the wives came over to inquire about us. They seemed satisfied by my answers that I was new to the international stage and had not yet learned to dance. They expressed confidence in Elisa's talents to teach me. Elisa did drag me onto the dance floor at one point for a slow fox trot, managing to guide me in one direction, then another. I eventually got into the rhythm but was exhausted from the intense concentration.

The evening ended at midnight. Upon our departure, the ambassador, his hand on my shoulder, invited Mitsu and me to have dinner with him one evening soon. He kissed Elisa on both cheeks, much to her obvious delight.

The gas lamps on the street matched her glow as we boarded our carriage. Elisa rested her head on my shoulder; on my other side, Mitsu gently rubbed my thigh.

9. A TRACE OF REALIZATION THAT CANNOT BE GRASPED

New ways of living fell into place. Lying entwined under our covers, morning was an intimate time for us. We would wake with the *muezzin* calling the *Fajr* morning prayer. Snuggled, we would whisper, waiting for the end of prayer at sunrise. My hand would lazily massage Mitsu's smooth chest as it reminded itself of his body. I didn't need vision to identify this body as his, the boniness of his shoulders, the firmness of his thighs, the meatiness of his stomach, the thick smoothness of his hair, the delicateness of his nose and the roughness of the overnight growth of stubble on his face. Yes, it was all Mitsu.

After completing this corporal journey, I would pull him closer, spooning his back into my chest, kissing his neck. My lips had their own sets of memory of the back of his head, the nape of his neck, his right earlobe. I checked each body part off the morning list to verify he was the same Mitsu that I fell asleep with the evening before. As I clutched him closer, the heat emanating from his body warmed me up. Our legs wrapped around each other, the bottoms of his feet touching mine, shivers of joy announcing our connection. We would lie like this until we roused or became aroused. Either way, these luxuriant mornings were the only part of the day without the intervention of anyone else.

As we emerged from bed, we would wash up, shave, and dress. We reserved western clothes for special occasions; otherwise, we would slip on the *juban*, the white undergarment. Then we would tie our *hakama*, a long skirt containing two straps that wrapped around our torsos. Finally, we put on the *haori* on top, an open robe with wide sleeves. Unlike our western clothes, I appreciated the loose fit, which allowed for easy movement. Without external pockets, our robes had wide sleeves to store small objects. Your *samurai* great-grandfather would have finished by sliding a sword through a belt.

Dressed, we headed to the kitchen, where we would have an informal breakfast consisting of rice or rice gruel on cool mornings, miso soup, fish, pickles and vegetables. I say 'informal' because other meals were served in the dining room. Except for the large tubs of miso and the sake shipped from Japan, everything else was local. Each morning, the cook's assistant scoured the market before we awoke to buy fresh fish and vegetables. The pickles were made and left to ferment until they were ready. Japanese kitchens had this mixture of salty, spicy, and vinegary smells, so even here I was reminded each morning of your great-grandmother's kitchen.

Breakfast eaten, we would head to our offices, where the paperwork of the Japanese bureaucracy kept us busy for a few hours each day. We accounted for each item we purchased in large, leather-bound ledgers, down to the exact weight and price of the local rice and fish the cook procured. We notated every meeting we had (save those informal meetings at Maxim's), with whom we met, and the topics of discussions. The Foreign Ministry was particularly concerned about our observations of the British, French, Italians and Americans stationed in the region. We were expected to have rough counts of the numbers of armed troops, the size of the delegations, and any gossip about local or international politics. Finally, we had to follow up on any contracts or sales.

If urgent news broke, which honestly was quite rare, we were supposed to telegram Tōkyō immediately. We sent two such messages when local nationalist fervor was heating up and Mustafa Kemal was rumored to be near the city. We would in turn receive information about changes to the cabinet of Prime Minister Hara. Although telegrams took a mere few hours to be delivered, being so far removed meant that essential information in Japan was often meaningless to us. Rarely did personnel changes affect our daily concerns halfway across the globe.

Once a week, Mitsu, Gül and I would roam the dusty narrow streets of Stambul. On one particular day, we headed to the famed Hagia Sofia, a sixth-century basilica turned into a mosque. Unlike other more prominent mosques near the shore, the Hagia Sofia is hidden in plain daylight in the middle of the old city, surrounded by buildings, markets, *hammams* and houses. The mishmash of busy streets did not allow for a clear view as we wandered from the Galata Bridge until we reached the south side. Standing there, its grandeur was revealed.

The mosque loomed over the neighboring structures, resembling a man-made mountain surrounded by four guard towers—minarets added almost nine centuries after the original building was constructed. The round dome formed the top of the mountain, wide and frankly inconceivable in size. Staggered around it were a number of other hills - other domes of various heights. Just as our temples recreate nature in our gardens, this magnificent structure mimicked the foothills of Anatolia, the blue tiles and brown and white walls representing the sky and land respectively.

Gül gained permission to enter the temple between prayers. An unremarkable narrow hallway did not prepare us for the magnificence of the prayer room. I caught my breath as I followed the soaring stone walls to the dome, illuminated by a series of windows encircling the bottom. We were inside the mountain itself, gazing toward the sun. Gül translated the Arabic writing on the dome, which announces God as the light of the universe. Neither Shinto nor Buddhism has a concept of an omnipotent God, so this was still curious to us. I felt uplifted by the very expansiveness of the temple and saw that Mitsu was likewise transported as he gazed over the chamber. Maybe this was the spirit of 'God.'

As we were starting to be jostled by the hordes of men entering for the afternoon prayers soon to come, we followed Gül out. The heat and noise of the dusty streets were more dramatic after our time in the cool sanctuary. A few minutes later, he led us into a low building.

"Here, come in, the *dhikar* is about to commence," Gül announced. "To the Sufis, *dhikar* is a practice of the consciousness of divine compassion."

We doffed our shoes and stood quietly against a wall. Ahead of us, about thirty men dressed in a fashion I had not observed on the streets, arranged themselves in several lines. Each had a white *hakama* that reached the floor, the top covered by a short, white, matching jacket. On their heads were tall, brown, camel-hair hats, each about two *shaku* high. The men were standing completely still, eyes closed, arms crossed against the chests.

The quiet was broken by several musicians strumming on stringed instruments as they accompanied a group of singers. Imperceptibly, one by one, the men uncrossed their hands and raised their right hands up while pointing their left hands down. If that was not odd enough, they did the most astonishing thing: They began to twirl. Initially, they spun slowly around the same spot, increasing speed as the music's tempo intensified. As they twirled, their *hakama* lifted, billowing out almost as wide as they were high. Their feet, clad in little black shoes, deftly moved rapidly, spinning faster and faster. Their tall hats, tilted back at an angle, seemed to move at a slower speed than their feet.

Gül explained, "These are Sufi mystics called 'whirling dervishes.'"

Mitsu asked the question whirling about my brain. "Why are they doing this?"

"Their practice is to revolve around their heart. By doing so, they encompass all of humanity. They do this to connect to the rhythm of the universe to find peace for the rest of us."

Entranced, I understood why Gül had taken us here today. The music pulsated in my entire body. Although sitting still, I was myself spinning, my heart beating in time to the music and these men. I closed my eyes as waves of energy passed over and into me, lifting me higher and higher until I was near the top of the Hagia Sofia dome, peering at the earth below. The crowd below me began whirling. From my vantage point, the individuals joined as spinning discs, indistinguishable, all as one being. For a brief second, I joyously understood life itself.

As the music gradually slowed, I floated back to the ground. I opened my eyes and saw the dervishes still spinning, yet more slowly, their *hakama* touching the ground again.

"They come back to us, back to our reality to serve humanity. They show us possibilities, then they return to practicalities. No one can stay where they were forever."

As my heartbeat slowed, I felt more alive than I had ever been. Their message penetrated the deepest reaches of my body, although much time would pass before I understood what I had experienced. Yet once it entered, the feeling never left.

10. THERE IS A PATH AND PLACE

Gül knocked at our door early one morning. "A telegram for you, Sir, just arrived from Tōkyō."

Groggily, I arose to let him in. "Have a seat. What can be so urgent?"

I scanned the page he handed to me, and while I let the words sink in I carefully folded the paper back up.

"What is the news?" Mitsu asked, noting my change in demeanor. "We have never had any urgent telegrams from Tōkyō."

I unfolded the telegram and read it aloud.

"'You have been appointed Consul-General to the Republic of France stop Report to the Ambassador in Paris by 17 May Taishō 9 stop Deputy Consul Katayama Mitsu will accompany you stop' We are going to France!"

Mitsu jumped up to give me a big hug.

"France. What a fantastic posting! We have three months until we have to be there. That's not enough time to buy tickets, pack—"

I planted my hand on his shoulder. "My dear Mitsu, you are ever the practical one. We don't have to rush these decisions. Gül will manage the logistics and hopefully will accompany us on at least part of the journey. Let's enjoy the time we have remaining in Constantinople. We will continue the adventure we started. I look forward to viewing what unfolds."

"What about Elisa?" he asked. "Will there be the three of us? If so, the trip will be quite different."

"I had not thought about her. Hmm, I suppose we are in the exact situation we discussed previously. Edmund will know what we should do. Gül, would you please make an appointment to get his advice this afternoon? Official business, of course."

"Of course, Consul. We have an appointment at 3 p.m. today. I took the liberty of making one for you following the arrival of the telegram. I assumed you would seek his advice, no matter what the situation was."

"Between your ability to guess our very needs before I even speak, and Mitsu's practicality, sometimes I am not sure what my role is. You both cover whatever needs to be done."

With his arm around me, Mitsu responded. "Without you, we are nothing. I mean it. I am here to make sure that you are happy and successful."

"Gül, what do you have to say about our transfer? How much have you traveled outside of Turkey?"

"Following the war, I traveled around parts of western Europe. I am guessing life has changed significantly since those days. I would be more than curious to discover how these regions have been rebuilt. I am also here to serve and assist you, in any way possible. I have no family here to make me stay. If you so required, I would enjoy accompanying you as long as you would like."

"You have no one here at all? Family or special friends?"

"No, my parents and family are gone."

"I am sorry to hear that, and even more sorry I did not ask previously. Given what you just told us, I hope you will join us. Your considerable skills will be of great utility, even more so than here."

"Thank you, Consul. Honestly, I hoped you would invite me, but I dared not ask. As Mitsu stated, we are an excellent team. I would be sad to lose you both, now that we have found each other."

"Let's get dressed. There is much to do. The other week you helped me contemplate the connections of the universe; today the possible universe widened significantly."

Edmund had a spacious, well-appointed office in the British Embassy.

Reflecting its military might, each office projected the mores of the ruling power. Without ever having been in the Ministry of Foreign Affairs offices in London I suspected his office would not have been out of place there. The walls were covered in striped wallpaper upon which a grand portrait of the king was displayed, in addition to large, signed proclamations of some sort. A hefty wooden desk occupied a substantial portion of one side of the room, while several dark, overstuffed leather chairs were clustered about a small table on the other side.

Waving his hand, he invited us to have a seat. "Would you gentlemen prefer tea or whiskey this afternoon? Officially teatime just commenced, but it's also late enough for us to have the first glass of whiskey for the day."

"Well," I replied, "there really is no choice here. Somehow you Brits have destroyed the wonderful tea we grow by adding milk and sugar to make an abysmal drink. I'd rather sip a drink incorporating much more refined qualities."

"You realize, my dear Kenzo, if you were not a foreign emissary I would have you court-martialed for your impudence. On the other hand, I applaud your recognition of the centuries of effort that have gone into the distilling of malt into an unparalleled drink. I must admit, I do appreciate you for introducing me to sake, the best way one can consume rice."

He clapped his hands, and a man appeared at the door. "Drinks, please, for our guests."

As the man returned with a bottle and glasses, Edmund turned to us. "What brings you to the seat of civilization on such a dreary afternoon? Honestly, I was relieved when Gül contacted me for an appointment, as it gave me an excuse to cancel a boring meeting with some British trade representatives who want my insights on the Turkish textiles market. Talk about bringing coals to Newcastle, I can't visualize locals wearing British tweeds in this ungodly hot weather. The stupidity of these people…"

"I have good and bad news, Edmund. I received word of our transfer to Paris in May. Our tour here is almost finished. I am being appointed to head the consulate there."

"Jolly good, chap. Great news, but what is the bad?"

"I regret that we will be missing your company following our departure."

"I am not so naïve to believe such bosh, yet I appreciate the boost to my ego, having you acknowledge our friendship. I have enjoyed educating you both to our ways here."

"We have come to seek your advice, Edmund, regarding Elisa. You have watched her over the past months at social occasions. For the reasons you originally suggested, she seems an appropriate companion. Should she accompany me to Paris?"

"Indeed, yes. Indeed. She has shown quite a capability to put others at ease. She has mastered the pleasantries of the boring and sophisticated banter on which women will judge her. Men are captured by her allure, by how she makes each of them feel special. She has been the ideal partner for you. Even her flaws make her a better match."

"What do you mean? How can her flaws be assessed as a positive thing?"

Edmund paused as he pulled out a cigar. He carefully clipped the end prior to lighting. He took a few puffs to make sure it was drawing properly before he returned to the conversation.

"Proper society can easily discern that she was not born wealthy, by the way she speaks and puts on airs. However, these qualities make your liaison more realistic. Wait a second, don't leer at me—I am not insulting you. I am honestly telling you what the sophisticated class will observe. Most of them believe anyone not born and bred in certain circles is of a lesser state of being. For the Brits, the further from Kensington you are, the lower the class you are considered.

"Yet even for us, the Japanese are treated as a special class of people. Your culture has a refinement and a style which remain popular in the upper classes. They are intrigued by a society bound by so many rules and a strict hierarchy. Unlike, say, when appraising the Indians, they make note of your acumen and appreciate your sense of beauty. So, they may scrutinize you, yet only had you been born British could you be any better. Instead, you provide a thrill as a mysterious sort of being who has refinement, maybe more refinement than they do."

"Although I have come to understand you since our first meeting Edmund, I still get confused as to whether you are insulting or complimenting me. Yet I do understand what you are saying. Ironically, we Japanese have perceptions akin to those you described. The rest of the world seems brusque to us, lacking care and cultivation. We spend centuries tending to our temples and their gardens. What you call art is simply our way of being. Everything is made purposefully, elegantly, as if nature itself is responsible for the creation. Our gifted artisans, statesmen, geishas, swordsmen, and actors reflect the essence of life as we perceive it.

"Throughout history, adventurers set forth from our island. Upon return, they brought back new ideas, tools, and inventions. Yet when foreigners arrived on our shore, they could not appreciate our culture. They ignored how each custom makes the whole of our culture. Since the British, and even worse, the Americans, forced themselves on us, we have had many opportunities to study your ways. Western technology boosted us to modernize. The younger generation, including Mitsu and me, are enchanted by modern life, yet we do not desire to forsake who we are as Japanese. Naturally, we are leery of others and their ways. Although I do not believe in such prejudices, too many Japanese believe we are naturally superior to any other race, especially those nearby us in Korea and China. I perceive how we stratify our relationships. However, I am not sure how Elisa fits into this."

"Let's go back to the last point I was making. You are unusual to us, but unlike other races we encounter, we want to appreciate you. If you had a Japanese wife, that would make you seem too foreign, too standoffish. However, Elisa provides an opening for the acceptance of the two of you as outsiders. They view her as a bit brash, someone who does not properly fit within high society. Your presence provides the sophistication she lacks, and her presence provides you the entrée into society you lack as a 'single man.'

"As a final point, I must say I am giving you the British view. The French are much more accepting. They are intrigued by the different races—the Africans, the Muslims, the Orientals. They are more daring and appreciate foreign cultures much more than the British. To top it off, they love women of all types. Elisa will find paramours among French men. You will be able to live there gaily."

"Thank you, my friend. I have learned much from you. I suspect our diplomatic careers will cross again."

"This is not a wake, nor am I dead. Enough talk. I suggest we have dinner at Maxim's tonight, where we can toast your entourage as you launch your journey. Perhaps I can lure Mr. Gül from the Consulate now you are leaving. I can always use such a trustworthy man on my staff."

"Gül will be joining us in Paris," answered Mitsu. "A man of such talents is priceless."

"Mr. Gül, if you change your mind, the British Embassy has a position for you. Okay, gentlemen, see you tonight."

Gül sent a message to Elisa to meet us at Maxim's for supper. She had stopped working there quite a while ago, and on her last day, Frau Helga held a going-away party. Her former colleagues were jealous of her new status, although, according to Frau, their jealousy was tempered by more than a bit of disdain about her willingness to consort with a Japanese man.

My Nina, you have already discovered the bite of racism. The little I have learned about you–more meaningfully, all I have learned about Americans–point to great suffering in your life, being born in New York City when you were and as you were. But I am getting ahead of myself. Racism was rampant; we experienced its stings in how we were treated and what was said behind our backs.

That evening, we met Elisa at the British salon. As she entered, I kissed her cheeks on both sides, a more sophisticated greeting she had recently taught me. Stealing my thunder, Edmund spoke up.

"Let's raise a glass to our dear friends, Kenzo, Mitsu, Gül, and the incomparable Mademoiselle Elisa. May they have wonderful adventures on their way to Paris."

Elisa was shocked by the announcement.

"Paris? What does he mean? Kenzo, what is he talking about?"

"As usual, Edmund runs ahead of the rest of us," I said, giving him a dirty look. "We have not had a chance to talk, so I must do this publicly. I would be pleased if you would join us as I take my post as consul-general to the Republic of France."

"Of course, my dear Kenzo, I would travel to the end of the world with you, but of course Paris is perhaps better considered the beginning, *n'est-ce pas?* How soon do we go? Why didn't you tell me sooner? I would have dressed better for such an announcement. From the time I saw a picture of the Tour Eiffel, I knew that one day I would be there. Promise to take me to the top as soon as we arrive."

My face flushed, as she kissed me in front of everyone.

Fortunately, Frau entered with a bottle of Champagne in her hands. "On the house tonight. Let's celebrate the wonderful news of my young Ukrainian protégée. Drinks for all."

Everyone came by offering congratulations. A number of men told me what to expect of Paris, especially regarding the large homosexual community in the spheres of arts, ballet and music.

11. NOTHING AT ALL HAS UNCHANGING SELF

In a few short months, I have already become accustomed to this cold, barren room consisting of nothing more than a bed, toilet, sink and my little table, upon which I am writing to you. The barred windows originally overlooked a similar-sized building across the courtyard. I would peer longingly at the bits of lives visible on the other side—families in their flats, shutting the curtains at night to keep the light from escaping, opening them in the morning, revealing everyday patterns as they exist in times of war. Children would run and play games in the courtyard for hours on end.

My life has taught me that humans seek to create permanence where it does not exist; we cling to what we think we have. I sometimes think of this place as home to give it a veneer of familiarity. Yet I have no home in the sense of a physical place, filled with a sense of ownership and security. I believe that none of us do. Home is a concept of the mind imbued through imagination. For each of us, home constitutes a bundle of accumulated experiences mixed with desires and fears. Believing you have a fixed, unchanging home is a delusion.

I have always been an explorer while simultaneously being a homebody. Once I settle in new accommodations, I put my mark on them, arrange my things and find a place for my clothes and futon. My needs are simple—an area to store, cook and eat my food; a seat on the floor to meditate; a table to write upon. Little by little I become comfortable in my established routines. Soon, that space pretends to be home. As soon as it does, I will seek a reason to leave for its inability to be everything I desire it to be.

The moment we found out that we would be leaving Constantinople, our routines began to feel precious. I wanted to hold onto them and make sure I was appreciating this environment which would soon disappear. The more I wanted to remember and hold on, the further the present flew away. I was clinging to a present at the same time my mind started clinging to a future. In this condition, time is endless, yet slips by quickly.

We returned often to watch the dervishes' prayer dance reverie. Gül translated for me as I spent hours quizzing the mystics for answers to questions I had difficulty even forming. They met my anxiety with a deep serenity as they attempted to explain the unexplainable. Once, I tried their dancing myself, spinning and spinning, but I just became dizzy rather than transcendent.

"Patience," they would tell me.

"I am leaving soon," I would reply.

"Patience. You will have time—we all have time to observe what is within us."

Patience was not easily come by. In my youth, my father and his wife were gone for extended periods during his overseas diplomatic posts. I was left in the loving care of my grandmother. Until I was four years old, all I knew was her small house in a quiet neighborhood. Then one day, without warning, I was thrust into the lives of these two unknown adults.

A call summoned my grandmother from the front entry. She slid the door open while I shyly hid behind her kimono. An elegant horse-drawn open-air carriage came to a stop in front of the house and I could see the neighbors gawking at the unusual sight. A formally dressed man descended and gave my grandmother a carefully wrapped package. Before she untied the bow and folded the paper back, she quietly read an enclosed note. When she finished, I thought I saw a tear in her eye. Wiping it away, she turned to me and exclaimed, "Oh look my dear, what nice, beautiful clothes your father has sent you! Let me dress you up so he can see you in them."

I stood there shocked and said nothing. At four, I did not know who she was talking about. Although my grandmother had told me about him, up to this point he was merely a fantasy like people in her other stories.

"Come, my dear, let's get you dressed. We don't want to be keep him waiting."

"Keep waiting? Waiting for what, *Oma*?"

"Your father is back in Tokyo and wants to see you. He wants you to live with him for a while."

"But why?" Disoriented and afraid, I pleaded, "I don't want to leave you."

"*Mago*, your father is back home now, and it is time that you get to know him. He is an important man. I cannot go with you, but you are a big boy now. Remember, he is your father and you must obey him. Be the good boy that you are with me and all will be fine."

I had never worn western clothes and shoes before, and they felt stiff and uncomfortable. My grandmother put a few other things in a bag for me and walked me out. She hugged me one last time before the man lifted me up to sit on the wide upholstered seat all by myself. I began to cry but she shushed me quiet and the carriage took off with a start, nearly throwing me out.

Down the street, the neighborhood vegetable seller looked at me with wonder in his eyes. I wanted to wave, but I was too busy trying to hold on. Within minutes, we were away from my street and everything I knew. People were walking and whenever we passed, they peered at me - likely wondering who this rich kid was, alone in a fancy carriage.

Finally we arrived at an intimidating western-style house. I had only seen such homes in books and did not know that we had them in Japan. The driver lifted me out and walked me to the door of the house. Another man appeared to let me in.

"Good afternoon, Father," I bowed, remembering my grandmother's words. The man laughed and said, "I am not your father, young boy. I will bring you to him."

We walked through several large rooms. I wanted to ask questions about all of the things I was seeing but knew that would be rude. If my grandmother were there, she could have explained everything. The man who was not my father knocked on a door and a voice from inside called us in.

My father was seated behind a large wooden desk. I stood by a chair and waited for him to give me some sign of what I was to do. Finally, he looked up and smiled.

"Kenzo, my son, you have grown. When I last saw you, you were a baby in your grandmother's lap. Come here, let me look at you."

Hesitantly, I walked to the side of his desk and bowed.

"Yes, you certainly look like my boy. I hope you are excited to be here."

I must have had a strange look on my face because he suddenly got annoyed.

"Why is your face so crooked? The first time you see your father you should be happy. Why do you think I brought you here? I am only back in Tōkyō for a short time and wanted to see my son, not some sour-faced boy."

Honestly, my Nina, I am not sure how I managed there. After a short interview, he summoned his wife in, who from the first stared down at me, making it clear that she did not want me there. Although I was upset, I tried to remember my grandmother's face and her parting words. I hid away my tears, but this was the moment that the ache of fear in my belly began which I have carried through much of my life. These people were strangers to me, sadly, just as I am a stranger to you, my daughter.

After a few days together, I fell into a routine and knew what to expect. No one held me like my grandmother, and instead I spent more time around indifferent servants than my parents. This was a loveless household.

One day my father finally announced that he was leaving for America to his next post, and as quickly as I had been commanded here I was sent back to my grandmother's. I ran into her arms and burst into tears.

"What did I do wrong? Why do they hate me? Please don't make me go back there again!"

She wiped my tears with one of her silk handkerchiefs and sat me on her knee. "You did nothing wrong. Your father went back overseas to be Ambassador. You will see him again one day, when he returns. He doesn't really know what being a father means and he was always too important to take care of people around him. But I am here and love you."

I nestled into her arms, able to let down my guard. But even back home, I often became anxious, worried, and sad without any particular cause. Unable to get enough air into my lungs, I would panic. My grandmother could still comfort me, yet from that day I felt alone. Unfortunately, children like me and maybe you, never knew the security and happiness that nourished others of our age. I don't have to be a clairvoyant to realize you must have felt abandoned not merely by me but also later on by Elisa.

Even when he returned, my father cared little for caring and was distant around me. His attention was occupied by ideas and the political intrigue of the day. To be the success he was he had a price to pay. Japanese politics were not a war of ideas—they were literally a battleground of life and death. While our *samurai* past was shrouded in tale and had officially ended, brute force still ruled the day. Political leaders were assassinated, from the prime minister on down. The government would change often, which ultimately led to the military taking command of the political structure. My father survived and fed on the confusion. Children were not his focus. I was afraid of him and struggled having no reason to believe that he cared for me in any way. Eventually I learned that affection toward me was not an option for him. His version of love was focused at directing my life, pushing me forward toward goals only he knew and which I neither understood nor had control over.

Much of the fear disappeared after meeting Mitsu, but some of it remained even when we were happily in love. Yes, Mitsu helped nudge away some of the hurt inside me and demonstrated how I could be cherished without judgment. You, too, will find unconditional love one day, in addition to the tenderness existing in my heart for you. However, love alone does not heal pain. It has its own limitations, most of which are created in our minds, then translated into behaviors.

Looking back, I see this period as the beginning of my pilgrimage, of my growth as a human being. In those days, I had more questions than answers yet had surrounded myself with fellow travelers who would guide and accompany me each step of the way.

Elisa suggested we gain contacts for our journey from other European emissaries. From her acquaintances at Maxim's and through the social scene, we received invitations for stays on our way to Paris and letters of introduction to key movers and shakers.

Since the ball, Mitsu, the Italian ambassador, and I, dined together weekly. He was an extremely well-educated, experienced man, hailing from a line of diplomats stretching back centuries. He enjoyed sharing his encyclopedic intellect of art, music, and opera as well as the ancient history of the Mediterranean region, the intricacies of Venetian politics, and the intimate details of the lives of the famous and infamous. His voice lowered when he related bawdy tales of his 'conquests,' as he called them. He insisted we take a steamer to Venezia. He promised to make sure our visit there would be enjoyable.

The more we learned, the more we wished to experience, and the more we felt impatient to leave. The urgency Mitsu and I felt prior to departure now seems like a premonition.

We were each immersed in our own thoughts as the steamer passed the Golden Horn for the last time and the noises and sights of the crowded city began to fade into the distance. I looked at the people I now considered as my family: Mitsu, my life-long companion; Elisa, my consort; and, Gül, my aide-de-camp.

Elisa broke the silence.

"Constantinople represents the dawn of the life I yearned for since I was a child. I forced my way through a riot of terrified people to get on the boat leaving Odessa. Arriving here knowing no one and being without any plans, I fought to get what I needed. I am a woman holding her head up high. Soon enough I will forget this city as I have already forgotten my homeland. Memories have no use for me."

Mitsu responded. "But Elisa, how can you forget your home and your family? My own history is attached to the countryside where I was born. My parents are proud of my accomplishments and encouraged me to quit the farm to have a future they could not provide for me. They count on me to tell them about the world, so I carry them everywhere I go. As we talk, I am composing a letter describing our departure. From my parents I will learn of the harvests, births, deaths and recent gossip. Despite the vast distance, each letter brings us back to each other.

"That said, each day here was incomprehensible yet inviting, so different from Japan. Isolated from what defined me before, this unfamiliar environment pushed me to become more aware of who I desired to be."

"What others thought I should be—a housewife living in a backward city doing nothing of interest—was never my aspiration," Elisa quickly interjected, her hair blowing in the wind as the ship picked up speed. "Unlike your parents, Mitsu, mine held me back. Sure, my father encouraged my education, but his goal was an obedient daughter whom he could marry off to some stranger. From the day I foresaw my dismal future, I was determined to break free. I shall never adapt to anyone's norms, and I will make my own way in life, alone, and independent. That is how I will live."

His voice raised, Gül interrupted angrily, "Elisa, you are misguided if you believe you are independent. Without Kenzo's invitation to be his consort, you would not even be on this ship. Who you are has become intertwined with Kenzo and Mitsu and even me. As long as you continue to maintain the façade for them, you will be free to pursue your own desires. Independence is always dependent on something or someone. You are still part of this group."

Elisa nodded as if in agreement although it was clear to us that she was not convinced by Gül. I sensed that she was not a woman to be beholden to anyone. I could not yet know how that would play out for me and ultimately, you, my sweet daughter.

The three of them turned to me, waiting for my response. I was staring at the horizon and let the silence last, thus prolonging the feelings circulating in my mind.

"We are on an adventure together. Our coming together was not predictable, nor can we foresee what will become of us. If I had the ability to peer into the future, what use would portending the future be, if it is unchangeable. Like cicadas finally emerging from their shells, I wonder who we will become."

"What do you mean, Kenzo?" asked Mitsu, his brows furrowed in concern.

"Back home, I knew I was Kenzo, an individual who made his own decisions and choices. Yet once we departed, I was able to identify how much of Kenzo was shaped by being Japanese. While my thoughts or actions often differed from Japanese expectations, the Japaneseness of life defined even these thoughts. Removed from our island nation, my own mind and being are behaving differently. Maybe my dervish friends have influenced me more than I thought. Through them, I have tasted life beyond comparisons. But now I worry, who am I becoming?"

"Ever since our days at the university," Mitsu replied, "you have utterly been Kenzo. Even your current questions are ones Kenzo alone would raise. Leaving Tōkyō, our desires were answered—to live more fully than we could there. We can never turn back now, no matter what happens. We change and grow, whether we notice it or not. Even old wounds heal with the scars to remind us."

The steamer sliced through the quiet waters of the Sea of Marmara as it narrowed into the Dardanelles. As we entered the strait, the battle scars on the hillsides from the Battle of Gallipoli four years previous were still evident. Craters pockmarked the hillsides, exposing rock and ruins. Our ship zigzagged around the remaining hulks of warships sunk in the channel during the early battles. So much of history is defined by war; peace is but a pause, a recovery and preparation phase for the next skirmish.

Gül, usually stoic, became uncharacteristically emotional. "Too many awful memories still haunt me here. I thought I had put this behind me. My family home was located in a village nearby. The Çimenlik Castle—its rounded walls are coming into view—was the Ottoman military headquarters, where I reported for my military service."

"It seems so calm from our distance," your mother said soothingly. "Look at the fishing boats and the little houses on the hill. I am sure living here must have been nice."

Gül responded, his eyes suddenly tearing. "The value of the Dardanelles is not its inhabitants but its sea route to the Black Sea. Whoever has control of the strait dominates the movement of cargo and people. I've lost the ability to observe what you are describing, Elisa. I still behold the large cannons on that hill shooting at the ships approaching in the channel. Over there," he pointed, "the invading force of British, New Zealanders, Australians and French was being slaughtered one by one until hundreds of thousands of bodies—yes, hundreds of thousands—were writhing in death throes, piled on top of each other on the bloodied ground. Their screams carried across the water, even silencing the gulls into a stupor. Can you imagine the death calls of so many men? Why did they even come here? Who would send their child to fight a meaningless war, in an unknown country, far from their home? I cry for the mothers, fathers, aunts and uncles who lost so much for no reason. I feel their pain as equal numbers of Turkish young men and civilians were also killed here. My village hardly exists due to the sheer toll."

"What about your family?" Mitsu quietly asked.

"We Turks were proud to protect our land, as we have been doing for millennia. The ancient city of Troya was located to the south over those hills; its siege and the untold number of deaths were celebrated in the *Iliad*. We all stupidly have been raised to accept the maxim: To fight is to live. I wish I could say my family was innocent, but none of us were. When the army recruiters on their fine horses trod into our village, my parents gladly volunteered their three sons. Since I had the best education, I was assigned to the military headquarters. My two brothers became cannon fodder. During one of the first invasions, they both were killed.

"Upon hearing of their deaths, my anger was so great that I tried to flee, vowing to avenge their murder. My commander held me back, telling me, 'You have work to do here which will bring us victory and make your brothers' deaths meaningful. Stay.'

"I complied, but was increasingly unsure why. My dreams of growing old in my village, surrounded by my family, died alongside my brothers. The final blow came right as the war was ending. Surrender was announced, and on one of the quiet days thereafter my parents came into town to sell vegetables at the market. A final errant cannon blast was lobbed across the strait—maybe a deluded soldier's parting shot. The bomb hit the square, and thirty died, my parents included."

Dumbstruck by his story we could find no words to soothe his pain. Mitsu simply put his arm around Gül's shoulders and Elisa held his hand as he continued.

"Numb and grieving, I abandoned my homeland and meandered through North Africa, Spain and into France. Certain places were untouched by the slaughter, whereas others were completely destroyed without any means of discerning why one area was annihilated, while its neighbor had been passed over. I wanted no part of the strife, no part of weapons and killing. I dared not travel farther than Paris as I dreaded facing the devastation of the northern battlefields. So I stayed there, learned the language, and found solace in the arms of other men who also needed to heal. Eventually I made my way back to Constantinople, feeling a safety in big cities that the countryside could not provide."

The words stumbled from my mouth, "Why...why then did you allow us to go by sea? We could have gone by the Orient Express directly to Paris."

"I needed to say farewell one more time, maybe for the last time. It's a reminder of what I am leaving behind. I did not want to face this alone."

Elisa snuck away for a minute and returned with a handful of flowers. Handing several to each, she said, "Throw a flower overboard, and make a blessing for yourself and those who are gone."

I studied my flowers and thought of my mother and my grandmother. As I tossed each one, I remembered what I learned from them. I said blessings for each of my traveling companions, most of all Mitsu. As I whispered his name, I tossed the flower into the wind. Unlike the others, Mitsu's flower flew upwards, lofting above as if it had wings. The others, immersed in their own thoughts, did not notice. I know birds fly and fish swim, but here was a flower on its own, floating in the endless sky.

13. THE BOUNDARY OF REALIZATION IS NOT DISTINCT

Our Lloyd Triestino Lines ship steamed on through the Aegean to the Ionian and onwards to the Adriatic Sea. So many names for the same body of water. As we passed ancient islands, Gül would recount the tales of the Greeks, Romans and others who fought for these lands over the span of countless centuries. Ruins of temples and buildings, columns fallen, roofs missing, and huge blocks of marble and limestone strewn about the shore were visible along the passage. Did centuries of wear, or war, create these ruins? Perhaps they are one and the same. Maybe the human penchant for war is as natural a force of destruction as are earthquakes, storms, and waves. Perhaps war is time compressed for an equally destructive effect. Naively believing that we were done with wars in our century, I put these thoughts aside.

About seventy of us were on board. Each evening we were served dinner by formally dressed waiters in the wood-paneled ornate ballroom, lit by sparkling glass chandeliers. As diplomats, we joined the captain at his table. A venerable Italian with a neatly trimmed black-and-grey beard, piercing brown eyes and a muscular build that I easily noticed under his impeccably tailored uniform, he was glad peacetime sailing had returned.

Elisa grabbed my hand as the band played a waltz. One two three, one two three—it was the simplest of dances for me. We spun about the floor, joined by several other couples, performing our best. After several dances, Elisa was scooped up by the captain. I broke in for a mazurka, and the captain took over anew once I was done.

She was enjoying herself, enjoying his attention. One would have to be very attentive to notice the slight differences as she and the captain took the floor. Their bodies were much closer than hers and mine; she settled more easily into his arms; her smile was bigger; and her eyes focused on her partner's face. I was glad she was happy and thought she might be invited for a drink and a private tour of the upper deck and his quarters. Since we made our decision together, she was at liberty in her relationships. She would tell all her paramours that I would not be upset. Indeed, the next day the captain complimented me by saying, "I am glad I did not have to fight you for the honor of enjoying Mademoiselle. Women as beautiful as she deserve to be spoiled."

During their dances, Mitsu, Gül and I talked about the other men on board. Gül had already made friends among the crew, who hailed from all over the former Ottoman Empire. His easygoing manner and Turkish manliness allowed him to approach men confidently. His ability to differentiate which men desired a more intimate connection allowed him to effortlessly make his way. I envied this talent of his.

At the table, Mitsu would lean back, his legs brushing mine, his arm occasionally grazing me as he pointed toward the object of our conversation. These apparently innocuous gestures covered the covert excitement I gained from simply touching my loved one. Only back in our stateroom were we truly intimate. We lived two lives: publicly, we existed within the constraints of culture in how we interacted; privately, we cultivated one of intimacy, where we thought solely of each other. Privacy is a human need and the reason closed doors exist. When we needed to express personal information in public, we resorted to speaking Japanese.

Nina, while I want to communicate honestly with you, I hope I have not disturbed you by my words. Parents are usually not so explicit with such things to their children, at least Japanese parents are not. But you are an adult in your twenties if this missive ever arrives for you to read. Intimacy should be cherished and never considered shameful. Normally, one learns about love and intimacy from experiencing its varied forms as one grows up. I despair about the person you might have become based on exposure to your mother's struggles to find love and satisfaction, her emotional distance from you, and her eventual disappearance from your life. Let me add to this list the feelings of abandonment you must have suffered without a father. For these reasons, I believe it to be vital to let you know that love can help heal our lonely childhoods. On this, I speak from experience.

As we steamed into the harbor of Dubrovnik, the ship's claxons announcing our arrival, the tall ramparts built during the 12th century rose high above us from the water's edge. Anxious to be on land, we hustled down the gangplank. Inside the gated city, we found a guide, and the two of us accompanied him. We invited the captain and Elisa to join us, but she announced they were going shopping. As usual, Gül had business of his own making to attend to. We departed, agreeing to meet for dinner at a tavern Gül knew.

Inside, the walls were thick and tall. As a young child, my father had once brought me to the Imperial Palace, where I was entranced by the high walls made of polished stone reflecting the morning light. Sometime later, a Zen priest explained how walls create an inside and outside, making emptiness and space definable.

Walls enclosed the entire city of marble streets, opulent buildings, houses, and shops, each abutting the other. The city was beautiful yet strange. Every inch was filled in; no trees or plants grew directly from the ground. The sun above was the sole reminder of the environment from which we had come. A contained, manmade city was the opposite of eight days on wide-open sea, which exemplified space itself.

We scrambled up steep stairways to the ramparts, where we regained the vista of the blue sea reflecting the bright sunny sky. I enjoyed circumnavigating the city from above, passing guards standing ramrod at attention, assigning a mere movement of their eyes to acknowledge our presence.

My Nina, I cannot separate the memory of the place from the magical dream state of its existence. Clean streets of white marble and limestone echoed with the muffled footsteps of its residents. No horses or carts interrupted our way. Our guide identified the differences of apparel—young Bosnian girls in white dresses, embroidered vests and banded headscarves that puffed up in front, then fell down in the back; Macedonian men in their dark, round flat caps, wearing short white kimonos embroidered in red and black thread; a Montenegrin man in dark pants tucked into white leggings, black boots and a long coat, who was playing a *gusle*, a single-stringed instrument similar to our *ichigenkin*, but bowed, not plucked.

"Each village has their own styles and colors. I can distinguish particular ones from others and can more broadly distinguish regional features," our guide commented. "The city is the regional market. Today you two are giving them something different, a novel sight."

"Ah, the seer is being seen himself," Mitsu joked. "We visitors believe our passage goes unnoticed, busy as we are taking in the sights. Meanwhile, those we are observing are discreetly nudging each other as we pass."

"Yes, think of the tales they will tell about you when they return home."

Right as he spoke, an old man limped over and talked to our guide in a language I could not pinpoint.

"This man asked where you were from. As a youth, he took off from Croatia to visit his relatives in Russia. There, he was conscripted against his will and sent to the Far East to fight against Japan. He saw their soldiers from afar and wanted to keep that distance. Despite his misgivings, he thought you might be Japanese. He asks you to join him for a drink."

We shook hands and followed him to a nearby bar where we perched on low wooden benches set on the street. The barmaid poured an amber-colored liquor into small glasses for each of us.

"*Zivjeli*", our host exclaimed, gazing directly into our eyes. We each followed suit and swiftly drained the sweet yet strong drink.

"He wishes you long life," translated our guide. "How do you enjoy our *rakija,* Kenzo? It's a local plum brandy containing a touch of anise."

"We have nothing to compare this to. The aroma and taste stimulate my nose as much as my tongue—simultaneously bitter, sweet, and even spicy."

The bottle was passed around once more, and more drinks poured.

The old man commenced a rambling speech, stopping occasionally when the guide cut in to translate.

"The earth's bounty is remarkable. I was saying to my daughter Esiaka this morning, something exciting and different is nearby. She scorns me, '*Otestka,* nothing is new—it's the same each day.' 'Is it?' I ask her. 'Look at your own daughter. Every day she is changing. A short while ago, she did not know how to stand up; suddenly, she is running and exploring where her feet can carry her. She learns more words each day and has such wonder in her eyes. That's the way to approach living.'

"She did not care to heed me and went back to her chores. 'Why don't you go find what is new and stop talking nonsense.' I decided to wander up to the market here. Then you gentlemen appeared."

He paused for several moments and poured another round of drinks. Gulping his down, he cleared his throat, spit, and began his tale.

"I was lucky to come back alive from the Russian front in 1905. My future was altered irrevocably from the day I was grabbed from a Moscow street on a cool October night to the heartbreaking return following the Battle of Mukden—"

"Mukden, you were at Mukden?" Mitsu exclaimed. "I was just fourteen during the Russian War, but all students learned about Mukden. More than 100,000 men lost their lives."

"Ah, you recall the name of that horrid place. I thought you might be too young. A stain on history, another mark of craziness and greed hardly remembered by anyone anymore. I was conscripted and forced on that damned railroad to hell for ten days. Bitterly cold as we embarked, the temperature crept downward even more as we crossed kilometers of barren tundra. I barely spoke Russian but met another Croat fellow who also got caught in this madness. We became the best of friends on the outward journey. Unfortunately, he was not to return.

"Eventually we arrived in Vladivostok filled with damaged warships lined up in its limping harbor. That should have been our warning to sneak back on the train, but they had pushed into our heads how it was upon us to provide victory to the glorious motherland. If you ever hear those words, my boys, escape as fast as you can."

He poured another drink for us all.

"*Zivjeli* ... yes, we must remember to live long lives. If we forget, we make stupid mistakes over and over. They sent our platoon to the countryside near Mukden in Manchuria. During our two weeks of marching, I realized that the life of country folk everywhere is identical. They carry life's burdens, growing and harvesting their crops, maintaining the land and caring for animals. The clothes they wore were different, the faces were different, but their lives were like those of my parents.

"The fighting began and men about me dropped, moaning and screaming in pain from bullets and mortar shots. I was stunned by the noise, sounds and smells. From the freezing cold, my body became numb, and I was barely able to move. Suddenly, the man beside me blew up, splattering me in warm thick blood. I collapsed behind a low wall and waited for death myself. Night was falling, and no one in my family even knew where I was. As streaks of lights suddenly swept across the sky I became mesmerized by the beautiful, red flashes and the whooshing noises, which sounded like the waterfalls of the Ibar River where I used to play as a child.

"Shouts of soldiers retreating woke me from my reverie. An unknown force within me pushed my frozen body upright and I followed them running as fast as I was able to, jumping over dead and dying bodies. Raw instinct carried me as I scrambled uphill in deep snow, running until I was exhausted. I saw what I thought was a church or mosque and ducked inside.

"It was dark, lit by candles. A priest dressed in a grey robe noticed me. Despite my condition, he did not seem surprised or even afraid. He took my hand and brought me into the main hall. On an elevated altar, I beheld a statue of a half-naked man. He had a robe drooping off his chest, one hand on his lap facing upward, the other touching the earth. His eyes had a strange faraway focus, as if he was seeing simultaneously all of universe and nothing. The priest lit two sticks of incense and gave me one. He chanted for a minute, then stuck his glowing stick into a big pot crammed with other sticks, some burning, others extinguished. I said a little prayer and crossed myself from head to the shoulders before I added my incense to the kettle. He pointed to the man and said 'Budva.' I remember that clearly because it's a city down the coast from here. How amazing that he knew the region where I was from. I took this as a positive omen, even though we did not speak each other's language.

"He gave me food and a warm spot to sleep. The next day, we both lit incense together. This time I said 'Budva, yes, I know Budva.' He smiled and bowed to me. He walked me down the road; shortly afterward I ran into a band of comrades being assisted by the Red Cross. I followed them to the garrison at Vladivostok, where I recuperated for several weeks, until they sent me back on the train.

"As soon as I got back to Moscow, I jumped on a train to Split, making my way along the coast to Budva. I marched into the first church I encountered, yet found no such statue inside. I asked around yet was stared at like I was crazy. I searched every church and mosque to no avail. Nonetheless, Budva became a sanctuary for me. I married a Montenegrin and soon had a family. Despite the ravages of combat, the peaceful part of my heart was saved by that place."

His monologue had a greater emotional impact on me than I could imagine, and it seemed to have a corresponding effect on Mitsu. He stood and said, "Please, sir, wait here. I have something I must retrieve on board our ship. I will be right back."

I had no idea what caused Mitsu to rush off—it was uncharacteristic of him to do so without explanation. Therefore, I was relieved when he returned out of breath after about fifteen minutes.

"Are you okay?" I asked worriedly.

"Very much so." He smiled at the old man. "I have the object you have been searching for." He pulled a package wrapped in paper and string from the sleeve of his kimono. "Here, please consider it a token of friendship from me."

The old man carefully opened the package and went wide-eyed. He stared at Mitsu, then back at the gift, then at me.

"It's him! It's the statue I was talking about. Where did you get this from?"

"He's Buddha. He came from India, and his teachings spread to China and Korea where you met him, and Japan. He shows us insight and the peace that comes from enlightenment. The temple you entered was a Buddhist temple. You can find Buddhists throughout Asia. He was an actual person who after learning the lessons of life and death taught humanity how to live with that knowledge. He's not a god, but we honor his wisdom for bringing us the Way."

"Buda, Budva ... You have healed an old man so he can complete his time on earth. My family will be shocked to discover I am not as crazy as they thought I was. I knew this was a special day. *Zivjeli!* My search has ended since you answered the question remaining for me. Thank you from my soul."

He gave Mitsu a bear hug and kissed him on both cheeks, then did the same to me. The man took off with a spring in his step as he greeted passersby on his way.

Now dark, our guide walked us from one narrow street to another until he left us at an ancient-looking tavern. Elisa was sitting arm-in-arm beside the captain, surrounded by a mound of bags and boxes.

"Look what we found. There was a beautiful Italian fashion shop, where the captain was so generous he did not allow me to spend a dinar," she gushed. The captain tipped his hat at me; I nodded back, smiling.

Gül entered, accompanied by a handsome man his age and presented him. "This is Zoran from the Maritime Trade Organization. He asked to meet our dignitaries, so I invited him to join us."

Introductions made, we settled into an evening full of conversation, tasty food, much *rakija* and cheers of long life. Later, a band of three men bowing or strumming stringed instruments, one playing a flute and another a drum, began to play.

After the opening bars of one tune, Zoran announced, "This is one of the Croatian traditional dances, reserved exclusively for men. Please, will you join me?"

I had never danced in a group of men and was reluctant. The rest of the table insisted I participate.

Zoran gave us instructions. "It's a simple dance, just follow me. Take the hand of the man to the left of you. Don't be shy, Kenzo, Mitsu won't bite you. First, step forward with your right foot and step behind with your left. No, Mitsu, your other right foot, that's it, you have it. Repeat that three times as we move in a circle. One and two and three, and ... repeat in the opposite direction. Good, one and two and three and ... As you finish the third step, lift your hand upward without letting go, swoop forward and swoop back two times, then we repeat our steps again, but this time with our arms around each other's shoulders."

It was thrilling, my dear, dancing alongside the man I adored on the right and Gül on the left. We began to sweat in the warm evening as we strained to follow Zoran's directions. A powerful masculine energy flowed from man to man as we were interlocked, weaving back and forth, from side to side. I felt a kinship with the Sufis as we twirled about as well as one with my *samurai* forefathers. Even Gül's usual stern face had softened into a wide smile.

Over the course of the evening, as soon as the band played one of their dance tunes, we would follow Zoran's guidance. Equally exhilarated by the men and the *rakija*, I was in heaven.

Around midnight, Zoran suggested that we relax in the *hammam*. Elisa bade us *adieu* and took the captain's arm as he carried her bags. Our footsteps echoed loudly as we wandered the quiet streets lit by gas lamps until we reached a building marked *Banya*. As we entered, we were met by a group of boisterous men in various stages of undress.

With the glistening of sweat accumulated from our night's activities and the heat of the space, I soaped my hands and rubbed Mitsu's back. Switching places, feeling his hands and sensing him close behind, was divine. Zoran motioned for us to move to the adjacent room full of steam, with a low ceiling and lit by candles on the wall. We joined a group of men talking, singing and playing as men do when they enjoy being together. I won't go into much detail except to say, men can pleasure other men. Men fathom the minds of other men in bringing out feelings of bodily joy.

Walls created this space where the energy of *shudō* and male sexuality are experienced away from the prying eyes of outsiders. Similar haunts existed in Yoshiwara, the famed 'Floating World,' where men or women could immerse themselves in pleasure. The area was greatly diminished by the time I reached adulthood, but its allures were not yet lost. Theaters, bars and restaurants, in addition to special places for sexual engagement, had the power to suspend time.

Men who desired men, women who desired women, men searching for women and women searching for men had their own quarters in the Floating World. Outside the gates, we were expected to act according to our societal roles. Inside the gates, other rules applied. No weapons were allowed; social class was extinguished. Fashions here were set by the high-ranking courtesans and eventually spread to the rest of the country. *Wakashu*, young men between puberty and adulthood, could take on both men and women's roles in dress, in comportment, and as lovers. Numerous famous *wakashu* became actors or musicians, publicly keeping their lives in a suspended state as neither male nor female.

As a rite of passage, my father took me to Yoshiwara after I turned sixteen. He secured an attendant at one of the halls of pleasure, who took me back to her den. I was nervous, unable to defy him. She invited me to come closer, but I balked. She took my behavior as shyness and told me in a soft voice. "It's okay, young man. You have no reason to be embarrassed."

I still refused and eventually blurted out, "Madame, I don't mean to insult you. I would be false if I tried to respond to you. If you were a man, my reaction might be very different."

To my surprise, she gently said, "I sensed that when I saw you outside. You don't have enough experience yet to know that other men exist with similar desires to yours. I will give you the address where you can become acquainted with male pleasure. Meanwhile, let us stay while we converse for a bit. When we go back to the waiting salon, I will give your father an honorable report so he will be proud of his son."

Feeling relieved and understood for the first time, we talked freely. I was curious about her work and dreams. She had hoped to become a singer and demonstrated her talents by singing a popular love song for me. As I listened to her words, an ache shuddered deep in my soul. A sadness welled up that I would never have such a deep experience; I would forever be lonely. She anticipated my thoughts, whispering to me that love and contentment would one day come. She was the one who told me about *shudō* and its honorable history of male bonding, a history my father would not have shared as he was not a practitioner. Finally, our conversation gave me words for the feelings I had sensed inside me.

Tempting as it was, I never visited the address she gave me; the knowledge alone that men existed who felt like I did was enough to make me happy and confident. When Mitsu and I finally met at the university, I knew love was indeed possible.

So much time has passed since those days, my dear Nina. The war between our countries keeps us apart. Imprisoned, my fate seems never to meet you. As I wrote earlier, many stories arose between then and now. I share this particular one so that even in the depths of war and destruction, you can envisage that your own dreams of romance and adventure can come true.

14. ASH CANNOT BECOME FIREWOOD AGAIN

Based on the Italian Ambassador's letter of introduction to the Morosinis, a distinguished Venetian family including ancient doges, dogressas, artists and benefactors, we made plans to meet them following our arrival at the Excelsior Hotel on the Lido. A messenger met us there with an invitation from the Morosinis to join them for the opera, followed by a formal dinner. They would send a carriage at 6 p.m.

Although Elisa wanted to decamp right away to the beach after scanning the well-to-do guests, she realized that she did not have the right clothes. Honestly, we were all astonished by the scantily clad women lounging in brightly colored bathing pajamas along the sandy shore. We would be staying for two nights, not enough time to immerse ourselves actively in local social life. Instead we went on a tour of the old city.

From one fantasy city to another, my daughter, both built on the unexpected. Venezia is a city not just built on the water but truly defined by it. Once we had crossed the Grand Canal, we were traveling in an exotic land of rococo palaces, ancient churches and other stately edifices, all designed to demonstrate the grandeur, wealth and beauty of its inhabitants. Constrained by narrow streets between multitudes of canals, even the wealthiest strolled or were transported by small boats from one place to another.

Ambling along quiet streets where laundry hung from building to building, women sang to one another across alleys and canals in this densely populated musical village. Even fish and vegetable vendors announced their arrival in song. We often heard melodies bouncing off the surroundings before the gondolier, dressed in a traditional blue-and-white striped shirt and blue-trimmed straw hat, came into sight. Singing as he oared his boat, he was accompanied by an accordion, a strange instrument producing loud, entrancing music. Your mother, needless to say, appeared to have won the heart of at least one such musician along the way.

Finishing our tour filled with vast opulence, we came back to rest up for the evening's events. Mitsu and I fell into our bed and nestled together for a short nap, my arms enveloping him, taking in his Mitsuness. Our breathing synchronized, and soon we both fell into a deep slumber. I dreamed that the two of us were the guests of honor at a ball at the Cà Rezzonico. We were the first ones to dance, gracefully spinning about the floor as we peered into each other's eyes. Gradually other couples joined in. At one point, I lifted Mitsu, twirling him into the air as if he weighed nothing. We both floated above the dance floor, spinning and spinning. Finally, slowly descending back to the ground, I planted a big kiss on his waiting lips.

Mitsu shook me and I awoke. "What were you dreaming about? You had the biggest smile on your face, and your legs were in constant motion."

"I had a premonition about this evening and our life together. Let's get dressed."

We put on our formal kimonos as it was a special evening on which we were representing Japan. We joined Elisa and Gül in the lobby. She wore an elegant blue- and cream-colored dress. In the packed lobby, a group of fashionably dressed women were curiously watching our unique group.

"Wow, you are more beautiful than ever," Mitsu gushed. "Those must be the designs you bought the other day."

"Yes, I was told this is *tres chic* these days. I didn't want to resemble a peasant girl. Everything I have done has been practice for tonight: how to act, what to wear, and whom to meet. The types of people on our set in Constantinople are in no manner comparable to those we will meet here. Gossip travels faster than any train or telegraph. As we make our debut, I aspire to be remembered and talked about."

"Talked about? I hope you don't cause an embarrassing situation."

"Oh, Kenzo, how can you be so mean? Of course not. Tonight will be the real birth of our new lives—we will be remembered for our sophistication and grace. Your formal manners and the uniqueness of dress will set the bar for me to be recognized as the woman who has the proper bearing and composure to accompany such an exotic creature."

"Let's go to the pier. The carriage has arrived," Gül said, pointing to an elaborate open-air carriage pulled by two well-groomed horses.

The driver watched us approach, then called out Elisa's and my names. "I am ready to take you to La Fenice on behalf of the Signor Morosini."

"Thank you, Sir. We are looking forward to a fine evening."

"Excellent. Please let me assist the Signorina and Consul into the carriage, and we will bid *arrivederci* to your friends who have accompanied you."

"Oh, I thought…Okay, just the two of us. Of course…" The invitation was for Elisa and me. The disappointment was apparent on my face; however, we had no choice but to continue.

Reading my mind, Gül said, "Don't worry about us. Mitsu and I will make do by ourselves tonight. The ambassador gave us tips. Later, you two can tell us the ways of society while we share tales from other realms."

We were off. I turned back as we set forth and met Mitsu's eyes, which were misty. Elisa squeezed my hand, whispering, "We'll have fun. I understand who has your full attention, but tonight let's pretend we are a devoted couple. We will be the only ones who know our secret."

"I will do my best," I sighed, "I feel bad for Mitsu, but I can't change what happened. Yes, Elisa, we will make it our own evening."

The city became even more magical at sunset when the boat took us across the Grand Canal and the Rio de Santa Luca to a small canal, where we stepped off. Along the way, each building was lit from within as if presenting a show for us to view. Elisa oohed and aahed over elegantly dressed inhabitants, the chandelier-lit lavish parlors, and gilt-framed paintings on the walls.

"One day, Kenzo, that will be us. I know it."

The exterior of La Fenice was relatively restrained—a simple square front facing a modest *piazza,* the entrance framed by four columns and flags of Italy and Venezia on the balcony above. A man bowed in greeting as we entered.

"Consul-General, Signorina, I wish to welcome you to La Fenice, The Phoenix. I believe this is your first time visiting our esteemed hall. If you will, please let me take your arm, Signorina, as we go to the doge's box. The Morosinis are awaiting you."

Our escort brought us to a gilded doorway on the second floor. He discretely knocked and then opened the door. An elderly man and woman stood as we entered.

The man, wearing a quasi-military uniform with a large medal attached to a yellow and blue sash in the colors of his family, approached. "Welcome, Consul-General, to Venezia. We are glad you are joining us. My dear friend, the Ambassador, told us so much about the two of you. Yet Signorina, he did not mention you were a woman of such beauty."

He kissed Elisa's hand and she blushed. Even she was overcome by the moment. "Grazie, Signor Morosini. I am unworthy of your compliments. I am honored to meet you."

"Please let me introduce you to Signora Morosini." Elisa curtsied, bowing her head slightly at the introduction.

The old women scrutinized her from head to toe as she spoke. "I adore your dress. You have been here for a short time, and already you reveal to me that you are familiar with our best designers."

"Thank you, Madame. I do enjoy fashion. Although given everything I saw in the shops today, I wouldn't even know where to begin. Yet, from the instant I set eyes on it, I was smitten by this dress and hoped it would be appropriate for tonight."

"Oh yes, my dear, very chic. A bit modern for me, but you are not my age. I could not carry off a dress like that these days. I mean, what would people say? I try not to let my age be a barrier to appreciation. At one time, I, too, was the plate of fashion. All of the designers would beg me to wear their latest creations. Now I find myself in a state of decrepitude, barely holding myself together and sticking to the fashions of the past epochs. Beauty is fleeting, so take care while you have it, and remember one day beauty will abandon you like a cat jumping for the new toy over the old.

"Speaking of fashion, *Signor* Consul-General, I admire a man who can dress in his native costume with panache. Consider those peasants wearing their traditional garb, unaware that ancient history is wrapped around their bodies. If your history amounts to an embroidered bib on a rough cotton dress, that tells me nothing. However, you, Sir, are so elegantly attired in silk, I have nothing but admiration. If I were younger, I would be as anxious for your attention as your young lady."

His tone reminded me of Edmund, and I was not sure whether I had been insulted, complimented or both. As she gave her hand to me, I raised it slightly for a kiss. I was getting used to this odd custom and would get much more practice soon.

"Please have a seat. The opera should commence soon. 'La Wally,' by Alfredo Catalani. Are you familiar with his work?'

"I am afraid not. This is my first opera."

"I am glad *La Wally* is your first. Similar to most operas, it reflects on unrequited love and the choices we make for the one we discover."

Elisa shot a quick peek at me.

"Natalina De Sanctis is wonderful as the lead singer. She has the most beautiful aria at the end of the first act. You will meet Natalina and Maestro Guido Farinelli as the guests of honor at our table. The lights are dimming, as it's about to begin."

As we sat, I examined the theater. We were sitting on the first tier of a large hall, above the main floor seating. Our tier together with the one three levels above us were arranged in a semi-circle looking out to a plush magenta curtain almost two stories high, where I imagined the stage to be. White stucco and gilt decorations of flowers, grapes, nymphs and fanciful creatures covered the entire auditorium. Just below the curtain sat the orchestra of string, brass and other instruments, almost none of which I could name at the time.

The production commenced after a little man crept through the orchestra to climb on the podium. That must be Farinelli, I supposed. He led the orchestra as the musicians first tuned their instruments, which I later learned was not part of the show; they then played a spritely tune. The curtain opened revealing an Alpine scene, reminding me of our mountains. Several groups of people, dressed for the cold weather, were mingling and chatting. At one point, instead of speaking, one person broke into song which was answered in song by others. Despite not speaking Italian I managed to discern that they were enemies.

Singing followed more singing. Finally, the woman whom I guessed was Wally sang a hauntingly beautiful song, reminding me of the one the geisha sang in Yoshiwara. Although the singer sung loud enough for her words to be carried like a bird on the breeze to each of us assembled, her voice was nonetheless both delicate and intimate. Not understanding the words, I followed her voice with my heart. Regardless of the libretto, the music was bringing tears to Elisa.

The second she had finished, the audience, who had been following every word breathlessly, exploded in cheers of '*Brava*' and thunderous applause. The singer acknowledged the audience and tried to continue, yet the applause would not let up. Eventually, the clapping died as the curtain closed.

After such an impressive performance I felt elevated and ready to go, but discovered three more acts were to follow. During the intermission, some of the Morosinis' friends stopped by the box to introduce themselves, as they would also be attending the dinner party afterward.

I found the combination of music and theater fascinating. Each by itself would have made for a wonderful evening. Of course, my brain automatically compared the production to our *kabuki*, which can be translated as the art of singing and dancing.

Maybe you have learned about opera already, my daughter. I assume English was your native language, maybe you also learned a bit of your mother's Ukrainian, a language she hardly spoke during the period in which I knew her. Hopefully she taught you French, a language she spoke so beautifully.

Finding a school to teach you my language was likely out of the question, yet the romantic part of me envisions you cultivating your Japanese heritage, so that you feel closer to me. I picture you in a school not unlike the one I attended as a child, a teacher showing you how to write *kanji*, an ink brush in your small hand. You try to write your name Uchida; after several attempts, your teacher congratulates you on your natural ability. Elisa is proud of you, as she realizes you will be the one who eventually reconciles our family.

Realistically, I am aware Elisa was not this type of parent. I can't be sure she would have even told you my name, let alone much about me. If Japanese schools existed there, they would have been shuttered as soon as Japanese was equated with the enemy. No, I can't assume you were schooled in your father's culture or language. I can't assume you know anything about me, which is why I continue to write.

Kabuki was our theater teaching us about the ways of life. Similar to the opera I was engrossed in, *kabuki* combined music with a small amount of speech. Indeed, the differences were minor—the sound of the music and how the parts were acted out. Watching *kabuki*, I can hear the sounds of Japan and its history; watching opera, I hear the sounds of Europe and its history. *Kabuki* is opera and opera is *kabuki*. Yet the two are not equal: one is ingrained in my soul, while the other is an art form I appreciate from afar, connected to another way of being.

Your mother was engrossed, watching the audience as much as she was paying attention to the stage. For weeks afterwards, she would recall the jewelry, dresses and hair styles of the most stylish women as well as the way men and women interacted with each other during the intermissions. She was constantly alert to the theater of life and her role in the performance.

I admired her self-knowledge: To be an actor is better than to be acted upon. Since she was an outsider, she needed to master all aspects of the environment. Outsiders survive with this knowledge; without it, they get run over. She was not one to get run over.

Her observations are what guided us in managing the minefield of the rest of the evening. You may have noticed from my rendering of this tale that without Mitsu and Gül, I would likely be lost. I regularly needed someone to help focus me on the particulars of daily activities. The big picture I sense well; the minute details and next steps are not my expertise.

By myself, I would not have been able to follow the lead of our hosts and the minute protocol of the dinner afterwards. While everyone was rushing about, I probably remained seated, marveling at the beauty of the space, dwelling on the music which lingered in my mind. Elisa was the one who grabbed my arm and led me into the crowd, acknowledging the couples we had met during the intermission. Employing her talents I had observed early on when she was a cigarette girl, she had memorized their names and key attributes she had learned from Signora Morosini. She would whisper their names and titles so I could appropriately greet them. She had already gleaned who was advantageous for us to know and who was not.

She knew just how to flirt so as not to be rude or aggressive, and to make sure she got noticed. She enjoyed being complimented (as do we all, I must add). She told me that all compliments are baseless, and that to accept them is dangerous. Dangerous because taking someone's words to be truthful seduces you to trust them. By trusting them, you cede your power.

I sometimes worry that Elisa passed these attitudes on to you. The real danger, though, lies in never trusting. I hope you understand this better than your mother did. Despite the ways she failed you, I truly hope you were able to intuit those times she was trustworthy. That said, I hope you trust my motives from afar. I recognize that a letter from your father cannot atone for my absence in your upbringing, but I must try. I must try because you deserve to have better influences; you deserve to hear that you have always been loved.

The evening was over the top, to use a phrase we recently learned from Edmund. At the close of the opera, following numerous cheers and bows for the performers, we were escorted across the plaza to an ancient *palazzo,* aglow with gas lamps. We were both relishing the experience, riding a wave of drink, food, art and conversation. As the newcomers, we had a role to fulfill and did our best to be witty and entertaining, as we provided a perspective the 'regulars' cannot. Inevitably, most Europeans did not understand the differences between Japan and China and thus made the assumption that our cultures were indistinguishable. To clear the confusion, I simply needed to point out that the two countries were as distinct as Italy and France.

Only if I was asked whether we were traveling alone or as part of a group did I remember the disappointment of leaving Mitsu behind. I felt anguished, realizing I was so enveloped by the evening's events that I forgot about him. I wondered where he was, what Gül had found for the two of them, and whether he was angry for being abandoned. Even these thoughts were fleeting because there was always another question to be answered, a new person to be met.

No one remembers exactly what happened; all we remember is the flames. One moment the murmur of convivial conversation filled the hall; minutes later there were screams of terror. Whether a candlestick, a gas lamp or someone's cigar initiated the inferno, no one knows, but the room suddenly burst into flames. An entire wall behind the head table where we were sitting blazed and the fire spread quickly.

Elisa jumped up, pulling me along as we rushed to the door. Bedlam reigned as the two hundred guests simultaneously scrambled for the exits. The screams of men and women, the sounds of the flames, glass breaking and timbers popping assaulted our ears. Nearly through the door, I glanced back and saw the Signora passed out, her face down on the table. Instinctively, I swung back to swim upstream through the masses. I didn't notice Elisa following me.

The smoke was getting so thick I could barely see. Elisa cried to me, "Over here, come over here to the table." A hand reached out of the darkness and pulled me over. "Follow the table!"

We inched our way, coughing from the dense smoke. The intensity of the heat was getting greater, requiring great effort to withstand. We reached the Signora, who was unresponsive. Thankfully, she was slight so that I was able to easily pick her up. Elisa gathered her dress from around her.

Your mother steamed ahead; her bravery was amazing. She kept calling back to me, to make sure I knew where to go, in addition to encouraging me. When we got to the exit, a wall of flames blocked our way with no way to go back.

"We have to jump through it," were her words before she disappeared. For a short yet strangely lingering period of time, I was alone, surrounded by smoke and fire, the crackling of wood, the sounds of plaster falling, an old woman in my arms, not sure if we would make it. The fire had a particular color that still makes me uneasy. Maybe it wasn't the color but an intensity of color, a vividness that was electric. Firefighters have described large infernos as living—a living and breathing energy threatening my own life.

"Kenzo, quick, jump across the doorway. You will be okay. Listen to me. Go!"

Your mother's voice woke me from the fire's enchanted spell. I jumped into flames, its heat surrounding me, as I was enveloped by the very fire-being itself. Suddenly, coolness eased my body. I saw Elisa and ran toward her into the plaza. I carried the Signora, who was stirring in the fresh air, to a bench to ease her down. Elisa sought the Signora's husband along with a doctor she had met earlier.

"What...what...happened...where..."

"You are safe now. Please keep calm—you are okay. Oh, your husband is coming over."

Signor Morosini and the doctor rushed over to examine her. A crowd of the other guests gathered.

"They both went back to rescue her while everyone else was fleeing."

"Such bravery by both the Consul and his consort. Where were our men? We should be ashamed!"

"He plunged right through the fire. I have heard the Japanese have the ability to withstand all manner of what would be torture to the rest of us. From their youth they are trained in these powers and sometimes turn them onto their enemies."

Signor Morosini turned to us. "The doctor says she is fine. The smoke caused her to faint. You two saved her from death. No level of thanks and gratitude I can express would equal what you have done. We will forever be in your debt for your courage. Whatever I can do for you, I will. Thank you, sir, and thank you, Signorina. You will not be forgotten."

The crowd surrounding us broke into loud cheers. Both of us were embraced and kissed over and over. Honestly, I was a bit embarrassed by the attention. The Signora herself rose to her feet and spoke privately to Elisa at length. She then came over to me.

"I owe you my life. There is nothing more profound one can ever say to another. You will forever be part of me, the both of you. When everyone else thought of their lives, you did not. I have made arrangements for your lady to be taken care of. Whatever is within my power is yours."

"Thank you, Signora. Seeing you alive, standing and talking to me, is the sole gift I choose. I had no thoughts except to save you from suffering. I could not have lived with myself had I not done so. That is my way. I hope you are not harmed physically or mentally."

"I will forever remember you picking me up. I thought that I was being lifted to the care of heaven. The heat got stronger and stronger as if I was nearing the sun. I saw *la Fenice* nearing the end of its existence in combustion and flame. At death, I was reborn in the coolness of my own ashes, my spirit arising. I awoke right here, and you, you handsome man, were the first person to peer into my eyes. I thought I might have been reborn to a land far from the Venezia. I wondered who I would be in this incarnation, whether you were my father, my brother or my *amante*. Upon viewing your face, I understood how much I yearned to live, wherever I was. You have given me a gift, and I promise not to waste my second chance at life."

She re-joined her husband, who escorted her away. I noticed the dark smudges on Elisa's face and dress.

She saw my concern and responded, "We both look like we have been to hell and back. Let's get back to the Excelsior."

We dragged ourselves arm in arm down the dark quiet streets to catch a *vaporetto* back. A bond was created between us, a bond deep and unbreakable.

15. THE WHOLE MOON AND SKY ARE REFLECTED IN A DROP OF DEW ON A BLADE OF GRASS

Returning to the hotel, Mitsu and Gül were nowhere to be found. I truly desired Mitsu's comforting embrace, yet instead washed myself as best I could, dropped into bed and fell into a deep sleep. I was vaguely aware as Mitsu joined me in bed. He smelled of alcohol, and his movements were clumsy as he tried to curl up beside me. I wanted to talk but was too exhausted to utter a single word.

The morning was awkward. The news of the fire had rapidly spread. From early morning, everyone in the hotel from the manager to the guests was sending us notes of congratulations and gifts. Amidst everything that was happening, Mitsu and I had no privacy to talk. Since our first days together at the university, nothing momentous had ever occurred when we were apart.

He was full of praise and affirmation for me once he heard what occurred. Yet he was more circumspect about my inquiries of his evening.

"Another time, I will share more. Given your experience, what I did was inconsequential. Even your father will be proud of you once he hears the news. You have upheld the best of the *samurai* tradition. How are you going to inform him? We can send a telegram right now."

"I won't say a word to him or the Foreign Ministry. It's better that they don't hear about this. They might inquire more, and since you were not there, the Ministry might wonder why my deputy was not present. No, let's just let it be."

"Why are you hiding your heroism? You should be proud of what you did."

"Neither the Ministry nor my father would want to discover I have a consort who is not Japanese. You remember how they warned us during our training? Women can be spies. Non-Japanese women are not to be trusted. As we know, they could never be brought back home. No, it's better to be silent on this matter. To change the subject, where did you and Gül go on your rounds? Tell me about the men you met. Between the Ambassador's suggestions and Gül's instincts, I am sure you had an enjoyable time. With our limited time here, I won't have a chance to explore the nether regions of Venezia. I can only relive your stories."

Mitsu blushed and his eyes darted. "I prefer not talking about last night. I feel ashamed."

"Ashamed, what would you ever be ashamed about, Mitsu? You are the most honorable man I have ever met."

"Please, my behavior was hardly honorable. I was very angry and jealous that you rolled away without me…No, you don't have to apologize. The situation was beyond your control. Despite that, I could not push back my feelings. I wanted to be alone, but Gül convinced me to go out. We were already dressed up, so we went to the tea dance on the terrace, where we had several drinks. Within a short time, Gül made friends with a group of handsome young men our age from all parts of Europe. After some more drinks, we took dinner together.

"One of them knew of a secret music club on the Lido, away from the socialite crowd everywhere else. Of course it was on the list the Ambassador had given us. For several hours, we drank, listened to singers and drank even more. The more we drank, the more sociable and happier I became."

Mitsu was interrupted by a knock on the door. An attendant brought in a gigantic bouquet of white flowers from the hotel management. The young man with a twinkle in his eye and an inquiring smile on his lips lingered for a minute, as he regarded Mitsu, then me. Seeing no response from us, he quickly turned and quit the room.

"Hmm, that was interesting. That man seemed a bit flirtatious. Anyway, back to your story."

"I had noticed that groups of the men would head off to what I assumed was the bathroom. At one point, I had to use the facilities, so I got up. Opening the door, men were clustered in twos and threes. Maybe it was the drinks or my loneliness; whatever it was, I wandered closer, joining them. Others saw me as a curiosity and gathered around. Giving myself over to pleasure, I immediately felt so guilty for betraying you that I felt sick to my stomach. I bolted out without saying a word to Gül. He ran to catch up and attempted to calm me. He assured me you would not be angry; I was sure I had undermined our relationship.

"By the time I got back, you were asleep. I stared at your innocent sleeping body, the body I know so well. All I could think about was how I had been unfaithful and how disgusting I was. I crawled into bed, nestling up to you, stifling the tears welling up. Will you forgive me, my dear Kenzo?"

"Forgive you…forgiveness is not needed," I told him. "While *shudō* between us is sacred, pleasure itself is not. You did not harm our relationship. I suffered as badly as you did while we were apart, enjoying myself so much during the evening. If there is a lesson, it is to trust each other. Even if we are apart, our devotion remains."

Nina, the fear of losing love is built into the emotion. Ironically, fear makes love appear more precious due to the doubt it raises within ourselves. If we believe ourselves to be unworthy, even the most fervent expressions of endearment can be batted away. I grew up with a distant father, someone I could not trust, one that did little to guide me through life's changes. Despite his lack of affection I knew who he was, what he looked like, at least. I could recognize his voice amongst others and pick out his visage among a crowd. But you do not even have that experience of me. At the very least I hope your mother showed you our pictures. There were several taken of us, including the one on the front page of the *Corriere della Sera*.

We met Gül and Elisa on the large open-air veranda facing the sea and the thousands of bathers. We were shocked by a huge crowd under a banner that said, 'Welcome Consul Uchida, hero of Venezia.'

"News travels fast," Gül remarked. "The Morosinis are an old, well-connected family. His brother is the mayor. I see him coming."

A delegation rushed over to us followed by reporters and photographers.

"Consul, as the mayor of Venezia, I offer my personal thanks to you and Signorina Elisa. Your deeds are being talked about throughout Italy. Our members of the press are eager to interview you both."

He shook my hand and gave your mother a kiss.

"Signorina, your bravery and strength are matched by your beauty. Tonight, we are hosting a banquet where you and your friends will be our guests of honor."

The reporters had a lot of questions for both of us. Naturally, her story was the one on which they decided to focus. We were practically blinded by the photographer's flashes, although the photo they used for the newspapers was taken later.

Every politician and prominent citizen was at the banquet. Even more impressively, ordinary citizens lined the canals, hoping to catch a glimpse of us as we rode by. Elisa responded by waving regally, her hand upright and moving so slightly as if she had been prepared for this occasion.

As we entered the hall, the photographers were waiting for us.

"Signorina, please look here...One of you and the Consul together... closer, Signorina, rest your hand on his shoulder, yes, perfect. Consul, please smile at the Signorina."

The picture that appeared in Italy and afterward in Europe was the one where I was sitting on a gilded chair with your mother standing behind me, her hand on my shoulder, her face radiant in a beautiful smile. We were dubbed the 'Heroic Fire Couple.' The article chronicled the fire, including fanciful additions about the secret powers of the Japanese, how Elisa's dress was nearly scorched off, as well as other dramatic elements. The article also mentioned how we met as a couple 'in a dark Constantinople nightclub, where the East met the West and passion ensued.' Fortunately, none of the substantial details of our life emerged. Nonetheless, any hope I had that the attention would soon fade dissolved.

The celebration lasted until the wee hours of the morning. We slept late because the *Simplon Orient Express* did not leave until noon. After saying our farewells, we boarded the train, which would transport us to Paris early the following morning.

16. WHAT IS INCONCEIVABLE MAY NOT BE APPARENT

Wrapped in each other's arms, Mitsu and I slept soundly as the train slowly rocked us back and forth. Our reverie was broken when the conductor rapped on our door, announcing our arrival at the Gare du Lyon in thirty minutes. We quickly donned our kimonos to meet the embassy officials who would pick us up. The Embassy here was one of the largest diplomatic legations we had, therefore the most formal. The four of us assembled ourselves as we arrived at the station. Mitsu and I took the lead, while Gül and Elisa would go their own way to the Hotel Plaza Athénée, where she had booked rooms based on Signora Morosini's suggestion.

Waiting stiffly on the *quai* were three officials, two in military uniforms. As we stepped off the train, the man in nonmilitary dress stepped forward and bowed deeply. We returned his bow.

"Welcome, Consul-General Uchida and Deputy Consul Katayama. Egashira Yoshinori, Assistant to the Ambassador. I am pleased to welcome you to Paris. We will immediately take you to your residence. Later, you will have a reception with the ambassador. Excuse me to say so, the embassy staff is excited to meet the 'Hero of Venice,' as the papers here are calling you."

I glanced at Mitsu, who kept a straight face. "Please, I am not a hero. Any Japanese man would have acted similarly. I am sorry if this incident caused any trouble for the Embassy. The press made much more of it than they should have."

"Consul-General, please, we are honored to have you join us here. We have received visits of congratulation from the Italian delegation and from French citizens. You have made our country proud in a critical point of our history. I have said too much and do not wish to steal the words of the ambassador. Please follow me. The soldiers will attend to your luggage."

The two men jumped up to retrieve our bags from the car. As we stepped away, Elisa discreetly peered from one of the windows, mimicking the demeanor of any well-to-do tourist curious about goings-on. She was learning the mannerisms of the class to which she aspired. She had confided, on the train, that the Signora had given her a gift of expensive diamond jewelry and gold pieces to support her journeys as an independent woman.

The grandeur of the station struck me as we craned our necks taking in the features of the main hall. I wondered aloud to Mitsu, "If this is just a train station, what do their palaces look like? This magnificent ornate temple can only be a gateway to a city beyond dreams."

Heading outside, I stopped to inhale the Parisian air. You may think your father odd to say so, but air is different everywhere. We often sense the difference of air in the mountains and by the sea, yet each spot has its smell. Paris air is a mixture of sweet perfume, soot, marble, fresh bread and sophistication. Yes, sophistication has its particular smell—a mixture of tart, perky and louche; the smell of purpose and lack of purpose, time and no time, leisure and preparation for leisure, arts and debauchery. The rest of my senses were equally stimulated: the sights of the grand boulevards that would displace the tiny lanes in Venezia, Constantinople or Tōkyō; the sounds of trams and cars as they rolled, honked, and clattered by; and the feeling of the early morning's glimpse of heat on a summer day.

Humans have a sixth sense–what can be called object of mind–how our body puts these perceptions together, interpreting our sensations into features and emotions. After we make an observation or note sensations, we instantly replace the immediacy by an idea of what we just experienced. The description I just gave you of my first minutes is merely a memory of what

I noticed. I have frozen Paris into a ball of attributes called Paris. Yet at the same time, my mind believes in my recollections as it holds onto that perception. I also hold another ball of frozen perceptions from our time there. I prefer not to think about them right now, but sadly will come to those soon.

A car pulled up; the chauffeur opened the doors and, bowing obsequiously, bade us to enter. If I had just arrived from Japan, I would not have even noticed their behavior. However, being apart from other Japanese for a few years, I was exceedingly aware of the changes in demeanor we would find working here. A counterforce of culture and mannerisms was already pulling me back home even though we were thousands of miles removed from our island nation. Eons of acculturation developed my sense of Japaneseness, which unbeknownst to me, had slowly changed while in Constantinople. The mind works thusly. We believe everything is fixed, for example our character and how we act. Yet, under different influences and environments, the mind adjusts bit by bit, transforming our expectations and ways of being. We become our own object of mind and do not discern how we are gradually changing until a specific event brings the change to light.

I wonder what your experience of Japaneseness is, born as you were in America without any direct influences from the country of my birth? Others likely assume much about you, just from your facial appearance. I doubt you have inherited Japanese culture, but maybe, just maybe, you somehow take after me. How is that possible, you ask? My life and decision-making have been influenced by my grandfather's grandfather, in addition to the adaptations within Japanese society over time. As you will find out, you come from a lineage of strong women including your grandmother. Perhaps we are like generations of animals bred over and over to gain certain traits. While these animals are reproducing, I doubt they perceive their purpose or how their species has changed over time. They simply are as they are. Or maybe we resemble the bonsai, whose original seedling changes form over its lifetime not by changing its innate treeness but by external limitations on its growth. I suppose a third possibility is through hearing my tale, or should I say *our* tale, recognition of the inherited conditions might spring forward in you or change your perceptions of the outside forces acting on you.

We soon arrived at the residence of the Embassy in the 8th arrondissement. Our adjacent apartments on the third floor had large windows from which we could survey the green and grey rooftops and the cathedrals hovering above them. Thirty minutes later our trunks arrived, and a valet stored our belongings.

Precisely at 2 p.m., we entered the office of the Ambassador *Danshaku* Matsui Keishiro, who had served previously in Korea, the United States, Peking and London. Considered a preeminent statesman, he was our representative to the Paris Peace Conference following the Great War. In his middle fifties, he regally stood by his desk in a silk-embroidered jacket topped by a Baronial sash. He had a thick moustache showing a bit of grey, a long nose and black hair cut short on the side. Honestly, he was intimidating by dint of his connections to my father and the older generation.

"Ambassador Matsui-san. Uchida Kenzo." We bowed to each other. "My deputy and confidant, Katayama Mitsu. We are honored to serve you."

"It is my honor to meet you again, Uchida-san. I first saw you as a baby, a distinguished son of a great man, our Foreign Minister. Regarding you here after three decades reminds me of the shortness of our time on earth. I was your age when we met. Now you are me. Your father and I have been friends, colleagues and political allies as well as opponents. Having you serve under my administration here is a testament of his trust."

"Thank you, Ambassador. My father's accomplishments have shaped our country's history. Sons are faded echoes of their father's abilities and stature. I cannot expect to be compared to him."

"Uchida-san, you ought not be so modest. We are very aware of your recent heroism in Venezia. The son of Kōsai saving the life of one of the doyennes of Venetian society—that is an account I was not expecting on the front pages of both Le Figaro and the New York Herald. My sole complaint is you did not inform the Ministry immediately. We had to learn of your grand feat from the press and visitors to the Embassy congratulating us."

"I am very sorry, Ambassador. I did not want to appear as if I was bragging about such a minor event."

"A minor event! Young man, you must be cognizant that your conduct is always important to your country. How you act reflects directly on the image and power of Japan, especially as we are conducting negotiations. For too long, the Great Powers have peered down on us. They take us for granted and have attempted to emasculate us since they forced their way into my father's world. We thought we had proven our worth during the Great War, but the Powers are still trying to keep us subservient, refusing to appropriately reward us for our accomplishments.

"You have shown the strength of the Japanese male. While those pampered, debilitated Italian men ran for their lives and were willing to sacrifice one of their benefactors, you were the one to go back to save her. How typical of these Westerners. I saw what they were like when I was stationed in London and Washington, D.C. Their racism and snobbishness do not appear to have any bounds.

"We are proud of you, young man. Given the interest within the diplomatic community in your exploits, I plan to have a special dinner where we can honor the innate bravery and strength of the Japanese man. As we enter into critical negotiations, this incident can be used to our advantage. This is not about you but your country. However, I do have a sensitive question I must ask you."

I already knew what he was going to ask. Putting on the mask of attentiveness we must wear for our superiors, I waited. "Yes, sir, of course, please ask. My deputy is my confidant, do not worry about being sensitive in his presence."

"The news articles show a white woman alongside you. From the photo, she seems very attentive. Is it true that she also ran into the burning room? She must be quite extraordinary. Japanese men, especially those of us from the former *samurai* class, are truly more virile than your typical man. You appear to have made an exceptional choice. Westerners are disturbed by us having a way with their women, so politically, you are also making a point. I won't discuss more about your consort. Just be discreet. You are first and foremost a diplomat. As I have served as a diplomat for quite a while, let me say I recognize the needs of a man. I trust you will not develop any feelings for her, because that will cause you trouble."

I finally broke through my mask and acknowledged his words. "We see eye-to-eye on this matter, Ambassador. Yes, in Constantinople I became cognizant that this woman, Elisa, would serve a valuable purpose. She is independent yet very trustworthy. We have an understanding which I think I don't need to explain. You are a wise man, and I appreciate your perceptiveness. I have learned much about Western society. Men often reveal secrets to women, which can be very advantageous."

"Well said. You clearly are your father's son. Someday I will tell you more about the adventures we had in our younger days. This conversation at the initiation of a meaningful part of your career has been very enlightening for me. What do you require to get going in your position?"

"I do have one request. I brought our special liaison from Constantinople, a Turkish man who has contacts everywhere we have been. He would be a vital addition to my staff, as he can operate at levels to which you and I have no access."

"I am aware of this man. Gül is his name, I believe. The Ministry recognizes his work in Constantinople. Another sign of your excellent skills, choosing the right aides. Of course, he is welcome here."

The Ambassador rose to his feet. Mitsu and I bowed deeply as we exited. We were silent until we got back to my room.

"Kenzo. You were very skillful in the combat of words between the two of you. The conversation ended in the ambassador showing his respect for you as a peer. Originally, he was treating you as a young child of a political colleague. You were properly deferential while showing your own abilities.

Little does he know, and the better that he does not."

"Thank you, Mitsu. Being my father's son is onerous enough in this political world. Being compared to him is hard for me to swallow. Who is this man that others respect and fear? The small amount I have learned from him can fill a sake cup. Yet others have long shared histories. I would not want my child, if I ever had one, to experience what I did. Our conversation was a case of accepting one person's delusions to another's advantage. He did surprise me by his acceptance of my having a consort. A surprising and welcome reaction. Even better, I was able to be somewhat honest about Elisa. What a turn of events."

"Indeed, you are right. I did observe you chafing under his assumptions."

"Although I will have to get accustomed being surrounded by our countrymen again, the interaction felt like second nature, much easier than those with Westerners. I quickly comprehend what to expect, and what is expected of me, as well as the boundaries. Speaking to outsiders, I am constantly guessing as to what I am supposed to do and say. With the strange stereotypes of the foreigners or the constrictions of our own people's expectations, I struggle to be honest and true to my words. *Shudō* requires nothing less."

"You have three of us who count on your honesty. That is more than most ever have."

"And the most extraordinary one glows before me in all his beauty. I never want to let you go."

Those words echo back to me often. I still don't want to let them go even though he is gone. I certainly have no desire to revisit the next part of my story in what might be the last days of my own life. Yet I must if I am to reveal myself to you.

17. SEEING COLOR AND HEARING SOUND

We took up residence in no time. Gül found a garret on the fourth floor of a building three blocks from the Embassy. Elisa established herself at the hotel as a long-term guest, which meant she had others to manage the daily maintenance of living. She had a late breakfast brought to her room; lunch would be at a widening circle of cafés that she attended; and dinners quickly became boisterous affairs surrounded by friends and acquaintances.

True to my promise, the four of us went up the Eiffel Tower, its iron lattices reaching into the sky. The massive grinding of the cables pulled us higher and higher as we were transported up toward the sky. So far up, the lights of the entire city flickered to the horizon and its sounds blended into a hum that was neither natural nor human. The wind buffeted us so much that Elisa held onto me as I held onto Mitsu, who held onto Gül. Above us the stars were abundant in the heavens, and for several minutes our bodies had melded as one. The essence of Sufi feeling, which I had tried so hard to recreate, came over me. Eventually I learned that one cannot grasp onto such a feeling, and more so, the feeling itself cannot be recreated. Searching for it, one can never find it. Dropping the search opens the possibility of experience.

In the twenties, Europe was rebuilding, following the destruction of the previous decade. Cities were growing as did the infrastructure of trains, roads, and harbors, fostering quicker and easier movement around the continent. Gardens and animals sprung up in the countryside; food was plentiful again. The places that had been bombed in Paris were speedily rebuilt. Theaters reopened, and the art scene on the Left Bank blossomed.

The madness of the previous decade was replaced by a fervency to enjoy each day as much as possible. We witnessed many of the leading entertainers, and I still remember the rapturous voice of Ninon Vallin and the free-flowing dance of Isadora Duncan. Once the performances were over, we would be ushered backstage to meet the stars, lounging in their dressing rooms. You can imagine, my dear, what a heady time this was for us.

Jazz had recently arrived, and so many new clubs opened on the Left Bank that we rarely went to the same venue twice. Following the sounds of saxophones and trumpets, we would stumble down tiny, dimly lit steps leading to a stage and a bar. Often, we would encounter friends of Elisa's who were drinking and smoking and carrying on in such a manner that some nights later at the opera I would have to be reintroduced.

Almost weekly, Elisa and I or Mitsu and I - or sometimes all three (Gül was not a big fan) - would go to the Palais Garnier for opera and ballet. These events were the strutting grounds for the upper classes as well as the legions of international diplomats, League of Nations officials, and others who were negotiating peace treaties and accords. A high degree of seriousness of work seemed to be matched by equal attention to opulence and leisure. Over time, Elisa made sure to become personally known to the movers and shakers of society. She was thrilled over meeting the royalty that were still abundant in Europe and soon counted baronesses, counts, and the occasional dukes and duchesses as friends.

Slowly climbing the white marble Grand Staircase lined with its red and green marble balustrades, Elisa would carefully survey her surroundings. At the right moment, she stopped, not for any particular purpose, rather for others to admire her. She would inhabit those stairs until her friends approached. Cheeks would be kissed, hands shaken in public displays of affection and camaraderie as the upper classes are wont to exhibit. During their social engagement with my consort, I was studying the frescoes and art on the ceiling, marveling at their beauty and wondering how they were created.

Eventually we would move *en masse* to the Grand Foyer, an even more decadent display of art, marble, glass chandeliers and gold leaf.

As her list of friends grew, Elisa would flit from person to person, dragging me along until the usher rang a bell, indicating we should take our seats in our box commanding over the auditorium, the largest in Europe. Elegantly dressed patrons filled the gilded red velvet seats until the seven-ton chandelier of brass and crystal dimmed. A hush came over the hall. The orchestra conductor entered the theater to thunderous applause to begin the opening music of Puccini's *Madama Butterfly*. Composed about two decades previously, our friends assumed I had already seen this doomed Japanese-American love story.

The stage curtain, which itself was painted to resemble a draped curtain, parted to display an Italian-French version of Japan, a country the composer had never visited. The women had heavily caked white faces and kimonos which were the wrong color, worn and tied the wrong way. The main character was fifteen years old, too young to be a geisha. The high-pitched sounds of the women laughing would have horrified anyone at home. Astonished and appalled, I burst out in laughter, and was shushed by Mitsu on one side and Elisa on the other. At least Mitsu understood how wrong the scene was.

Yet at the intermission, Elisa was sobbing, "It is so beautiful. I was so sorry for her when the American captain left her."

"What are you talking about? Everything I have seen so far is insulting to Japanese culture! I am over ignorant Westerners loving their exotic Orientals, as they call us. They themselves are also exotic to me. I don't make a fetish of them. I'm leaving!" I found myself shouting.

Mitsu gently touched my arm, "Kenzo, people are staring at you, please quiet down. You're making a scene. We don't understand Western culture enough to appreciate the absurdity of opera stories. Remember your description of *La Wally*. We laughed about the avalanche of snow that conveniently killed her suitor. Let's examine this with the eyes of a scientist ... how do they view us?"

As usual, Mitsu interceded to show me a different perspective on the situation, so I agreed to go back. Despite the beautiful music and dramatic scenes, Chio-chio-san's *seppuku* made me recognize I should have departed earlier. Our ride home was quiet, as Elisa was afraid to speak, and I was not able to let go of my own thoughts. The Americans were the ones destroying our traditions, in what you, Nina, were taught was the 'opening' of Japan. We weren't closed—the West wanted to conquer us. They forced their way in via gunships and took advantage of our leaders, who were weak from infighting in our government. My generation grew up living between two worlds. Nights like this one made the contrasts very apparent.

I suspect you are also living between two worlds, yet you must be woefully unprepared, knowing little about Japanese customs and history. What can you draw on, except your own inner strength, when reacting to rude comments and stereotypes? If I had been by your side, I could have supported you as you navigated the racism and sheer stupidity of the ignorant. While neither of us can change the past, perhaps my writings can deepen your understanding of who you are.

18. THE FEATURES ARE INFINITE IN VARIETY

My daily work routine was interesting yet forgettable: Meetings, attending industrial exhibitions in Paris and around the continent, and hosting Japanese industrialists and ministry officials were the norm.

One day, Gül introduced us to a completely different part of society.

"You must come along to a most interesting gathering. A group of artists, poets and writers meets weekly at the Left Bank apartment of an American writer. I won't say much more, except that she is extraordinary."

Mitsu and I were intrigued as much by the mystery surrounding Gül's invitation, as by the idea of meeting actual artists and writers. Whenever we strolled the Left Bank, we observed them–or who we thought they were–in outdoor cafés, arguing, drinking and smoking. They seemed to be the soul of Paris. We had yet to venture into any galleries, although what we viewed from the street was intriguing.

The three of us (Elisa was dining with a count she had recently met) headed across to the Left Bank. Although we had chauffeurs ready at the Embassy, we preferred to go by our own means. As students, we depended on the trams and trains to get around Tōkyō, and an underground Métro was a new experience. We were thrilled by the enchanted realm that existed under our feet with its white tile-lined staircases and platforms. Standing arm-to arm with us were men and women returning home, stalks of bread under their arm, bags of vegetables and meat at their feet, and sometimes well-behaved, curious children surrounding them. The professions were often identifiable by their uniforms: rotund bakers in their white jackets, fishmongers still smelling of their wares, fine merchants in impeccably tailored suits and bowler hats, and police adorned in their elaborate uniforms.

In certain quarters, especially on the Left Bank where we were headed tonight near the Luxembourg Gardens, the train was packed. Most passengers were students buried deep into science and philosophy books, their friends arguing nonstop about any number of topics. Everywhere we went, we would encounter artists sketching their friends and the subway scene.

Outside the Rennes Station, among a multitude of boisterous passengers, we were treated to an old man playing accordion as a monkey scampered by his side. The monkey would sidle up to passersby and attempt to put his little hands in their coat pockets. Despite being done in good humor, the little guy earned his keep over the evening. Depending on how a particular suspect appeared and acted, the crowd often shouted warnings. Should a supercilious gentleman, his nose high in the air, parade by, expecting the masses to part way, he would receive no such warning and depart missing a watch or billfold.

The Left Bank exuded boundless energy as ideas brewed and the young experimented in finding meaningful ways of living, following the deprivations of war. We bumped our way through the crowds during our short walk to 27 Rue de Fleurus.

"Ah, gentlemen, here we are. The home of Gertrude Stein and Alice Toklas, our hosts. Are you ready?" asked Gül.

"Ready?" I responded. "Ready for what?"

"That you will discover soon enough."

We rang the bell. A thin, diminutive woman answered the door.

"Mr. Gül, I am so glad you came tonight. I see you have brought your friends along. Such dignified and handsome men. I am Alice Toklas—you may call me Alice."

"This is Kenzo Uchida, the consul-general of Japan, and his deputy, Mitsu Katayama."

"We tend to an informal American style here, so I hope you are okay with us introducing you as Kenzo and Mitsu to the others."

"Of course, Madame." I answered.

"You can start by not calling me 'Madame,'" she giggled as she bade us in.

The apartment was unlike any I had ever witnessed. From floor to ceiling hung paintings on top of paintings, filling every inch of wall space - all modern, very different from the classical style I had seen in the Louvre. Shapes and forms encompassing nudes and portraits, each bewildering in color and intensity, leapt off the canvas and assaulted my eyes and expectations.

About a dozen guests were milling about, talking, drinking and gesturing. At the center of the activity was our other host, Gertrude Stein. She was round and had the shortest haircut I had ever noticed on a woman until much later when I met female Zen monks with shaven heads. She had an open waistcoat made of coarsely woven material that a mountain peasant might wear, over a colorful striped shirt. Her skirt was heavy and dark, falling to the floor, unlike the modern style Elisa preferred. Thinking about Elisa, she is perhaps the complete opposite of her in almost every conceivable way.

Despite the crowd, she espied us the split second we stepped into the parlor.

"Gül!" she cried. "Is this the present you promised me? Intriguing what I see, what do I see?"

Gül made our introductions as she released herself from the group and strode over. She clasped my hand firmly, exhibiting more masculinity than Edmund or his compatriots. I had not met any American woman at the time, so I incorrectly attributed this to American feminine behavior.

"I will let Alice introduce you to our other guests, although freeloaders might be a better description of several of them. However, I do wish to introduce you to Pablo. He would enjoy you very much. Pablo, please come over here to meet my newest best friends."

A captivating man strode across the thick carpet. Compared to the other men, he was dressed quite formally in a dark suit and buttoned waistcoat. He had a white shirt, yes, I do remember these details quite clearly, I can usually remember what any man was wearing. Picasso was one of those men whose looks gave me a particular jolt of desire. He had thick black hair brushed across his forehead, making his head appear lopsided, all hair to one side. The muscles of his lower face outlined his protruding lips. His nose was bulbous and equally unforgettable. His dark eyes pierced the room with the intensity of their gaze.

"Bonjour, monsieur. Êtes-vous Japonais?"

"Mais bien sûr, je m'appelle Mitsu et voici mon ami Kenzo."

"Picasso, Pablo Picasso."

He firmly shook our hands, though not as strongly as our host. His hands were smooth and had a slight smell of linseed oil about them.

"My favorite Japanese artist is Hokusai Katsushika—are you acquainted with his work? The *Diving Girl with Octopus* is my favorite. I was inspired to try one of my own. You can see my attempt on Gertrude's wall. Do you think I captured the style?"

He continued without letting us answer.

"Togo Seiji is one of my friends here. He is a wonderful artist, a young man with great potential. I told Gertrude the first time I met her, 'He is very nice, your brother, but like all Americans, he shows you Japanese prints. Moi, j'aime pas ça, nonetheless I do enjoy the raw érotisme of *shunga*."

"*Shunga*," blurted Mitsu. "How did you learn of *shunga*?"

"It has been very popular here since the turn of the century. The French and Spanish enjoy *le sexualité*, yet we do not have art as explicit as yours. I can paint nudes with abandon but to show actual sex acts like your artists do crosses the line. *Shunga* is so alive. Tell me what you think of Gertrude's art collection. She is one of the biggest supporters of living artists."

"Well, sir," I began, "I can hardly say much about art, especially European art. May I be honest, Monsieur Picasso, the classics appear dark and foreboding, besides being flat and lifeless in their studies of men and women, royalty and merchants, all in the heavy, outlandish costumes of the day. I don't understand the bloody pictures of Christ. Your Western god reminds me of temple diagrams of the levels of hell in Buddhist mythology. Is your god the devil?"

Picasso burst out laughing so loudly that all conversations stopped, and the guests twisted their heads to figure out what had caused his outburst. Gertrude, who knew Pablo's antics, glowered at him, causing even greater laughter.

He was almost unable to speak. "Can I quote you on one of the best observations I have heard? Tell me more."

"The majority of paintings depict the ownership of objects. Were all artists merchants? I hope I don't sound uneducated or badly opinionated. Our art gives me an awareness of how humans and things are portrayed. We will not produce a Michelangelo or a Goya. They were fully of their period and centuries later can still be easily appreciated by those connected to that history.

"Maybe our art containing animals can be directly compared to European paintings. Even there, our animals appear more vibrant, active even if they are lying still. The focus on older European art for capturing the exact detail of a bird's feather means the bird itself as a life form is missing. Maybe that is what I perceive as different. The very energy of even ordinary Japanese portraits is evident, at least to us. Portraits of a particular actor or *samurai* or warlord aim to capture the energy and movement I rarely observe here."

"Monsieur Kenzo, your observations may change my opinion about the Japanese. I and my friends have stopped trying to match our pictures to reality. We have photography to do that for us. Yes, you are right, we are trying to capture the energy of the moment, the vibration within."

"As soon as I entered, I was drawn to the movement and lively spirit of the pictures on these walls."

We talked so much that my head was spinning by the time we retired. As she escorted us to the door, Gertrude told us we were always welcome back. Picasso promised to show us the hidden galleries of the Left Bank. Gül also introduced us to his friends, including several novelists and poets who showed great interest in meeting us. They explained the relationship between the two women, Gertrude and Alice, lovers, friends, and confidants. Each was their own person, although Alice took the supporting role.

My own insight into the province of women was extremely limited, and honestly, I learned more from your mother during this time than I did from any other woman, except perhaps my grandmother, whom you will meet later. Growing up, most men learn to take women for granted. My father's wife was devoted to his career. She was intelligent and well-regarded, yet solely an adjunct to her husband, not her own person.

Despite the increasing likelihood that my death will soon come as the bombing grows, I will discuss this in further detail later…Sorry, I am just laughing, realizing the ridiculous nature of the statement I just wrote. Clearly, I have no control over the bombs raining on the city every day, yet like every other inhabitant, I still approach life in the naïve belief that I control time in the hope to carry out everything I have planned. My prison guard arrives at her job every day, ever surprised by the destruction of another nearby building. She asks me, 'how did that happen?' rather than acknowledging, 'Of course more buildings will disappear by the German bombing.' Despite my circumstances, my mind believes I will somehow outwit death. The impossibility of doing that is unquestionable—it's a fundamental awareness of Buddhism that we all will die. Nonetheless, here I am saying to you I will get to that matter later, assuming I can guarantee you I will. Under these circumstances, I will accept this way of thinking. I still have so much left to tell you, so much to share, so let me keep writing.

To me, Paris will always be where one argued ideas in the midst of a changing ragtag group of characters until the early hours of the morning, under the influence of the warm weather, wine, and music. We were so alive. Like any feeling, this did not stay and proved unreliable, unstable and unworthy of confidence.

19. FLOWERS FALL EVEN THOUGH WE LOVE THEM

Shortly after the New Year, Mitsu became ill, complaining of lung congestion. We blamed the cold weather, but he was the only one who so suffered. Weeks passed before he consulted the embassy doctor who expressed concern about his lungs and ordered immediate bed rest.

"I can't do that," he complained, "I have too much work to do."

"Nonsense. I am your boss and your dearest companion. You must stay in bed until you get better."

Although a nurse attended to him, Elisa volunteered to come by during the day to sit with him. Despite our efforts, he just became weaker and weaker.

The doctor was recalled, and he examined him thoroughly. Shaking his head, he announced a diagnosis. "He has influenza, which is compounded by pneumonia. He must be taken to the hospital immediately."

The diagnosis took us aback. "Are you sure?" I asked. "Can't it be something else?"

Sighing deeply, the doctor shook his head. The word influenza alone struck fear into our very being. Each of us knew victims of the Great Flu Epidemic that ravaged the entire globe, leaving more than 50 million dead in its wake. Minor epidemics still erupted, increasing the toll of death.

I was ready to transfer Mitsu to a hospital. Despite being very weak, he protested in a voice so quiet we had to lean in to hear him. "Please let me stay here. I don't think I have long to live. I feel a strangeness within me, a transformation—already part of me is gone. I wish to die among you all, not among strangers, alone. Please, please don't force me to go, please."

His tears showed his desperation. We reached the conclusion to trust Mitsu and to take care of him where he was. We divided our time, assuring someone was always by his bedside. I didn't want to leave him, and the others had to force me away to eat and get a few hours of fitful sleep.

True to his intuition, he did not live much longer. For five days he lay listlessly. Suddenly, he sat up with a renewed sense of energy. "Kenzo, please bring me paper, ink and a brush. I need to write."

I hesitated, as if denying his wish would stop the inevitable. Instead, I brought a large sheet of paper, ground and mixed the ink, and handed him a brush. He did not hesitate. Showing more energy than I had witnessed in him for months, he brush-stroked calligraphy. Once he finished, he was ready to let go of this world.

I sent word for Elisa and Gül to come quickly. I held his hand and whispered, "I love you, Mitsu. These are not words I say enough to you. I love you more than you can possibly know. I long to hold you here forever, but I cannot. I want to always see your smile, but I cannot. I desire for you to never leave my side, but I cannot halt the inevitable. The only thing I can do is remember you and tell others of our life together."

As I talked, he gazed directly into my eyes, a faint smile on his face. We stared at each other, not blinking. His breath was getting uneven, yet his eyes never flickered from me. His hands turned cold so I rubbed them, to no avail. I never realized a person could be so cold; I was shivering holding on to him, yet I just kept looking into his eyes.

"I love you, Mitsu," I whispered, "I love you, I love you, I love you, I love you..." Nothing else was running through my body except for my devotion to him. We were completely, universally together, unbreakable as a unit.

Then he was gone. Life drained from his hand. Where does it go? He was still staring at me, his eyes open, his lips still forming into that special smile of his, yet no air moved in his lungs or out his nose and mouth. His pulse was gone. "I love you, I love you, I love you, I love you..."

Gül ran in to find me crying, slouched over his body, tears falling on Mitsu's face as if they were his tears. Sobbing deeply, feeling the heartbreak within me, I was still screaming, "I LOVE YOU, I LOVE YOU," over and over and over. Gül tried to move me away, but I resisted. I was not ready to leave Mitsu yet; I wasn't sure I would ever be able to. Instead he let me stay, running his hands through my hair and across my shoulders. We cried, holding each other. I finally touched Mitsu's cold, cold face, shut his eyes, and kissed him on the lips. As I stood up, Gül chanted as he sprinkled some kind of dust on him. His chanting was low and serene.

He leaned over to retrieve the paper that had fallen to the floor. "It's his death poem, an old Buddhist and *samurai* tradition. The person writes their final statement before he dies."

"What does it say?" he quietly asked.

"In the light of the day, shadows are illuminated."

According to our tradition, I sent Gül to get towels and warm water to cleanse and prepare the body. Following his return, I asked him to retrieve Mitsu's best kimono. I wet his lips, as custom required, attentively wiped his face and hair, knowing I would never again see his body. I disrobed and washed him. No one else knew about the mole on his left shoulder blade or the straight line of black hair down from his belly button. I rubbed the soft skin around his nipples, which I had often caressed as that pleased him immensely. After cleaning his feet, I had to kiss them one more time, as we often did to each other.

Gül returned, carrying the carefully folded garments. I finished washing his body and lifted Mitsu up, while Gül arranged his *kimono* and *juban* under him. Lifeless, his body felt much heavier. We carefully dressed him, layer by layer, the kimono tied in reverse and a pair of white *tabi* on his feet. Finished, we cleaned up and I informed the Embassy of his passing.

The ambassador and his wife soon arrived. The Buddhist priest attached to the Embassy was contacted for the ceremony the next day. Mitsu's earthly body would be cremated, according to our traditions. The ambassador instructed his assistant to make the funerary arrangements. We moved Mitsu to a small hall in the Embassy, which served as a shrine for occasions such as this. We laid his body on a white-clothed table.

Elisa discretely entered, after the others had exited. Distraught and apologetic for being late, she kissed Mitsu and offered a prayer from the Kaddish. For the night and day, as is our custom, either Gül or I sat by the body to oversee Mitsu's transition.

The embassy staff gathered in the afternoon and rose as the Buddhist priest, draped in his brown robes and *okesa,* arrived. Lighting the incense, he began to chant a sutra as the smoke, scent and sounds enveloped us. He gave the signal, and I approached and bowed at the altar. In a daze, I pinched incense in between my fingers, touched it to my forehead and dropped it on the burning coal. I repeated this act two more times. As the smoke wafted up, my heavy spirits were briefly overcome with a lightness of being, evanescent and free. The ambassador and embassy staff came forward to offer incense, followed by Gül. Although our friends were informed of Mitsu's death, the Embassy preferred that the service be private. Naturally Elisa was upset but understood the protocol. She did slip in later, and the three of us offered incense together.

The next day, we took him to the crematorium. The priest recited a sutra as the body was slid into the oven, my last view of Mitsu in human form. The breathing, living Mitsu was gone from this body. I was sad, yet recognized this body was not Mitsu. When the oven was opened, I scooped the ashes into a temporary urn, treating his former body respectfully as it makes its transition into the dusty earth. Utilizing a special set of chopsticks, I picked up the larger pieces of bones, placing them on top of the ashes. We do so as a reminder that our time on earth is fleeting—our bodies change as we age, and at death we change completely in form.

My duties were almost complete. The French urn that was used - marble and gilt bronze - seemed so wrong to my sensibilities. However, a proper *raku* urn would have to wait until I returned to Japan, although I had no idea when that would be. This strange urn sitting on a shelf observed my every stroke as I wrote to his parents. How do you break the news of the death of a son? Words can only express the inadequacy of the moment, no matter what I could say about his strength, the care he received and his last moments with me. I promised to bring his ashes back upon my return. Until that time, I assured them, I would guard them closely.

20. ALTHOUGH BEFORE AND AFTER EXIST, PAST AND FUTURE ARE CUT OFF

Oh Nina, what have I done? I am doubting myself right now. As much as I wanted to tell you my saga, maybe I was not thinking straight. For a brief flash, you met Mitsu, and now he is gone. You only have my word for who he was and the impression he made on others. But it's not fair to you. Of all people, you don't need any additional pain. Here I am reliving those worst days of my life, not thinking of your feelings. I was about to write that if you were Japanese, you would understand, but I don't know what solace that would bring you.

Let me just say, without Mitsu you would not exist. Please let me continue and explain.

My emotions were akin to the rollercoaster we rode in the Brussels exhibition the year before. Once Mitsu died, I was helpless to stop the pain, fear, sadness, loneliness, and guilt as they passed in and out of my body. Yet these emotions were intimately connected to love and compassion. Without our deepest connection, I would never have experienced such despair; one side heightens the other. They appear as opposites and merge into parts of the same feeling.

Grief becomes its own experience of the world. Each of my thoughts, emotions and actions were overcome by the missingness of the moment, feeling the presence of the Mitsu who was no longer present. I am sure that at times you have had similar feelings. The pain and loneliness would surge within me sparked by a memory, by opening a door, by an errant smell. Walking on one block on Faubourg St. Honoré, he would come into mind, while the adjacent block caused no such reaction.

I lost the ability to discern time—minutes and hours disappeared. I would find myself fixated on an object, feeling the depth of emotions rising, and somehow two hours would have passed. At other times, I would refer to an event, and Gül would remind me that it had not occurred yesterday but an hour ago. Sleepiness and sleeplessness stopped correlating to day and night. I went out and seemed to maintain my job; however, without Gül following me, I would have been incapable of keeping track of what I was doing.

The constant uncertainty that I harbored as a young boy re-emerged. Unspecified fear deep in my bones radiated out, reconnecting the loneliness from my youth to now in a tale of nonstop sorrow, ignoring the happiness Mitsu and I had shared for these last years.

I was also leaning on your mother much more. Overcome by grief, I was not able to discern that she and Gül were also suffering. She tried to keep me interested in daily activities and kept up our schedule of opera, theater and dinners. Her friends, who had no idea of my connection to Mitsu, did not mention him after their expressions of condolences. I suffered their cheery, vacuous chatter in silence. I wanted to scream, "You and everything you know will end. This is what you pay attention to?" Fortunately for my work and our social standing, I resisted such impulses.

Music alone had a timeless quality that bypassed my brain, going directly into my body and soul. At the opera, whenever a tenor or soprano sang a particularly beautiful aria, each note would crawl under my skin and permeate my whole being. Sadness and joy were united by the beauty of melody and the skillfulness of the singer. On many an evening, the music transported me out of my body, so that I floated with it as a melody cloud up to the ornate ceiling of the auditorium. Each time the music ended I felt the pangs an opium eater must feel. I desired, I needed more, yet felt even emptier. Yet the second the ensuing aria got under way, I would get my injection anew and wait for my high.

Les lapines, one of the terms used by my French friends on Rue de Fleurus to describe themselves, were willing to listen to me reminisce. They had adored Mitsu and his gentle ways. They knew he was absolutely loyal to me, so although they often flirted, they did so knowing they had no chance. As they described him, I recognized the deep impression he made on others who dearly missed him. In such a short time, we had found many friends.

About six months after Mitsu's death, Gertrude approached me. "Kenzo, you need to get out of the city. I have a country house in the south outside of St. Rémy-de-Provence. Let's make an excursion and invite *les lapines.*"

"I'm not sure I am ready to do that. It is nice of—"

"I have never been known to be nice and won't let that start now. We are going to the country, and you are coming. That's it."

Elisa was already a semi-regular at Gertrude's salon. Not surprisingly, she enjoyed being the object of attention, particularly by the artists. "Kenzo, Gertrude is right, you could use the country air. By the way, I asked Pablo if I could pose for him. I adore the idea of him painting me in the countryside."

Gertrude looked at her in amusement. "Elisa, only you could turn the classic artist opening line around and use it before him. Either way, one or both of you will wind up naked to the wind. I am one of the few women that he has painted fully clothed."

"Oh, I know he prefers nudes. I told him, 'I will pose for you any way you wish—why not?' You are right, Gertrude, why does he need a nude model if his paintings don't even resemble humans?"

"Okay we are all in agreement then. Kenzo, now you have to go. You wouldn't want to disappoint Elisa's rendezvous with fame."

A caravan of three vehicles made their way to St. Rémy with Gertrude taking the lead. The lengthy trip was made longer by her well-known lack of direction. Rather than argue with her, we understood that getting lost and finding our way anew constituted part of the adventure. We arrived at the estate midafternoon.

Away from our regular haunts, I looked forward to traveling someplace which did not hold any memories of Mitsu. Yet I found myself interpreting my experiences through his eyes, noticing what he would have enjoyed, the way a garden framed a house, the shape of the shadows below the ancient plane trees, the smell of lavender. This is one way we carry people with us after they are gone. The danger is that thoughts can create a yearning and conjure fantasies of what we would have done were the person still alive.

Gertrude spotted me wistfully gazing into the countryside. "Kenzo, you are alive. Mitsu would wish for you to enjoy yourself. He would be hurt to think his death put you in such a state. You can remember, and you can live anew simultaneously. The past has ended. There is no there, there. Take life back for yourself, don't be misled by your imagination." She paused, "To assist in that, you can carry our luggage into the house."

In France, my dear, *une maison de campagne* can refer to any manner of buildings from a broken-down farmhouse to a castle of fifty rooms. Gertrude's *maison* was a stone building built two centuries ago. The dark kitchen was the center of action with an old-fashioned wood fireplace that had numerous pots hanging over the flames, overseen by a local woman from the village, who was engaged by the couple whenever Gertrude and Alice were in St. Rémy. Her comportment was no-nonsense as she bustled about, known to be the best cook in the region. Maybe for these reasons she was the sole person on earth able to boss around Gertrude, without her protesting.

The rest of the house was notable for the ancient, exposed beams of wood, cut from the local forests and crafted into shape without the use of nails. The dining room had a hefty wooden table, on the surface of which bruises and bumps revealed a century of meals. Only the walls anchored us in the present day as paintings by her various guests were hung in no discernable pattern. There seemed to be at least five bedrooms, yet there could have been more—iron beds, thin mattresses and enough covers to keep one warm in a blizzard. Finally, an expansive salon replete with overstuffed chairs and a sofa seemingly as old as the house itself.

The house was set in an olive grove of ancient, twisted trees, and as we arrived, we observed workers picking the fruit to be pressed into oil. Outside the entrance to the *maison* stood an ancient chestnut tree, its giant, gnarled branches shading the ground below. Spikey seed pods hung low and heavy and littered the ground and the large table situated underneath.

Gertrude pressed me and one of her favorite *lapines*, Robert, a lanky poet with a handsome face, big ears, and an impressive Gaelic nose, to go into the village to gather food for dinner. She had sent over the orders when we arrived; all we were required to do was to stop at each of the shops on her list.

We built up a sweat as we ambled on that hot summer afternoon, woven baskets in our hands. Robert, who had been there previously, told me stories about the villager's reactions to Gertrude, the unusual *Américaine,* who acts more like a man than a woman. But he added, "Somehow she manages to win everyone over, no matter how outlandishly she behaves."

The quiet of the countryside was comforting. Except for time spent with Gül, I had not been alone with another man, since Mitsu's death. We chatted amiably, occasionally touching each other's arm or shoulder. The village was big enough to boast a bakery, green grocer, meat shop, and wine shop besides a modest hotel and a fairly active café. We made our rounds and retrieved all our items. We even added a delicious *gateau* and additional bottles of wine.

Our baskets were full and heavy, so we stopped to rest by the Roman Triumphal Arch that marked the edge of the town. Robert pointed to the sculptures of Gaulish prisoners being overseen by the Roman overlords. As I was inspecting the life-size sculptures more closely, he pulled me in from behind. I must have acted surprised because he quickly dropped his arms.

"I didn't mean to scare you," he said. "You seem so lonely. I thought you might care for some attention."

"You know…um…you know what happened…and except for, well, no one has caressed me…except for Mitsu."

"Let me try again, okay?"

This time, I sighed and leaned into him, his chest meeting my back. He kissed me softly on the neck and my ears, yet I involuntarily tensed up.

"It's fine, Kenzo, I recognize the feelings. I lost my lover during the war. We were serving together at Verdun, in the battle to save France. We had survived the entire nine months of fighting, yet as we regained Fort Vaux and ended the siege, he was killed. We often discussed our plans for our return to Paris, hoping to buy an apartment on the Rue de Bretagne, where we could stroll to the opera. Unexpectedly, our dreams died. I bought the flat anyway and often go to the opera. But the dream is empty without him."

A villager trudged by pushing a haycart, its contents billowing upward twice his height. A young girl perched on top softly sang a song.

I peered into Robert's deep-set blue eyes. "I understand empty dreams. I live these days in a fuzzy realm where clarity seems close, yet as I approach, it recedes into the distance. Is the pain you feel now the same as when he died?"

He sighed. "In the midst of war, you can't grieve, and you can't stop surviving. To my comrades, Louis and I were supposedly just *amis*. Hundreds of soldiers from our platoon were killed, and Louis was just one more to them. No, during war, anger and rage counteract grief. Fortunately, the battle ended soon thereafter. I was a madman, shooting at the slightest movement on the other side. In retrospect, I was probably trying to get killed so I didn't have to worry about a future without him.

"In Paris, I tried to get back into life; that's when the hurt appeared. A battle where France and Germany each lost so many men makes you indifferent to death. Am I better off as a survivor? Most days I say yes. Today, with you so close, the answer is certainly yes."

I spun around and spontaneously kissed him.

"Let's get back to the house before Gertrude comes searching for us herself."

We gathered our baskets and strolled back feeling a jolt of electricity in our steps. A car pulled into the yard as we entered. Picasso vaulted out to greet us.

"*Bonjour*, Kenzo, isn't this enchanting? You probably heard that Van

Gogh was treated in the valley, right over there. Those buildings are the Monastery Saint-Paul de Mausole. This evening the stars will emerge, and we will experience the famous sky he painted. I saw his work in 1901, right as I arrived. Vollard, my art dealer, had a number of his paintings and enjoyed showing them to me. It's too bad we never met; I eternally feel his presence here."

Elisa came over coyly and put her arm in Picasso's. "Gertrude set up a place for Pablo to paint me. If I am going to be nude at least the temperature is warm. That way, I won't shiver and make him lose his concentration, isn't that right?" She pecked him on the cheek.

"Oh, your wife is not joining us?" Robert inquired impishly.

"*Mais non,* I have painted her too many times already; she is ready for me to move on. I promised the Mademoiselle her own special time. I daresay you have no objections to our plans, Kenzo?"

"Elisa is her own person and always will be. I have little or no say over her activities and do not desire to begin now. That is why we get along so well. I will be interested to see what comes of your session."

Alice poked her head out of the door. "The meat will go bad if you linger any longer in the hot sun. Please bring in the food so the cook can get our dinner started."

Underneath the chestnut tree we were joined for dinner by several other artists and writers, all men—three Americans, an older Italian sporting a large, pointed moustache and a monocle, and two young Frenchmen from the village. We opened the wine and gave toasts in the four languages represented by the group. I was seated between Gertrude and Robert. As course after course was presented, and more wine was poured, a peace that I had not felt for too long came over me. I noticed that even laughter came forth naturally in the back and forth of the conversation. For a short time, I was completely present—no past, no future—a warm evening, delectable food and fascinating companions.

I don't remember much of the discourse, yet the memory of camaraderie among kindred spirits remains. On occasion, Robert would gently nudge me with his hand or foot. Even Gertrude was uncharacteristically gentle and noncritical. One of the Frenchmen brought an accordion and sang popular Italian, French, American and even Russian songs. We would join in, often inventing ribald verses as we went along. Robert kept prodding me to contribute something Japanese. Against my better judgment, I launched into the song the geisha had sung to me in my youth.

"Chiru wa uki, Chiranu wa shizumu, Kouyou no, Kage wa Takao ka, Yamakawa no, Kawa no Nagare ni Tsuki no Kage..."

To my surprise, I felt a release of grief, and longing disappear into the dark skies.

Elisa was the first to speak. "The song was beautiful, heartfelt yet sad. What do the words mean?"

"Scattering and falling are the cherry blossoms under the light of the moon," I translated. "The most beautiful things in life are fleeting. We perceive their beauty, and before we are even finished, the conditions change. Yet beauty still exists in its falling away. In the moonlight, everything is ephemeral. Nothing is what it appears."

"Oh, Kenzo, you are more romantic than you let on. I sensed, yet rarely see, this side of you."

"Bravo," Picasso chimed in. "Bravo. By your singing you share your sense of beauty. I am honored. The French may be fascinated by *le fétiche japonais,* yet witnessing your song I am captured by *l'instinct japonais,* the real thing."

I didn't want to say any more, I had revealed too much. I believed that the pain I faced was mine alone. The uncertainty and the fear were also mine. I hardly knew what to do on a beautiful evening in a wondrous environment with friends, and I was torn between my memories and the possibility of future love.

Gertrude signaled the end of the festivities. "It's late for Alice, so I will bid you adieu." We arose and kissed each other on the cheeks. Elisa and Picasso snuck off as the other guests made their way.

Robert was waiting, watching me. "May I invite you to stay with me?"

"My mind says I shouldn't; my body is telling me to ignore that. I've learned to follow my body for the best advice."

In his room, we undressed slowly, luxuriating in the sight of the other's body, observing what we could not hitherto. The moon provided our illumination, our clothes falling and scattering on the floor. I pulled him to me and held onto him for a minute. His heart pounded as he surrendered to my arms. He guided me over to the bed and we too fell down without a sound. *Chiru wa uki…*

In the morning, I awoke in a panic. Where was I? Who was this person? I dressed and ran from the house. The sun was rising over the mountains, the air was chilly. Without paying attention to where I was going, I ran until I was exhausted. At a quiet spot near a little stream I leaned over for a drink of its cool waters. Who was this worn and disheveled man staring back at me? I could see the trees, sky and his face. In my state of mind, I was not sure which was the original and which the reflection. I poked the water, which made the image wavy, distorted, and full of texture. This distorted Kenzo was the fearful little lonely boy without a mother, waiting for his father to appear. The other Kenzo was just a confident mask I wore to fool the rest of the world.

I didn't tell you the full truth earlier, my Nina. This story was so practiced that even I was deluded into thinking I was revealing the truth. I am truly embarrassed. Of anyone, I need not hold back from you, the person who might understand me, the person having a perspective that I did not have at your age. I'm sorry.

I did mean to lie to you when I told you about my grandmother. My mother died shortly after I was born; my grandmother intimated it was from shame. Her seduction by my father, the well-known politician with the beautiful wife, left my mother pregnant. Unlike the miserable Chio-chio-san, she had no promises of a future. Instead she was sent to the Floating City where herbalists and skilled women could end pregnancies.

Apparently, my mother instead went back to her parent's house and confessed her situation. She was adamant that I was to be born and, as my grandmother told me, was convinced I would be a boy. They had ways to tell that which now are mostly lost to us. Her parents were embarrassed and worried about village gossip, thus sent her to the city to her grandmother.

As soon as I was born, she contacted my father to tell him he had a son, his first and only. Maybe she thought he would assist her, maybe she even thought he might come back for her. There was only silence until one day a letter on fine stationery arrived for her enclosing some money and nothing else. The silence of the note was all she ever heard from him. My grandmother said that soon afterwards she stopped suckling me, then stopped eating herself. A month passed and she died.

My grandmother remembers hearing me crying. "Unusual, since you were such a quiet baby, always thoughtful-looking," she said. She came into the room to find my mother on the tatami, cold and motionless, as I was squirming and crying nearby. I had heard this account so often that as I got older I began to believe I remembered it. What I surely felt was the emptiness—the disappearance of my mother's affection. Even a baby learns to identify its mother by the feel of her softness, the shape of the nipple, the smell and taste of her skin. Those memories still reside within me.

I told the truth when I said my father would come to visit me when he returned to Japan, and I did live at his house for short periods. But his wife was not my mother. She recognized that, as did I. Although our blood lines were connected, my father was not my father, either. As his son, he cared for me as a concept and an object but never as a person. Our souls were not connected.

I wanted to have a father, especially since I was motherless. I yearned for him to pick me up, to play with me. I craved to be by his side so I could imitate him and learn to be like him. I wanted him to care for me and care about me. None of that ever occurred. I must have irritated him or maybe irritated his wife also, for when he would get his next assignment, I was sent back to my grandmother. He provided money for my upkeep and schooling. I would write to him often. I hoped he would comment on my penmanship, on my ability to write the complex kanji. But no compliments ever came.

This was the pattern as I grew up. Every few years, I would be sent to his home in Ushigome, when he was back. He would closely inspect me for I do not know what. As I got older, he would test me on my history and math, and make me write poems and essays that he would critique. He provided a tutor and made sure I got into the best upper school that would prepare me for Tōdai. Everything he did was on his terms. Unlike Mitsu, who was accepted at the school by his own intelligence, I entered on my father's connections. Anytime I visited him, he would remind me of his influence and tell me this was how politics worked.

"Intelligence is fine and proper, Kenzo, connections and wealth get you further. Remember that and remember who helped get you here."

I felt worthless until I met Mitsu. He saw something special in me that I could not. He was the sole person (except for my grandmother) who saw me for who I was; the others merely saw me as my father's son and treated me with care to curry favor.

I am sorry I am proving an untrustworthy narrator of my own tale. I don't mean to be. If I were an author, I would rewrite and edit these bits to make the narrative more coherent. Yet in our minds, until our end, the story changes along with changes in our environment, perceptions, and memories. Urgency prevents me from going back and presenting you with a more cohesive narrative. We are all part of constantly changing, unstable conditions. If I were not a prisoner, would I be writing to you? What if I met you that fateful day? These questions are meaningless, simply delusions. Conditions brought me to this place, just as others brought on this war.

Reality is unreliable and untrustworthy. I hope you don't find me that way, although I would understand if you did. Humans desperately need to rely on others, especially our parents. Even though I had my grandmother as my steady and loving influence, I yearned for more. I ached for a kind and loving father who did not exist in real life. Ultimately, I suffered greatly from this delusion. I hope through my writing you will avoid a kindred fate, but despite my best desires I am not sure that is possible. Maybe those are the conditions under which we are both working.

My existence was an open secret in my father's world. His colleagues knew I was his son, and I benefited from that fact as I reached the university. They accepted me into their political and diplomatic world, knowing he was watching over their shoulders. The professors at the university never pushed me too hard as my privilege already guaranteed my graduation. They needed me to succeed so that in my father's eyes they could succeed. These were the conditions of my father's world.

All of these memories were interrupted by a hand on my shoulder—it was Robert.

"You have been sitting, staring into the water for the last 30 minutes. At first, I was afraid of interrupting you as you seemed to be in another world. Then I called your name, and you didn't hear me. I was worried so I decided to approach. Are you okay?"

I was pulled back into the present and struggled to remember why I was even there. "I am sorry, Robert, I don't comprehend what is going on. Am I okay? I can't say for sure. My perceptions of myself seem to be coming together and then apart. I am sorry for acting so strangely."

He crouched down and pulled me into him. "You just described my life at the end of the war. Here, lay your head on my lap. Let me soothe the scared look on your face; you need someone who can take care of you. Don't think about the future or the past. I feel your pain and sorrow. You miss your Mitsu—of course you do and ever will. I miss my Louis. Re-opening one's heart is hard. I can see yours—open, tender, and guarded. You won't be stuck forever."

He talked to me for a lengthy time. Eventually, the softness of his touch warmed a part of me, little by little, as his voice quieted my inner voices and memories. At one point, he laid beside me and held me. His warmth filled me with hope again. Our passion erased the pain, so much so that we almost tumbled into the stream. I stopped thinking about Mitsu and paid attention to the feelings that Robert aroused.

Afterwards, we lay side-by-side contemplating the sky above. Lazy fluffy clouds floated above, and cicadas buzzed, rising in intensity, then slowly dissipating. Eventually, we decided we were hungry and put on our clothes, knocked off the dirt, and made our way back to the house. Lunch was just being brought to the table, and we joined the group.

21. WE MISTAKENLY BELIEVE THE SELF-NATURE OF THE MIND IS PERMANENT

Nineteen twenty-two was the year everything turned upside down.

Gül announced he was leaving. Although he did not specifically say so, he remained until he sensed I could manage myself again. He had had his own special bond with Mitsu as the only other man who put order into my daily activities, and had promised him that he would take care of me. Perhaps sensing big changes soon to come—he consistently had an intuition of what was next—New York would be his destination, working at one of the grand shipping companies where he would utilize his vast knowledge of the Asian, Middle Eastern and European markets. Although I understood his rationale for leaving, I was devastated. More than just a colleague, he was a friend, my first western friend. As you may detect from my anecdotes thus far, his worldliness, in addition to his openness which had served in guiding us, framed our experiences since we arrived in Constantinople. Deeply indebted to him, the loss of his companionship overwhelmed me. We promised we would see each other again. The two men who made me whole were now both gone almost at once.

Elisa originally had a plan for a private dinner to celebrate our second anniversary in Paris, which, as was her want, blossomed into a bigger event. Your mother had created quite the social life. Her artistic admirers competed for her attention after Picasso's portrait was hung at Vollard's gallery. She informed each of them that I was her number one man but that there was an opening for a number two. She would tell me about her different suitors, their attributes, approach and, occasionally, other more intimate details. She was so skilled at getting attention, sometimes she did not pay equal attention to what type of man she was flirting with. Following several disastrous encounters, she asked me to be a sounding board for judging their characters. Given the importance of maintaining our public relationship, she needed to be a bit more discreet. We became closer as we understood more about each other in our interesting, intertwined lives.

"This will be the *fête* to end all *fêtes*!" she grandly announced. "People will rave about this party for a long time."

To my surprise, she decided the Morosinis would be the guests of honor. The Signora had the idea to have a party where the old Paris elite would meet the younger artistic set. "Let's enliven things a bit," was her soon-to-be infamous quote.

Since our time at Gertrude's country place, Robert and I had been circling closer toward each other. We were spending more time together as I reluctantly opened myself to him. Meanwhile, Elisa was a favorite of Picasso until she moved on. Nonetheless, we still saw him whenever he was in the city.

The Morosinis arrived a week ahead of the party. Naturally, the Signora took Elisa shopping as soon as she descended from the train, visiting the most fashionable couture shops. The Signora treated your mother similarly to a living doll, adorning her in the latest modern fashions. Naturally, Elisa enjoyed the recognition and acclaim she received.

Robert and I met her on the evening of the party at her apartment. Guests were streaming into the second-floor ballroom. I was therefore surprised she was wearing an unremarkable cloth coat for the big event.

"Don't worry, dear, I won't disappoint my fans."

Indeed, she was correct. At the coatroom, I slipped off her covering, handing it to the attendant.

"Now I am ready, are you? Please take my arm."

The instant we entered into the hall, all eyes were on your mother. The women immediately recognized she was wearing a dress by Paris' most desirable designer. A crowd rushed to surround her.

"You are wearing a Madeleine Vionnet design—it can be no one else," gushed one woman.

"Yes, you are right. She is one of my favorites. I was at her shop two days ago. As soon as I saw this one, I knew it had my name on it. Vionnet just needed to make a tiny adjustment for the fit to be perfect."

"I adore how the crepe de chine drapes across your body, and the color is beautiful. She alone tries such unusual fabrics. I heard she models her styles after Isadora Duncan, natural and free-flowing."

"Apparently Isadora was just here on her way to Moscow," Elisa confided. "I wish I had come in a day earlier, so we could have met again. Did you hear what she told Vionnet? They were having a discussion about men. She said, 'Any intelligent woman who reads the marriage contract, and then goes into it, deserves all the consequences.' Can you imagine? She is certainly right. I think my Kenzo agrees..."

The women giggled and nodded their heads in agreement. At times like this, I was merely a decoration for her as she held forth. The Signora noticed the commotion and came over. She greeted me effusively, offering her hand and kisses on the cheek.

"Doesn't she appear *favolosa*? Of course, you two are always the most interesting couple. I joke that she is so wild she needs two men to accompany her wherever she goes. Are you not going to introduce me to your friend? Elisa was telling me he is quite the poet."

"Signora Morosini, please meet Robert."

"*Enchanté, madame.* Elisa and Kenzo often laud your kind spirit and generosity."

"I am hardly kind to them—I am indebted to them both. They were *eroi* for pulling me to safety that horrible night."

As we were talking, a tall, striking man accompanied by an entourage of rough types entered. Justin, a mediocre poet who occasionally appeared at Gertrude's salon, was a former paramour of Robert's and still bore more than a bit of resentment about how their relationship had ended. His group was boisterous and obviously had been drinking.

Robert appeared concerned, and Elisa came over immediately.

"Who invited them?" she asked angrily. "Justin is not on the guest list, and I would certainly not invite his type of friends. He is so boorish and is a troublemaker. Kenzo, you have to tell him to go."

I raced over to the men.

"*Bonsoire,* Justin. What brings you here? This is a private party for invited guests."

"It's the Princess himself," Justin sneered. "We were invited by Robert—didn't he tell you?"

"I don't think so. You two are not exactly on speaking terms."

"Ask him yourself. He's coming over here."

Robert stepped into the circle, and Justin gave him a kiss on both cheeks. "Tell your Jap friend you invited us. Don't you have certain things you need to inform him of?"

"Justin, this is not the time for this. Please go right now! You are embarrassing me—everyone is staring. Please leave now. We will finish this later."

"What? Are you afraid I might say something you prefer I kept secret, like you are coming back to me, moreover planning on leaving your Asian doll-man? Or have you not told him you have spent the last week at my apartment? By your gaping mouth, I am guessing not. Oops, sorry, I suppose I should let Robert give you the news." Justin grinned evilly.

"Kenzo, ignore him, he's been drinking."

Justin pushed Robert aside. "I know what I am saying. You can't pretend otherwise. I am not going unless you come along. You have no future here. You've had your taste of the exotic. You need to come back to your own kind."

Robert was silent and stared at the floor, not regarding either of us. Justin was speaking the truth. I became infuriated.

"Out!" I pushed Justin hard in my fury. "No dogs are allowed, so you and your pack of curs better scat."

He dove at me, fists extended. "No boy talks to me in that way."

Although I had never fought before, as a youth I was trained in *jujitsu*. I was also aided by Justin's inebriated state which made his reflexes slow. As he lunged, I spun sideways, tipped his fist with my arm, easily brushing him away. He jumped at me again, and my response was a kick to the solar plexus. He rolled on the floor, moaning. One of the other men jumped into the melee, and I dispatched him just as fast.

Instantly a crowd encircled the fight. Robert pulled Justin onto his feet, and they stumbled off. The other men retrieved their companion, still rolling on the floor in pain. Amidst shouts and curses, they quit the building. I never saw Robert again, and no one talked about him any longer, at least when I was present at Gertrude's.

I was shaken, embarrassed and upset. Elisa handed me a drink, which I threw down in a gulp, the alcohol burning my throat. A second met the same fate. The party guests were chattering, animatedly recounting their version of the fight. Whereas they were thrilled by the unexpected event, I felt humiliated.

"I'm leaving. I can't stay here. Please give my apologies to the Morosinis and other guests. I feel a bit ill and unstable. I will catch up with you later."

"Kenzo, are you sure? Why don't you sit for a little bit? You were amazing. Just as I think I know everything about you, you surprise me." She gave me a kiss on the cheek and the group cheered while raising their glasses to us.

"No, you didn't hear what they said. I have never been so insulted. I can't remain. I must go."

"Okay, the guests will forgive you. Please stop by my apartment later, so I am sure you are okay. I am so sorry I asked you to get involved. You are a strong, beautiful man whom I admire. I care about you deeply. I mean what

I just said to you."

I barreled out, leaving no opening for further conversations. Directionless, I ran into the street, my adrenaline surging from anger, betrayal, humiliation, fear and sadness. I had trusted Robert and was beginning to unlock my heart. Without even a premonition, he slammed it shut. How could I be so blind?

Sinking into remorse and pain, I roamed aimlessly toward the Left Bank. I crossed the Pont Au Change, staring at the cold waters of the Seine below me. The usual nocturnal merrymakers packed the streets, their joy pushing me deeper into a funk. I hesitated as I passed my favorite cathedral, Saint Chapelle, its intimately beautiful stained-glass windows reaching to the heavens. Mitsu and I often sat silently side-by-side for hours, entranced by the wonder of its magnificence.

Once I thought of him, my senses were overwhelmed by Mitsu-ness. Heartache, loss, and anguish surged like a tsunami. Temporarily Robert had been a bulwark, holding back the swelling tide; now the flimsiness of our relationship was revealed. Much time went by, my dear one, to accept that such grief never heals, remaining, tingeing my feelings in every circumstance. I don't mean to scare you by saying this. I was able to become happy again and was not constantly consumed by grief. Yet once you lose the one you cherished the most, everything is different. Even love is different.

I ran across the bridge, struggling to escape these sensations. The crowds were bigger and more raucous on the Left Bank. I almost caused several fights as I bumped through the crowd. Fortunately, everyone treated me in the happy bemusement that comes from alcohol and amiable company.

Music was coming from a basement, so I followed the notes of the trumpet down to a dark and sultry space. A woman, caked in makeup as thick as a *kabuki* actor, sang under red lights on a tiny stage in a low, deep voice, a cigarette hanging from her mouth. Men packed tightly, mostly ignoring the singer, laughing and drinking. As I ordered a drink at the bar, I felt a pat on my back. When I turned, an unknown man gave me a kiss. We chatted; I don't remember his name or even what he looked like. He bought an additional drink, lessening my anger.

I watched myself without judgment as I followed his entreaties to a back room. In a scene from a Greek frieze, men were on top of each other in every which way. I didn't feel any shame or inhibitions; I only desired to inundate myself into the depths of physicality so I could forget everything else.

In the midst of the frenzy, a voice yelling sounded above the din.

"*Gendarmes, police. Allez, allez.*"

Bedlam ensued; escape was impossible as the club only had a single exit. The police drew out their wooden batons, beating whoever was in their reach. The chanteuse defended herself by brandishing a chair against anyone who approached. The scene descended from one of indulgence to one of hell as the panicked men were beaten one-by-one. I escaped, relatively unscathed by the brawl, to the stairs, only to run into a swarm of angry *gendarmes* at the top, arresting every man that came out. Along with dozens of others, a number of them bleeding, others sobbing, and most of them full of rage, I was shoved in the back of a truck.

At the police station, the charging official paused as I told them my name, whispering something I could not hear to his companions before I was thrown into a crowded jail cell. I found a spot in a corner and collapsed asleep in drunken shame and exhaustion.

I was awakened by a jailer who called my name and silently led me to a bleak, windowless room. A minute passed, the door opened, and in strode your mother.

"Elisa, is that you? What have I done to myself? I am ruined, my career is ruined, I can never show my face again."

"Trust me, I've handled the situation, my Kenzo. You have had a hard-enough time. We are going to my apartment straightaway."

"But—"

"But nothing. The police chief is a dear friend of mine...He recognized your name and contacted me as soon as was possible. The charges have been dropped—your name was not entered in the records. You can come back to my suite."

"What can—"

"Shh...No more chatter here. Wait until we get to my place and get you cleaned up. It's been quite a night."

As she promised, we were able to walk out the door, the police chief winking at her as we passed. A taxi took us directly to her apartment. The streets were empty of revelers, and a quietude prevailed as the sun cast its early rays over the city. She opened her apartment door, leading me in.

"Sit here. I will go run a bath so you can get cleaned up."

She left, and I heard the water running. I sprawled disoriented on a settee and stared at a painting on the wall.

She found me that way when she came back from the bathroom. "What they turn me into when I pose is a mystery to me. Cubism, Dadaism, surrealism, I can't even identify myself in the completed pictures. I treasure them anyway. Poor baby, here I am chatting, and you are not hearing a word of what I am saying, are you? Oh, Kenzo, you are a mess. Come."

She led me to the tub, and in my dazed state, I stood there, still in shock. She disrobed me, steadying me as I stepped into the tub. Painfully, I submersed myself in the steaming waters. She laid my head back on a towel and washed my body. She shampooed my hair and rinsed me tenderly. I wept softly and then more intensely.

Eventually, I was able to stand as she gently dried me as one would a baby. She brought me to her bed, pulling the duvet over me. She slid in the other side and snuggled beside me.

"It has been difficult for both of us. Let's rest for a while. Sleep, my Kenzo, sleep."

We must have slept until the afternoon. At one point, I groggily opened my eyes, sensing her soft body close to mine, her arms clutching me. I kissed her hand and rubbed it against my face. She stirred a bit, snuggling even closer. I wasn't even sure what I was doing, but she knew. She kissed my back softly and turned me over. She massaged my whole body, kissing me, caressing me. She guided the way through the only instance I made love to a woman.

We briefly napped once more. Your mother called for a pot of tea and sandwiches. After they were rolled into the room by an attendant, we talked about our lives and how far we had come. We had been together for such a short time, yet for both of us our previous lives seemed like a dream. We think we are fixed in one place and then before we know it all has changed, and we are different. Or not.

It was the closest the two of us ever were and ever would be. For once the unexpected shows up, and we cannot count on remaining the same.

22. HERE THE WAY UNFOLDS

Although some time had passed, I was still nervous when I was called into the Ambassador's office. Upon entering the room, I was shocked to find my father standing alongside him. He said nothing as I bowed; he acknowledged me by his return bow. As I took a seat, he began pacing the floor.

"Kenzo, I have been hearing favorable news about your performance as Consul both in Constantinople and here. The more I hear, the more I can see myself in you. I was especially proud of your bravery in Venezia. You proved to these worthless Westerners that the true character of the Japanese man is fearless, strong, and moral. Yet in the diplomatic sphere where we work the cowards are in charge, preventing the strong from getting our deserved rewards. I am here to boost the current negotiations on the peace treaty and gain what is rightfully ours. From the Russian War to the present day, the Western powers have refused to reward our contributions for containing their enemies. Big changes are materializing at the highest levels."

"What sorts of changes are you talking about?" I asked.

"The discussion about our identity and our deserved global role has been going on since I was your age."

"As students, we spent hours discussing whether military might, or economic might, would make us succeed."

"Yes, those who believed in economic strength prevailed until after the Great War. We provided the armaments, the cotton and the food that maintained the Allies. And yet, at war's end, they spurned our contributions and gave us almost nothing. We are still looked down upon as lesser beings than the white race. Our citizens face discrimination in the United States, and racism prevents us from our fair share of the victor's rewards. Those of us who wish to have a stronger military securing our destiny are emboldened."

He stopped pacing and stared at me. "You and I are the progeny of the *samurai*. We must reinvent the *samurai* for the 20th century. The West will soon realize the mistake they made by rejecting our fair demands."

With no reaction from me, his face grew red, and he became agitated. I thought he was going to bang on the table in front of me. The Ambassador pretended to examine a document on his desk.

"I am bringing you home for a special assignment. I need someone I can trust, and there is no better person than my son. You will go to Manchukuo, where you will conduct confidential groundwork on local military preparations. As the sole great power in the region, this territory is within our sphere, and one day soon will be annexed to Japan. Our neighbors are weak, and now is the time for us to strike. Although the U.S. and Britain will do anything to prevent us, we are strong enough to push back on their interventions."

"Father, I am honored you think so highly of me. But I'm not the right person—my expertise is in Europe."

"That is an interesting point you bring up. Those of you who have been living removed from Japan are now indeed suspected of being influenced and weakened by Western culture."

"But…but you spent much of your career in Washington, D.C., London and Budapest," I loudly interjected. "I don't mean to question you as my father, but aren't you also included?"

He stopped for a minute, shocked by my question. He smiled, first at the Ambassador, then at me.

"Lesser men might take the outburst as an inappropriate way to address your father, a government minister; I accept you as one *samurai* speaking to another. I want you to be part of the emerging vision. By appealing to nationalistic feelings, we can erase the shame we have carried since Perry's black ships appeared on our shores threatening to attack. We are compelled to prove ourselves, me included. Those of us who have lived in the West have learned about its strengths and its debilities. I use my position and worldliness to exploit the latter, to create a stronger country. Politics is the art of knowing what to say at the opportune time, and how to say it.

"This brings us to a very serious matter: The Ukrainian woman you brought from Constantinople. I can guess what attraction you find in her. Nevertheless, you must get rid of her. A Japanese diplomat cannot be seen with someone like her these days."

"Sir, you don't under—"

"What is there for me to understand? You should know a powerful man cannot be limited to one woman. I have had many of them in each of my posts. I was always discreet and required discretion from them. You have failed to do that by flaunting her in public. I won't mince my words and demand that you get rid of the white woman without delay. Your affair is harming both of us. My enemies would care for nothing better to say than, 'Look at Uchida's bastard son, who is acting like a Western man under the thumb of his white consort.'"

"Father—"

"No more discussion. Get prepared to return home by mid-July. Your position is finished here."

I arose from my chair without acknowledging my father. I bowed only to the ambassador and brusquely dashed out. I was furious. How can a father who barely has been part of my life cause so many problems? As I write this sentence, I pause: why wouldn't you have the same thoughts about me? Sadly, my dear, as I reflect on this, I can accept why you would harbor similar grudges. I try hard not to be deaf to my own thoughts, yet they spring up unbidden and sometimes escape unnoticed.

As angry as I was at my own father, I am now afraid that I have re-created a similar relationship with you. Writing to you is forcing me to comprehend the truth of my ways, even where I had been sure of them before.

I am sorry–have I already apologized? I am sorry for the pain I am sure I have caused you in the chain of events, and for the mistakes and regrets that I passed down from generations of old. I have vowed to put an end to them. Hopefully my letter will make a difference in your life. I hope that you can forgive this wayward father of yours.

I searched for your mother. She was at her favorite café, surrounded by several friends. Despite their entreaties, I asked her to come with me privately. We strolled to the Luxembourg Gardens, where despite the cool, cloudy day we rested on a bench in a quiet part of the park. The flowers were bursting into bloom, their joyous colors belying the conversation I was obliged to begin.

"My father arrived here today."

"You didn't tell me he was coming. I hope I can meet him. His picture is so handsome, not as handsome as you, of course—"

"Elisa, please don't interrupt me. I have very serious news. I am being sent to Manchukuo–Manchuria, you call it–and I will have to go in July."

"How long will you be gone? I can stay here meantime."

"I said you mustn't interrupt me. You are making things harder. I have been ordered to end our relationship. As my father said in his usual delicate manner, 'Get rid of the white woman.' You and I can't be seen together any longer. He has his spies watching me, probably even as we talk. I did not foresee it coming, just as I could not foresee Mitsu dying or Robert being such a cad. This might be our last chance to talk."

Seemingly unperturbed, Elisa picked a pink camelia blossom from the bush alongside our bench, pinning it behind her ear. "My dear Kenzo, unlike you I have anticipated this possibility from day one. I knew you might abandon me when I was no longer needed. I have always been the most practical one, except for Gül who was the most practical of us all. I won't be an abandoned woman and have my friends pity me. That is not my way. I am leaving you."

An elderly man walking his large dog entered our secluded spot, accompanied by a younger man. They both fell silent after they noticed us and waited stiffly until the animal finished his noisy sniffing of the scattered leaves before they exited.

"Leaving me? You make it sound like you have been preparing for this all along. What do you mean?"

"I will forever remember you as the man whose large, beautiful heart was never meant to be mine. I admired the bond between you and Mitsu and have desired to cultivate such devotion for myself. Men seem to love each other better than they can love women. You were bonded to each other in a way I doubt I will ever experience. I fancy men, I savor the pleasure and adoration I get from them, I even delight in how easily I can manipulate most of them. To be with one of them as beautifully and naïvely as you two fit together is impossible for me.

"I am not sure what else to say. You opened me to the universe of my dreams. We both have grown since we met. I am unlikely to find another such friendship. As much as I might be self-centered, meeting you was one of the instances when that impulse was married to a better impulse to support someone else's needs. I doubt I would still be selling cigarettes at Maxim's, yet you were the elegant gentleman who opened the door for me. The people we have met, the places we have gone, the experiences we have had were priceless—this being said by someone who calculates the price of everything. I am sure it will be a turning point for the beginning of another adventure."

"If you are not staying here, where will you go? Back to Venezia and the Morosinis, or maybe to southern France?"

"Even prior to Gül's departure, I was dreaming about New York. The best ideas come from across the sea. Gertrude's and Alice's American friends have refreshing ways of living. An independent woman can thrive in Manhattan."

"Elisa, I have never inquired into your finances. Do you have enough savings?"

"I will be fine. I spent most of what I brought from Ukraine, and Signora

Morosini has been quite generous. Maybe I should have saved more, yet why would I do that? It's not Elisa's way."

"You know I don't have much on my salary, but I can at least help you on your next step and buy you a first-class ticket on a steamship leaving from Le Havre. You will travel in style, your own style. In America, you can write me and tell me about your successes. I will be waiting to hear about your future adventures."

"And I, too, Kenzo. Honestly, I can't imagine you being part of the war machine. Don't let them harm your soul. I have witnessed firsthand how the military can destroy lives. I will leave before I cry. I'd prefer tears not to be your last memory of me. *Adieu,* my Kenzo. *Enchanté,* my love. *Adieu.*"

She kissed me goodbye and strode down the shaded path. I was sure this would be the last time I would ever see her. I was wrong about that, we would have another chance at it in the distant future. Through my tears, I tried to follow her as she disappeared toward the Metró. Like dewdrops, tears both distort and amplify all that we can see.

23. A FISH SWIMMING DOES NOT REACH THE END OF THE WATER

I never completely believed your mother with regards to the emotions she showed. While she had an internal strength, no doubt, her external toughness was a façade, hiding the wounded animal, the fearful child, and often the insecure being within. So I learned to distinguish between the real courage she displayed amidst the fire from the feigned courage she showed at our last encounter. The latter was an attempt to demonstrate her independence. The truth was we both needed each other.

She did not, however, disclose the tightness of her finances. Only much later did I discover that Signora Morosini had stopped her financial support after the last party, once she came to the conclusion that Elisa's needs would repeatedly be greater than any sum of money available. Before she vacated the hotel, she sold most of the jewels to pay off her debt.

I bought her a first-class ticket on the SS *Paris*, the finest steamship of its day, and gave her what little money I could. We had mutual friends on the ship so I knew she would not be lonely—not that she could ever be lonely. She had so many potential suitors that I honestly assumed being free from me would allow her to move on to someone else on board and be set.

As for myself, I had my own farewells to conduct. My remaining weeks were made miserable by the presence of my father. He seemed to have decided he would atone for the lack of attention he had shown me in the previous decades by insisting on a nightly dinner. He spent most of each evening pontificating about one point or another of the byzantine political machination of the times. The more we were together, the less interested I was in returning. Fortunately, he was called back early, due to yet another political emergency.

After our dinners, I snuck back to my old haunts—Gertrude Stein's salon was the one I was going to miss the most. The conversations, art, poetry and even the replay of petty rivalries were music to my ears. I knew it was ephemeral, but that is what I would miss. My way of being, as I had come to enjoy it, would soon end.

Despite my arrest at the men's club I still had to pay it another visit, not particularly to see anyone, yet to bid farewell to being surrounded by dapper men my age, feeling a furtive freedom, a freedom to be cherished even more for its furtiveness. Truly, it was a place to become aware of the moment. Once one entered the door, there was no future left, only a present waiting for a man to wander into. Whatever occurred ended with departure, and thus had no past.

I was saying goodbye to my youth. I was thirty-one years old and already had suffered the death of my lover and the disappearance of my closest companions. The very excitement of the Left Bank was a celebration of the rich possibilities of youth. Although quite a few of Gertrude's friends were older they too set the tone to think and act differently. Nothing in Japan could match the youthful fervor here. Expectations for me to fit in would be large as my father talked incessantly about what he and I would do when I got back.

Returning Mitsu's ashes to his family was the one task weighing on me. Visiting them would be one of the first responsibilities I would undertake upon returning. Then I would determine my future direction.

Before I left, I received a letter from Elisa.

June 1921

My dearest Kenzo:

I am writing you this note to tell you I had a wonderful voyage across the ocean. Very soon we lost sight of land and then nothing, nothing, nothing but sea. Fortunately, the SS Paris *is such a fine ship with so much to do. I was pleasantly surprised at all of* mes amis *I knew on board. The ones I didn't know but should know—soon enough we were having dinner together. The dinners were the highlight of the trip, and I spent much of the afternoon preparing myself for them. Fortunately, before I left I had bought an entire new wardrobe because each night was an excuse to get dressed up.*

As a single woman, I was often at the captain's table. He was sweet enough to introduce me to any of the well-to-do single men on board. Of course, most of them were like you, so we had lots of fun. I did meet one eligible man, the right age with the right wealth, and we hit it off. We chatted about what he would do in New York, and he suggested a proper hotel for me.

I am wary of the women because they get very jealous if their husbands pay attention to me. To be able to enjoy the attention of the men during the night I ingratiate myself to the women in the day. Most of the time I do fine.

I so enjoy the fine society and Champagne and dancing each evening until late. The voyage went by fast. Madame Rostrovska, you remember her from my parties, the widow from St. Petersburg, invited me to stay in her apartment on the Upper East Side of Manhattan. Since my funds were a bit limited, I thought this was the perfect place to stay until I could meet my new gentleman friend again. I was told that her area is an exclusive conclave.

Bises,

Elisa

Her letter eased any concerns I had for her future. Your mother had landed on her feet as I expected.

My own departure day came soon enough as I caught a train from the Gare du Lyon to Marseille. Four of us had made the voyage on the trip to that station, yet I alone remained to make the return. As the train puffed out of the station, winding its way out of the city into the countryside, a deep pang hit me—I was going back home without Mitsu. You might have thought, my dear, I would have recognized that already. Alas, I did not. Until then, I was involved in the activities of going home; now, those activities were done. My protracted trip back would be accompanied by my utter loneliness.

The SS *Nagoya,* a medium-sized P&O Line steamship, would be my new home for several weeks. As a high-ranking official, I was treated respectfully and routinely ate at the captain's table, my sole source of conversation on this voyage. Frankly, I did not wish any other interactions. From the moment our ship slid out of the Suez Canal into the Red Sea, I was on a journey of irretrievable memories, a journey of desperation, a journey of solitude and contemplation.

I was worn and tired. Day after day, I perched at the rail on the stern, watching the waters churning into a powerful wake. If I jumped in, would anyone notice? I did not want to end my life. No, I was curious whether anyone would care. My father likely would not; maybe my disappearance would even eliminate me as a problem for him. The captain would notice I was missing from dinner, yet an alarm would only be sounded after a second day passed. Except for my grandmother, no one else was waiting for me anywhere. I had likely entirely disappeared from Gertrude's circle; indeed, when she wrote her famous autobiography, my name was not included. Your mother was establishing her own fashionable lifestyle in New York.

The prior trip was about excitedly watching the land go by and wondering about its inhabitants. This trip was about the water; water surrounds all continents, as rivers cascade to the sea. We take water for granted, even though we depend upon it. Like an arrow sprung from a bow, rivers have one direction from high to low. Once shot, the arrow flies in one trajectory, eventually hitting the earth. Yet once rivers hit the sea, the quality of water itself transforms as purpose and directionality are lost, as sweetness becomes salty, as form becomes shapeless. Water is its own kōan—by its nature, water is water, yet each of these connected waters around the earth have their differences.

Those new qualities create a power far beyond its previous state. The waves pounding our ship were more powerful than the strongest raging river.

Our gigantic vessel merely bobbed on the powerful sea. You may ask, 'Father, what about the coastlines? Don't they contain the sea, as the banks contain the river?' Your question is a land question, my darling, one borne from the existence of landed-ness, of living on the solid ground, applying your perspective to the sea. The coastlines themselves are formed by the sea, pounded into submission, knocked in and worn down. No amount of human energy can ever overcome this force of nature.

The sea is formless; nevertheless, it changes. As one heads south the water becomes warmer and warmer past the Canal. Passing by India to Malaya and Indo-China and heading toward Japan, its temperature drops. The water changes colors on a daily basis in myriad indescribable blues, greens, browns and yellows.

This object of mind which we have of the sea cannot remotely be the sea which is too big, too all-pervading, too expansive. Yet for all of its size, somehow fish discern limits we cannot perceive. While we experience all waters as the same, they find barriers to their travel that prevent all but a few of them to explore its vastness.

We think we know it, yet we know nothing. A cup of water is not the sea, just as an ocean full of water is not the sea.

I can hear you laughing, 'Such a silly father who doesn't even know what the ocean is.' I can laugh along because it is silly to think you know, then to think you don't know what you thought you knew. As an adult, this pertains to living beings in addition to objects, and to ourselves.

Observing the endless waves, each different yet similar in its wavy quality, kept me sane during the weeks of the voyage. Doing so, I was calm, without worries, not thinking much about what would happen once I returned home. I knew what my father wanted me to do and assumed that is what would result. I had no intention of being belligerent or a bad son, as I had no intention of being obedient or a good son. The days of intention would come soon enough.

WHAT IS THE PURPOSE OF PILGRIMAGE?

24. DEATH IS AN EXPRESSION COMPLETE THIS MOMENT

Tōkyō was sweltering on the morning of my arrival. The *Nagoya* had docked in Yokohama the preceding evening, and I took an early train north. After an absence of five years, the changes I saw astonished me. How did Tōkyō get so big and crowded? The streets were jammed. Wading through the milling multitudes, I made my way to my grandmother's house. I had telegrammed her from Singapore where the ship stopped for a day as I did not want to surprise her at her age. I had to search for her house, as the neighborhood had grown so much. Foodstuffs and supplies spilled out of shops which had opened on the block. Bicycles, carriages with vegetables for sale, pedestrians and a few cars all competed for space on the small street.

Her house had remained the one constant on her block, although it was a bit more worn for wear than I recalled. In my absence, I had been paying a young woman to stay and assist her. I shouted greetings at the doorway. Miki answered, beaming.

"Please, you are home, Uchida-san, welcome back. *Obāchan* has been waiting for you since your telegram arrived. I tried to explain you would not arrive until today, but she insisted on getting dressed up as soon as she heard you were coming. Please, come in."

I removed my shoes and peered inside. Now the inadequacy of this house, which had once been the entire universe for me, struck me. I was immediately ashamed of that thought.

My grandmother shuffled into sight and, as I was told, was wearing her most elegant silk kimono tied with a large *obi*. The huge smile on her face and the glint in her eyes erased any signs of aging as she bowed. I returned her bow with an even lower one, then broke formality by hugging and giving her a kiss. She smelled of powder and roses, exactly as I remembered. She pretended to be taken aback by my embrace yet would not let me go.

"My grandson, I can die now, happy to have seen you again. Each day, I have made offerings at the altar for your safety. Let's light incense for your return."

We faced the altar on which Buddha and a vase of yellow flowers stood and knelt on our knees. Each of us lit a stick of incense on the altar, bowing three times. Our ritual thus completed, I guided her over to a chair; however, she insisted on bringing me a snack.

"*Obāchan*, let Miki get the food. You don't have to do it."

"My dear grandson, please let me serve you myself. I remember what you like. Miki is a fine person—I am your grandma."

Another of my regrets, Nina, is that not only were you fatherless, but had no grandparents or other relatives either. You were cut off from the generations that raised your mother and me. You grew up devoid of any relatives to tell you your history and connections, except for the little Elisa might have shared. A world without my grandmother, especially given my circumstances, is unthinkable. She always talked about my mother, and even though I was too young to have my own recollections of her, she instilled memories of her in me. Although our situation is different, one hope for my writing is that I may fill in some gaps for you.

Grandmother fed me my favorite foods and sweets and took me on a tour of her garden. Despite the summer's heat, her prize roses were blooming. "Just for you," she said, "just for you. They have been waiting along with me and just came into flower yesterday. It was only then that I could believe you would arrive home. My flowers are never wrong. We have both grown old together and can read each other's minds."

"I had forgotten about your conversations with your flowers, trees and birds in your garden, *Obāchan*. As a child, I could vividly hear the conversations, not just your voice but also the responses you heard. But at some point the voices of the plants and birds disappeared."

"Oh, my dear *mago*, my heart is so full to be able to hold your hand in mine and to hear your voice. With everything else changing so much, thoughts of you have been my constant companion reminding me of the purpose of my life."

"I could barely find your house. The quiet street I remember is gone. It seems everything is more prosperous."

"There is more available, and food is plentiful, although the price of rice has doubled in recent years. With my savings and your contributions, I live well. But some of the older neighbors without children to support them are hurting. I share what I can, and they do the same with me, filling my house with flowers or helping me out with some more strenuous chores."

"Obāchan, you look as healthy and beautiful as the day I left. It is like you have not aged, whereas I feel so much older and weighed down by my experiences."

"I sensed that from your letters, my dear *mago*. The memories of those who we loved and died, like Mitsu, always stay with us. A day never passes where I don't think about your mother. She was a kind and open woman yet took on life's pains too deeply. Despite her strength and wisdom, she followed her heart and took on everyone else's pains. One can't live like that, we have to keep space for ourselves and our own nourishment. She is the complete opposite of your father who is in the papers every day now. He was just appointed as the acting Prime Minister again, but I suppose you know that."

"No, I didn't. That is a surprise. He left Paris a few weeks before I did but did not let on what the reason was. I am supposed to meet with him now that I am back. He wanted me to go to Manchukuo for him, but maybe this gives me an excuse to wait a little longer. Nothing has changed in our relationship, *Obāchan*. No matter what I have accomplished, I still feel that in his eyes I am a pesky mosquito, buzzing about him."

"You are no mosquito and he is prouder of you than you imagine. Yet he is a hard man in a cut-throat world. He is always waiting to make his next move. While this is his second time as acting Prime Minister, he knows that he will never be chosen for the actual position. That must pain a man like your father, who does not know how to accept defeat."

"Or responsibility."

"You are correct in that. You are now a man and have proven yourself in the world. Let go of your comparisons to him as well as your desires for things that he cannot give you. You have the heart, intelligence and grace of your mother. You may not realize that, but I do, and I believe those around you see those characteristics. Unlike with your father, people are attracted to you because of your wise and compassionate nature. As a young child your inquiries revealed that. You are young and have far to go and, yes, much to learn. Yet I have complete trust in your path. Take this time to discern your own future. You will hear the voices of the flowers and birds again one day, trust me on that."

"Thank you. Except for my late friend Mitsu, *Obāchan*, you were always the one that knew me the best. With everything that I have seen and experienced, there is much I want to tell you.

"Yes, my dear, I want to hear your stories."

Just as I started to recount my adventures, I noticed that she began to tire, and her eyes would close in sleep for a moment or two. I made an excuse for myself, suggesting she take a rest and for us to continue the conversation in the evening. While she napped, I unpacked my bags in my old room, which was untouched since the day I went to the university.

The house lovingly encircled me. While physically diminutive, it appeared to me as expansive as the ocean. I hope you have at least some joyful feelings and memories of home. Your household circumstances were troubled and unstable, as your mother moved you from place to place, while the numerous men in her orbit paid no attention to you. Sadly, Elisa, who was always trying to keep her head above water in these times, could not ensure a life providing the safety any child needs. Here, even as an adult, even with my doubts, I could feel my grandmother's safety, stability and devotion.

However, she had little to offer as I faced my prospects. Lying in my room, I felt claustrophobic. If I couldn't return here, where else could I go? I tossed and turned that night, visited by Mitsu and Elisa, both encouraging me to enter a large, mysterious edifice. Each time I tried, they would disappear, and reappear, beckoning me from an equally intriguing, strange building. On my third try they were pleading, "Come in, Kenzo, come along," and yet I still failed to follow. I awoke sweaty and anxious.

Quiet conversations, short strolls in the neighborhood as my grandmother greeted neighbors for the sole purpose of showing me off to them, eating meals together, occupied our days. She inquired little about my experiences overseas as that period was finished and did not need to be revisited. I had brought her some small presents, including a miniature Eiffel Tower, which she put on the altar by Buddha. She often asked whether I would be remaining here in Tōkyō or at least nearby. I did not answer that question nor broach the topic of my father and his entreaty that I go to Manchukuo. Each evening, my disturbing dreams would haunt me.

On September first, I rose early for the task I was loathe to face. Days before, I had replaced the garish urn I had carefully transported here with a pale blue, glazed one in *raku* style. I tenderly moved over the ashes and bones, carefully wrapped his remains up, and departed for Mitsu's parents' farm about an hour west of the city by train. The rice fields were green, and in the gardens surrounding the earthen houses, vegetables were lushly growing. After asking for directions along the way, I finally found their small farm. Mitsu had been sending money back to them, and they had invested in the house, adding a tile roof and other improvements, in addition to buying a cow and other animals.

I called into the house. His father emerged, looking at me curiously.

"Katayama-san, it is Uchida Kenzo. I hope you remember me."

He bowed, "Of course, Uchida-san. My eyesight is failing me these days, so I couldn't quite tell for sure. *Okāchan,* come quickly. Uchida-san has come to visit."

His wife shyly peered out the door. "It is you, Uchida-san. Thank you for visiting us here. *Otōchan,* get our guest a chair." She disappeared into the house and came back shortly afterward with tea.

We exchanged pleasantries, and the conversation promptly fell silent, a silence I hated to break. I finally mustered my courage.

"I am so sorry for the reason I have come here today. Mitsu made me promise to visit you as soon as I returned to Japan. During our travels, he frequently talked about you both, how honorable you are and how he hoped you were proud of him. I can tell you that he died peacefully without significant pain or discomfort. He was too young to die."

His mother began to weep softly. I continued. "I have his ashes here. I promised him that I would bring them home to make sure he joined those of his ancestors."

I unwrapped the urn and delicately set it on the table. Instinctively, both of his parents touched the urn softly as though it were alive.

"Otōchan, go tell the priest Mitsu's ashes have arrived." She turned to me. "We held the funeral services as soon as we received word of his death, and we postponed the forty-nine-day anniversary until the ashes arrived. Now we can complete the rituals. Let me change and we will go to the temple."

His father headed for the village temple while his mother went inside. I sat and let a tear fall on the dusty earth. Death is a given for all of us and is itself not a cause for tears. Yet my desire for his death to be erased and his living body to be accompanying me for a different celebration with his parents was what passed through my thoughts. Wanting the impossible is another cause of suffering.

His mother and I painstakingly made our way up the dirt road to the temple perched halfway up the hill near the village limits. The neighbors who saw our procession - his mother in her mourning clothes, a walking stick in her hand and me carrying Mitsu's urn - bowed as they realized why and where we were going.

We passed under the *Sanmon,* the tall gate leading into the temple yard. The modest temple, built more than five centuries ago, served the local region. In addition to the *Butsuden,* the main hall, there were a couple of adjacent buildings, including a residence for the priest. The grounds were carefully raked, and the trees clipped back. The priest in his brown robes bowed in greeting. He took the urn and went inside the temple. Shortly after, he invited us to join him. Taking our shoes off, we stepped onto the *tatami* mats and sat on our knees in *seiza* as the priest lit incense and chanted. On the altar was a *sotoba,* the wooden funerary stick on which Mitsu's *kaimyō,* his Buddhist name, was written. Except for priests or other Buddhist practitioners, we only receive our true Buddhist names after death. I smiled as I read the kanji, *Shin Ki, Profound Capacity.* The local priest certainly knew my Mitsu.

Once the ceremony was over and we each had lit incense, I handed the priest an envelope containing money on behalf of the family. They would have been too proud to object and had prepared one of their own. We followed the priest who solemnly carried the urn and *sotoba* to the graveyard, crammed full of stone markers, most of them very old, in addition to hundreds of *sotoba,* fading under the harsh sunlight.

The priest had barely positioned the urn amongst the markers for Mitsu's ancestors when the ground began to rock. The earth rumbled as it moved and swayed, throwing things askew. I lurched forward to save the urn from falling. The *Sanmon* swayed vigorously, creaking loudly as did the entire temple. Branches fell from trees, and the multitude of *sotoba* clacked as they fell to the ground. Mitsu's parents grabbed each other as we heard a crash coming from inside the temple. We were fortunate to be in the open air where the danger was diminished.

Earthquakes here are common, so we thought nothing was unusual. Yet in this case, the temblors did not stop. For more than four minutes, the earth rolled with wave after wave of pulsations, their intensity increasing. The priest began to chant the soothing sound of the *Enmei Jukku Kannon Gyo* to remove suffering and calm our fears.

"Kan Ze On
Na Mu Butsu Yo
Butsu U in
Yo Butsu U En
Bup Po So En
Jo Raku Ga Jo
Cho Nen Kan Ze On
Bo Nen Kan Ze On
Nen Nen Ju Shin Ki
Nen Nen Fu Ri Shin."

We joined him, chanting repeatedly until the rocking stopped. We ran into the temple where the Buddha was knocked over, as were the rest of the altar implements. One of the walls looked precarious, and rooftiles were shattered. We became aware of the wailing of people and the sounds of animals that had been hushed into silence during the quake. For a time, the entire earth was screaming. Some houses in the village had collapsed, and a fire ignited. Neighbors who were able threw buckets of water at the flames and successfully kept the blaze from spreading.

We staggered back to the farmhouse, fearing the worst; around us it looked as if a giant had trod the countryside, smashing every structure with his big feet. The family home was not as badly damaged. The beautiful tile roof was shattered, tiles strewn for thirty *shaku*. The glass windows were cracked, and the entire house was slanted sideways, as if waiting for another rock of the earth or a strong wind to knock it down. Ignoring the danger, Mitsu's father and I carefully entered, carrying out undamaged belongings.

The family's possessions were few, so the losses were minimal. While we were doing that, his mother gathered the roaming animals, making sure they were accounted for.

An ominous cloud of smoke was rising into the sky toward the east and south where the city was. I was not comfortable leaving his parents, but I suspected the conditions in the city were much worse. I had to get back to my grandmother's house, which I discovered would be no easy task. The main road to the railway station two kilometers distant was already clogged as desperate people fled into the countryside. I managed to get on a train for three stops before we skidded to a halt. Ahead of us, the tracks were twisted, bridges lay collapsed, and trains had tipped over. Fires were burning everywhere, and the screams from the thousands trapped under the rubble were terrifying.

I had about five kilometers left to my grandmother's house, and my hellish journey lasted for hours. Aftershocks were toppling buildings that had managed to stand during the initial temblor. Block after block of blaze and rubble obscured the streets and obstructed my way. I was a madman amongst an entire city of madmen and women, all of us trying to get somewhere in order to survive. A number of times I stumbled, my lungs aching from the acrid smoke, the streets smelling of death.

As I neared the neighborhood where my grandmother lived, my pulse raced and my mind slowed to snail's pace. Nothing was left standing. I searched and searched for her street, in futility. The houses, trees and gardens had evaporated in the ubiquitous destruction of the fires. I ran one way, then the other, then another, calling her name, invoking Kanzeon, searching for anything familiar. Nothing remained.

That night, darkness never came; the fires in many parts of the city lit brightly the still unfolding horror. The sounds of suffering, wood burning and crackling, and buildings collapsing was too much to bear. I tripped over the dead in the streets, the tar having melted as they tried to escape, trapping them upright in the face of the inferno. No place was safe as a tsunami inundated the harbor, and collapsed bridges blocked the escape routes of entire neighborhoods as the fire incessantly raged.

The Great Kanto Earthquake leveled the entire port of Yokohama, destroying the industrial power of the nation and our biggest seaport. Almost 150,000 souls died, and 60 percent of Tōkyō's residents were homeless. The fires burned out of control for three days before they were finally extinguished. At one point, rumors spread of Koreans poisoning wells and setting additional fires. Thousands of Koreans or those thought to be Korean were killed by incensed mobs and police alike.

I spent those days aiding the suffering as much as possible as a way of avoiding the grief which began to overwhelm me. None of us could make sense of the losses we suffered. Dazed, exhausted and unable to think about the future, I kept active, clearing rubble where we heard victims cry from inside; carrying water for fire brigades; clearing bodies from the streets; and gathering them at makeshift morgues.

Later that week, I picked up a newspaper and noticed an article mentioning that my father's last day as interim Prime Minister was the day the earthquake hit. The paper reported his home was still standing and his wife was safe. I had been sleeping on the streets and eating from some of the food stations that had been set up. I was tormented about whether or not to go to his house. I had not been invited there as an adult, and this did not seem to be the best time. However, in desperation I made my way to Ushigome.

The large, solid mansions were intact; even the trees appeared unruffled. The streets were guarded by police checking everyone's identification to prevent refugees from streaming into the area. I found his house and talked to the guard, who examined my dirty clothes and haggard appearance suspiciously. I convinced him I was a Ministry employee. He went inside and returned, directing me to the back of the house. Minutes later, my father appeared. "You look horrible," were the first words he uttered. I turned to leave, and he grabbed me by the shoulder. "I am not rebuking you, son. I didn't mean to sound so harsh. What happened, where were you?"

I gave him a rough account of what happened. Honestly, I have no idea what I said to him. I hated him for being who he was and having a home and family when I lost every bit of what I had. He called over an aide and gave him information to write up.

"Here, take this message to the Ministry forthwith. They will provide you with housing and food. Afterward, when you are clean and rested, we will talk more. I'll summon you in a few days. The Manchukuo assignment is still waiting for you once conditions get stabilized and back on track.

"I am saddened to hear about your grandmother. She was an outstanding person, to you and even to me. She had little reason to be nice to me, yet she was always cordial. She aspired for you to have the best possibilities in life through me. Your own mother was a beautiful, smart woman, I wish she had been there as you grew up. In another setting, we might have been together—that was not to be. These two women are gone but I still have plans for you. Now that I have retired, it is your time to follow in my footsteps. For now, go and get some sleep."

He bowed and returned to his house, leaving me standing alone, pieces of paper in my hand. I didn't move from that spot, his words spinning in my head. His aide came back to escort me to the Ministry building near the Imperial Palace. He brought me to an office, where they assigned me a room and procured a vehicle to take me there. A kind, gentle young man who obviously had been seeing numbers of others similarly traumatized, escorted me to the *sentō*, the communal bathhouse on the grounds. We both entered and removed our clothes. Mine were thrown in a garbage bin, as they could not be laundered; the stains, sweat and rips rendered them useless even as rags. We entered the washing area, and I plopped down. The young man poured tub after tub of hot water over me. He soaped my hair and massaged my head. He scrubbed my body, over and over until I was practically raw. The water was black from the soot. After the third or fourth washing, the water was flowing clear. He supported me as I limped into the tub to soak. I could barely stay awake; he kept up the conversation to make sure I was okay.

Eventually, I had enough and stood up. My knees trembled from exhaustion and every part of my body ached. He rinsed me under a stream of cold water, which I barely even registered. I put on the clean kimono they gave me, and he escorted me back to my room, where I later was told I slept for two days straight.

25. HOW DOES THE WIND PERMEATE EVERYWHERE

I awoke to a devastated world. All I knew was gone; the dearest person in my life was not to be found. Fortunately, I had savings protected in a bank so unlike a significant number of others, I still had resources. I mulled over my uneasy conversation with my father but put that out of my mind for now as I had a more important priority. Although my grandmother's body was presumed to be consumed by the fires as was the fate of her entire block, I still had to arrange a funeral service. Locally, temples were destroyed, and the number of funerals outmatched the available supply of priests. For that reason, I arranged to have the service for my grandmother at the village temple where Mitsu was interred.

I went back to help Mitsu's parents rebuild their house. The damage was less than we initially assessed, and we easily managed to straighten the building up. Retiling the roof took several more days of work. The manual labor momentarily distanced me from my trauma and grief. His parents were grateful for the assistance, treating me as their son at a time I needed human connection the most.

On the day of my grandmother's funeral service, they joined me as my family. The community had committed the effort to secure the temple as one of many such reconstructions over its venerable history. The service brought my emotions to the surface as tears fell. The priest revealed my grandmother's new name on her *sotoba, Bu Zan, Dancing Mountain*. From my description, he explained to the mourners that she was as solid as a mountain, unchanging and steadily present in my life. Yet the skies around a mountain are in constant motion, thus changing the mountain itself. The mountain cannot be taken from the sky, nor the sky from the mountain. For the second time, he seemed to be remarkably clairvoyant to choose such an unusual, yet perfectly fitting name.

As we were chanting and the temple bells rang, a line of doves appeared on the horizon and circled the village. The pain I had been carrying since the earthquake struck dissipated slightly at the sight. Following the ceremony, I briefly spoke to the priest about my feelings. We decided to continue the talk the following day.

Our conversation continued for hours as I shared my story and what I thought I understood about my past. He was a kind man whose gentle laugh invited me to trust him. I told him about my connection with Mitsu and how bewildered I was without him. I even told him about Elisa and how she was another part of our created family. He listened openheartedly but spoke little. He invited me to light incense and to chant the evening sutra. Afterwards, he suggested I sit zazen with him in the pre-dawn hours.

You probably don't know this, my child, Japanese families do not go to temples daily or weekly like Christians, Muslims or Jews. The temples are supported by the community and major life events —births and deaths— are celebrated by services. Our homes have altars, which you have heard me describe already; for Buddhist ones, we light incense and set flowers or even fruit on the altar. Buddha is not a god. Buddha is an embodiment of spirit itself, a way of being in the world. This is about as much detail as I knew, as much as most Japanese know about the religion. Buddhism and Shinto are integral parts of our traditions.

I awoke with the rooster and made my way down the dark road to the temple. The priest was lighting a candle on the altar as I entered. He bade me to sit on a round cushion, *zafu,* on the *tatami* mat. I watched as he demonstrated how to sit, my legs entwined with each other, my back straight, my hands cupped on my lap. He rang a bell three times.

"I invite you to breathe deeply and to follow your breath in and out.

Shikantaza or zazen aligns the body, the breath, and the mind altogether. The mind's job is to think, just as the heart's job is to pump blood. While we cannot stop the mind from thinking, we can stop our attachment to the thoughts. Visualize your thoughts as clouds floating into view and then away."

After what seemed to be about ten minutes, which was actually closer to an hour, he rang the bell once. We stood up. He taught me a walking meditation, *kinhin*, as we silently paced around the temple aligning our breath. The sun was rising higher as we sat for another meditation. He rang the bell again. We repeated another interval of sitting, and finally he signaled for me to rise as he conducted a simple service of incense and chanting. After two and half hours, we were finished. He offered me rice gruel and pickles to eat for breakfast.

I was anxious to recount my experience, but he had other ideas. We spent several hours in silence, reserving words for explanations of what needed to be done as we cleaned the temple grounds, pulled weeds and cut wood. Only when our tasks were completed did he invite me to talk.

This time, he took the lead.

"Zazen is the key to experiencing the Buddha's teaching. We are born, age, suffer from illness, and die; the nature of life is ephemeral. Human nature makes us rebel at every stage of the cycle. We continue to believe that things stay the same, including our bodies and minds. As difficulties and suffering appear, we deny their existence instead of recognizing them for what they are. We live thinking we will be the one to outfox death. None of those delusions works, and we suffer even more greatly."

My daughter, you probably think this grim. Yet accepting grimness opens a door. My life even after Mitsu's death had happy events, yet the hard ones reverberated the most. If zazen was a means to transform those horrible events, I was ready.

I came back each morning, following this routine for several weeks. The priest, whom I called *Oshō-sama*, or 'Teacher,' invited me to move into the temple. He no longer had a family and appreciated the assistance in maintaining the upkeep. He also saw a yearning in me, of which I was not yet aware, for deeper practice. His invitation surprised me; as I contemplated the offer, I decided why I should accept it. I had no home and no desire to follow in my father's footsteps and to accept the assignment to Manchukuo.

Mitsu's family was pleased by my move.

"Did Mitsu reveal that he planned to become a priest at one time?" his mother asked me.

"No, although it makes a lot of sense now that you mention it. He had the demeanor of a Zen practitioner—patient, generous, refusing to judge anyone. Offhandedly, he would mention a Zen teaching or use a Zen phrase, but I never thought of asking him about the origination of his insights."

"Yes, he took his first steps along the path of training. His training made him realize that he did not desire to become a village priest and rather wanted to explore the world. From an early age, he was a very smart, industrious boy, so we supported his decision. He used the Zen training to be less distracted than other boys his age in his studies. He was accepted to the university, which set his course forward."

"And that is where ours joined and continued."

"Yes, my son, if I may call you that. I am grateful for our time together. He told us about your friendship from the day you met, and he wrote about you constantly when you boys traveled in the West. We previously met you once, yet through Mitsu's letters we enjoyed getting to know you a lot better. The stories he told about you are obviously true. Maybe you will take the steps in Zen practice which he did not complete."

She gleamed at me. "Don't forget us here. You always have a home waiting for you."

I bowed deeply. "Yes, *Obasan*. You gave a despairing homeless man sustenance. Your generosity of spirit will eternally be with me."

I wish I could tell you, my daughter, that I was a good Zen student. Alas, I was too full of my thoughts and my suffering. I thought that no one else had ever suffered the way I did. Given a chance, I recited my sufferings like a sutra. *Oshō-sama* would patiently acknowledge what I said. When I asked what I should do, he would tell me: 'Sit *zazen* more.' His answer seemed reasonable; moreover, the practice did not add any more hurts.

Bit by bit, he trained me to assist him at funerals and anniversaries. Eventually, I learned about arranging the temple, lighting incense, and hitting the bells and various drums during the ceremonies. I was a sponge absorbing everything he showed me.

Learning was my way forward until one day, during our morning chant, he whacked my shoulders with the *keisaku,* a long, flat stick used often to remind me to straighten my posture or wake me up if I was tired.

"Wake up, Kenzo. Awaken to your practice. What do you think you are chanting?"

"The renunciations, *Oshō-sama.*"

"Have you ever listened to yourself? We chant to let the words burn into our body, our breath and our mind. You are doing none of that."

'What more can—"

"Listen to yourself—don't make excuses. You are complaining in the middle of the renunciations. You are not paying attention."

"What do you want me to do?"

"I never want you to do anything because you have so much you want or don't want to do already."

I was hurt. He had never spoken so harshly. I was also embarrassed. I wanted to do everything right, and I was ruining it. I was foolish for following this path.

"It hurts my ears to hear you thinking, stop. Stop your thinking!" The *keisaku* came down harder, another whack.

How did he know what I was thinking? Was it an advanced Zen trick I would learn?

"You still have a question mark on your face. The *keisaku* is not punishment—it is the stick of enlightenment which says, 'Wake up, wake up to your delusions.' Let's go back to the renunciations. Let the words in, as though the *keisaku* were speaking them."

We repeated the verse together three times. "All my ancient, twisted karma from beginningless greed, hate and delusion, born through body, speech and mind, I now fully avow."

By the end of the second round, my body released the pent-up tension, and, during the third round, a positive joy took over. Yes, I was full of greed, hate and delusion, and as *Oshō-sama* had previously told me, we store these in our bodies and mind. Each time we speak, they arise through our lips as a reflection of our inner state. Despite not wanting to be greedy, hateful or delusional, being stuck in my own version of pain kept me from paying attention to others.

This was a vow of renunciation. I was vowing to become aware so my inner nature would not continue to control me. By acknowledging the behavior, I had the options to either stay how I was or change. Of course, changing is not simple, yet the hardest part is to view change as a choice, rather than the hopeless endless cycle of repetition of mistakes. Joy and hope entered my body. Yes, the *keisaku* was still needed to wake me on occasion, and each time its slap came, my reaction was not to wonder why, but to pay attention to the lesson at hand.

Time goes by fast if one is not following a calendar. As fall moved to winter then to spring and soon back to fall, I lived by the sun and moon, the warmth and cold, snow, rain and wind and the natural cycles of growth.

Living alongside *Oshō-sama,* I came to understand his patterns and habits, although I knew little of his previous life. Once, while visiting *Obasan,* we had a brief chat about *Oshō-sama.*

"Oh, Kenzo, poor *Oshō-sama.* He was married; his wife was very nice and helpful to all of us. They had a daughter who possessed a beauty beyond her surface. She was generous and so intelligent that she left the village and went to Tōdai. Except for one time, she never returned. Shortly after, we heard that she had died. People like to gossip, of course, but no one knew of her ultimate fate. *Oshō-sama's* wife was heartbroken by the loss of her daughter and never recovered. She herself died within the following seven months. Since then, he has never uttered his daughter's name or referred to her. For more than thirty years, *Oshō-sama* has been alone in that temple. I am glad you are there to keep him company."

I was not reading newspapers, so I knew little about the recovery from the earthquake except what I observed in our village and heard about our region. I had no connection with the Ministry or my father and was content to be out of their sights. Due to the overwhelming number of burials in Tōkyō, more than a year passed until the memorial stone for my grandmother was completed. *Oshō-sama* and I installed the stone in a prominent spot by his family's section, among markers dating back centuries.

He told me we would schedule a private service the following day. *Oshō-sama* approached me as we finished our temple cleaning, *sōji*, to say he wanted to talk.

"Kenzo-san, I have been talking to my superiors about your progress. You have grown considerably. We believe you are ready to make a commitment for the future. You shouldn't be surprised. I care deeply for you. A lifetime of pain and sorrow has been lifted from me since you arrived."

"*Oshō-sama*, how is it possible that I have comforted you in such a way?"

"You still believe you are the only person in the world," he said, giving an exuberant laugh. "Maybe I am mistaken about your preparedness. Ha! No, you are ready."

"Ready, ready for what, *Oshō-sama*?"

"I have recommended that we initiate priest training. Once finished, if you want to proceed, you can attend Eiheiji Monastery. You have the capabilities of being a teacher, in addition to priesthood. I saw the potential in you the first day I met you three decades ago."

"You met me? I was a young boy. I don't remember meeting you. You must have known my grandmother, yes?"

"Yes, your mother also."

"My mother, how would you know her? You hardly ever go to the city. What do you know about her?"

"I know everything and nothing about her. The first time you entered the temple, I sensed that we had a profound connection. As much as I examined you, I was not able to determine how we were connected; I could only imagine it was from a previous lifetime.

"Once you told me the earthly name of your grandmother for her funeral service, I immediately recognized who you were. The person who you thought was your grandmother was not related to you by blood."

"What, what are you telling me? What do you mean?"

"Hold on, Kenzo-san. Give your grandfather a minute to explain."

He paused to catch his breath. His compassionate, wise eyes peered into my own. For some minutes we wordlessly shared the sorrow and joy in our gaze.

"You likely have heard that I had a daughter. When Michiko was born, my wife and I were very happy and content. As she grew up, I saw how her curiosity and intelligence would one day carry her out of the village. While I didn't want her to go, I had no power to prevent her eventual departure. Therefore, we made sure she had the best education possible for a girl and accorded her the privileges usually associated with boys. Growing up, she was happy and self-confident. It was our fault to not recognize that she would have difficulty finding someone to marry as she did not conform to the expectations of women. Despite what befell her, I would not have changed how we raised her. However, my wife lamented this decision until her own death.

"She was accepted at Tōdai. As one of a handful of women, the pressure was immense, still she was successful. She dreamed of joining the diplomatic corps, a dream that was all but impossible. Her talents became known, and she found what she thought was a mentor, an ambitious young man who was moving rapidly upwards in the ranks of the Ministry of Foreign Affairs. He was full of ideas of women's equality, which encouraged and equally misled her. With her hopes sufficiently raised, she failed to notice his true intent.

Since he himself was married, he wanted to conquer her for her talents and beauty. He had no intention of supporting her.

"All of this she grasped too late. She came back to the village one day, pregnant, distraught, and confused. My wife and I did our best to comfort her, yet knew that if she stayed here the village might abandon the temple, and worse, she would have to face the gossips and evil-speakers every day as an example of someone who dared to dream above her position in society."

Spellbound, I listened as he continued. Fear began to seize my body. My breathing was shallow, and I wanted to block his words from coming out.

"*Mago*, my grandson, you are my grandson because your mother was my daughter. We sent her to the person you called your grandmother - her life was dedicated to caring for women in need. She was a former geisha, well-respected, generous and kind. Following your mother's death, she kept you as her own grandchild. We were forever grateful."

The bubble of fear in my body burst at hearing his words. A million thoughts raced through my mind. I tried to speak, however no words would form. I caught myself and slowed my breathing, asking "what now," "what next," as I breathed in and out. As compassion and gratitude emerged, I could gaze into *Oshō-sama's* eyes.

"I saw you only once, as we assented to your grandmother's recommendation that we not be involved in your upbringing. Due to your father's desire for a claim over you, we were afraid that you would be confused if we said we were also grandparents, in addition to the grandmother raising you. I was visiting Tōkyō for a rare meeting and came by your house; you were about six. I recognized my daughter in every move you made and your confident answers to questions a stranger was asking. Most of all, I saw my daughter's eyes in yours. You also had her color, brightness and intelligence. In retrospect, that is what I noticed when we met as adults. I realize this is too much information. I hope you don't hate me for telling you this."

"*Ojīchan*, why would I hate you? You must have struggled here each day, unable to tell me who I was to you. You, who reminds me daily of our ancient, twisted karma, observed the karma of our own family. Ultimately, karma is karma, neither good nor bad, our backward path leading to the future. You have helped untwist a few strands of that karma. Even more importantly, your karma twists into mine and into my mother's and that of the woman I will still call my grandmother, and even into my father.

"This also means the karma Mitsu and I shared extended back lifetimes. Our bond was deep, we were preordained to reconnect. We shared an indefinable sensation and now you confirm our feelings. I may need lifetimes to accept all—"

"Don't worry, you are on the path of acceptance. Assuming you are willing to begin, the path will be made wider since your vows are strong and your intention is sound. Practice never stops pain from arising. Even I still have regrets —I wish my wife were here to meet you. As hard as we try altering reality; the past cannot be erased. The present can be transformed by acceptance. Over time, our mind rewrites the past and the traumas."

"I have one question. What happened to my mother?"

"She died from complications of childbirth. Your grandmother made the arrangements as the family member seeing off the earthly body at her cremation. She brought the urn to us. Come, I will show you it."

I followed my grandfather - the first time I used that word to myself - over to the cemetery. He pointed to an urn adjacent to my grandmother's *sotoba*.

"Limitless Wind is your mother's Buddhist name. She is among our family and your grandmother. One day, you will join us here."

"Grandfather, she only has a *sotoba*!"

"Yes," he sighed. "It pains me each time I come here. I have held this secret for too long. Secrets are never truly secret. They burn endlessly as long as they exist."

"Grandfather, let's add her name to my grandmother's marker to honor her as she deserves. Would that be okay? In the bright light of day, secrets dissolve."

We brought the stone cutter back, who added Limitless Wind to Dancing Mountain. *Oshō-sama* was happy as the circle was completed, which would eventually include the interlocking circles of Mitsu, your mother and generations known and unknown. At the ceremony, *Oshō-sama* had me lead the procession, light the incense and recite the sutras. Thus began my training as a priest.

26. THIS PATH, THIS PLACE, IS NEITHER BIG NOR SMALL

Time flew by as I learned to be present. Each moment was a time for practice. What I did not do became as significant as what I did. Over time, I became aware of the fears and desires occupying my thoughts. The delusions *Oshō-sama* talked about referred to our attachments to ideas and perceptions we think of as real, yet which exist solely in our minds.

"Zen is a body practice," he would often repeat. "What is happening in your body right now? Pay attention, but don't hold on to it. By paying attention, you will notice the changes. Change is the only constant. When you don't notice change, you are fixated on an idea which is not reality."

Too many dismiss this as nonsense, but I hope you can grasp at least a piece of what I am describing. To learn how to perceive is a gift, and these insights I hope to share in my writing to you. Perception is power. Do your best to be open to your daily routine activities. Working, playing, loving, sleeping, eating, writing, sitting, driving, listening, studying, speaking, hearing, feeling, laughing, and crying are all states of perception.

I will admit one regret I still cling to—I wanted to share these teachings with you in person. One day, my wish is for you to find a teacher, so you can experience this thing your father deemed vital. For now, you just have me planting the seed.

Oshō-sama–I continued to call him that publicly, and reserved *ojīchan* for our private conversations– introduced me to his teachers. A number of them had concerns about the direction in which Japan was headed in its interactions with the other countries of the world. I occasionally saw my father's name in the newspaper. He appeared to be a voice for signing a peace treaty, while concurrently being a major player in our territorial claims on Manchukuo, Korea and parts of China. So many contradictions, yet that is true for every person.

The Sōtō Buddhist leaders and teachers *Oshō-sama* knew hoped that international and cooperative views in the civilian government would lead to a more peaceful world. The perspectives gained from my diplomatic career were perceived as valuable insights by them. Even though I was in a remote temple, senior teachers sought me out for an explanation of certain aspects of foreign policy and to ask my advice about how the policies might impact our practice.

In formal *dokusan* or practice discussions, *Oshō-sama* guided me in my training.

"*Mago*, as one of the last acts of preparation, you will sew your *rakusu*—the small bib we wear every day. I will order the larger *okesa* for you."

"*Oshō-sama*, I thought you told me that Sōtō Zen had given up the practice of hand sewing since the Meiji Restoration."

"Yes, that is correct. However, unlike most priest candidates who are the sons of priests and have been preparing for the role since childhood, you have arrived via a different pathway. For this reason, I am looking back at our ancient traditions and believe that sewing your own *rakusu* will help you discover your intentions in becoming a priest."

"Sewing my own robe? I know nothing of sewing..."

"Ah, even better. You know nothing of becoming a priest and know nothing of who you are. The Buddha asked his followers to sew their robes from discarded and useless rags to distinguish themselves as practitioners. Since they were using rags, the bib itself is made of tiny pieces of material sewn together into little patches. These patches are sewn to each other to create a pattern resembling rice fields. You will use new cloth, not rags, and with each stitch you will chant—*Namu Kie Butsu. I take refuge in Buddha.* I can help guide you, but this is something you must learn through practice.

Sewing was not something I had learned as a youngster, and the exacting nature of the effort was exacerbated by the scrutiny of *Oshō-sama* and, even worse, by the visiting teachers. They seemed to take delight in pointing out my mistakes, requiring me to undo my hard work to re-stitch correctly. My ego was angry at their comments. Eventually, I learned that concentrating on each stitch would lead me to the robe. Worrying about my progress took me away from the focus on stitching. My teachers were trying to show me how my errant thoughts emerged in my sewing. Stitching and removing stitches, making mistake after mistake, allowed the robe to emerge. Finally, I sewed the last stitch on the neckpiece completing the robe: the Pine Stitch, a broad, open stitch that resembled a slanted arrow, an insignia representing the Sōtō Zen sect.

I had more than a bit of trepidation when I handed over the finished robe to *Oshō-sama*. He examined my work closely, noting uneven stitching and a spot where I might have missed a stitch. My heart sank as I wondered if I would ever get it right.

And then he said, "Mistakes are life. The mistakes will remind you that your robe was made by a human. Good intent is not perfect intent; perfect intent is meaningless. Enlightenment includes everything including mistakes, pain and suffering."

He took my robe, which would be returned to me at my ordination. Leading up to it, *Oshō-sama* added more sittings and prostrations, conducted in absolute silence. Any anticipation or worry I had was tamped down by the continued sitting and meditation.

The sun rose on ordination day, no different than on any other day. The temple needed special cleaning since our local supporters would be witnessing the ceremony that would formally include me as a member of their *sangha* or community. As *Oshō-sama's* only student, my ordination was a big event. Local women arranged flowers on the altar and in the temple. They also prepared food for a feast afterwards.

My hair was shorn, and I shaved my head smooth, leaving one lock on the top. My last act before ordination was to chant and make full prostrations throughout the temple. As I made these rounds, doubts surfaced. 'What am I doing?' I thought. 'Mitsu never finished his ordination—did he observe a warning I also should have noticed?'

Following the last prostrations, the bell rang, marking the opening of the public ceremony. As my head raced, 'Flee while you can,' the instant I doffed my sandals to step on the *tatami* in the *Butsuden*, my brain fell quiet. I followed the steps we had practiced over and over. Each phase of the ceremony was repeated three times to allow me to reconsider my assent to following the Bodhisattva precepts and the ways of living as a priest. *Oshō-sama* lit incense, spritzed me with water, and shaved the lock of remaining hair. He gave me the *rakusu* I had sewn, the *okesa*, a larger robe that would hang over my shoulders, my own eating bowls, and the *Kechimyaku*, the bloodline transmission of every teacher from Buddha through Dōgen to the teachers in Japan to *Oshō-sama* himself. My name was the last entry on the grand lineage of teachers.

As he handed me my *rakusu*, he revealed my Buddhist name, written on the back. Homecoming Moon, Profound Mountain. I recognized the connection of my names to my grandmother's and Mitsu's. I would carry them close by forever.

Mitsu's parents were the first to greet me. His mother presented me with an *okesa*, one she had sewn. With my own sewing challenges, I appreciated her effort even more.

In a lowered voice she told me, "I started sewing the *okesa* for Mitsu. When he left the temple, I kept it as a memory of him. Once *Oshō-sama* announced your ordination, I hurried to finish it on time. You will be carrying my care for you and Mitsu in the same robe."

I surprised her by giving her a big hug, almost lifting her off her feet. Others followed suit, offering their congratulations, handing me envelopes containing money. During the feast I was surprised by how many villagers made toasts and offers of congratulations. *Oshō-sama* gave a speech where he welcomed me to the family of the village *sangha*. He recalled his wife and daughter, the first public mention of his daughter since she disappeared, which perked the ears of the older members. He also welcomed me as a grandson to replace him one day when he retired. I doubt anyone suspected my true provenance. What they understood was the old man's close attachment to me.

Nina, by this time you were five. If you are similar to me (and how I wish that to be true), you may be wondering why I am not yet talking about you.

The reason is simple: Elisa and I had completely lost contact. Her first letter left me feeling good about her future. I had written back to her but did not know that she never received that letter. Much later–and yes, we will get there soon enough, and let me say your assumed impatience is natural–a large packet of letters she wrote me was eventually delivered. Thanks are due to the fastidious bureaucracy of the government, which files every piece of mail ever received with the intent of delivering it to the rightful owner. All her letters were addressed to the French Embassy. These letters were far from being delivered, so between Elisa's abrupt departure, my unexpected departure, the Great Kanto Earthquake, the slowness of mail, her pride in not telling me the truth about her financial circumstances, her movements in New York, the death of my grandmother, and the reunion with my blood grandfather, a lot happened which caused not one but multiple letters to not be delivered.

I had often thought about Elisa and wondered what she would think of my current status. She would have been proud of my mother and her independence. "A woman just like me," she would have said. It cannot be a coincidence that the only female relationship I experienced was a woman who was in some ways like my mother, whom I never knew. My grandmother's own independence and the way she described my mother might be what originally attracted me to Elisa. Our not-so-ancient, twisted karma brought us together. You have a connection to all of these women who created the situation from which you were conceived. You are part of a grand lineage of women whose experience and love lives within you.

The timing from your point of view gets worse as my memoir continues. *Oshō-sama* recommended me for study at Eiheiji, the Sōtō Zen Monastery in Fukui. Located on the other side of the country from where I lived, it is where our first ancestor, Dōgen Zenji, brought Zen over from China. From the stories I heard, Eiheiji was intimidating, adhering to strict rules and a stricter schedule. Once I crossed the gate, I would have no contact with external life for at least a full year. Depending on my abilities and interests, training might last for much longer. In the end, I would be assigned a temple or, in the case that *Oshō-sama* was ready to retire, would become his replacement.

Traditionally one arrives at the monastery by a several hundred-kilometer pilgrimage up and down the mountains and valleys of our country. I was strong and enjoyed hiking, so the journey would take me about a month to complete. I would depart in September to avoid early snows. As tradition is deep and complicated, the pilgrimage required particular clothes. A conical, woven bamboo hat would protect my head from sun, rain and snow. My black-and-grey walking kimono and robes would keep me warm, along with my white leggings. My feet would be bare except for thin rope sandals, *waraji*, which easily break in a few days and of which I would require many pairs over the course of the pilgrimage. Finally, I would have a folded and knotted backpack to carry in front of me which would have my eating utensils and my letter of recommendation. On my back, my *okesa* would be carefully folded and hung around my neck.

My eating bowls would double as begging bowls, as I was expected to depend on strangers along the way for food and shelter.

On a sunny morning, the second day of September, *Oshō-sama* accompanied me for the early kilometers of my pilgrimage. We passed Mitsu's family's house, where his parents came running to donate food for my begging bowls. They were not the only ones who did this. By the end of the day, I had food to share with the family who let me sleep under their roof. On the second day, I left the region covered by our temple, therefore no one was looking out for me. The poor farmers I met were enthusiastic to see me striding by, although they had much less to offer. I slept in a thatched hut, tightly nestled in among a family of five. I had less food to share, but my contribution was appreciated.

On the third day, the rain poured hard. The fields were empty, and I was forced to clang on my bowls in front of houses to receive food. My feet were getting sore from the rough sandals I wore, and I was completely drenched. At the end of the day, I was invited into the very comfortable house of a local landowner, who saw me as an excellent way of gaining merit. How odd to be seen as a means to better the karma by someone who had more resources than the poor tenant farmers on his lands. Nonetheless, I was grateful for a warm spot to sleep and the chance to dry my clothes.

Each day brought gifts of food, warmth and acquaintances. For remote families, I was a wonder appearing out of nowhere to recount stories of faraway places. For others, I was a listening board of the suffering they were facing. Still others asked me to heal sick family members, say prayers for the dead, and even marry a couple without the means to afford the ceremonial costs at their Shinto temple.

My travels brought me to Shinto shrines along with temples of other Buddhist sects. From the latter, I would learn about what we share and the doctrinal differences setting us apart. I discovered all were generous within their limits. As I entered the mountains, my trip became somewhat more strenuous. The terrain was more challenging with people fewer and far between. Several evenings I slept outdoors under massive, centuries-old pines. Thousands of stars shimmered in the cool, moonless sky. The mountain people whom I met shared stories of their lives very unusual to me who they called the 'flatlander.' I was glad for my multiple layers as each day was getting cooler.

I hiked through the mountain pass where Mitsu and I once got caught in a snowstorm. Fortunately, just the gold and red leaves on the trees were lazily falling and accumulating on the ground. I found the *onsen* that had sheltered us so many years before and spent the night appreciating the soothing hot waters. I thought about staying another day, as I had no fixed arrival date. Awakening in the bright mountain sun, nothing pulled me to dally. I was carrying Mitsu's robe and therefore did not need to stay to remember him. I kept moving step by step toward my destination.

Up and down valleys I trekked. My *waraji* kept breaking, and for several kilometers I hiked barefoot in streams and soft grass. Occasionally I would run into hikers enjoying the outdoors. As they usually packed just enough provisions for their short jaunt and most often were city dwellers who had no interest in the begging bowls of a rural monk, they were the only ones who snubbed me. I wondered how I might have acted as the old me, and recognized that no matter what I did, Mitsu would have been generous.

As I made the final descent into the lower mountains and valleys where Eiheiji was nestled, I began to run into more people. Here they were accustomed to pilgrims and would beseech me, 'Come, pilgrim, tell us a satisfying tale and we will feed you. If you do not, another will get your food.' Truth be told, they were amiable and willing to share generously. They marveled at the distance I traveled. One of the more stubborn men demanded I give them a better account than the mere journey that took me here. So, I told them about the earthquake, my losses and how I found family at the end. My story silenced the laughter, and they gave me food and money to spend on myself before entering the monastery.

On the thirty-third day, I entered the village fronting the tall gates of Eiheiji. To celebrate the completion of my trek, I joined a number of men wearing similar garb gathered at a busy noodle house, slurping noodles and drinking *sake*. These were some of the men I would train with for the foreseeable future. Sensing that our upcoming step might be more challenging, we took full advantage of the warm night to sate ourselves.

27. TO STUDY THE SELF IS TO FORGET THE SELF

Finishing our last meal, we walked to the *Sanmon*, the large entrance gate, flanked by statues of three guardians. Students who had arrived earlier were sitting in the lotus position, both legs crossed, their backs upright and hands folded into a *mudra* on their laps. For generation upon generation, pilgrims have awaited their entrance to Eiheiji in the same manner. I handed over my admission papers, my name was checked off, and I was directed to a spot to sit *tangaryō*, the ritual waiting period. *Tangaryō* had no set time. Generally, it was three to ten days, different for each practitioner. Each day I was to knock at the gate to find out whether I was allowed in. If the answer was no, I would return to sit further. We would be brought food twice a day and were allowed to use the bathroom.

For a Zen practitioner, sitting comes naturally. Sitting for extended periods at the temple is broken up into breaks, walking meditation, silent work, and eating. Without any breaks, *tangaryō* was pure sitting. I soon discovered that sitting without knowing when I was to finish was significantly challenging. In my regular day-to-day sitting, no matter how uncomfortable I might become, I could remind myself, "this will end soon." Simply believing it would end at a certain time created an artificial goal in my mind. Without such a goal, I had to accept I had no control of my time, except to face the present continuously. Despite my many seasons of practice, I found it terrifying.

Several hours went by easily. Finally, I was sitting at the gates of the place I had dreamed about since *Oshō-sama* made mention of it. I kept visualizing what life would be like inside, whom I might meet, what I would do, whether I would become enlightened. I made an effort to let these thoughts go as I had been trained, yet in my excitement they kept coming back. I no sooner told myself to let go when the next thought came in. Even just noting my feelings of excitement cascaded multitudes of thoughts of the future.

At last, I was prepared to focus on the present. I felt my legs ache from the prolonged sitting, especially after a month of hiking and active daily use. Gradually the ache became a sharp pain. *Oshō-sama* often reminded me that pain is another product of the mind. He taught me to notice the pain without adding any urgency to it; in those early days of *tangaryō*, that seemed impossible. My mind would not let go, suggesting if I moved my leg a little, nobody would notice. When I did not, it invented dire stories—if I didn't move my leg, surely my leg would be harmed, likely permanently. Once the stories began, old stories arose about past pains. Soon enough, I was witnessing Mitsu's death. Pain upon pain upon pain stacked up. My ancient, twisted karma felt like a boa constrictor strangling me—tighter and tighter, each second worse than the previous. My body was convulsing under the flood of memories, carrying me off in a nightmare.

Pain at the forefront, blame filled my body—this time going back to my very conception. If I had not been conceived, my mother would have lived to break ground for other professional women. If I had not met Mitsu, he too would be alive, not exposed to influenza. I was so self-centered that I saw myself as the cause of suffering for others. No matter how I shifted my mind away, additional horrors would spring up.

Breathe, I told myself, just breathe. Did these hallucinations go on for minutes, or hours, or days? I honestly cannot remember. I remained trapped until a spark of awareness occurred. I became aware that these were only visions, not the transpiring of real events. While part of my brain was still controlling the thoughts, another part was observing my mind. I started to separate 'myself' from my thoughts. Without mysticism, and merely through observation, we can easily distance ourselves from what arises as emotions or beliefs.

As I was congratulating myself for detecting the tricks of my mind, I stumbled right into the mind's next trick—judgment. My congratulatory mind quickly morphed into a judging mind. We have limitless ways of severely judging ourselves better than any outsider.

I watched myself judging myself for my actions and for the actions of others—my mother, Elisa, Mitsu, my father, grandmother, and *Oshō-sama*. The judgments pushed back the pain, which brought me to a different level of hell where I became, and seemingly had been for eternity, a complete failure. Anything positive I had managed to accomplish was overshadowed by even greater harm.

Meanwhile, I continued to observe the mind judging. First, it created stories about the emotions arising within me, then it judged me for having such stories. I began to laugh a series of loud bellowing guffaws at my realization, laughing so hard that I began to cry from the joy of laughing at my delusions. Breathing deeply once more, the laughter subsided. My brain went quiet.

I cheered this event before I discovered that my mind was again one step ahead of me, congratulating itself for overcoming the previous obstacles and *for being an excellent Zen practitioner, no, not just that, but maybe one of the best practitioners sitting here, a Zen student on the way to enlightenment, maybe, maybe a Zen student achieving enlightenment, here on the steps of Eiheiji. The others sitting here will be jealous they did not achieve enlightenment as easily. Look at the guy who is snoring, he certainly won't ever be enlightened. I hate the way he wheezes as he breathes. How can he do that to me? His wheezing is destroying my enlightenment. How dare he! He's such a slob I don't want to be near to him. How will I ever endure, if he is assigned to a tatami near me, I will be hearing his wheezing for the next…*

That easily, my judging mind took charge.

This is the reality of the human condition, my dear. Even at your age, I expect you have been stung by the lashes of your mind's judgment. I wish I had the power to banish these thoughts from your mind, just as I'd like to banish them from mine. The satisfying news is that we don't need any special powers to learn to notice and not react.

Every day I knocked at the gate; each day I returned, feeling failure. After seven days, I gave into the feeling of hopelessness. I spent that day and night acknowledging my imperfections, hurts and delusions.

At the deepest point, Mitsu's voice came to me. "Kenzo, I am accompanying you on your journey. I've never judged you. You have the fortitude to end the delusions of suffering and judgment. Let go of your thoughts and let your body guide you. These are the teachings *Oshō-sama* taught us both. Trust those teachings."

This vision quieted my mind. I sat two more days, peacefully and without expectations. The thoughts, pain and delusions still arose. I simply noticed and let them pass as thoughts. They lost their power to take over.

On the ninth day, I knocked on the door. The young monk responded, "Homecoming Moon, please follow me. *Tangaryō* has ended for you. Welcome to Eiheiji."

I was ecstatic, but my legs were unsteady. The young man propped me up.

"All of us have endured the waiting. What you may not have noticed was how we all accompanied you on your journey. You became part of Eiheiji when you departed from your home temple. From that point on, you joined the lineage of bodhisattvas and practitioners, initiated before Dōgen, even before memory. Watch your step as you cross the *Sanmon*. You have arrived. Your path led you here and will carry you forward. I will take you to the *Sōdō*, the Monk's Hall, where you will sleep."

Those simple words opened my path to the unimaginable.

28. WHEN YOU FIND YOUR PLACE WHERE YOU ARE

The monastery was bigger than I expected—a small city larger than the village. Hundreds of monks and dharma-transmitted teachers, led by an elderly abbot, comprised this city of men. As men, we practiced together, worked together, ate together, bathed together and slept together. Men dominate the external world; here in a community solely composed of men, that form of domination disappeared. I began to sense what communal life might have been for my *samurai* ancestors. In cases where women are not present, men have to adjust the way they behave with each other. Authority no longer exists solely based on being male. We lived dedicated to the benefit and well-being of others.

Like any village, we had to grow and prepare food for three meals a day on top of maintaining the grounds and structures from the ravages of torrential rainstorms, the burning sun, and snow. Bathrooms needed to be cleaned, *tatamis* swept, garbage emptied, vegetables chopped, rice cooked and kitchens cleaned up. Outside, certain of these roles might be defined for women; here, they were done by men. According to Zen practice, no task is menial—each is an opportunity for the practice of mindfulness of the present moment.

We had specific ways of being that had been passed down by generations, often originating from Dōgen himself who founded the monastery in 1244. In addition to his more philosophical texts, Dōgen wrote directions for applying Zen practice to daily tasks. His *Instructions to the Cook* guided every aspect from the planning of meals to the placement of bowls, the correct way to cut vegetables and the preparation of the rice gruel. He gave us instructions for washing and bathing. Our washing basin was to be seventy percent filled. Every morning, I would wash my face and turn the bowl toward myself as I emptied most of the water. The rest I would pour on the plants as recognition of circulation of water from the stream back to the earth. On days ending in 4 or 9, we bathed in the large *sento* and shaved our heads.

The seventy buildings comprising the compound were connected by roofed, open-air hallways and stairways, which protected us from the elements. We spent so much time indoors meditating, carrying out work assignments and studying that our only witness of the passing seasons was through these walkways. The red maple leaves I saw framed by openings of the corridors as I arrived were soon replaced by flurries of snow.

Unlike earthly cities, ours was unusually quiet and peaceful. The sound of the human voice was the rarest of noises we heard. Even with one hundred monks shuffling by, only their muffled footsteps and the swishing of their robes competed with the wind blowing in the pines or the birds singing from high reaches. I distinctly remember the cicadas buzzing when I entered, and the day they stopped as the temperature dropped.

The passage of time was signaled by bells from the tiniest *inkin to* the gigantic kettle in the *Butsuden* or clangers of metal or wood. Without any visible clock, each bell told us what to do—stand from zazen, eat, start and end work, start and end chanting. The easiest to remember as well as the most annoying was the *shinrei* at 4:10 a.m. in the winter and 3:10 a.m. in the summer. A runner would whisk through the hallways of the *Sōdō,* loudly clanging the bell for us, not to get us up, but to get us to jump up. Within a minute of the bell, we arose, stored our futons in the cabinet, and formed a line to the bathroom.

Nothing in my previous experience prepared me for the communal living of the *sangha,* a Buddhist community of practitioners. As I stepped under the *Sanmon,* I was absorbed by Eiheiji itself. We functioned collectively, letting much of our individuality drop off. Each individual role was a part of the whole.

For example, the monastery had its own set of carefully choreographed rituals and services, very different from the simple services *Oshō-sama* conducted at the temple each day. The morning service required sixteen monks to assist the Abbot, banging drums and cymbals and bells, lighting incense, and distributing sutra books. Each role had to be executed correctly at the proper time in concert with others. We were a living embodiment of Indra's web, the symbol of interconnectedness, a web containing a mirror which at each interstice reflected every other mirror, as we view our actions endlessly playing out. Our moves were choreographed precisely—a single step too soon or too late would ripple through the service, bringing a rebuke from the *Ino* in charge, followed by several hours of practice so as not to repeat the mistake. Simultaneously, we were individuals and a group without distinction.

This was as true in our daily work activities. Everyday a crew of us cleaned the massive wooden stairs connecting different buildings until they shone brilliantly, reflecting the dappled light. Despite the mindful nature in which we approached this task, we quickly clambered up the long stairways, swabbing the treads back and forth as a unit. With sweat pouring off our foreheads, we focused on the act of cleaning, not the energy being stirred up or even the accomplishment of the work.

It's ironic that despite the present peacefulness we ran quite a lot. The inscription on the *han*, the wooden block summoning us to morning zazen, captured our effort:

Great is the matter of birth and death, quickly passing, gone, gone. Awake each one, awaken. Don't waste this life!

Foremost, Eiheiji was a training monastery—classes, readings and memorization were key aspects of learning. Adding to the sutras I already chanted were an entire canon of other longer sutras, a few in Chinese and even one in the original language of Buddha, Pali.

Dōgen's most influential work, the *Genjō Kōan*, was the center of our studies. Our principal teacher was a robust man in his sixties whose accent identified him as being from the south near Fukuoka. His contagious smile and glowing eyes grew even brighter as he lectured. We would recite the *Genjo* Kōan aloud, the words of which still burnt in my mind, after which he would review and comment on the text, syllable by syllable; the sounds of the words and their origin were as valuable as understanding the context of the entire piece. In class, we poured over the original Chinese characters in addition to their translation into Japanese. Written characters generally have several possible pronunciations, which leads to multiple definitions of any word. The juxtaposition of these interpretations would reveal the meaning behind the meaning behind the meaning.

The passage of time is of little importance at Eiheiji. So immersed in our monastic life, I did not question why I was here, what I was doing or what I left behind. The regimentation, the schedule and rules became a part of me. By focusing on the task in front of me I became more aware of random fleeting thoughts, and feelings and memories that raced through my mind. Previously, I would have spent time analyzing these, trying to figure out what they meant for me. In this more limited physical and communal setting, I became aware of how my own reactions and perspectives affected the other men. The 'me' and the group were now one.

Ironically, the man that upset me so during *tangaryō* did occupy the *tatami* adjacent to me. Nobuo became a close dharma friend. Yes, he struggled to keep his possessions orderly and was often reprimanded for being the last to store his futon. On occasion, he did snore loudly during the precious hours we had for sleep, yet I learned to accept him. He, too, was a follower of *shudō*, as were quite a number of the men.

Learning was augmented in *dokusan*, where I would discuss my practice with my preceptor. At the appointed time, I waited for the three bells summoning me into the *dokusan* study. I responded by ringing the high-pitched *inkin* three times and entered the alcove where our teacher was serenely sitting facing an empty cushion in front of him. The light streamed from an open window to a spot on the floor near my teacher. I bowed at the altar out of respect for the dharma, made three prostrations and a final bow, then sat. We peered into each other's eyes, before settling into our conversation. His face drew me into trust and compassion.

"*Rōshi,* before we talk about our lesson, I would like to ask you a question about my vows."

"And what is that, Homecoming Moon?"

"I must ask about our vows of cultivating honest relationships. I feel a little embarrassed to talk to you about this."

"Don't worry, you are not the first to have questions and I imagine some feelings as well. I have noticed how you and Nobuo have been interacting these last months. Am I correct?"

"Yes, I won't ask how you noticed, except to say the *sangha* is small."

"The *sangha* encompasses us all. Nothing occurs outside of it. Each addition or subtraction changes how we are together. How each one of us acts affects the entire group. What is true here is true for the entirety of humanity."

"I thought my question was outside the purview of the *Genjo Kōan,* but quickly I see it is just another manifestation of its teachings. He and I have recognized that we seem to share a connection and a commitment to *shudō*. Obviously, we have many constraints here on our time. That said, we seem to be getting closer to each other. The code of behavior—*shingi*—requires that I talk to you before anything occurs."

"Yes, that is true. Our time in the monastery is different than the outside world. Every minute is practice, and every action is practice. Taking on a relationship, especially a sexual one, while you are here must occur within the expectations of practice. It is not easy, and any mistake or fallout affects us all, not just the two of you."

"We made a personal pledge to be observant of how we treat each other. Our practice has heightened both the feelings and the attention we give one another as well as others. Through my daily activities of work, study, eating and sleeping in the *sangha,* I am growing more fully as a human. The grief from the deaths of Mitsu and my grandmother, along with the trauma of the earthquake, seem to be lessening as I start to heal. Many a session of zazen has focused on these unfinished stories in my body. As I accept grieving as a process, the emotions, physical pains and stories arise within my body, where I can let them go. Zazen provided the way to heal more deeply. Although our time together may be brief, Nobuo and I care and feel strongly about each other."

"You were right to say your question is encompassed by the *Genjo Kōan.* Dōgen tells us that we experience the world in two ways which appear to be in opposition but are not. The absolute is the entire universe in which we exist. The absolute is perceived by the body through our senses, consciously and unconsciously. The relative is our individual perception of what we consider our sphere, including a 'me' and 'you.' Perceptions of the relative are produced in our mind, which tries to make sense of the sensations we have felt and weaves them into stories, theories and ideas.

"Dōgen says, accept these simultaneously; do not compare them. What you experience is not either or both. It just is. Any relationship is the same; it exists on all levels. To commit to a relationship with Nobuo cannot be seen as separate from yourself. It cannot be seen as separate from the *sangha.* Dōgen does not tell us to judge the relative as wrong—we need the relative to differentiate, the me that is me and the you that is you. Only you and Nobuo can determine the extent and the manifestation of your relationship."

While he was speaking, a crow landed on the windowsill and curiously peered at us. Just as sudden, he squawked and took off.

"Experiencing the relative self and what is called the interpenetrating, connecting or empty self, is enlightenment. Dōgen uses poetry to illustrate his thesis.

To study the Buddha Way is to study the self.
To study the self is to forget the self.

To forget the self is to be actualized by myriad things.

When actualized by myriad things, your body and mind of the self as well as the bodies and minds of others drop away.

No trace of enlightenment remains, and this no-trace continues endlessly.

"Homecoming Moon, let practice be your guide and let zazen be your means. It's how we let the mind of the self drop off. As it quiets, you will feel through the body. That is the absolute or the ungraspable no-trace of realization. Thusly you experience Dōgen's message in zazen as well as in your relationships."

"Thank you, *Rōshi*. We will do our best."

"Although we generally do not use *kōans* as teaching tools, let me give you one to ponder. *When a child cries in the night alone across the seas, can you hear her?*"

"Thank you, *Rōshi*. You have given me much food to nourish Buddha-nature."

Despite being a closed city, numbers of spots existed where Nobuo and I sought solitude during the breaks we received during the day. Since we laid side by side at night, when the lights had gone off, we often cuddled for a number of hours.

More than one warm summer evening, we jumped across the high walls after the sleeping bell had rung. We snuck through the corridors, being careful to avoid the squeaky floorboards we knew intimately from daily polishing. We scampered along the wall, enjoying the slight breeze and smell of the pine trees, looking for the spot where one could jump over.

Being on the other side of the wall was liberating. The forest was no longer something to be viewed as the backdrop to our daily life. Instead, we felt part of the expanse of unending wilderness. Similarly, the furtiveness required to conceal our connection inside the monastery dissipated. We fell into each other's arms, kissing as if nothing else was possible. We rolled in the grass enjoying the softness on our bare skin and the fullness of the warm summer breeze. What remains with me today is the blending of our bodies, the ease and the enjoyment, the ways we complemented and completed each other. We were present and together.

We both knew our time together would be transient as he would be leaving in less than a year. Like most monks from villages, he was preparing to take over his father's temple, which had been part of the family lineage back into history. Although I too had a family connection, I was not raised as a young boy to take on this role. My path was more open.

Over time, my teachers decided I was ready to receive dharma transmission, which would allow me to become a teacher. My robe would change from black to brown, and I would be considered for special positions within the monastery. This momentous transition would bring unanticipated changes. *Oshō-sama* attended the ceremony. I was taken aback by how much he had aged since I last saw him. One of the original observations by Buddha is that we age and grow infirm.

He was proud of my ordination, yet he did not ask me when I was coming back to the village. Instead he asked about what I was studying.

"*Rōshi* gave me a *kōan* that I have been considering: '*When a child cries in the night alone across the seas, can you hear her?*' I have been mulling this over and over. I glimpse a response, but still lack the precise words to express it."

He paused, as he always did before answering, his kind eyes gazing into mine. "*Mago*, you don't need words. Unlike me, you have been across the seas, yet even I can hear her. What don't you hear?"

"I am comfortable in accepting that my path is indivisible from all beings, known and unknown. Yet once I think this thought and feel content in that knowledge, my contentment disappears in seconds. Earlier, I might have described my experiences as unconnected to my journey to where I am now. But still…"

"But nothing," he interrupted. "You have ears, you have eyes, you have sensations. You have traveled far and wide. What is the purpose of your journey? Let go of your grasping for understanding and let the voice come in from across the sea. You have nothing more to learn, you must only accept and share what you have experienced."

With that he bowed and left me to consider his words.

Months after the ordination ceremony, I moved to private quarters within the monastery. Eiheiji had a number of staff members who were interacting in the external world. The head of monastery operations called me into his office one day.

I knocked on his door.

"Come in, Homecoming Moon. I hope your transition is going smoothly. Please have a seat."

"Thank you, Director. I am enjoying not having thirty other men snoring and tossing around me."

"Ah, it's been ages since I routinely slept in the monk's hall, yet sometimes I miss it. I have a bigger change for you to consider based on your diplomatic history and your connections."

"I have not paid much attention to such things since I entered into practice after the Kanto earthquake, eight years ago."

As he talked, he poured me a cup of tea. "So, I am curious about your father. Are you in contact with him?"

I almost spit out my tea in surprise. "My father? I know nothing about him and have been happy about that. We have been estranged for quite some time. I have little respect for him, and he has even less for me! I doubt he would even listen to me. Why do you ask about him?"

I could see that he noticed the anger in my words, yet he continued. "From our earliest conversations before you were a priest, you were actively interested in the questions of how democracy develops, particularly as related to the military. Most of us supported a greater civilian role. Unfortunately, those discussions seem to be over."

"Over, what do you mean?"

"The military is now the de facto force behind the civilian government.

We are no longer talking about simple politics. It's now a matter of war and peace. The military point of view is superseding all others."

I was shook by his words. "Have things changed so much since I entered these doors? Didn't we learn any lessons from the tens of thousands of Japanese soldiers that died in Mukden and the untold millions that died in the Great War? I saw the aftermath of those deaths in the destruction of cities and the trauma that they left behind in the living. What can anyone possibly do to prevent that from happening again?"

"We are not sure, to be honest, except that Zen Buddhism has been an essential part of our culture since Dōgen returned from China. Our voice is needed."

He paused and unconsciously looked around, lowering his voice. "Unfortunately, that is not so easy now—anyone who speaks directly against the military is cast as a traitor and their voices are shut down."

"What? How can that be?" I interjected as I jumped up. I began to pace the small room. "It's not like the old days when Zen priests were attached to warlords and *samurai* families, providing justification for the barbaric practices of killing and fighting as a way of gaining power or settling disputes."

"Homecoming Moon, please lower your voice and sit down."

Sheepishly, I realized how my emotions had overcome me. As I sat, he continued.

"Fear is causing some Zen leaders to rethink how we can relate to the military. With newspaper editorials implying that Zen Buddhists are anti-Japanese, an ugly mood is developing in the country. Remember how during the earthquake Koreans were blamed for causing the fires? A single spark was all that was needed to ignite the riots that killed innocent people. We must examine our part in creating the conditions that are prevalent in our government, society and the world."

"As you say that, I wonder if a single spark can ignite compassion as easily as hate? Do you think that is possible?"

"You have outlined the task I wish to ask of you, Homecoming Moon.

You have taken vows to save all beings. You know that the Buddha's Way is the path out of delusion and greed. Your foreign exposure informs your Zen practice, and your Zen practice will inform your foreign exposure. You are the best person to lead our internal discussions about Sōtō Zen's position in society. Eventually, you will seek guidance outside the monastery."

"I am honored you have thought of me, although I wish I had better clarity about the next steps. So, how will I begin and when?

"Your role commences today as director of the Office of Buddhist Peace and National Culture. You are relieved from *sōji* and unnecessary ceremonial roles. You should first meet with the influential teachers at our temples. Since the upcoming generation of priests who will head temples in all parts of the country come here or to Sōjiji, we must focus on training them in the best ethical and cultural skills to counteract the growing militarism. With their strong relationships within their temples, their *sangha* and communities seek their wisdom and guidance."

My path to you, my daughter, was forming. The *kōan* that *Rōshi* gave me and that I have been pondering would soon find a resolution. Thank you for being patient.

29. FULLY ENGAGING BODY-AND-MIND, YOU INTUIT DHARMAS INTIMATELY

A new position, authority, and a blank slate—this is a description of Zen itself. As I talked to senior teachers, I discovered how controversial this effort would be. Men whom I greatly respected were concerned that the office would send a signal that Sōtō Zen was at odds with the country. Others were even more defiant, justifying how Zen coexisted during the time of the *samurai* and was part of military culture itself. Listening to discussions of 'compassionate wars' ridding societies of bad elements or even ridding the earth of bad societies was painful. I still have trouble believing that trusted people could think in this way.

In these initial discussions, I heard a myriad versions and visions of Zen and living in the world. Whereas my focus since I walked across the *Sanmon* had been on Eiheiji as a community, I fell into the delusion that we were separate from the external world. The doors of Eiheiji do not prevent contagions from slipping through. None of us are uncoupled from others. So my new question was how my actions could affect the affairs of humanity?

Personally, the most jarring change was being one of the select to read the dizzying litany of sufferings in the daily newspapers: a major economic depression hitting the world; our military takeover of Manchukuo; the continuing disarray in the government; the growing influence of the army and navy; and untold numbers of political and social movements worldwide.

I discovered that my father had been appointed as the director of the Southern Manchuria Railroad. The railroad itself was one of the causes of the invasion of Manchukuo, and he defended the military's role there. Apparently, many politicians initially had concerns about the invasion. However, those concerns were erased once Japanese troops easily overtook the area. Manchukuo was being called our 'lifeline' for its richness of minerals, grains and other natural resources. The use of the term 'lifeline' was deliberate. Who could support cutting a lifeline? The memory of Gül's tears as he told the story of the Dardanelles served as another lifeline which helped me comprehend the power of words to shape perceptions, thoughts and reality.

Gül would have understood another word gaining traction –*gekokujō*, a willful disobedience due to moral principles–which also played a part in the turn of public opinion. The Manchukuo invasion was incited by an explosion secretly set by Japanese soldiers, then blamed on the Chinese. Without authorization by the government or the emperor the military invaded. The so-called moral principles invoked were the saving of Japanese lives, our inherent right to the territory and, of course, our need for our lifelines. We would soon find *gekokujō* being used to justify the assassination of leaders in the civilian government who were identified as not sufficiently supportive of the military. But who gets to decide these moral principles?

My father was rewarded for his efforts by receiving an appointment to the House of Peers, which added *Hakushaku*, or Count, to his honors. He was also named the Minister of Foreign Affairs for the third and last time before he retired permanently. The newspapers said his health was deteriorating rapidly.

I wondered how life felt for him. Was he proud of his achievements, especially his longtime dream of the Japanese occupation of Manchukuo? Or was he occupied by the aches and pains of aging and declining health as the public stage on which he had acted was disappearing? Maybe he encountered loss, as many do as they approach old age and death, unable to accept the changes in their bodies.

I wondered about one other thing, my daughter, something that is perhaps familiar to your struggles. I wondered if he thought of me. Did he think of me as much as I have been thinking about you since I became aware of your existence? Did he wonder where I was or why I remained distant from him? Did he understand the hurt he caused me by his absence when I was young? My view was limited and selfish; I realize that. In that period, I could only view his suffering through my own lens. I needed to believe that he was regretting what he should have done differently for me and my mother.

Knowing what I know now, I also think of what I should have done differently. Foremost, I should have paid more attention to Mitsu as soon as he became sick, making sure he had better medical treatment. As I write these words, I still slap my head for being so stupid. Yet without Mitsu's death and all that followed, you would not have been born, or at least not under your circumstances. Without you, I would not be where I find myself presently. One cannot unravel the pieces of twisted karma. No matter how much we try, the past is done.

As you can tell from my writing, Zen training does not eliminate confusion. The mind continually works to preserve its sense of self at all costs. Stepping back, I can see clearly that I was writing about my own suffering, not my father's, not Mitsu's. Unresolved feelings often show up in the blame of others.

Reflecting on what I had been reading in the papers and hearing, I went back to Dōgen for guidance, thinking of a passage I had often recited:

Now if a bird or a fish tries to reach the end of its element before moving in it, this bird or this fish will not find its way or its place. When you find your place where you are, practice occurs, actualizing the fundamental point; for the place, the Way, is neither large nor small, neither yours nor others. The place, the Way, has not carried over from the past, and it is not merely arising now.

Frankly my learning told me that considering ourselves apart from others is a delusion. The question I was facing might be better stated as: How did I support the creation of the causes and conditions now arising? How are my thoughts and actions contributing to the increasingly warlike nature of our society and other nations far from us?

So, accepting my responsibility for creating our conditions, I worked to change those conditions. Within the Buddhist world, we had our own set of words shaping our perceptions of reality. How might we use these words and our practices to counteract the propaganda immersing the popular imagination?

If I needed to meet Zen teachers, I would have to visit them. So, I embarked on a pilgrimage to Sōjiji, the other head Sōtō Zen temple, located in Yokohama. Along the way, I would visit other prominent temples. My journey would end at Tōdai, where I hoped I still might have contacts.

On a late spring day, I set off in the manner I had arrived - as a pilgrim. In preparation, I prayed for peace and well-being at the *Butsuden*, an ornate building housing statues of the Buddha of the past, present and future. I had spent much time here, and a pang of uncertainty arose in my leaving. As I crossed the *Sanmon*, my mood changed to excitement and anticipation of my pilgrimage.

My first temple visit was at Kōshōji, a five-day hike to the city of Uji. My senses were assaulted by the sights and sounds of the world I had been sheltered from for almost six years. The streets were bustling as tourists, arriving monks, and visiting dignitaries thronged the entrance to Eiheiji. The noodle shop where I had my last dinner before entering the monastery was full. As much as I thought about stopping, thinking I could relive my experience there, I realized both the futility of that thought and the urgency to spring into my journey.

Quickly enough, the environs of the monastery fell behind as I followed the road through tall pine trees to scattered clearings where farmers were toiling in their fields. After living behind cloistered walls, my domain was suddenly expansive. Fresh air and the blue, cloudless skies were the backdrop of my first full day outside the gates.

I was unaware of it at first, but my mind shifted to memories of the fields near Mitsu's family village along with the lavender fields of Provence. As my memories took over, I stopped noticing what was present. Emotions welled up, reminding me of my loneliness and those whom I had lost. I probably ambled more than an hour before I was approached by a farmer who was holding out food for me.

"Pilgrim, you are headed in the wrong way. Eiheiji is behind you, not in front of you. Are you okay?"

His words snapped me back to the present.

"Thank you, sir, for your generosity and your directions. Actually I am coming from Eiheiji and am on my way to Uji. I am on a different sort of pilgrimage. Yet you are right. My mind was lost and not concentrating on my path."

He filled my bowl full of rice and vegetables as we chatted. He told me about being a farmer and his concerns for his children and their future prospects. While he was far removed from the conversations in Tōkyō, he reflected on how the economic and social changes were negatively affecting him.

I bade the farmer farewell. His intervention was what I needed to get back from the meanderings of my mind. Just as in the start of a *sesshin*, the mind fights the efforts to quiet its power.

I hiked through fields and forests and eventually some smaller cities. The leaves were ready to burst on the trees, and the grass was turning green. Everywhere farmers were getting the spring fields prepared for sowing crops. Toward the evening, I found shelter at a temple near Mount Hino.

The next day dawned with a lengthy ascent up a mountain pass from which I saw the Sea of Japan separating us from China. Once upon a time Eihei Dōgen and his colleague Myōzen set sail to China, searching for a Buddhist teacher to answer their questions about authentic practice. I tried to imagine the sea through his eyes, the vast expanse of rough and pounding waves, the long voyage testing his endurance.

His journey lasted five years as he sought out the right teacher. He must have been a demanding or maybe even annoying pupil, continually asking questions, not content to accept the practices as given. Eventually, he met a teacher, Nyōjo, on Mount Tiatong. Nyōjo practiced a form of meditation that satisfied Dōgen's queries and the reason for his pilgrimage. After receiving dharma transmission, he returned, and in 1243 initiated the building of Eiheiji Daibutsu Temple.

Hiking downward, the scenery changed as I neared the coast. Gone were the tall pines, replaced by compact reeds and bushes waving in the windblown landscape. The salty air was my first alert as the path opened to follow the shore. Striding by numerous fishing villages, where small boats tied to wharves bobbled in the tides, I was a curiosity to the locals who stopped me often to offer fresh fish and seafood to eat. Rarely did they see pilgrims here, and several children accompanied me from village to village, peppering me with questions about where I was going and what I was doing. I enjoyed their imaginative questions and the willingness to show me the way. However, because I was unaccustomed to such vigorous physical activity, I was exhausted when I arrived in Tsuruga, the largest regional city.

The few steep mountains on my path the following day challenged me greatly, as I doubted my ability to climb up one more steep path. But the last descent provided me with relief as well as a sweeping view of Biwako, a vast lake. There I encountered several families from Kyoto, who were enjoying a short holiday. In contrast to the farmer I had met earlier, these educated people knew quite a lot about foreign affairs and had opinions, positive and negative, about Japan's growing influence in the region. They expressed some concerns about the military's increasing role in the government yet were worried about the increasing political violence and wanted to feel stability and safety.

When I arrived at Kōshōji, I was effusively greeted by the head priest, who showed me about the grounds. The early *sakura*, cherry blossoms, were opening in the extensive gardens surrounding the main building. As we entered the *Butsuden,* I was met by a group of monks from village temples who came to Kōshōji for lectures and consultations. Preceding our talk, we conducted a service and sat zazen for two periods.

Afterward, the monks talked about the increasing responsibilities they faced as Buddhism was coming under attack from the government and military. I was surprised to hear these priests were already feeling pressure. Each community was expected to establish a military support committee to aid in recruitment and logistics. Although the government promoted Shinto as the face of Japan's pride and nationalism, a number of the priests already had been asked to participate in the support committees. Going about their regular lives as they have done for decades was not a good enough response. The inherent dilemma in my mission sharpened into view as I pondered what can be done to support our priests who are being forced to answer these questions on their own.

Although I would have enjoyed a week in the quiet beauty of Kōshōji, it was just my initial stop. From ancient times, this well-traveled route contained many small, ancient Buddhist temples that sheltered me each night. Wherever I stopped or visited, the local priests were very interested to hear about the reason for my journey and, more than once, talked my ear off about the problems of maintaining a community temple.

Arriving at Shōbōji on a warm day, sweaty from the strenuous scale over Mount Gozaisho, I was greeted by the abbess. Even though Buddha had included women among his students, I had not met a Zen nun before. Shōbōji had been established for several decades, and additional buildings to house and train the 140 resident nuns were still being constructed. The women there conformed to the schedule that we followed at Eiheiji. As they had no chance of leading a temple like their male counterparts, I found their devotion to the precepts was stronger than in most of the men I knew.

In an animated conversation led by the abbess, the women were adamant that Zen must serve as a force for peace. As sisters and aunts of men conscripted to fight in Russia, China, Korea and Manchukuo, their focus was on the trauma which warfare causes families and villages. They encouraged me to speak with other women, not just the men on my pilgrimage. I'm embarrassed to say, my daughter, I had not thought about doing that previously, being so much a product of my culture. I apologized for my ignorance and told them my own mother and grandmother would have been exasperated by my behavior.

Chastened, I vowed to listen more deeply to the women and men I met on my journey as I headed out again. As the days increasingly became warmer, the pink *sakura* petals painted my pathway, their sweet perfume bringing forth memories of my grandmother, and our springtime strolls. As a child, I would scoop the 'pink rain' into the air and scamper as the petals rained down on us.

Chiru wa uki...the song welled up unannounced. Beauty, sorrow and wonder accompanied me as I wandered through the evening.

On the Pacific Ocean coast, small villages were interspersed among growing cities. For the first time, I began to see some soldiers on the streets of the cities and military vehicles streaming down the major roads. The economy was booming and more prosperous than in the other regions I had walked through. Most local people I talked to connected the increase in jobs and livelihoods to the changes in government. They spoke of the improvements a strong Japan would bring to their lives.

I was pleased to stop by Rinsō-in where a friend, Shunryu Suzuki, was heading the family temple. He introduced me to a group of his students who were facing the military draft. Under Suzuki's tutelage, they were a refreshing group, wide-eyed and not yet stained by attachment to any particular institutions or ways of thinking. Due to the nature of their discussions, they secretly met on a regular basis to debate alternatives to the government policies. They were encouraged by my efforts and talked to me about how the Buddhist precepts and the eight-fold path helped to guide them.

Their suggestions gave me food for thought, as Suzuki accompanied me for the final days walk to Sōjiji. Although we spent much of the time in silence, we had several serious conversations as we climbed the mountain behind Rinsō-in across green tea plantations alternating with tall trees and mountain streams. From the top of Maganho, Fuji-san rose toward the sky in the distance. The mountain became our constant companion, and I marveled at the continual dance of clouds around it.

"Suzuki, what about your dream of establishing a temple in America?"

"It remains a dream. It is hard to see it happening right now. My responsibilities for the sangha here seem to grow, especially in these hard times. I was invited to set up a temple in Manchukuo and even went there for a short time."

"Really, I am surprised to hear that. I suspect the circumstances there were trying."

"My desire for going somewhere new obscured the challenges of going to a place where I was not wanted. I quickly realized that the military authorities saw the establishment of a temple as a way of stamping the territory as Japanese. I would be dependent on them for everything and as much as I wanted to help, it became clear to me that I could not follow the Way in this manner."

"I often worry that I am blind to my desires and can't trust myself to know what the right Way is. Despite years of sitting, accepting my own delusions continues to be a challenge."

"And it will be so for our entire earthly lives, my friend," Suzuki continued. "After I came back, I was approached about being the leader of a regional military support committee. Here I was back home, facing the same dilemma that I was faced with in Manchukuo."

"So, one part of the sangha supports your peaceable intentions while another wants you to prove that you support the military. Please tell me your answer."

"I felt forced to accept the role as the leader of the support committee and we had a community meeting in which I insisted on letting others speak. The next day, I quietly resigned from the role, citing my family and spiritual responsibilities. My resignation was accepted, and no one lost face in the process."

"Thank you, Suzuki-sama. Your words and those of your students have given me more guidance than any of the talks I have had with senior leaders. I am starting to imagine a path forward."

We parted ways as we entered Sōjiji, the training temple that had co-equal status to Eiheiji. Yokohama had rebuilt itself since the earthquake, its famed shipyards were filled with new military vessels and cargo ships. The iron mills and other heavy factories were belching acrid black smoke, so that the air was acrid and pungent. In contrast to the rural setting of Eiheiji and all the other temples on my pilgrimage, Sōjiji had found itself in the middle of this noisy and dirty city over the years. As I walked under the Sanmon, the sun was blotted out by ever-present smoke.

Given their proximity to the seat of the government, the leadership at Sōjiji was not as conflicted about the role of Zen. Many saw no problem in aligning Zen to what they called the 'requirements' of the nation, which included the expansion of the Japanese influence throughout Asia.

I was particularly surprised by one dharma teacher who directly criticized Suzuki. "Zen priests cannot act in isolation of the government's will. By abandoning his important role of founding a Zen presence in Manchukuo, he brought shame on himself and to Sōjiji itself. We cannot have individual village priests acting on what they think are their convictions. He has created danger for all of us thought his traitorous act. Because of him, we took it on ourselves to convince the military authorities of the sincerity of our support for the good they are bringing to our country."

I found it very difficult to listen and not to react with my own set views. I longed to speak for peace, yet in my role I listened as intently as I could. For our program to be successful, I had to understand all viewpoints, not just the ones I preferred.

My pilgrimage ended. I took the train to Tōkyō. Tōdai was transformed by the politics of the day. Almost no one was willing to discuss publicly the possibilities of peacemaking. *Kenpeitai*, the secret police, was on the watch for any public or private pronouncements they considered treasonous. Several professors were afraid of meeting me; although it did not cross my mind, they assumed I was being followed. The academics willing to talk insisted the civilian government institutions were still in control and that the military had an essential role in keeping the government stable. The chaos created by the changes of prime ministers and their cabinets over the last couple of decades, they argued, made the military a benign force of continuity.

Secretly, a few did share writings which were more pacifist and argued for a different course of action. These tracts were carefully printed and distributed to those who were trusted. I found them interesting yet useless. When dissent is banned, communication often occurs solely between people who already think alike. Talking and writing become dangerous, too dangerous for sharing with strangers, the very ones who need to be reached.

So, how do you speak out about something you cannot put into words? That's a *kōan* in itself. I suspect, Nina, you have faced this very issue yourself as a female who is half-Japanese, living in a society that does not care to see or hear either of those two parts of you. In Buddhism, the term 'skillful means' connotes reacting to a situation with compassion and appropriate action. As the slow train to Eiheiji left behind the dark skies over the coast, my mood brightened in the sunny skies over the mountains, and I began to ponder our next steps.

30. BIRTH AND DEATH; DELUSION AND REALIZATION

I briefed the director on my findings and observations, especially about difficult conversations I had in Sōjiji and Tōdai. The more we talked about the suggestions of Suzuki's students about an emphasis on the eightfold path, the more we thought this might be the way forward. No Buddhist can deny the importance of theses teachings. The eightfold path, my dear, is Buddha's practical way of living an honorable life: right view, right intention, right speech, right conduct, right livelihood, right effort, right mindfulness and right concentration.

Of these, I suggested we focus on right speech and right action, emphasizing the process of listening, speaking, not defaming, and being compassionate while facing complex ideas and emotions. We both realized how the military might find right speech and action very dangerous concepts in the current political climate. Thus, we set about finding ordinary non-threatening ways to discuss them.

Working within a tradition centuries and centuries old, as Zen is, the measurement of time is different. Three years of travel, writing, training and discussions were needed to implement the program. I became a visiting teacher roaming far and wide, talking about these precepts.

I went back to *Oshō-sama's* temple, where the whole village came to hear me. I was touched by the homecoming to a degree I did not expect. Once I began speaking, the *butsudan* went quiet. Mitsu's parents sat up front on the *tatami,* their smiles and attention encouraging me. Zen language can often be the opposite of simple and clear, so I found examples from the village to illustrate.

"Buddha gave us guidelines for compassionate behavior emphasizing the benefit to the entire community. If a farmer grows nice big healthy radishes, we all will have tasty pickles. I have been away from the village for some time, yet I assume this is still true?"

Laughter filled the hall as I continued. "Can someone falsely claim, 'That farmer stole my radishes?' Of course, everyone understands radishes cannot be stolen from fields. Once planted, they grow and grow until they are ready. A stolen radish would be hard to hide."

More laughter.

"If the farmer does not steal a radish, and instead he says, 'That radish is bad, coming from bad people who don't plant radishes the right way,' he might find he can get a few listeners. He might find he can build distrust. Eventually, he might use so-called moral principles to convince someone else to dig out the radishes, telling him the village would be better off or that he was owed these radishes. This would result in some who have good pickles, others who have no pickles, and the farmer who incited the accusation accumulating the most pickles. I think we all believe this is not wholesome for the village.

"Now, can we think of another example, maybe about stories or slander? The Buddha says right intention or thought is the first step. We must be aware of what goes on inside our minds. Holding ourselves to the right intention, we can engage in right speech, using words which do not hurt others and speaking truth compassionately. Buddha specifically decried gossip or libelous speech which accuses someone of a bad deed without justification or incites harm against them.

"Finally, Buddha had another key guideline—not to kill. We are connected to each other, so taking a life is to cut out part of our own. We would never kill anyone over a radish, yet we have heard of lives ended over words.

How can words be compared to a radish? A radish gives a flavor and crunch for our rice gruel breakfast. Words are nothing—they have no substance, they are less than air, yet words can kill. They can kill because they cause deep feelings such as fear and anger. Radishes are not dangerous but are real. Words are not real but dangerous."

One of the younger men raised his hand, "*Sensei,* thank you for your wise words today. Can't a radish also be used to kill?" Everyone laughed as he continued, "A big radish could be used as a bat to swat someone hard."

"Yes, a very good observation. If the mind is aimed at killing, any number of objects are available for that end. The radish itself does not have killing energy at its core. Solely a human can convert words into actions and killing. Left alone, a radish stays still where it is. Left alone, words should stay quiet until they are well-nourished. Once words are nourished and grown carefully, we have right speech. Unnourished speech can bring trouble to the community."

Another man raised his hand. "*Sensei,* how does right speech grow in the mind? If I have to wait until right speech is nourished, I might not ever speak. If that occurs, I might not get nourished because my wife will ignore me."

A few nodded at the question.

"Buddha did not say no speech, he said right speech and no harmful speech. Harmful speech often arises from the lack of knowledge because we do not think ahead, or we speak from anger or fear. Of course, if you speak from compassion and kindness, I suspect you will get the nourishment you seek." I smiled, letting everyone notice my words had more than one connotation.

"In compassionate speaking the other person will feel they can correct your mistake without fear even if you are mistaken. However, if you add fear to your words, fear is all the other person will hear. Fear is a sickness which spreads from person to person. Like a sickness, fear is better stopped by prevention than by cure."

"*Sensei,* where does fear come from?"

"Buddha tells us fear comes from self-clinging. What did he mean? He said our suffering comes from us holding onto our ideas, our sense of self and our culture, as if they are real. The more we hold on, the more we suffer. When we cling, we usually desire more and remain unsatisfied. Or we protect what we have—another form of clinging. One way we fear is believing we don't have the number of radishes we need. If we have a large crop, we might fear someone will take what we have, which makes us try to protect our radishes. Even in times when we have enough, we might fear someone else has better radishes or even a food better than a radish.

"Sometimes nations get caught out by fear, a national clinging, wanting to preserve scarce resources. The American president once said, 'The only thing we have to fear is fear itself.' He may be a Buddha. When we become afraid, we don't have the right thought, right speech or right action. We distrust others. Following the spread of distrust, the community begins to die, causing the ones who are fearful to say, 'The village is dying, so we were correct to be afraid.' They fail to comprehend that their fear is what is killing the village.

"We do not want fear to kill our country and our ways. Remember the strong, nutritious radish has no reason to fear, even though it will be eaten."

It was getting late. *Oshō-sama* rang the bell and in a powerful clear voice chanted for our well-being.

I remained for two days, assisting *Oshō-sama* and visiting Mitsu's parents. They both were still vigorous, and on arrival offered me radishes.

"The entire village is talking about your radishes. They must not feed you enough at Eiheiji, if your mind is clinging to radishes," his father joked.

"Are you coming back to the temple here?" his mother quietly asked. "It has been years since you went to the monastery—maybe you are too big for our village. It's okay if you are. Mitsu was not meant to remain here, so I guess this might also be true for you. Listening to your talk made me realize I have been clinging to the idea of your return. I expect you have other big plans. You boys yearned to be involved in big things to change the world. We just have radishes."

"*Obasan,* tending radishes is as important as tending what you call big plans, maybe even more important. At least you know if the radishes are big and tasty. Often, I cannot tell if the effect I am having is helpful or not."

"My son, all parents are afraid they are inadequate, did not provide their children enough or should have acted differently. Until you came, we blamed ourselves for Mitsu's death, for encouraging him in the wrong way. You helped us comprehend that we were wrong to think like that, and our lives are always based on positive intent. Your presence here made me feel alive again. That was the gift you brought. You are a follower of morality and forever will be. Please don't believe otherwise, or else I will come at you brandishing a radish, like *Oshō-sama* doing his *keisaku,* beating goodness into you."

For a minute her words released a flood of memories of those who were part of who I am. Although I did not know about you then, you have also always been part of me. There was no me, only a world in which a little speck named Kenzo moves around in throughout time among all other specks.

Before I left, *Oshō-sama* and I conducted our traditional service for my grandmother and mother. He no longer hides the secret of Michiko's return to the village. His secret gone, his burden was lighter. Most of the older villagers knew what had occurred but said nothing in order to preserve his honor. For him, fear is gone. I was happy for him and my mother.

Snow was falling hard in Tōkyō on the afternoon of February 25. I was staying at a temple headed by a colleague. Early that morning, the unusual sounds of gunfire filled the air; the radio soon announced there had been an attempted coup led by a number of young military officers. Citing *gekokujō,* they invoked their right to correct grievances regarding their perceptions that the military was not being respected. Several government officials were killed, including the Finance Minister. By the end of the day the rebels had been arrested except for several of their leaders who committed suicide. The city was nervous as the government vacillated between appeasement and horror at the killings.

Killing is an extreme that can erase everything else. For a brief time I considered postponing our plans. Once such a basic Buddhist principle is broken, can we even discuss right speech? Certainly I can connect the dots to how one believes that bringing death upon another is the answer; however, will right speech be the process that disrupts the killing cycle?

These thoughts were interrupted by a more immediate issue. I was scheduled to meet an old colleague at the Ministry who was also a friend of my father. Arriving at his office, his forehead was furrowed, a grave look resided on his face.

"Uchida-san, how horrible these days are."

"Yes, the whole city is talking about the coup attempt. We are lucky they were stopped."

"Stopping them did not alter the direction of events," he replied. "It is a bad day for the country, and I am concerned about our future. However, I have another more urgent matter concerning you."

"What is so important?"

"It's your father. He is near death. I think his heart is weakening. His last term in office was very demanding as he attempted to manage the political and military changes. Currently, he is alone in his house. I visited him the other day. He was weaker than ever. You should pay a call to him."

"Me, why me? I have not seen him since our unpleasant meeting during the Great Earthquake. While he helped me, I have not attempted to visit him again. I was supposed to be on an assignment to Manchukuo, yet instead I disappeared. Look at me in my monk's clothes—I am sure I am not someone he wants to meet. From what I read, he has become a Christian."

"Uchida-san, you are as stubborn as your father. He specifically told me, 'One regret I have is to not see my son before I die. I don't even know whether he is dead or alive, so my hope for viewing his face again is low.' I am not inventing those words. If you are willing, I will call a car to take you to him immediately. Dying men have a different perspective. As a monk, you must be aware of that. Let me take you."

As a son, I had significant doubts and noticed how easily old wounds rose to the surface of my consciousness. As a priest, I had to go where I was being requested. Within the hour, we were at his house, and unlike my previous visit, I was let in the front door. The house was dark and cold with all of the curtains shuttered. His doctor showed me to his bedroom. My father's eyes were closed; he was breathing heavily. I was shocked by his appearance, so drawn and withered. He was no longer the man that I held in my memory from our last encounter in Paris.

The doctor announced, "Uchida-san, the miracle you have asked for—your son Kenzo - has arrived. Open your eyes to see yourself."

The old man stirred and his eyes flickered. "Kenzo," he whispered, "are you truly alive, or is a dying man seeing a ghost? I hope you are not the latter, because a son never should die before his father."

"No, Father, I am here. An hour ago, I was informed of your state of health, and I rushed right over."

"Oh, Kenzo, you are here. You are wearing the robes of Buddha. Are you my son or an imposter? Why would Kenzo be wearing those robes? I didn't raise him to clean temples—he was to follow in my footsteps as a statesman."

"I myself had no vision of the path that led me to these robes and the period of study I have put into receiving the honor of them, yet here I am. My path has been long and the right one for me. Right now, we may not have the time for explanations."

He struggled to sit up, so I helped him up and arranged some pillows behind his back. His rheumy eyes looked at me intently. His voice was just a whisper and I had to sit closely to follow his words.

"I have much I want to say, and as you said, we might not have enough time. I have no strength for lengthy discussions and an argument. Look at me. I can sense the end of my days coming, which gives me a certain clarity of thought previously missing. As physically distant as I was from you, we were always closer in my thoughts. I asked you to go to Manchukuo as a chance for us to become better acquainted. I had heard favorable reports about you in Europe that reminded me of my own early tour as an ambassador. Even your choices for women lovers reminded me of myself. No matter what resides between us, I am glad you came here."

"My vows make me tell the truth, father. I never felt welcomed by you. I felt I was a mere curiosity. When I visited as a child, I behaved like a pet dog rolling over to perform for its owner, afraid of being kicked if I did the wrong thing. This house holds no good memories for me."

"I am not surprised by your honesty and feelings. I was not a good father. When your mother died, I was ashamed of leading an innocent, intelligent woman to her death. You were a reminder of her, both of how I used and later rejected her. I was a shallow man, unable to acknowledge nor accept my responsibility. Caught inside hurt and pride, I could not decipher the feelings of a little boy. I assumed you would hate me, yet I attempted my best for you."

"It was confusing to me. The woman whom I called my grandmother encouraged me to be closer to you—"

"Why do you say she was not your grandmother?"

"I know little about her background, except that she was kind and loving. I have met my mother's real father, a village priest. He told me about how my mother came to live in the city."

"So that is why you are wearing these robes? Your grandfather was indeed a simple man yet with unfolding kindness. He raised your mother as one would raise a son. He boosted her expectations in a culture not ready for her. My wife is well-educated too, schooled in America. Had I known your mother first, maybe things would have been different for me; though perhaps not, as she would not have withstood my inattention to family. Your mother's stay with the woman you called your grandmother was not accidental."

"What do you mean? I was told she was a geisha yet know little else about her background."

He paused for a minute, catching his breath before he continued. "Aikichi-san led one of the most renowned houses in the Floating City with the finest of women working for her. True to her name, Blessed Love, she treated each one with kindness and compassion, never allowing harm to the soul or body of her women. Her house had the best music, the best food and the best accommodation. As a young man, I was introduced to her house by one of my mentors. She took a liking to me, introducing me to her clients as a promising young university student destined for a great career. I met politicians of various parties, military leaders and government officials. Surrounded by such men, one's career is set. That is why later on I made sure you got into Tōdai and that my colleagues watched over the launch of your career."

His train of thought was interrupted by a series of deep, phlegmy coughs as he tried to clear his lungs. His eyes tilted back for a minute as he tried to regain his breath. I lifted a cup to his lips. He took a few sips of tea.

"Thank you, my son. It gets harder each day to talk. Please let me finish Aikichi-san's story. After one of the many fires swept the district, she decided she would not rebuild. She foresaw the changes coming and approached her calling differently. She wished to assist women wishing to make transitions to other lives. She opened her home as a school for women to gain manners and refinement, while her true purpose was aiding women who wanted to forsake the floating world.

"But Father, what does this have to do with my mother?"

"I am getting to that. When I heard your mother was pregnant, I asked Aikichi-san to take her in. They met, and she recognized your mother as a kindred spirit, another independent and self-confident woman. She also viewed her as the child she never had. Upon her death, she devoted herself completely to raising you. She told me and your grandfather her decision. I knew she was best suited to raise you and agreed to assist her over the long-term."

"Father, I often thought my grandmother was otherworldly as a child. I had a fantasy that when I was sleeping, she flew with the doves. Often I tried to stay awake to watch out for her transformation but fell asleep. Her knowledge on topics from politics to the esoteric to the ordinary was wide and informed. She seemed to intuit beforehand what trouble I might get into."

"And she told me you were an exceptional boy, and I can see by your observations that you were."

"She knew my mother only for those seven months, yet she told me stories for hours on end about her life and, most crucial, told me about her character. When I was reunited with her father a decade ago, their descriptions matched exactly."

"What I suspect you have not heard, my son, is that she initially survived the earthquake. Despite her age, she helped for hours, pulling neighbors from their crumbling houses and soothing the children. Neighbors who remember her last hours described strength beyond imagination for an old woman who was infirm. Several hours in, the fire stormed the area. Before the blaze hit her home she went back inside, no one knows why. She was never seen again. They did report that in the midst of the inferno a swarm of doves appeared and calmly flew over the crowd trying to escape, showing the people a safe path from the flames. It sounds like an unbelievable fantasy, yet dying gives me a fresh perspective on it. Your unexpected arrival confirms that."

I found myself moved by the story of my grandmother and by my father's condition. "What can I do for you, Father? I so yearned for you to see me as I am, and today my yearning has come true."

"There is nothing more, my son, nothing more we can do. We cannot change the past. What we can do is add our present feelings to the past ones. As for me, I will remember our conversation today and let the old ones and the desires for the ones we did not have disappear. Death is not a destination where one should carry his life's accumulations. I can now enter death empty-handed."

Those were my father's last words. He regarded me lovingly and closed his eyes to rest. He died two weeks later.

His funeral was grand, as befitting a man of his stature, held in the Christian church he had adopted, perhaps a strange choice for someone concerned with the traditions of our country. No human is ever consistent in their beliefs, I guess. I sat toward the back, a Buddhist anomaly in this environment. My mentor approached me at the service as my father's body was taken for burial.

"Uchida-san, come by my office tomorrow. I have a package from your father. The day after he saw you, he told me where to go in his office to find it so I could deliver it to you upon his death. He said nothing more, and I did not ask."

Intrigued, the next day I arrived and was led to his large ornate office, the wide windows commanding a view of the grounds of the Imperial Palace.

"Uchida-san, let's find out what the mystery is. Of course, I am curious, but I am sure not as curious as I expect you are."

He handed me a large, thick, sealed envelope. I opened the outer envelope, and another was inside, appearing old and worn. My father had written a note appended to the inner envelope:

My son, these letters appeared after you left France. The Consulate kept them and eventually sent them to the Ministry. Since you were nowhere to be found, they languished in an office until a few more unusual inquiries came from New York. In my final stint as Minister, the desk officer forwarded these to me. They have been sitting unopened, waiting patiently for you. They are now yours.

Carefully, I opened the inner envelope and out fell a dusty, yellowing stack of letters, two newspaper clippings and copies of several telegrams. I recognized the handwriting of Elisa instantly. The ink was fading yet legible.

"They are letters from an old friend from Paris who went to the U.S. Oh, and here's a telegram from Gül, an aide who worked for me. He was Turkish and moved to New York shortly after Katayama Mitsu died.

"Thank you for delivering these. They are finally reaching their intended destination. Viewing the handwriting alone is like regarding a long-unforgotten old friend."

"I hope they bring you welcome news. Please stay in touch. I might be able to assist you in your project, and you might be able to help me sometime too, possibly. Please don't disappear again, okay?"

"My disappearing days have ended," I assured him. As soon as the words came out of my mouth, a feeling arose that suggested I might be wrong.

I carefully slipped the packet into my satchel and departed. I wanted to read them immediately, but still had business to attend prior to heading back. I also needed the comfort of the monastery surrounding me in order to open this portal into the past.

31. THERE ARE THOSE WHO ARE DELUDED WITHIN DELUSION

July 1921

Kenzo:

I am so angry. I hardly posted your letter when the most demeaning and embarrassing incident occurred. As planned, Madam Rostrovska and I left, quite excited to be in New York. Such tall buildings everywhere. You have seen pictures of the city, in real life they are even taller, so big, so crunched together. The streets on a quiet day are packed. As we were taken by car, we saw the types of people change as the street numbers (each street is numbered) got higher. The higher we went, the more sophisticated the people.

At last we reached Madame's apartment building on 76th Street. The building, sleek and impressive, had a doorman, who tipped his top hat in greeting as he opened the door. He brought our luggage up to the apartment—so elegant.

Upstairs, Madame opened the door to a most luxurious entry and living room with Italian wallpaper and heavy, plush curtains. I was admiring the beauty when the shock happened. She offered me a closet to sleep in! A windowless space, off the kitchen - she called it the maid's room.

"You want me to sleep here? What do you mean?" I stammered.

She turned to me, "My dear, you were never one of us. From the beginning, we all laughed behind your back at your pretensions. I doubt you have a cent to your name, so I am taking pity on you. Fortunately for you, my maid left—actually the little whore got pregnant, so I let her go. She could not possibly work for me in such a condition, reminding me of her careless and dirty ways. You can begin tomorrow as my maid. I will let you get settled. Then I will show you your way around and explain the duties."

She left me alone crying through the night. I had no idea of what to do. I had the money you gave me but did not expect this sobering reception. I didn't want to stay, yet for the first time I felt I had no options. I was hoping my gentleman friend might call on me as promised but realized how awkward it would be if he did.

I will write you once this gets settled. I don't expect to be here long.

Your Elisa

November 1921

Kenzo:

I am finally gone from that witch's clutches. It was horrible from the start, and with each day it got worse. She threw a party, inviting everyone from Paris whom I knew, including the gentleman I mentioned. She made me wear a maid's costume to make sure everyone took notice of my status. Not a single person acknowledged me, not one! All of these so-called friends who ate and drank at my parties, none of them had the decency to say a word to me. They were whispering behind my back and laughing. I put on my strong face and stared each one right in the eye as I served them. I made sure they had no chance to avoid me. The party finished early, and Madame was very upset. I gave her a cold stare and said nothing at all. Can you imagine me saying nothing? If it were not so awful, it would be funny.

From then on, I never spoke a word to Madame. She learned not to say a word to me either. She was utterly dependent on me serving her, and I did nothing bad to her. My refusal to speak unnerved her.

I made friends with the other maids in the building, most of whom came from Russia or Ukraine. They were not the types I wanted friendship with, though they helped me to plan my escape.

I might have stayed longer. She at least was paying my wages, which was un-

like the experience of certain other maids. I saved up every penny. You know how I can be, or maybe you don't—despite what you may have thought, I constantly worried about money and making sure I had enough.

I left one day on my own before she had the chance to fire me. You see, I'm pregnant. For a few months, I have been feeling strange sensations in my body and assumed my bad living situation was causing the problem. In the times she did speak to me, Madame kept on accusing me of eating her food since I was getting heavier. I found a doctor, and he announced I was pregnant. I worked out the timing; you were the most likely suspect.

Of course, I cannot be 100 percent sure. Nonetheless, I am pretty certain you are the one. What a surprise for you. I am worried you have not responded to any of my letters so far, so please write back. I am now living in what is called a tenement. The Lower East Side is the opposite of the station I was used to. Every poor immigrant lives here. It's crowded, and I hear all sorts of languages. It feels just like being back in Europe except out on the back streets, not in the grand hotels we frequented.

The baby is due in March. Please send me money by Western Union. They are the most trustworthy.

Waiting for you.

Elisa

March 1922

Kenzo:

I am writing to inform you that you are the father of a girl named Nina, a nice name, one you can even pronounce in Japanese. I have not heard from you, so I assume you are abandoning me. You are not the first. Even as I entered the hospital, they kept asking, "Who is the father? Who is the father?" Like the father was going to have the baby!

I ignored their questions, and one of the nurses said, "You should be ashamed of yourself coming here like this. If there weren't so many of your types, we would take your child from you when it is born. You don't even deserve to be here." I was indignant and turned to leave the maternity ward when the birth suddenly started. I was unprepared for the pain. I felt I was being punished and was alone without family or any friends.

A few hours later, the baby was born, and the nurses and doctors were silent. "A girl or a boy?" I asked.

The doctor answered, "It's a half-breed bastard." They handed her to me.

Despite my pain and delirium, I thought she was beautiful. From the minute I saw her I recognized your smile on her. Her hair was black as night, her eyelids folded in. I held her in my arms, her warm body against mine. I remembered our one night of closeness which resulted in our daughter.

I wish I were madder at you, yet even more so I want you to see her. At least they won't take her from me, as not even an orphanage wants to take a half-breed. She is mine, and I remember you fondly whenever I look at her.

Please show me I am not wrong to believe in you. Please, Kenzo, don't be like other men. I hope you are not.

Your Nina awaits you.

Elisa

My Nina, that is how I learned of your existence. You would have been thirteen at the time I read these letters. I was sitting in my room and wanted to run and shout, "I have a daughter and she lives in New York." Had I done that, it would have been a first in the temple's venerable history that such words were shouted in the hallways, waking the abbot.

All lives are entwined, and, as Buddha realized in his awakening, all beings are connected and indivisible. Our delusion comes from the functioning of our mind, tricking us into believing otherwise. Yes, I was far in distance and time from Elisa, yet once she announced your birth, you became part of the sphere within my perception. As the connections were revealed between my mother, my grandfather, Mitsu, his family, my father, Elisa, Gül, and now you, what I might call 'my world' expanded exponentially. I carry you in my heart as my mother carried me and my grandfather carried us both. Even now, I remain surprised *Rōshi's kōan* would manifest itself in my life in such a literal way.

I cannot emphasize enough how much the discovery of your existence has completely changed my history. My biography suddenly includes a daughter, which changes how I think about the past. This drawn-out letter I am writing you reflects the story of you from the beginning. The first and longest part covers the forty-five years before I knew you existed. However, the account I have related would have been different if you did not exist. Your life changed my past, just as I expect your story may change if this letter gets into your hands. The final part of this account is what happened in the course of knowing that you existed.

Instead of screaming, I wrote Elisa a letter to the last address I found. She moved often, and I was afraid I would not find her, just as she had not found me. I still carry her last letter announcing your birth close to my heart in my robe at all times. The letter was there when I was arrested here in England, and it will be there when I die.

There were other letters in the packet, increasingly angry and upsetting. Your mother's predicament was escalating. Even though she worked as an English teacher to other Ukrainian and Russian immigrants, she regularly had struggles. Often there were problems regarding men, of which you must have been aware, even as a young child. You may or may not know your mother enjoyed sex. I cannot condemn an activity that brings happiness, excitement and satisfaction. Men have always been allowed to celebrate this act, and so should women. Whether she was seeking enjoyment or companionship or support, it appears she had no relationships that were stable for any period of time.

She complained about my abandoning her, not supporting you and for being the cause of her misery. I could not tell if she believed these accusations or was writing out of anger that I had not responded to her letters. I hoped it was the latter. Although I was hurt by the tone, I could understand the human response of seeking to blame one's misfortunes on another. Human communication is tough enough, and letter-writing requires stability. Unfortunately, neither she nor I had stable lives at the time where we could have engaged in dialogue.

In addition, the packet contained two articles from the New York Daily News. These articles were clipped and sent from the Japanese Consulate and contained annotations of questions they were asking. The articles carried a picture of you and Elisa. They claimed I had promised her money for what was called our 'Love Child.' I was confused by the articles because we had had no contact since she left. I admire your mother for trying to secure finances for your support. Her ingenuity of asking the Japanese government for money showed me the Elisa I knew.

While I took no offense, I immediately began worrying about the state of your upbringing and care. One minute, I discover you are my daughter, and in the next I am already worrying about you and despairing about your condition. Too much time had passed, and it was too late for me to be of any assistance. Worrying about the past is useless; the mind creates problems and tortures itself.

One of the articles mentioned an unfortunate marriage she had, adding lurid details that corresponded to things she made mention of in another letter. I now realize her storytelling was a sign of a deeper problem. We dream, and sometimes those dreams are nightmares. I fear she might have been descending into nightmares during her waking hours. Our brain creates stories of blame and incessant hurt, no matter the circumstances we are in. These stories take us further from perceiving the reality of the now. Instead, new occurrences add to the hurts of the past. Her letters changed from loving concern to disappointment, and later to anger and bitterness, lashing out at me and every man.

The final item, the most recent, was a telegram from Gül. He gave me his New York address, sending me best wishes for the 1934 New Year. Even assuming he moved, Gül would leave traces for others, so I wrote him, and he swiftly responded. He was now a successful shipping-company director and invited me for a visit should I ever have a chance. He had not seen Elisa and knew nothing of you. Given his skills, I asked him to track your whereabouts. I had no doubts he could find a needle in a haystack given time. After eighteen months of searching, he found your mother on Long Island. He was alarmed by her state of mind. However, she was excited to hear I was trying to find her.

I wrote her a letter, in which I apologized for the lateness of receiving her letters, explaining my circumstances since leaving France. Expressing my delight about connecting again, I asked her to give you my greetings.

January, 1937

Dear Kenzo:

As Gül had promised, you decided to write me back. I don't believe a word of your story about becoming a monk in a remote monastery. What kind of fool do you think I am? You ignore me for ages and suddenly you are interested. I know better than to trust you. Back at Maxim's, I was told to be careful of your type of people but you wined and dined me, promising me a luxurious life. You used me like other men did, and then you dumped me.

Whenever I tell stories of where we traveled and our adventures, people laugh, accusing me of arrogance and creating a fantasy. No one believes me anymore, including my dear Nina. I have trained her to be strong because her future will not be easy. No matter how much she achieves, no matter how smart she is at school, some ignorant teacher or administrator will put her down for her race. She and I are facing the world alone. The Jews and Ukrainians and other Slavs don't want any part of me. Countless times I have been spat on, spat on, for the crime of asking for assistance from a charity. I won't even dare talking to the Japanese here.

The lone group that accepted me as a member were the Socialists. Their Ukrainian Labor Home has lots of social support, cultural activities for Nina, and a bar where I can take a break. The men and women there take my story as one more example of being taken advantage of by the bourgeoisie. They see us as victims of the class war engulfing the world. I have a bit of respite among them, though they constantly lecture me about the falsehoods of my past in the upper strata of Europe. Honestly, Kenzo, if I had a choice, I know what side I'd take in a class war.

I don't know that I care to hear from you. Your naïve letter opened scars that cannot heal. The pain and rejection you caused was cruel. You must be joking, telling me you are a priest. If I did believe any religion, I would say you are the devil, sticking your pitchfork into me one more time.

What did I do to bring such pain? All I desired was making a way for myself, a beautiful life of elegance. Men may take my body, but they will never take my soul!

Send me money. Show me that you care. Ask your rich, famous father who does everything for you to give you money. Nothing else will be as useful. One more thing, forget about the child. She is mine, not yours. You did nothing but take advantage of me at a time I was weak. The one act of kindness I did for you has been repaid over and over in pain and suffering. You have done enough harm to me.

Maybe if you give me a sign of how you truly care, I might change my mind. Otherwise, don't waste your time trying to fool me for whatever reason.

Elisa

Many conflicting emotions arose from her letter. Sorrow and compassion were the first ones. Yet my own feelings of anger were even stronger. Her reaction was akin to an animal that has been tortured, whose sole response is to attack others. My practice does not eliminate my own pain and suffering; I am a human. I felt the pain of being falsely accused and having my intentions misunderstood. I sat on my cushion, tears streaming as I relived my own suffering, loss, and perceived lack of ability to control my life. Why was this happening to me? It was the identical question your mother had.

Yet I knew I had done nothing except to inherit this twisted chain of karma. I relived *Oshō-sama's* slap of the *keisaku* when I confronted my karma born of greed, hate and delusion. *Whap*, Kenzo, end your mind's frozen story now. *Whap*, breathe, Kenzo, breathe. *Whap*, as long as you are Kenzo, you will have a story you believe is unchanging. Once you give up Kenzo, you will let go of that story. All stories are by definition invented, therefore untrustworthy. Acknowledge the pain and suffering in you on top of what you have caused others. Acknowledge, don't hang onto it. Breathe and acknowledge. Breath and let go, breathe and watch what emerges from now. Breathe ...

What arose was compassion for myself and all beings. What arose was a plan to meet you, my daughter, and make our family whole. What arose was likely a delusion but a delusion worth pursuing. No matter the state we are in, we cannot predict the future. We try comprehending the conditions surrounding us; we attempt understanding the causes of our suffering; and we can put forth intentions of a better way forward. My intention of meeting you was created in this moment.

32. THERE IS DELUSION AND REALIZATION

The political situation was worsening daily. Once the China War was declared in 1937, the militaristic fervor rose, causing the ineffective civilian government to cede power and decision-making to the military. Every incursion, every conflict was a step that furthered the destiny of our people. The ability to express contrary positions was steadily diminishing. Newspapers expressing more cautionary views were closed by government censorship or adapted their editorial content to match the views of their readership.

Even at Eiheiji and Sōjiji, the willingness to speak out for our principles was diminishing. Few would directly acknowledge the madness seizing the country. Many expressed hope for the emperor and government to carry our best interests forward. I continued my teaching and outreach to our priests and temples to ameliorate the situation. We each are part of society; every little effort changes the course of the future. This is a fundamental truth.

Although I disliked going to the capital where military might was being exalted in movies, newspapers and on posters, I persevered. As I regularly did, I met my former mentor, who helped me stay abreast of the current political machinations.

"Welcome back, my traveling monk. I hope you are successfully amplifying the environment for peace. I am not sure what else can be done. The rumblings of full-scale war are apparent. Germany is invading country after country with virtually no reaction from the Great Powers. Now our military is feeling kindred urges. Knowing the Powers are focused on their European domain exposes Asia to our own bidding."

"That is awful news, I was hoping you would tell me at least one positive development. Even as monks, we can hope for things beyond our reach. Sadly, from my point of view even the religious institutions are following the government's direction. Shinto priests are conducting services daily for the benefit of the imperial destiny. Even within Buddhist ranks, I am observing deeper and deeper splits. Few dare to publicly speak for the sanctity of non-killing. I never thought I would see the day *gekokujō* thought would take over our temples. Such is the power of delusion."

"These are hard times, and I hope we will survive them. I am glad you came by. I enjoy hearing your voice of reason, reminding me of our responsibilities. To that end, I have a proposal for you. Honestly, I am not sure whether I have the right to even ask you this. The mission will be dangerous and may possibly achieve little."

"Tell me. I am always willing to listen."

"A group of us here at the Ministry are opposed to any additional military action. We want to contact certain of our compatriots overseas. Obviously, we cannot write much in official cables, as mail is being reviewed and censored. Any expression of potential dissidence is considered treason. Thus we need to communicate person-to-person."

"How could I possibly aid your efforts?"

"Obviously none of us can embark on a voyage to America and Europe without raising suspicion. However, a Buddhist monk visiting overseas Japanese would not be questioned by our military or civilian officials. I can tell them you are assessing the state of spiritual affairs and views of the overseas Japanese communities. Your cover would be as visiting lecturer. Given your diplomatic experience, you have the right skills."

"Where are you considering?"

"The obvious are cities where we have identified contacts in embassies or consulates where large Japanese populations live. High on the list are Honolulu, San Francisco, Seattle, New York, Washington, D.C., London and Paris. Assuming you agree, I will send a cable to those officials, informing them a Buddhist monk is visiting local communities and that they should assist you. By sending the cable under my signature, I am signaling to them that you are carrying a personal message from me."

Before I could respond, his phone rang. He picked it up and appeared bemused while he scribbled notes on a pad of paper. Outside the window, I observed the passersby below. A military official identified by the numerous decorations on his chest, reading a document as he dashed ahead, accidently rushed into a woman pushing a pram and spilled his papers.

"Where were we?" he asked as he hung up the phone. "The ridiculous requests I get here...anyway, what do you say?"

"What type of danger might I encounter? I assume I will be followed and my every move reported back to Tōkyō. Will any of your contacts be put into peril by my association? I cannot lie about my mission, even if lying is best for promoting peace. Ultimately, my goal to spread the dharma has not altered."

"For a secluded monk, you still retain your knowledge of how the government works. Yes, assume you will be spied upon. The contacts I give you will be secure, and you will also meet other embassy officials who are not secure. You will discern those with whom you can speak freely from those with whom you must be more guarded. As you said, your mission is spreading the dharma, a subject on which I personally need more education. Retaining one's true bearings these days is not easy. I envy you for your steadfastness."

"And how soon are you thinking?"

"Given the sensitivity and covertness of this mission, we cannot rush our planning. A year would allow both of us to make the necessary preparations. What do you say?"

"For my country, for my beliefs and for another ripple of peace, I am ready. I trust you will not lie about my motives. You have given me the explanation for the purpose of my travels required by my superiors. For some, a Ministry of Foreign Affairs sponsorship would demonstrate I am trusted by the government and our views will be considered aligned. The other school will claim my peace-making efforts validated."

"Great. Go back and prepare what you must—I will do the same. Thank you on behalf of your country."

As I parted, I had but one dream—to see you, my Nina. Tenderness flooded my thoughts as I glimpsed a future together. I imagined living in New York, introducing myself as your father. I would tell you and your friends about your grandmother and great-grandmother. Perhaps I could take you to an amusement park I read about, called 'Coney Island'. Oh, the things we will do!

My excitement and joy were almost impossible to contain. Our pathways would cross and interlink as they were intended to. A vision of a father and his daughter building a family anew took shape. I was so sure of our future that I ignored the possible obstacles. We often connect difficult emotions to delusion—delusion is just as present in hope and happiness. Seeking has delusion lurking in every corner.

As I predicted, the senior monks were supportive of my mission. I initiated the complicated process of writing to the local temples on the list. Eventually, each temple responded and was eagerly awaiting my arrival. I said farewell to Eiheiji, never to return. Any flickers of nostalgia or regrets were diminished by my secret.

Oshō-sama, Mitsu's parents and I spent a day together. They were all worried for me; nothing I could say made them feel differently. Our farewells were emotional, as none of us knew what the future would bring. The three of them were getting older, so every absence I had from them was a reminder of aging and possible death. Oshō-sama gave me an *omamori,* an amulet offering me protection wherever I traveled.

In Tōkyō, I received the list of planned contacts and meeting dates, and we debriefed on my message for them. Except for the list, nothing was written. I had a portfolio of the temples and monks in addition to an itinerary: a ship to San Francisco, a train to New York, and then a ship to Paris, finally ending in London. From there, I would find out whether more cities were added to my itinerary or whether I would return directly.

I was prepared to sail when Germany invaded Poland, forcing Britain and France to declare war in September. The Ministry was astir; the treaties we had with Germany required Japanese military support, although no one knew what this might entail. The European war seemed to have little impact in Japan, but my trip was postponed until the Ministry had more clarity.

I sent a telegram to Gül, informing him about the delay and asking him to inform Elisa. I stayed in the village to be close by and able to leave on short notice. Working alongside *Oshō-sama* had a positive and grounding effect on me. None of them expected me back, so my presence was a joy and relief. I returned to the simple ways of a village priest, greeting the sun in zazen, conducting a morning service, helping *Oshō-sama* expand a garden and retile the roof. I would have lunch at Mitsu's parents twice a week, the three of us often eating quietly, glowing in the comfort of our lives with each other.

Finally my contact informed me I would depart at the New Year. On this last day, members of the congregation did a thorough cleaning of the temple to prepare to start anew. Personal debts are paid off, and families come to the temple. Once the cleaning is completed, we eat long soba noodles to bring extended life.

Near midnight, we rang the temple bells 108 times, marking the birth of the Shōwa 15, or 1940. At the end, we built a bonfire outdoors, burning the records of the past twelve months.

In the morning, our goodbyes exchanged, I headed to Yokohama to set sail on the *Tatsuta Maru*. Despite my several months of preparation, I was still concerned about our impending reunion. Could we call it a reunion if we have not met previously? Still, given how much you were already occupying my mind, the word seemed appropriate. I was not sure what a young American woman of seventeen might be like or how you would react when we met.

Not sharing my covert purpose with my grandfather and Mitsu's parents weighed on me heavily. Hadn't I learned from unearthing so many family secrets that the power of secrets limits our true relationships and interconnectedness? Whereas I would give you a different answer now, back then my delusional focus on bringing closure between us blinded me…I was blinded by what I thought was love.

Gül told Elisa of my delay, and I also wrote to her with my plans. Given her previous letter, I was not sure how she would act; her letter back made me uneasy.

November, 1939

Dear Kenzo:

After what you have done to me, can you really be coming? Of course, you made a promise only to tell me you are delayed. What should I believe? Finally, after so many years passing, you are coming back. I'd love to throw you a party like in the old days. Remember the fun we had, dancing, attending parties and gossiping in the best of society? While those times have long passed, not a day passes that I don't think about them. I am constantly lecturing Nina about what she must do to gain a husband of good standing. She doesn't hear a word. She's smart and throws her learning back at me, as if I am a peasant from the steppes. She thinks I make up how I lived in that very special time.

When you are here, you can tell her about it. You can tell her how I was admired and how beautifully I dressed and all of the wonderful people I met. You can tell her how Picasso painted my picture or that men wrote poems about me in the cafes. You can set her straight. The half of her coming from you is as frustrating and naïve as you are, frankly.

I hope I don't sound bitter. I am waiting for you, my sweetheart, as I have since I last saw you in Paris. I knew one day you would come back for me.

I will be waiting for you.

Love, Elisa

NOT-KNOWING IS MOST-INTIMATE

33. HERE THE WAY UNFOLDS

Once the ship set sail, my home, my island nation, disappeared beyond the horizon. The *Tatsuta Maru* became my temple, surrounded by a deep, endless ocean. I sequestered myself in a *sesshin,* sitting zazen from early morning to night, stopping only for the meals delivered to me. Five times a day I would walk *kinhin* on the main deck gazing at the waves, simultaneously feeling like Dōgen's fish in its watery world, his bird flying in its spacious atmosphere and a monk walking a ship. My robes set me apart from the rest of my passengers, who let me glide by as a ghost among them. They respected my silence. If I had a begging bowl, it would have been overflowing from a partial circuit.

Several parts of Dōgen's *Genjō Kōan* use ocean imagery. The sea voyage to China and back was a pivotal experience for him. For a land person it can be disturbing to be in the middle of the sea. Peering into the distance, the ocean appears as a circle extending around the viewer. Yet Dōgen tells us the ocean is limitless and cannot be defined by any measurement. The ocean represents dharma, the teachings of Buddha which release the possibilities for each of us. When our mind limits the limitless, it reduces our ability to understand true existence.

Outsiders often question me about the seeming boredom of the routines of a monk, not perceiving the ceaseless, unthinking repetition of their own lives. For me, life is full and abundant as each moment is different, imbued with its own sense of time.

Each day passed like this: As was my practice, I watched my concerns arise, which allowed me to sense my own anxieties and hopes, the foremost of which was meeting you. I imagined multiple scenarios of how that occasion would play out, each time watching the results float up into the clouds. Thinking back to what I recall, my little one, nothing arose that foretold the events leading to my current incarceration. The mind is most useless in seeing the future, a lesson I have had to relearn again and again, failing each time as it clings to the belief of its independent existence. This is our nature as humans: We believe we can control our future and that of others.

On the eleventh day of our journey, the ship entered the port of Oahu in Hawaii. We passed the vast fleet of American warships as we docked, still quiet in the early morning. We were in port for one day, and several local temples invited me to speak to their large congregations. My limited time did not allow for much conversation and interaction except for my dharma talks. My contact at the consulate told me he was soon returning home. All he wanted to know were my impressions of the situation there. He was afraid of going back as he saw war as inevitable. He told me several of the consulate staff were spies who spent equal effort in surveillance of both the Americans and the Japanese staff.

The ship hove off, embarking on the remaining days of the trip. I went back into *sesshin,* accompanied by worries attached to every move and thought. Paranoia is powerful and contagious. These thoughts swirled, and instead of watching them floating into the sky, they sunk into the sea, staining the waters below our ship. I welcomed the solidity of our ship and my continued practice, yet I did so aware of the rising tensions underlying the state of world affairs.

On the fifth day of such thoughts and feelings, a set of islands then soon the Golden Gate Bridge loomed ahead, arching above the two sides of the bay. The fog we saw from afar was less solid and more diaphanous as we neared, shifting and dissipating as the sun burned it away. Traces of fog still clung to the tops of the hills as the bay sparkled, welcoming us into its world. However, preparation for war had already started here. Our entry into San

Francisco was delayed as we had to carefully sail through the underwater mines protecting the city. Sailing underneath the bridge, the honking and noise of motor cars passing above served as signs that we were nearing the end of our voyage. Feelings of surety of what I was doing grew in my body, as I saw myself spanning the divides of world views. From our distance, the rolling hills of the city appeared quietly auspicious, although the docks teeming with military vessels reminded me of the deadly seriousness of my journey.

Pulling into the port, the energy and confidence in the background hum of this compact city began to seep into my body. The air was fresh and cool. I felt ready for whatever was to come. I was met by a priest and several prominent members of the local congregation. We had not completed our introductory bows when one of the members asked, "What will Japan do since Germany invaded Poland, and now England and France have declared war?"

I was stunned by such a question, "W-w-what? Why are you asking me this?"

"Sorry, *Rōshi*, I apologize for being so rude prior to even introducing myself. I am Okamura, the president of the congregation. We are worried here about what is going on. I thought you might be able to tell us more."

The priest intervened, "Let's properly introduce ourselves and let our guest clean up and eat. Afterwards, we converse about current events."

We caught up with the formalities of my stay, as my hosts drove me to Japantown, as it was called. From the car the people on the street appeared to be Japanese and the signs on the shops were written with kanji; however, little else resembled Japan. I was a guest at the home of Okamura-san, a wealthy man who had come to the U.S. as a child. He had an elegant wood house, typical of San Francisco. The interior style was very American, offset by Japanese prints and other touches. He introduced me to his wife, who for the evening was dressed in a kimono.

My hosts were well-briefed on Japanese politics and the players from the local Japanese press. And, of course, they were aware that Japan had signed treaties aligning it with Germany and Italy in order to boast a united front against the Soviet Union. They related to me how Americans were looking mistrustfully at Germans, even those who had lived here for generations. Apparently, some German families were changing their surnames to deny their heritage, an option not available to the Japanese. With the greatest numbers of Japanese settled on the West Coast, some politicians were suggesting that Japanese-American loyalty was a problem.

There was great interest in my work, and everyone agreed that my efforts were needed. The local press had been alerted and would attend my lecture the following evening. They wanted assurances, however, that I would say nothing that might embarrass the community or link them to the military actions on which the U.S. press was vociferously reporting. I assured them I was well-practiced as a former diplomat in managing such issues if they came up. More importantly, the nature of my teaching was focused on the right pathway.

The next morning I was driven to the Consulate not far from where I was staying. I met my contact and discussed his status. The German alliance was overturning all my plans now that war was declared. The door was rapidly closing for diplomatic solutions, although the hope was that the United States would remain neutral. My contact's reading of the American sentiment was that most did not want any involvement in the war. However, the U.S. Congress had decided to ban sales of oil to Japan, which was considered to be an act of belligerence by Tōkyō.

The audience that night appeared to be quite receptive to my lecture. Maybe American culture made talking about right speech and speaking honestly less strange to the local congregation. The influence of democracy and particularly the guarantee of freedom of speech in your constitution fascinated me. I even used that as an example of the precept. The questions reflected an openness as members struggled to better utilize these precepts in their lives.

My press briefing was more challenging.

"*Rōshi*, your trip certainly comes at a trying period for Japan. What do you expect to accomplish here?"

"As I explained earlier, I have been developing a program to better share the dharma among Sotō Zen temples in Japan. By emphasizing right speech in all of its manifestations, we hope communities can discuss differences honestly and openly. The biggest challenge I have so far faced is to identify culturally specific ways that support Buddhist right action. As you heard me discuss earlier, right speech is virtually written into the U.S. Constitution. My practice will gain much by talking to citizens here."

"Your trip is being sponsored by the Ministry of Foreign Affairs, not something they traditionally would do. What is their involvement?"

"As a result of my diplomatic experiences prior to becoming a monk, I had observations about how Japanese who live far from their homeland, think. Therefore, the idea arose to explore the Buddhist connection in communities of Japanese citizens of other countries. My intent is to ripple the opportunities for peace everywhere by right action and speech. I appreciate their support in making my journey happen."

"What is your opinion of the Japan-Germany treaty? Will Japan take advantage of the war in Europe and expand the current fighting in China to other countries?"

"I am a simple monk who put aside being a diplomat decades ago. My expertise lies in the dharma and in encouraging practice. I abandoned political decisions once I put on these robes. I care about peace everywhere and encourage peace wherever I can. Each of us contributes to how our individual societies and the collective global society respond. You may be pessimistic and scared, which fertilizes negative seeds. As Dōgen said, 'Weeds will grow, even though we don't like them.' What he meant was our dislikes and fears have their own outcomes."

"There are those in Japan, *Rōshi,* who would consider those treasonous words."

"I deal solely in the dharma and have vowed to free all beings of delusion. Vows are not bought nor sold—they manifest themselves because of causes and conditions. I thank you for listening to me."

The conversation reminded me of what had been lost back home: an inquiring press. They had stopped asking hard questions of government officials, having taken on the role of abetting government censorship by ignoring or defaming voices questioning the events of the day. I observed how Americans took this freedom for granted, which also meant they might, under the right circumstances, easily be influenced by demagogues who manipulate the press to broadcast their dangerous views.

In San Francisco, a Buddhist priest apparently was not such an odd event. Substantial populations of Japanese, Chinese, Mexicans, and Irish, made the city its own League of Nations. Most of these groups had their own neighborhoods, and little infighting appeared among them. As immigrants or outsiders they shared similar hopes. The adventurous are the ones willing to leave behind their home countries to begin anew. However, I was told different groups were forced by law and societal discrimination to live together in certain neighborhoods.

Japantown was adjacent to the Fillmore, a Black community. One evening, as we were wandering the quiet streets of the neighborhood, the familiar sounds of a jazz trumpet came from a club.

"I have not heard jazz since I lived in Paris in the 1920s. Can we go in?"

My escort was shocked, "*Rōshi*, this is not a place for a Buddhist. Drinking, dancing and other sorts of activities are going on."

"My son, you have just described precisely where a Buddhist priest should go! Come on, I won't tell anyone you accompanied me."

Entering the club, my senses were assaulted by the intensity of the music, the smell of alcohol and marijuana, the sexual strutting of the men and women, bringing me back to my youthful nights in Paris. Without noticing it, my head was bobbing to the music as my foot was tapping. Some in the crowd noticed me and gave me an encouraging smile. As I surveyed the stage, I was shocked by what I saw.

"Wait, the trumpet player and drummer, they're Japanese!" I shouted over the music.

"Oh, yes, *Rōshi*...The band got its start here and tours up and down the West Coast."

"I could never imagine such a thing. How did this happen?"

"When my parents arrived in San Francisco, they were not allowed to live anywhere except in what was a Negro neighborhood. Originally, life was tough because we both had prejudices, but my generation broke the barriers. This band is one of the several mixed-race jazz bands receiving acclaim up and down the coast."

I did get my accomplice in trouble with the elders as news traveled fast in the tight-knit community. Upon returning late to Okamura-san's house, he was waiting for us and expressed his fury at the young man. I calmed him and took full responsibility for my actions. I let him know I forced him to enter. The look on his face was priceless as I had broken down at least one expectation of how a priest acts.

"Okamura-san, a Buddhist priest is not a fragile object needing to be handled like a precious doll. Buddha stole away from his father's palace to discover a humanity at large, and full of suffering. We go everywhere and are reminded that enlightenment can be found in music and in dance - even in non- Japanese music and dance. The energy and emotion of jazz is life itself. I am cognizant about what occurs in such clubs from my posting in Paris; nothing goes on there that does not go on behind closed doors of even the finest homes."

His face and body relaxed. "You are not your standard Eiheiji-trained monk, I can see. Thank you for opening my mind. The moon shines brightly tonight."

He bowed.

I traveled along the West Coast visiting temples in Seattle, Portland, San Jose, Fresno and Los Angeles for six weeks before heading across the country. Each city had its own flavor and listening to the old and young generations painted a picture of different Americas. I was especially interested in the teenagers, hoping to get an idea of what you might be like. As much as their parents were deferential, the second generation, the *Nisei,* were full of questions. They knew the old ways in addition to the modern and American ones. Oftentimes, they acted as intermediaries for their families. They translated for their parents and grandparents, helping them to navigate this unfamiliar environment. I am sure you bore these responsibilities for your mom. Sadly, I suspect she would have been resistant to recognizing the knowledge you had. Many of the *nisei* saw themselves as American, not Japanese.

As interested and curious as I was, my heart kept telling me there was one particular place and one young woman I yearned to see. I caught the transcontinental train in Sacramento heading east. We traversed snow-covered mountains, forests of pine trees, vast endless plains where the winter winds blew strong and hard. Huge farms where hundreds of cattle and pigs huddled to keep warm taught me that the size of America was one of its defining characteristics. The people were bigger, and the land was too big for me. Dōgen would describe the vast emptiness of existence while this grand country was revealing itself, mile after mile after mile. Maybe he had come to this continent instead of China as we were taught.

After a stop in Chicago, we entered barren expanses of forests where the tips of branches were about to burst into bloom in the warming sun. Among the forests were small farms on rolling hills, carved out of the surrounding wilderness. The houses appeared older and poorer, and the small towns we briefly stopped at were quiet in the middle of the day. This was a very different America from the cities I had explored and from the farms of the Central Valley; more insular and contained, less expansive. The land and environment affect our vision and world view.

The embassy officials in Washington, D.C., hosted me on my visit. After a formal luncheon, they took me on a tour of this monumental city, evoking grandeur and power and reminding me of my stay in Europe. The Congress building, its huge dome illuminated and visible from a distance, was a symbol of the power of a democratic people. The Embassy told me about the debates and how representatives from each of the states came together to discuss issues. In my younger days we often talked about democracy, a dream smashed by military control. My own father had been posted here and likely walked the streets I was on. Surprisingly, these thoughts came to me with a positive feeling of connection to him without my old overlay of hurt and suffering.

The signs of spring were appearing as daffodils and other flowers were pushing their way up. Early blooming cherry trees, a present from our old country to this new one, were bursting into flower. We ambled underneath the trees along the river on the petal-strewn path. The seriousness of our conversation belied the impression that we were not in Tōkyō walking around the grounds of the Imperial Palace enjoying the blossoming season. Our path took us to the most moving monument of all, the Lincoln Memorial, a temple to democracy with an all-knowing man, sitting and gazing into the distance; I acknowledged Buddha-nature permeating everywhere.

I had several contacts within the Embassy, and our meetings saddened me. My contacts were hopeless and discouraged by the events. They knew that one day soon they would be forced back home. The U.S. had not declared war on Germany, although it was assisting the British and French efforts by sending military supplies. The remaining hope they carried was that the Congress was against joining the war.

I was more than anxious to arrive in New York. As we chugged along on the five-hour train ride, we passed by large industrial cities—Baltimore, Wilmington and Philadelphia, as well as by airfields, and by military and commercial vessels lined up on docks. The flames of refineries shot into the sky. We crossed a large river, and the sign on the bridge said, *Trenton Makes and the World Takes*. Making and taking seemed very American–brash and transactional–and, sadly, a prelude to nations at war. No sharing, no relationship, no mutual benefit, a one-way direction from creation to disappearance.

Toward the evening, lights in the distance rose higher in the eastern sky as we neared our destination. Soon a whole city of buildings reaching as high as mountains gleamed in the setting rays of the sun, and the artificial lights adorning them switched on one by one. As quickly as they appeared, they disappeared as we plunged into a deep tunnel. The train clanged and banged as we entered near-total darkness, only a string of open bulbs hanging between the tracks, illuminating the way. We slowed to a halt at our destination of Pennsylvania Station. Clambering up the steps, hundreds of us, valises in hand, finally emerged inside a building where thousands more were scurrying to catch their trains. An anthill of activity engulfed us, maybe more making and taking, I was not sure.

Here I was met by the consul-general himself, a man who had served alongside my father at the initiation of his career. He led me out of this madhouse of a station onto the street where thousands more were running to catch buses and taxis, or perhaps just running for the sake of it. The blinking neon signs, huge shops and wide streets, thousands of cars, buses and trucks honking their way amongst the traffic, overwhelmed me. No wonder Elisa was hard to find. In a city where no one stood still, how could you find anyone?

My official plan was to stay here for several weeks. Unofficially, I had dreams that I shared with no one. I had several lectures planned, and the rest of the time I hoped to see you and Elisa.

Gül met me at my hotel. What a joyful reunion we had! He appeared more handsome and dignified than the last time I saw him in Paris, if that were possible. His hair had turned silver, and his beautiful eyes were as striking as ever, taking on a bit of softness. We talked as though we had been with each other just the day before. The previous decades' lack of communication did not matter as we restarted our lives from where we had left off.

"I don't know why," he said, "but it does not surprise me, seeing you wearing those priest robes. You are still Kenzo, no different. Maybe more content, more at ease, more aware. You seem to have found your way within our worrisome world."

"And you, Gül, you seem to have found happiness. Is there a man in your life?"

"I'm still independent and content to be removed from prying eyes. Early on, I explored every neighborhood. From the sailor taverns where men were seeking quick sex before they returned on board, to sophisticated clubs where men of power, enveloped in cigar smoke accompanied by the smell of leather chairs, the taste of whiskey on their tongues, share beds for the night away from their wives. Every evening, the theater lights extinguished and actors, their followers, stagehands and directors drink and dance until the wee hours of the morning."

"This sounds like the Gül who I remember. You always had that ability to know where to go."

"Here you can find whatever you desire, except maybe long-term affection." His eyes looked directly into mine at that moment. Then he changed subjects.

"My business has been successful, although like everyone, I am worried about what war will bring. Most of our clients are in Europe, so the U-boats, blockades and fighting have brought shipping to a near standstill. I'm a survivor. This is not my first war and period of instability. I have no idea what will happen next. Japan is not likely to sit on the sidelines as they did during the Great War.'

"You are likely correct, Gül. Japan has been fighting multiple countries over the past three decades—Russia, China, Korea and, recently, Mongolia. The talk of Empire is everywhere; empires need lands, bodies, and resources. And those resources–oil, coal, rubber and iron ore–are a spider's web of dependency, feeding the military. When the military is fed, war is always the result."

"Let's talk about the real reason you are here...Elisa and Nina."

"You talked to her, right? What did she say? And Nina, did you meet her, what is she like? As a monk, I may be trained not to act on emotions, but every time I think about her, care and concern well up in me, making me ignore everything else."

"I am sorry, I did not meet the young girl. Elisa didn't care to share much about her. I gather she is very smart, at the top of her class, and, from the pictures I saw, quite pretty. I recognized you in her face. She does have your features in her eyes, nose, and lips along with your black hair."

"Until you said this, I did not allow myself to think that she might look like me. I am now even more excited about meeting her. Did Elisa say anything more about her character?"

"All she wanted to do was reminisce with me about the old days. She lives in a dream of those times and is angry they are gone. While she has had multiple hardships, she told me that the foundation of her downfall was her pregnancy and birth of your child, which prevented her from scraping and scheming her way back into high society."

"Oh no, how can she believe this? Given the contents of her letters you are confirming that she is suffering greatly and creating additional and unneeded suffering for the child."

"What shocked me the most is that she kept referring to her as a half-breed."

"Half-breed? Gül, I don't understand. She used the same phrase in a letter to me."

"Honestly, I don't understand how a mother can say that about her own child. It is a derogatory word referring to a child with parents of different races. Elisa became so agitated when we conversed, I feared for her wellbeing."

"Her last letter echoed those themes. I am concerned she has different expectations than I do."

"I'm afraid you are right. I am not sure of the correct plan for meeting her."

"Your report makes me reevaluate my reasons for being here. My intentions were never to bring harm to Elisa, although it appears I have done just that. Also, my intentions are not to bring harm to her or Nina in the future, but listening to you now, I fear I might cause further harm. Here I have been lecturing on Right Speech and Right Action, yet our twisted karma does not show any signs of being relieved. Perhaps I should not meet her."

"Kenzo, I have known you since 1919. You are a man of unflagging decency, compassion and dignity. You used to say how Mitsu had those characteristics, but you yourself were blind to how strongly you reflected them. The two of you were so special. Surrounded by the honorable influences of you both, Elisa succumbed to them as did all of us. On her own without the backing of your compassion and stability, she is a planet spinning off her orbit, colliding into others on her path. If anyone has the ability to help her, you are the one. You must go for the sake of Nina."

I was silent as I pondered his words. Feelings of the loss of my mother and family filled me. My own path was burdened by unfilled wants and needs. Mitsu had supported me to act on my yearnings. Even his death brought me to his family and causing my own family to open the circle of love. Bringing you into that circle was my wish for you, my one and only Nina. I have treasured you and held you in esteem from afar. I wanted you to be freed from fear.

Intentions are powerful, yet I have no control over others. Believing that one's intentions are powerful enough alone to change others is misguided. How an individual reacts in the web of the universe will be based on their experiences, their perceptions, their delusions. If we don't recognize the fundamental tenet of interconnectedness, and instead choose to believe our independent lives as separate from all life, we are forever cut off from other beings.

"Well, despite my doubts I can't not meet her, not after the distance I have traveled. Although my words are measured, I am extremely excited by the idea, and I doubt that I will be able to sleep much tonight."

"Tomorrow afternoon, I will come by to take you to their apartment. I'll retire so you can rest and prepare yourself."

He started to leave and then turned around. "Maybe I should stay here with you."

Without another word on my part, we fell into each other's arms. His strength and stability were what I needed. We peered into each other's eyes and saw affection and understanding reflecting back. Without planning or hesitation, we kissed long, deeply, soulfully. We did not speak a word as we fell into bed. Surrendering into them now, his arms were as strong as I remembered them. Passion, laughter and even tears carried us that evening as time merged into being and being into time.

34. IN DELUSION THROUGHOUT DELUSION

I slept fitfully, dreams flying through my mind, dreams full of anticipation and longing, each ending without fulfillment or direction. Eventually, I fell into a deep slumber and awoke early as the sun was rising. The noises of the city, hardly ceasing during the darkness, slowly crescendoed as its residents prepared to leave their apartments for the day. I cuddled close to Gül, and he sensed my awakening. We hugged and kissed until he arose to get dressed to return to his apartment. I put on my robes and sat zazen for an hour, using my breath to keep my thoughts and desires at bay.

At 1:30 p.m., Gül arrived, and we headed to the train station. Thousands were in their midday routines, boarding and leaving trains, lugging briefcases, bags and boxes, scurrying up the stairways. We were fish swimming upstream as we made our way to the vast underground cavern where trains zipped in and out. As in the old days, Gül confidently led the way. We entered a Long Island Railroad train, and it quickly lurched forward. Ten minutes later, we emerged from the dark tunnel into the warm bright sun.

The ride to Mineola took less than an hour. The train crawled through Brooklyn and Queens, the vastness of the city taking on greater dimensions. Instead of open plains and endless forests, buildings leaned against each other, filling every possible space. Laundry hung from balconies; cars clogged the streets; store after store announced their goods for sale on large signs. Without any clear delineation, spaces between houses expanded, and I saw yards full of children's toys, bicycles, gardens, chairs and trees. Each house demarcated by a fence of wood, wire or brick was an individual palace compared to the multiplicity of apartments earlier.

Leaving the city limits, the vista opened even more as the space between the houses expanded and numerous leafy parks became visible. After several stops, the conductor called out, "Mineola, all off here."

Elisa's apartment was close to the station. Small shops, individual houses, and three-story apartment buildings were arranged along tree-lined streets. A gaggle of children, heading home from school, followed us for a block, giggling at the sight of a Japanese monk in robes on their street. Their parents and other passersby were somewhat more discreet.

Gül stopped in front of a café and pointed at an apartment building across the street, down the block.

"Elisa lives on the second floor, unit 203. Her window is right above the main entrance. Enter, and the staircase will lead you right to her flat. I will wait for you here. Good luck, Kenzo."

My heart was pounding as I penetrated into an unlit hallway. The building smelled of cooked cabbage and cigarettes. The wooden stairs were worn yet clean, and creaked as I ascended. Certain stairways at Eiheiji were constructed to make noise so no one could sneak up on the monks during the days of instability centuries ago. We would creep as quietly as possible on those steps as a test of our mindfulness. The senior teachers could do so without alerting everyone in the vicinity. I slowed my breathing and tried to concentrate as I tiptoed up; I didn't reduce the squeaking a bit.

I found her door and stood still for a second. My thoughts were solely concerned with seeing you, my daughter. Suffused by anticipation, I rapped on the door. A few seconds later, Elisa stood at the entrance. We stared at each other, neither of us moving, both taking each other in. The passage of time had been rough on her. Her face was worn and worried. Her skin was red and blotchy, which her thick and unevenly applied makeup concealed poorly. Her hair, tied in a bun and dyed an unnatural color, was limp and flaccid. She wore the Vionnet dress, which was now faded and had a torn sleeve.

She smiled, extending her hand.

"*Enchanté, Kenzo.* Did you forget how to greet a woman since you took on these robes? You were such a gentleman in those days, so handsome in your tuxedo. I must say you still are."

I took her hand and gently kissed it.

"Oh, you do remember. Thank God, none of the men in this country treat a woman properly. Please enter my modest abode. The maid is out right now—however, she left tea for us. Please come in."

I stepped into a maelstrom and wondered what it must be like for you, living in such a place. Clothing and some toys were strewn about the flat. The walls had taped-on pictures torn from magazines of fashionable women and scenes from Paris. Here and there I recognized knickknacks from her Paris suite. As I settled into the sofa, its big, bulging cushions sank around me and I felt the springs underneath. A Chinese teapot and two cups, one with a broken handle, were set on a small table that had one of its legs missing, propped up by a pile of books. I am recounting the space as it was, without judgment, taking note of the circumstances of her living situation.

"Let me pour you a cup of tea. I am so glad you are here, Kenzo. Ever since I received your last letter and Gül talked to me, I have been waiting eagerly. Every day I have been waiting, thinking this will be the day my Kenzo returns, my hero. Remember when we were heroes, Kenzo? I sometimes still feel the heat of the flames and remember jumping into them, waiting for you on the other side. You resembled a god, your kimono flying behind you as you emerged from the smoke and fire, carrying Signora Morosini. That Morosini, maybe we should never have saved her for all the help she gave me. Once you cast me out, she abandoned me, too."

I tried to respond, but Elisa continued, her words swirling around the room like smoke, blinding me.

"You were always my hero, you who rescued me from Maxim's where they made fun of my desires to enjoy the best that life offers. Who knows what I might have become if I had stayed? But you swept me off my feet, made me promises and carried me away like in a fairy tale. We had so many wonderful times, so many parties, and I lived in luxury. No one believes me, not even my own daughter."

"Yes, Nina," I interjected, "where is the dear girl? I can't wait to see her."

"Where do you think she is?" she snapped. "It's a school day. She won't be back until about three. She has no idea you are here, that you were even coming. I wanted this to stay our own little secret, just you and me, the way things were after Mitsu died. We have much to catch up on and prepare before she comes home."

"I told you I hoped to meet her."

"Yes, sure, of course you do, and what about me, did you care to see me, Kenzo? Or do you plan on abusing me again, by taking the girl from me?"

"Elisa, I missed you and knew nothing about you, where you were, what you were doing. I felt terrible forcing you away. I was powerless to confront my father. With Mitsu gone, nothing was right. My stay in Paris was completed shortly after you arrived here. Returning home without Mitsu was painful."

"Oh, pain and agony, poor boy. I didn't even tell you half of what I had to endure. You had an easy time in France, and I am sure your rich, powerful father took good care of you in Japan—the poor, weak son who refused to stand up for the woman he loved. That is the tale I have told everyone who cared to listen."

"What do you mean, 'the woman I loved,' Elisa? I cared for you as a friend, as a companion. Mitsu was the full focus of my love. You understood that and entered into our relationship under those conditions. Now you are saying we were lovers. As much as you meant to me—"

"You say we were not lovers? How was our child created? I didn't do that by myself. Once Mitsu was gone, you confided in me. Then you used me like other men before you, and like them you disappeared. Why do you have such a strange look on your face? We both know why you are here. You traveled across the waters to offer your overdue apology so we can live the elegant and cultured life we deserve. Okay, Kenzo, I accept your apology. Come here and kiss me and we will make up. I already have my valise packed and ready by the door. The girl is old enough to take care of herself. When I was her age, I ran away from home for the first time. She will be fine."

"Elisa, you are inventing a relationship that did not exist. You understood my intentions from the initial conversation that we had so long ago. We talked about my situation plainly, and you agreed. You didn't want a husband and preferred your freedom to choose your companions as you saw fit. From Constantinople to Paris, I was happy that you were happy. You offered me comfort during a time in which my heart was broken. After you rescued me from the jail, our connection made complete sense, but we knew that intimacy between us would never happen again."

"I thought better of you, Kenzo. I will ignore your nonsense. Let's go!"

"Elisa, how can I make you accept the truth? We are not going anywhere. I came to visit you and meet my daughter. I am a Buddhist monk—I am being honest. Are you okay? I am concerned about you."

"I am feeling fine and will feel better when I'm gone from here. You will never fully understand what a horror my life is here—caring for a child that has been called a half-breed from her birth, and the harassment and shame placed on me for being her unmarried mother, struggling to make ends meet when there is never enough money for the two of us to live in comfort. Oh, the things I was forced to do to survive."

"Elisa, I don't have the words to say how sorry I feel. I want to make up for it in some way."

"Well, you can make up for it by getting me out of here. These neighbors don't realize who I was and where I came from. One of them even called the police on me last week. I had not talked to the police since I hauled you from jail. The favors I was made to promise that ugly police captain were awful. The police have no right to tell me what I can or cannot do—to quiet down and take better care of my daughter. How dare they!

"Wait, Kenzo, wait. I see her coming from school. I didn't want her to find us here. Get back from the window."

"Elisa, you are being unreasonable. It's best I go."

"You can't. I knew one day you would come to rescue me and now the time has come."

She scanned the street from an open window, and I saw you for the first time. You had your schoolbooks in your hand and were singing to yourself as you skipped across the street. My heart leaped with joy. Never in my dreams did I imagine the fullness of emotion that came over me in that moment. After all of my travels, my years of planning, I would finally meet you, my daughter, my love.

But your demeanor changed just as quickly, as you studied the window where your mother stood, a frightened look taking over your face.

"Get out of here, you disgusting half-breed!" Elisa screamed. Your face crumpled. What was your mother doing? I jumped up and approached the window, but she shoved me away with such ferocity that I went reeling across the coffee table, causing the teapot and cups to go flying across the room.

"I told you this morning never to come back," she screamed. "You don't belong here anymore. You have caused me nothing but trouble from the day you were born. You and your ideas. Scram, you mean, thoughtless girl! I have given you everything, and what have you brought me? Misery, just misery. You deserve the pain I have suffered for the last seventeen years. You miserable bastard child!"

I gingerly rose and saw you on the street, shocked and embarrassed and crying. Passersby were turning their heads to figure out what the commotion was. The anguish and confusion on your face was agonizing. Along with you, my dreams came crashing down while Elisa continued her tirade. For a few seconds I froze as I began to recognize my inability to stop her. Then you did a smart thing—you ran away as fast as you could. Some neighbors started shouting from their windows at your mother in a number of languages. Their intent was clear: they had heard enough.

But what could I do now? Since you knew nothing of me, you could not be expected to develop trust in a strange Japanese man claiming to be your father - even had your mother introduced us. No, we needed time together to build a bond between us. But at that moment I was faced with the harsh reality that I could do little in the way of building a father-daughter bond, and only hoped you knew how to protect and take care of yourself.

Without saying another word to Elisa, I ran down to the street. You were already gone, nowhere to be seen. Trembling, I peered back at the window, where Elisa still stood.

"You cowardly, yellow-skinned son of a bitch. Yes, you better run away now before I have you arrested!"

Those were her last words; I never saw Elisa again. I hurried back to the cafe and found Gül. I fitfully filled him in on what had just occurred.

"What should I do now? I feel responsible."

"Kenzo, she's crazy. You needed to witness it for yourself. Originally, the neighbors said she was kind, if a bit pretentious. When she lost her job due to a series of arguments at her workplace, she became more belligerent to those around her, including Nina. She is still unemployed and has been pressuring her daughter to drop out of school to find work."

"I saw Nina's terrified look as her mother screamed at her. If I hadn't been here, things wouldn't have gotten this bad. From what you told me, she began to change once I started writing. Her letters sounded more and more unraveled over time. I thought I was helping, but now I see how wrong I was. What else can we do?"

Gül regarded me long and hard. "You did not cause Elisa's state of mind. She clearly never planned for you to meet your child. Her letters were a barometer of her inner turbulence and haphazard reactions. You are not to blame for her struggles. We can return tomorrow afternoon and wait on the street for Nina. That way we can at least meet her. There isn't much we can do. Let's go back to the city."

We headed back, heavy-hearted. My mind arranged the bits and pieces of Elisa's past into a fixed narrative. Of course, I would never know the complete story of what happened to her, just as your story is incomplete to me and even mine is incomplete to myself. The same Elisa who agreed to join us, two men whom she barely knew, who jumped selflessly into a fire, the same Elisa who would pose for Picasso, who freely shared her enjoyment of affluence and comfort, this same Elisa eventually finds her energy stifled, twisting her frustration onto herself and you. I kept wondering: Did I unknowingly encourage her? Could I have altered the awful scene which played out today?

Alas, hindsight is not related to foresight. Both are delusional states of the mind. Past and future exist in the mind only. My desire to fix your situation was linked to my desires at your age to change my own life, which was further entangled with the desires my mother had for her life. The lineage of our actions is endless. Awareness of our lineage can bring fateful obsessions as well as liberation. When our mind searches for answers within its realm, it usually veers toward fate. Buddha sends us toward liberation.

Gül stayed over with me and we returned to the apartment the next day as planned. The window of Elisa's apartment was open, the curtains blowing in the breeze. On the street we found a pile of your clothes, books and other objects strewn about. I picked up a sweater of yours, just so I could touch something that belonged to you. We went upstairs where the door stood wide open; I stepped into the apartment after calling out Elisa's name. Her belongings were scattered - perhaps the result of a skirmish - and some objects I had noticed the day before were missing.

A few minutes later, a neighbor appeared in the doorway.

"Ya lookin' for the crazy lady?" she asked. "She ain't here anymore."

"What do you mean?

"I live next door to here. Every day I heard tantrums. Yesterday's the worst. She's screamin' at that poor girl shakin' in the street, using words no mother should ever say at her own kid. The girl runs off, then I see you run onto the street. You must've been here."

"I was. I couldn't stop her."

"I don't know who you are, mister, but you must be related to the kid given your looks. After you left, all I could hear was bangin' and screamin' and stuff being thrown against the walls. That racket went on all night long. Finally this mornin', I sent my son for the cops. She was dumpin' her kid's clothing and stuff out the window when they showed up. The cops were here over and over, but this time they put the cuffs on her and took her away kickin' and wailin'."

I could not believe what I was hearing. "You say she is gone?"

"I don't think she'll be back for a long time. She was screamin' all night long,

'You promised to take me away! You promised to take me away!' I don't know what she was talkin' about but looks like she got her wish."

"What do you mean? Where did they take her?"

"They hauled her to Pilgrim State, you know, the insane asylum, and locked her up."

"An asylum? Things must have been worse than I thought. I was shocked by her behavior yesterday, yet I never imagined…"

"It's for the best, mister. Jesus Christ, none of us could pound reason into that lady."

"What about Nina? It must have been awful for her."

"I tried to protect the girl, but nothin' I said moved her mother. That young girl has strong will, otherwise she never could've stood up to her mother's crazy makin'. She never hit her, thank God. Still, she callin' her names, scarin' her friends away and gettin' into fights at school with teachers."

She walked around, picking up a few things and dropping them down again.

"Some neighbors who were sick and tired of her antics ransacked this place once they hauled her. I'm not that type of person, so I've been watchin' over her stuff, knowin' the girl is likely comin' back soon. I heard she's with Child Welfare now."

I looked at Gül to see if he understood what that implied. "Child Welfare? I am not from here—who are they?"

"It's where the county takes care of abandoned kids and orphans and such. They find families for them to live with. I'd take her on, but I barely have space for my own. She'll be a hard one to place, bein' a half-breed and all. Sorry, I don't mean to insult you, sir, that's what we call 'em around here. Most people won't want one livin' in their home. Likely she'll have to work, so at least she'll get some food and a bed."

Indeed, as she spoke we saw a dark green car with some type of governmental insignia on the door pull up. You stepped out, as did a severe-looking woman who held your hand. You rushed over to your belongings, glanced up to the window and began to cry. I am not sure whether you saw us. Although the woman tried to hush you, your tears kept flowing. Without wasting any time, she gathered your belongings from the street and put them into the trunk of the car. Then she drove off with you, drove you out of my life forever.

"Yup, at least God bless her, she's separated from that crazy mother of hers."

I thanked the neighbor for all she relayed and motioned to Gül that we should leave. Despite her curiosity, I saw no reason to reveal anything else. Had I thought that an explanation of who I was would have served a purpose, my dear, I would have told her more. As we departed, I realized I still carried your sweater. Do you remember the one I am talking about, soft, light blue, with a little stitched rabbit? Did you notice it was missing? I put the sweater in my bag and on the train ride back kept peeking to make sure it wouldn't disappear.

35. THIS PLACE HAS NOT CARRIED OVER FROM THE PAST

Back at the hotel, I was beside myself. I paced the room, heartbroken.

"Gül, I started this journey certain of my actions. Yet desire blinded me, and delusion took over. Just as I cannot redo and fix my relations with my mother and father, I can't undo Nina's. I have come to a dead end."

Gül grabbed me and forced me to stop my furious pacing. "There are still other alternatives. We can talk to the Child Welfare authorities. Let me go and investigate the situation."

He dropped his hands from my shoulders. "We can't give up now, Kenzo."

"I am not giving up, but we need to step back. Meanwhile, you are right. Why don't you see if you can find someone who can help."

Within two days, Gül was able to arrange an appointment with the County Child Welfare Department. Even though Gül tried to comfort me and would hold me close, I had barely slept the night before, my monkey-mind going over all the possibilities yet never arriving at a resolution.

At the Child Welfare office, we joined a long line of women who were waiting for their appointments, many with mauling children. Many pairs of eyes looked at us, continuing to glance backwards as they gossiped with neighbors on the line. One woman looked at my robes and politely asked me which Catholic church I was from. She wanted me to bless her efforts to get her daughter back. Our conversation reminded me of my pilgrimage to

Eiheiji, where so many people presented their problems to me. As I had the same wish, I could only bow and wish her hope.

We inched forward until we were directed to a small office. I recognized the stern woman as the one who had accompanied you the other day. She never looked directly at me and focused her gaze on the papers in front of her.

"Mr. Ushido, my name is Mrs. Francini. Let's get on with this. So they tell me you say you are the girl's father, is that right?"

"Yes. But my name is..."

She cut me off. "That's strange, Nina says she doesn't know who her father is. She said that her mother told her he was supposedly a Japanese diplomat that got her pregnant and then abandoned her. She doesn't even know his name."

"She is correct, we have never met. And I used to be a diplomat, but not any longer. Until four days ago, I had not seen her mother since 1923."

"When an unmarried woman like Miss Dobrovska has a half-breed kid, we just have to throw our hands up. I can't imagine why she would want to bring a child like that into the world. If she stuck to her own race, her life would have been much easier. But I can't undo her poor decisions. Anyway, what do you want from us?"

"I want to meet my daughter and take care of her."

"You want to do what? What planet do you come from? Are you nuts?"

"I feel responsible for Nina. I only found out about her a few years ago. I arranged to come from Japan just to see her. I want to get to know her and now that her mother is gone, take care of her."

"Mister, do you know the slightest thing about children?"

"I know a child needs love and support from her father."

"A child needs a mother and now her's is in the looney bin. How is a man supposed to raise a child alone? What type of work did you say you do?"

"I'm a Zen priest on a peace mission to stop the world from war. I don't earn anything. I ask for donations to support myself as I go along."

"Whoa, now that's quite a highfaluting answer. You take the cake, mister. Just when I thought I heard every crazy answer in the book, you come in and knock them all out of the ballpark. Given what's going on in Europe and Japan, you are not doing so well in that line of work. Maybe you should get a better job."

She laughed loudly at what she thought was a joke. I glanced at Gül and could see that he was getting angry. But I had to try to remain calm if I was to succeed.

"Mrs. Francini, I know my task to seek peace is never-ending. Yet I must try. Maybe my answer starts by having peace and reconciliation in my own family. I was raised by my grandmother, after my mother died. I know how Nina must feel, especially now."

"From twenty years of experience in this job, I can say broken families lead to broken families. Nina needs to experience what it is like to be in a normal family. Honestly, it's probably too late for her to get back on track, but at least she will learn a good trade. She will be required to work day and night as the family's maid. That will teach her good habits."

"But what about her schooling? I understand she is supposed to graduate high school soon. She is so smart she might be valedictorian of her class."

"There is no way that a half-breed girl whose mother is at Pilgrim State is going to be allowed to be valedictorian of her class. You don't seem to know much about this country and what we stand for."

I was aghast at what I was hearing. But before I could formulate a response, she continued.

"I'm a busy woman and have heard enough already. This case is already closed. Here is what I will write in my report, an unknown Jap claims to be the girl's father, claims to be here on some delusional peace mission, has no fixed job, begs for money and wants to take care of a child that he knows nothing about. Did I miss anything?"

"I know my situation does not sound good, but she should know that her father loves her and cares for her."

"She will know nothing of the kind. She will never know you were here. Let me be blunt. Even as a half-breed, she is an American. We are not about to let some Jap kidnap one of our children and bring her somewhere to do who knows what. You Japs may think we are stupid, but we know who our enemies are. I don't know who sent you here but as difficult as this kid is, I am no traitor and will never let you see the girl. My job is to protect children from people like you."

"But I am not your enemy and have no connection to the Japanese government. I am a man of peace and only want to do what is right for Nina."

"Say what you want, you will never see the girl and will be arrested if you try. Now I suggest you leave the building and scurry back to whatever hole you crawled out of. I've wasted enough time with you already."

She stood up and two burly men entered promptly, one of them flexing his broad shoulders and arms.

"These men will escort you to the door. Don't try to do anything funny, I wouldn't want any trouble."

Gül and I said nothing on our way back to the hotel. Only then I allowed myself to break down, crying for the first time since my grandmother's death. Gül held me tight.

"I knew it was futile to try, but I had to do it. And the woman was right about one thing… what can I provide for her? Nothing. It sounds like Nina knows little to nothing about me. Given Elisa's state of mind whatever she does know cannot be good. I must remind myself that reality as defined by my mind is untrustworthy."

"Is your heart also untrustworthy? Be honest, Kenzo. What is it telling you?"

"It tells me to hold on to my love for her, even if it is only at a distance."

Gül pulled me into an embrace. "I am here to do what you need," he whispered, "for as long as you need."

Nina, even with all my training and understanding, loneliness, hurt and loss are not vanquished from my body and mind. In the days and weeks after you were taken away, I could barely leave my hotel room. I would sit and meditate and recall the scene, trying to figure out what I could have done differently. I blamed myself for what happened to you. If I had never written to Elisa, she might not have nourished fantasies of running away and abandoning you. As much as your situation growing up was difficult, it was all you knew. Like me, we both felt trapped by our childhoods and blame ourselves for our loneliness, our fears, and our instability. Yes, the repercussions will be long-lasting; however, your story is not ending; your next stories are just being written. In the future and with any luck by the time you are reading this, you will understand the strength you gained from adversity. Even as you carry hurt and pain inside you, you carry the knowledge that you have survived.

As for me, the causes and conditions of the present brought me to see you briefly and brought me your sweater, which I will treasure forever. Its presence still comforts me in this cold, dark room.

In the following weeks, Gül patiently provided solace and made sure I was eating and cared for. He would watch me as I sat to meditate and when I arose he would gently take me in his arms, stroke my face and shoulders and quietly assure me of his devotion and care. Slowly, he helped me regain my sense of self. He was able to find out where you were sent and a little about the family with which you were living. He and I reviewed the possible scenarios over and over, but we could not figure out a way forward.

Despite the hurt pounding my very soul, I tried to carry out the lectures I had planned. As was the case after Mitsu died, Gül's support helped me through my misery once again. Despite his love and support, I told him one morning that I needed to continue my trip. His face collapsed and he jumped out of bed.

"What are you talking about? It is virtually impossible to cross the Atlantic now. German U-boats are threatening all vessels, including passenger ships. And no one can guarantee your safety if you reach Europe. What use will you be over there?

"We've talked about this. I am dedicated to peace, to saving all beings. Delusion is everywhere, as it always has been—"

"Then why don't you save yourself?" he pleaded. I had never seen Gül so exasperated. "You believe it's not a delusion that you can save the world? Think about yourself, Kenzo. I want you to stay."

He paused for a moment, sat on the bedside and looked into my eyes as he spoke.

"After I left Paris, I had no expectation that I'd ever meet you again. Although I had strong feelings for you, I knew you needed to heal. So I left in order not to complicate matters. Reading your first letter to me a few years ago, I felt my heart leap again. And when we did finally meet, I realized that our shared connection was still burning. For the first time, I dared to have hope of a future with you by my side. Have you considered that maybe the unseen purpose of your arrival was to bring the two of us together again?"

"You are right, my old friend. You always knew what I felt, and you still do, even before I do. My heart says 'indulge me, stay here in Gül's embrace. If you do, maybe you will find a way to Nina.'"

"Yes, your heart is telling you the truth. How can you think of leaving? How can you think of leaving me?"

"I initiated my journey not knowing and not controlling what might befall me. As much as I want to remain in your arms, I still have a mission to carry out. My contacts in Paris and London are expecting me. I cannot just ignore them. I know that I can't prevent a war once guns are already blazing, yet I am called, as we all are, to put my efforts toward peace. I move about not knowing what well-being I may bring yet continue to live to provide good."

He studied me for a minute. He responded, shaking his head. "A spark rekindled our lives. I instantly recognized you were the one I had been waiting for. What of our well-being, doesn't that count for anything?"

I brushed his cheek and pulled him in closer.

"Gül, I ask you to please assist me on this path. If it includes my return here for us to live out our lives together with Nina, we will find out soon enough."

"Kenzo, your steadfastness of purpose is a trait I have always admired. If I thought I could make you stay, I would do anything to keep you here with me. But despite the hurt I feel now and will feel when you are gone, I know I can't stop you. My only hope is for you to be successful and return quickly. Let me find a ship for you. Since you are used to waiting, we can use the time we have as best as possible."

He embraced me and we kissed as if it was our first and last. Neither of us wanted to break away as the pain gave way to the urgency of longing. Love and passion know no time when we let go of the future.

True to his word, he found a ship bound for Calais leaving in a month. I had a renewed energy for my lectures and spoke more about right intention than I had previously. I thought about you continuously and pondered the right action for you and I. I lived with the pain of unknowingness. There is a Zen phrase that says 'Not-knowing is most-intimate." Not-knowing is anticipation without anticipation. It is the space between our breaths, the space between experiencing our senses. Not-knowing is the lack of expectations while embracing expectations. If each day is lived fully, time has no meaning, and everything is being. Most-intimate is an intimacy without any measurement or bounds. It is an experience of immersion and suchness with an awareness filled with our entire bodies. All of our experience, our wandering, searching and being is the most-intimate, not partially intimate, not sort of intimate but most-intimate. Most-intimate is full of deep emotion and feeling of the moment ranging from happiness to grief, fulfillment to emptiness, beauty to revulsion. Most-intimate wraps its arms around and hugs your body with its knowledge. If each day is lived fully, time has no meaning, and everything is being.

Gül and I lived in not-knowing and most-intimate, and on the day of departure we had to accept that our physical separation was imminent. As we observed our final hours together, we walked through the motions of normalcy, knowing all would rapidly change.

On the pier, just before I boarded the ship, we had our final conversation.

"Kenzo, remember our old friend, Edmund Kinver?"

"Of course. He had such a profound effect on our lives. Without him, no Elisa, no Nina. Another person irrevocably linked to our lives."

"He is in London and has moved up the ranks of the Foreign Ministry. I telegraphed him so he can support you once you arrive. I suspect he might be very useful, no matter what you do."

"Ever the caretaker, thank you for watching over me. Please don't ever doubt what you have done for me and how twice now you have lifted me out of dark and despairing times. We have always done our best together. Distance will not weaken our bond."

We kissed and embraced for a final time, taking each other in, not willing to let go. Only when the ship's horns announced the final call to board was I forced to break away and began my lonesome walk up the steep gangway. As we steamed away and the city receded into the distance, the sorrow and pain of these last months welled up.

I was completing the incomplete cycle of the return trip Elisa could never make. However, return trips are an illusion; a return is impossible as nothing is ever identical. We cannot even return to the second that just passed us. I held onto the railing with tears falling into the vastness of the sea.

36. WHEN YOU RETURN TO WHERE YOU ARE

Even though the German army was approaching the French border, like all Parisians, Gertrude and Alice were so confident they would be quickly repulsed that they already planned a victory party. They still remained on Rue de Fleurus and had plans to move permanently to Provence. As their friends were caught up in the political battles of the Spanish Civil War and almost all Americans had evacuated, their weekly salon was diminished. Whatever place I once had in their lives had disappeared, but I suppose the same was true for me. They were amused by my changes and downplayed my mission. Although the two of them had been such an important part of my earlier life, now they were merely part of my memories of that life.

Walking through the Embassy's doors also brought back a jolt of memory—my old apartment which Mitsu and I had shared, the hall that held his body for the funeral, the Ambassador's office where I encountered my father. I even saw a few people who remained from the time of my posting. Again, memories mixed freely with present day observations, the familiar with the unfamiliar, the old and the new, people once present and people now present.

My contact was well informed about the German approach. Although he had little to fear, he was concerned about the greater political implications. The Germans were in secret talks with the military, and soon enough he told me, that Japan would officially join the Axis nations. Given the control the military exerted over foreign policy, the war certainly would widen. He had even heard that plans were being developed to attack the U.S.

Given the dismal outlook for peace, he felt that there was little I could do right now. I was planning to meet the Ambassador as news broke that German troops slammed across the Maginot Line and were headed for Paris. Because of my lack of diplomatic status, my contact had me evacuated to Calais, where I caught a ship to England. I was but one of thousands of refugees trying to escape. As we floated out, other boats waited offshore to pick up more people. But there were hardly enough to make a dent in the snaking line of agitated people, stranded on the pier.

Tensions were high during the three-hour trip. The Germans had been attacking ports on the British mainland, so we were not safe until we disembarked. I relived a memory of fleeing previously, until I remembered that I was recalling Elisa's tale of her escape from Odessa decades ago.

A cheer rose from all parts of the ship as we docked at the port of Dover. Due to the ever-present worry over spies and Nazi-sympathizers, everyone was being questioned before we could disembark. The officers peppered me with questions about my reasons for entering the country and told me to report to a police station within two days of my arrival. I boarded a London-bound train and went directly to the Embassy. My Paris contact had wired them, so they were expecting my arrival.

"You have come just in time," the Ambassador said instead of a formal greeting. "We are closing the Embassy."

"Closing the Embassy? Why? The British and the Japanese have had a close, fruitful history, no?

"'Had' is the correct word. We are on different paths at this point in history. The British Empire is blocking our necessary and natural growth in Malay, Burma, Hong Kong, and Singapore. These should never have become their territories. Each is a lifeline, especially for rubber, oil and other resources. We just received orders to close the Embassy and evacuate Japanese citizens."

"What now? I promised the Ministry I would finish my work for them."

"What work? This telegram came for you today." He handed me an envelope and watched me closely as I opened it and shook out its contents.

"Uchida-san. Return immediately with the Embassy. You have a new position as the Soto Zen liaison in the War Ministry. The Emperor and Nation await your service."

I had to read the telegram three times before its meaning sunk in. Everything I had worked for and everything I had believed in was erased in three short lines. The Ambassador continued to watch me with a smirk on his face.

"Uchida-san, now you understand."

"Sir, I understand nothing. Don't you see that everything that was good about Japan is collapsing?"

"Collapsing, just the opposite, my monk. We are headed for the destiny the ancestors foresaw for us. The Emperor will make us whole again, and soon our power will be unbeatable. Once Britain is defeated, Germany and Japan will be the most powerful nations on earth. All the territory on the Asian continent to the north and south will be ours. Russia will be contained on one side by us and by Germany on the other. Germany will take control over Europe, just like they are doing in France. We will then gain the peace you so want."

"Ambassador, action that is not right action is delusion. Delusion brings suffering. You don't know what level of suffering you are opening up."

"This old-fashioned Zen nonsense is exactly why the Emperor has forsaken Buddhism for Shinto, the country's true and original religion. Our *samurai* lived by the code of right action. We are simply returning to our path shaped by the ages and don't have patience for those who will not stand for the homeland in its day of glory. As the Foreign Minster recently said, 'We each must extinguish ourselves through service to the state.' Report back to me tomorrow and we will get you ready for your new assignment. The Ministry is waiting. Glory to the Emperor."

Before I could respond, he turned and left the room. I stood there alone for several minutes, trying to take in what had just happened. Despite the crushing news, the Ambassador's worldview was only an echo of what I heard in Japan before I left. While an echo is just a diminished reminder of the original, it is also real. Where was the echo from my efforts? Why did I feel so bereft and alone? Failure upon failure briefly welled up and washed over me. Then I watched failure wash away into the distance, disappearing into the sands of eternity. Without fear's hold over me, I was left with the question that always remains, namely, what is next?

My contact at the Embassy, who was also shaken by the rapidity of the unfolding of events, rushed into the room. Silently, he walked me out a back entrance and we walked a few blocks away. Only after looking around to make sure no one was following us did he begin to speak.

"You already heard the news from the Ambassador. The wheels of war are set in motion. Once Paris falls, the Germans will attack Britain. Do you know that our contact at the Ministry has disappeared?"

"Gone? Where?"

"I don't know. The military has installed operatives in every Ministry post to do their bidding. Those who refused to go along were arrested and some were even killed on the spot."

"What will you do?"

"I have no choice but to return to the country I won't recognize. Working for the military is an impossibility for me. I am sure I will be removed from the Foreign Service. Or worse, they could decide that I am a traitor. But I have my family there and must go back for them. What about you and your War Ministry assignment?"

"I left Japan not expecting to return. My dreams were destroyed in New York, and now what little I had left of illusion has come to an end too. I am homeless and can only accept that fate for me. Yet despite feeling empty and drained right now, my peace mission is unchanged. I don't know the way forward, but that is not new for me. I have never known the way forward, except that I must take the first step."

"Are you saying you won't go back?"

"I can't return and go to the War Ministry. If Soto Zen has lost its way,

I have lost my place there. I will tell the Ambassador my answer tomorrow."

"If that is your answer, then we need to get you in hiding now. You cannot trust what he might do. Some of my other colleagues are going back in chains because they spoke their true feelings."

"Little surprises me anymore, although I have to admit to being a bit confused at the moment. I appreciate you helping me out. I hope this will not cause you any problems."

"We need to find you a place to live, although staying in London offers no easy solutions. Japanese foreigners must register at a police station and report there at least once a week. There is a curfew, which recently changed from 10 p.m. to 8 p.m. If you are caught on the streets later for any reason, you will be arrested."

"Ah, yes, the immigration officials told me I would have to register."

"I know where we can seek help. Let's get dinner and talk some more. There's a Japanese restaurant close by. The owner will be staying because he has a British wife."

We walked the several blocks to the restaurant. The sun was still high in the sky although it was nearing 6:30 pm. The houses were sturdy, made of stone, and the neighborhood appeared quite prosperous. As we poked through the *noren* of the *Fuji-ya*, a voice greeted us, "*Irasshai-mase,*" and a middle-aged man stepped forward and bowed.

"Consul, welcome back. I see you bring a visitor." He bowed a second time. "Kobayashi, pleased to meet you."

"Uchida, traveling from Tōkyō. I am glad to meet you."

"You come such a distance at a vexing time. Please sit. We will bring you *sake* and food shortly."

Fish, vegetables, rice, miso soup, pickles and several other items soon filled our table. Kobayashi-san joined us.

"What brings a traveling monk to England? The numbers of visitors have dwindled in these last weeks, and now the embassy will be leaving shortly on the *Fushimi Maru*. As the final passenger ship to return, I assume you will be leaving with them."

"I can honestly say I don't have specific plans yet."

"You have no plans? You are in London, there is a war going on in Europe, Japan is an ally of the Germans, and you have no plans? Excuse me for being so rude but I am a bit shocked. What kind of world do you think exists these days?"

"Maybe I also am shocked. I have traveled across the U.S. and then to France and now here. My purpose is to speak about the dharma of peace. Given the state of the world, my message is boundaryless. I arrived here today, escaping from France before the German troops reach Paris. Of course, when I made my plans, no one foresaw any of this."

"Yes, you are right. Surely you knew when leaving the States that you were coming into dangerous territory."

"I am not ignorant, as others may claim I am. I understand that war is a horrible, maybe an inevitable force for humans, a force not dissimilar to an earthquake. In Japan, we live daily knowing an earthquake may appear without warning, right?"

My listeners nodded in agreement.

"We prepare for them and build our buildings strong. Yet the moment the earth shakes, we can react from the spot we are at, both physically and spiritually. We cannot prevent earthquakes and cannot prevent a war which has already begun. We all contribute to war and subsequently we all contribute to peace. The conditions which brought me here are hopefully supporting the latter. My actions will be determined by what I find here."

He bowed. "I honor your resolute spirit, my friend. Yes, we need healing. About half of our community is leaving, including those who have lived here for decades. However, that is not a choice for me, as London is a home for my family. My children can barely speak our language and know nothing of Japanese life except for what we do here. They are British, as am I. I can't go to a place so foreign— despite being born there, it no longer exists for me. Here is where I will stay."

The consul spoke. "Kobayashi-san, our friend needs a place to hide for the next few days until the rest of us leave, can you aid him? I can identify some housing for him to move to once we abandon our living quarters."

"I understand the seriousness of the times, so of course he can remain here. We have an extra room in the back. Later, the charity society might also be able to assist. We had our heyday during the Emperor's visit just a few short years ago, when London was awash in Japanese painting, culture and food. That seems like another lifetime now. But we still take care of each other and will need that care even more now."

"Thank you, Kobayashi-san, for being willing to take care of my friend."

"Yes, thank you for your generosity," I replied. "I look forward to being of any service I can."

"*Oyasumināsai.* Roshi, I wish you the best, and please say some prayers for me and my family."

We bowed, and as soon as he left the owner took me to a room and introduced me to his family.

Another room, another home, another moment.

37. THE WIND MAKES FRAGRANT THE CREAM OF THE LONG RIVER

I did stay in London. In any moment, there are unlimited possibilities. Our mind tries to limit them and convince itself that the best outcome will be chosen. Later, decisions are revisited, and either the mind chides itself for making the wrong decision or praises itself for making the best.

When I left New York, my sweet, dear daughter, I decided the time had come to stop such endless beating up of myself. Glimpsing you briefly demonstrated that my longings and desires were indeed endless. While you and I come from a family lineage full of complicated stories and unanswered questions, so does everyone else. I believed I was the only one, the only one who did not know his mother, who never enjoyed the love of his father, the only one who endured the death of a loved one. Writing this sentence reminds me how ridiculous I can be and how lonely I can make the world appear. Yet how can I be lonely if we are all connected, and part of the same world?

The Kenzo I knew changed the instant I knew of your existence. Writing to you has revealed to me how you have transformed the earlier parts of my story without ever physically meeting. You are imbued in everything I have ever done and thought about. I want you to understand how life-changing you have been for me.

As to you and your reactions to my letter, I vainly hope you can learn from my mistakes and delusions. As you read this, your vision of your own personhood will change. I have always been part of you since before you were conceived. We were never separated. You carry the history of thousands of generations from different parts of the world within you. You are a continuation of lives long gone and lives yet to live in the future. One day you may have children, and your children will have children. Your story is being written as you live. New chapters will be added on each step of your path. Your life will make sense one day and appear meaningless the next. That is how we humans are.

The truth Dōgen revealed is: Everything we need we have; everything we need to know, we know. We are just asked to accept that truth. The entire search for enlightenment comes down to accepting that we are already enlightened. Enlightenment will not prevent you from hurt, and feelings of loss and sorrow. Acceptance will allow you to live a wonderful and miraculous existence and to feel joy even within pain.

None of the recent events has convinced me that Dōgen was wrong. Although all of the Embassy left on the *Fushimi Maru*, the joy of rebirth, present in each moment, kept me going. Even without any Buddhist temples, I found Buddha-nature everywhere in the people I met and the places I visited. As the war announced itself by the bombs, explosions and devastation, we practiced compassion and sharing. Fear was rampant, and so was the desire to live. I have a memory of those first days of the bombing, before everyone got used to the randomness of the noise of the bombs falling, numbed by the screams and the sounds of broken glass, crumbling buildings, and fire roaring through neighborhoods. What I remember is the sound of a woman singing, a song declaring that she was alive and still had hope and joy within her. Her unknown voice spoke to my heart and the hearts of others, holding us secure as debris was raining down.

Fear is ever-present as an emotion that drives desire. Fear that we are lacking and missing out, fear that others already have what we need or want, fear that life will end. Fear breeds fear. Fear can also be a warning. What is changing now? What is arising that I must pay attention to at this very breath?

Kobayashi-san was very helpful getting me established and taking care of me. I gave several talks at University College regarding the dharma during wartime. I appreciated that I could publicly speak about the dharma and peace. I knew the British government was following me and attending my lectures. Immigration officials and police interviewed me numerous times, trying in vain to understand what I was doing here. Most foreigners from Germany, including Jewish refugees, in addition to British anti-war intellectuals, were being interred in camps on the Isle of Man. I knew my time was limited, yet, my dear, I always have known that.

I was not afraid when the police knocked on the door of my little flat, and searched my belongings and papers. I was not even afraid when they arrested me, interrogated me and decided to hold me prisoner in this humble room. I could not fear dying because I already knew death would be my end. So, when they assigned me the job of cleaning the debris to search for the bodies of the injured and dead, of young children and adults of every age, I was joyful. I remembered the tale my father recounted of grandmother and the doves. Each day here I feel her presence among the doves flying above us as we work. Although the work is arduous, the task is much easier for me than for the women who work alongside me. I don't know the stories or the relationships of any of the bodies I find in the way they do. I approach each discovery in equanimity without having to face someone I knew from my school days or from the greengrocer's. My daily life is a prayer for the dead and the living. This is my gift. This is what I do.

I am unafraid of hard work; digging, searching and hauling debris reminded me of assisting *Oshō-sama* on the temple grounds. The work was never finished there, nor will it be finished here.

I am not living better or worse than my neighbors. When bombs pummel the streets, the prisoners and the free live equal lives. I lived on a *tatami* at Eiheiji; here, my narrow bed and room are spacious. I awaken at sunrise, as is my habit, and do not require any light in the evening to prolong my day further. I have a short period to write before exhaustion takes over.

After the adjoining building was incinerated by the bombs, my windows were blackened by the inferno. The next morning, the sun's light barely came through. I wiped away the char and now faced a mass of rubble. Nothing remained, and we could not find bodies within the smoking rubble.

The children returned days later, playing on the concrete slabs that were once walls and ceilings, digging out pieces of debris, turning broken pieces of wood into rifles for their play battles against the Germans. They play quietly, worried to disturb the eerie silence which has settled over most of the block. A scrawny orange tabby cat hunts a rat for breakfast. The rats are the only animals flourishing these days. Despite their equal weight, the cat wins that battle, triumphantly parading his meal prior to relishing his feast.

Last night I heard a voice outside my window. "Kenzo," it meekly cried. "Kenzo, we are waiting for you."

"Who is this?"

"We have always been here calling for you. This is the first time you have answered. In the daylight you will see."

Although unexpected, the voice was somehow familiar and comforting and it gave me a peace of mind as I fell asleep coddled by its familiarity. The next morning when I was allowed out, I called out. "Mysterious and comforting voice, where are you? You promised to show yourself in the sunlight."

I didn't receive a response, yet I was motivated to carefully walk around the ruins where the children had played. There I saw a pink rose poking around some fallen blocks.

"Yes, here we are," the flower replied as I approached. "Our voices are always here."

"But I hear you now. How is that?"

"Despite this unfortunate rain of concrete, our roots are deep and continue to nourish us. Our tendrils search for the warmth of the sun. This life is hard, yet we know no other life. But you know that from your own life. Despite your years of wandering and questioning you now know that the little boy who once talked to us alongside his grandmother is still the same boy that can hear us now."

"You say 'us', who is 'us'? I see you alone."

"We are always present, our roots spread around the world, our wings cross the skies, and our fins swim the eternal sea. You have similarly roamed the earth, connecting the Kenzo from birth to the Kenzo standing before me. Your grandmother's grandmother and your daughter's daughters surround you in this moment, as they always have and always will. You too have roots that will live on when you fade just like we are fated to do soon."

The ease which had come to my body and mind in the last weeks suddenly grew more profound. A gentle wind arose and one-by-one ruffled and lifted the petals of the rose. One landed on my shoulder while the rest floated into the morning light, dancing and twirling until they disappeared from sight.

I take solace in Gül's knowledge of my whereabouts in London. We telegraphed each other almost daily from my arrival until the day I was arrested. Our simple daily words provided comfort. From afar I feel his attachment, as he feels mine. We have lived enough to recognize that physical togetherness is not needed in order for love to be shared.

I warned Gül that he mustn't worry should he not hear from me. The most likely reason would be my arrest. Once I stopped telegraphing him, he contacted Edmund, who came on a visit. He was a man beaten by the effects of the bombing and war. For a short period, we resumed the *joie de vivre* we had at Maxim's, and laughter brightened this dreary space. Then the seriousness set back in.

"Kenzo, I am afraid for you, old chap—I have no power to get you released from here. I have tried and been rebuffed by my superiors."

"Edmund, I am not afraid, so do not fear for me. I have one request that I hope you can fulfill. You will be shocked to hear this: I have a daughter named Nina. Elisa is her mother. If you can come back, I can tell you more."

"Now that is something I am curious about which, besides, seems even more implausible than viewing you in priest's robes. What is your request?"

"You can see this stack of paper that I have been writing. I am writing Nina and telling her my story as best as I can...actually our story—you too play an influential role early on. I will be finished in the next days. Can you retrieve it and, once the war is over, send it to Gül? He will assure that one day Nina will be able to read it. Assuming you can agree to this, there is nothing else I will need."

"Of course. I'd be honored to do that favor for both of you."

We bade each other goodbye and swore we would meet at least one more time.

If these pages ever get to you, dearest Nina, it means that the war must have ended and that you have met Gül. Think of him as your father, as he is the last survivor of our group, and hopefully physically present in your life. He is an honorable, kind and loving man. He will have his own version of our shared history to impart.

As I write these last words, I have the package neatly waiting to be tied up, with Gül's name and address on the cover. The rose petal is pressed into the first pages.

Even when all is bleak, hope drives us to act as if the bright future were near. Punna, one of Buddha's earliest students, wrote this poem reflecting on everything she had learned:

"...When you are as full as the full moon—burst open. Make the dark night shine."

Nina, burst your heart open. When you do, you will feel mine beating as one with yours. Your father has always been part of you and therefore never distant from you. Your father's love has grown and multiplied in tandem with your own love. You only need to think of me, and I will be beside you. I know this to be true because that is what I am doing right now, and you are here. So close, so still, so dear.

Appendix 1: *The Genjō Kōan*: Actualizing the Fundamental Point Written in 1233 and revised in 1252 by Eihei Dōgen, Translated by Robert Aitkin and Kazuaki Tanahashi

1

When all dharmas are Buddha-Dharma, there are delusion, realization, practice, birth and death, buddhas and sentient beings.

2

When the myriad dharmas are without a self, there is no delusion, no realization, no Buddha, no sentient being, no birth and death.

3

Buddha way, basically, is leaping clear of abundance and lack; thus there are birth and death, delusion and realization, sentient beings and buddhas. Yet in attachment blossoms just fall, and in aversion weeds just spread.

4

To carry the self forward and illuminate myriad things is delusion. That myriad dharmas come forth and illuminate the self is enlightenment.

5

Those who have great realization of delusion are buddhas; those who are greatly deluded about realization are sentient beings. Further, there are those who continue realizing beyond realization, who are in delusion throughout delusion.

6

When buddhas are truly buddhas, they do not necessarily notice that they are buddhas. However, they are actualized buddhas, who go on actualizing Buddha.

7

When you see forms or hear sounds, fully engaging body-and-mind, you intuit dharmas intimately. Unlike things and their reflections in the mirror, and unlike the moon and its reflection in the water, when one side is illumined, the other side is dark.

8

To study the buddha way is to study the self. To study the self is to forget the self. To forget the self is to be actualized by myriad things. When actualized by myriad things, your body and mind as well as the bodies and minds of others drop away. No trace of realization remains, and this no-trace continues endlessly.

9

When you first seek dharma, you imagine you are far away from its environs. At the moment when dharma is correctly transmitted, you are immediately your original self.

10

When you ride in a boat and watch the shore, you might assume that the shore is moving. But when you keep your eyes closely on the boat, you can see that the boat moves. Similarly, if you examine myriad things with a confused body and mind you might suppose that your mind and nature are permanent. When you practice intimately and return to where you are, it will be clear that nothing at all has unchanging self.

10B

Firewood becomes ash, and it does not become firewood again. Yet, do not suppose that the ash is after and the firewood before. You should understand that firewood abides in the phenomenal expression of firewood, which fully includes before and after and is independent of before and after. Ash abides in the phenomenal expression of ash, which fully includes before and after. Just as firewood does not become firewood again after it is ash, you do not return to birth after death.

This being so, it is an established way in Buddha-dharma to deny that birth turns into death. Accordingly, birth is understood as no-birth. It is an unshakable teaching in the Buddha's discourse that death does not turn into birth. Accordingly, death is understood as no-death.

Birth is an expression complete this moment. Death is an expression complete this moment. They are like winter and spring. You do not call winter the beginning of spring, nor summer the end of spring.

11

Enlightenment is like the moon reflected on the water. The moon does not get wet, nor is the water broken. Although its light is wide and great, the moon is reflected even in a puddle an inch wide. The whole moon and the entire sky are reflected in dewdrops on the grass, or even in one drop of water.

Enlightenment does not divide you, just as the moon does not break the water. You cannot hinder enlightenment, just as a drop of water does not hinder the moon in the sky.

The depth of the drop is the height of the moon. Each reflection, however long or short its duration, manifests the vastness of the dewdrop, and realizes the limitlessness of the moonlight in the sky.

12

When dharma does not fill your whole body and mind, you think it is already sufficient. When dharma fills your body and mind, you understand that something is missing.

For example, when you sail out in a boat to the middle of an ocean where no land is in sight, and view the four directions, the ocean looks circular, and does not look any other way. But the ocean is neither round nor square; its features are infinite in variety. It is like a palace. It is like a jewel. It only looks circular as far as you can see at that time. All things are like this.

Though there are many features in the dusty world and the world beyond conditions, you see and understand only what your eye of practice can reach. In order to learn the nature of the myriad things, you must know that although they may look round or square, the other features of oceans and mountains are infinite in variety; whole worlds are there. It is so not only around you, but also directly beneath your feet, or in a drop of water.

13

A fish swims in the ocean, and no matter how far it swims there is no end to the water. A bird flies in the sky, and no matter how far it flies there is no end to the sky. However, the fish and the bird have never left their elements. When their activity is large their field is large. When their need is small their field is small. Thus, each of them totally covers its full range, and each of them totally experiences its realm. If the bird leaves the air it will die at once. If the fish leaves the water it will die at once.

Know that water is life and air is life. The bird is life and the fish is life. Life must be the bird and life must be the fish.

Besides this, further steps can be taken. Thus there are practice and enlightenment which encompasses both eternal life and unlimited life.

Now if a bird or a fish tries to reach the end of its element before moving in it, this bird or this fish will not find its way or its place. When you find your place where you are, practice occurs, actualizing the fundamental point; for the place, the Way, is neither large nor small, neither yours nor others'. The place, the Way, has not carried over from the past, and it is not merely arising now.

Accordingly, in the practice-enlightenment of the Buddha Way, to attain one dharma is to penetrate one dharma; to meet one practice is to sustain one practice.

Here is the place; here the Way unfolds. The boundary of realization is not distinct, for the realization comes forth simultaneously with the mastery of Buddha-dharma.

14

Do not suppose that what you attain becomes your knowledge and is grasped by your consciousness. Although actualized immediately, the inconceivable may not be apparent. Its appearance is beyond your knowledge.

Zen master Baoche of Mount Mayu was fanning himself. A monk approached and said, "Master, the nature of wind is permanent and there is no place it does not reach. Why, then, do you fan yourself?"

"Although you understand that the nature of the wind is permanent," Baoche replied, "you do not understand the meaning of its reaching everywhere."

"What is the meaning of its reaching everywhere?" asked the monk again. The master just kept fanning himself. The monk bowed deeply.

The actualization of the Buddha-dharma, the vital path of its correct transmission, is like this. If you say that you do not need to fan yourself because the nature of wind is permanent and you can have wind without fanning, you will understand neither permanence nor the nature of wind. The nature of wind is permanent, because of that, the wind of the Buddha's house brings forth the gold of the earth and makes fragrant the cream of the long river.

APPENDIX II JAPANESE WORDS

Butsuden- Buddha Hall, a teaching hall in a Zen temple

Dokusan- a teaching meeting with one's Zen teacher to discuss one's practice and questions that arise.

Kaimyō- a Buddhist name given at death

Kanji- a system of Japanese writing using Chines characters.

*Kanpai-*a salutation when drinking

Kechimyaku- the bloodline transmission of every teacher from Buddha through Dōgen to the teachers in Japan

Keisaku- a long, flat stick used in Zen temples to whack a meditator's shoulders if they are slouching or falling asleep

*Kinhin-*walking meditation

*Mago-*grandson

*Obāchan-*grandmother

*Ochaya-*teahouse

*Ojīchan-*grandfather

*Okāchan/Okāsan-*mother

*Okesa-*a Zen priest's mantle or robe that is worn draped diagonally over the left shoulder and under the right armpit

*Omamori-*a small amulet from a temple that resembles a tied bag which offers protection

*Onsen-*a hot springs bath

*Oshō-sama-*teacher

*Otōchan-*father

Noren-A small curtain over the entrance of a teahouse, restaurant or bar

Raku-a type of pottery

Rakusu-a traditional Japanese garment worn around the neck of Zen Buddhists who have taken the precepts.

Roshi-teacher

-san-a formal honorific added to names

Sanmom or *sammom*-A large gate of a Zen temple

Seiza-a sitting position on one's knees with the legs folded underneath

Sensei-teacher

Sento-a bathhouse in building

Shinkantaza-sitting meditation; Zazen

Shudō-samurai same-sex relationships

Shunga-Japanese erotic etchings

Soji-the ritual cleaning of a Zen temple and its grounds conducted in silence as another form of meditation

Sōtō-the main branch of Zen Buddhism in Japan

Sotaba-a funerary wooden stick inscribed with a person's name and dates

Tangaryō-a ritual waiting period before entering a monastery for a practice period

Tatami-thick woven straw mats that cover the floor of Japanese homes and temples

Zafu- a meditation cushion

Zazen- seated meditation

ACKNOWLEDGMENTS

One of the blessings of writing this novel is that every day it gave me a reason to reflect on my Aunt Nina Friedberg Uchida, who died in 2016. Nina was with me from the moment I was born and there was not a world without her love, her smile, her restless energy and her optimism that we shall overcome some day. She engaged with everyone wherever they were and sought out those that were alone, needed help or wanted to change this world. With all our current uncertainty, I feel strengthened by her guidance, commitment to the movement and struggle and her every ready activism. She is not gone, her energy is there when you call on it, just like Joe Hill in the old folk song. Say her name and your fears will be vanquished and your direction will be clear.

Nina never knew her Japanese father, but during a visit when she was 91-years-old, she told me that her children had discovered that in the 1930s her father had traveled from Japan to NY where she had been living with her mother. With a gleam in her eyes, she said, "I know he was looking for me." Instantly, I had a vision of his story and why despite this journey, did he not find his daughter. I told Nina that I wanted to write this story and she unsurprisingly replied, "Alan, men are always appropriating women's stories. I have tried to write my own story for many years. But it's too late now and I know I will never do it. You are a good writer and so please do it."

Little did she or I know the journey this story would take me on. And unfortunately, she died later that year before I had a chance to begin writing. Inspired by the little I or other family members knew about Nina's parents life, I threw myself into research and the history of the times in such disparate places as Constantinople, Paris, Japan and New York between the two world wars.

An early discovery was of biography of Frederick Bruce Thomas, by Vladimir Alexandrov called "The Black Russian." Thomas, an African-American opened a nightclub in Constantinople called Maxim's, where in real-life Nina's mother briefly worked as a cigarette girl and supposedly met her Japanese diplomat lover.

Later on, another key moment occurred in an email exchange with Dr. Rustin Gates at Bradley University, perhaps the foremost U.S. expert on Kosai Uchida, the Foreign Minister and two-time temporary Prime Minister of Japan, who the family and Nina assumed was her grandfather. When Dr. Rustin said Kosai only had a daughter with his wife, although there were some rumors of illegitimate male offspring, as a novelist a new storyline emerged for me.

In addition to the historical period between the two world wars, I needed to learn more about same-sex male relationships in Japan. In 2017, the Japan Society of New York, hosted a groundbreaking exhibition called "A Third Gender: Beautiful Youths in Japanese Prints." This exhibition broke open the previously unnoticed art of *wakashu,* teenage boys who could live as a man or a woman. Additional research led me to "The Gay of the Samurai" by Koichi, (tofugo.com/Japan/gay-samurai) summarizing the scholarship of same-sex relationships prior to the Meji Restoration.

Most of what I have learned about writing has come from reading novels. The Gay Boys Book Club in San Francisco, of which I have been a member for 23 years, provided useful feedback and criticism in an early draft and was the encouragement I needed to continue on.

Special thanks are due to my Zen teacher Kikū Hōetsu Christina Lenherr for encouraging and guiding my entry into Zen and opening my life up to the living everyday with an open heart. Former San Francisco Zen Center (SFZC) Central Abbott Rinso Ed Satizahn introduced me to the wonders and beauty of Dōgen's "Genjo Kōan." Curious readers should seek out Shohaku Okumura Roshi's book, "Realizing Genjokoan" which unlocks the meanings behind meanings of Dōgen's text. Zen Monks Rev. Daigan

Gaither, co-founder of SFZC Queer Dharma and Myogan Djinn Gallagher, resident teacher at Black Mountain Zen Center, Belfast provided valuable insights into life as a Zen priest and temple rituals. Hoitsu Suzuki Roshi and Shungo Suzuki Roshi and their family hosted me on my visit to the Zen temple Rinso-in in Yaizu, Japan. The detailed descriptions of life at Eiheiji would not have been possible without a retreat at the monastery supported by Eiheiji's International Department. Finally, Leo Egashira provided valuable guidance on the validity of my Japanese cultural references and use of terminology.

Over the last several years, I am thankful for a number of other readers: Kathy Anderson, Joe Okonkwo, Sylvia Furstenburg, Jose Medio, Joel Evans, Gary Nielson, Deborah Isaly van Dommelen and R'Sue Caron. Edmund Preston served as a model for the British Deputy Ambassador in the book with all of his mischievous and loving intent.

Jim Currier has always been a wonderful supporter of my writing and published an early excerpt called *The Kenzo Kōan,* for the Summer Edition of Chelsea Station Magazine.

Special thanks go to Shana McNair and Scott Wolven at The Writers Hotel in New York for their detailed feedback and the opportunity to workshop the book with other excellent writers. When I was scheduled to give a reading at the KGB Bar in New York's Lower East Side, I discovered that the bar was the building that originally housed the Ukrainian Labor Hall, a place well known to Nina's mom and my family. My grandfather spent many hours in that building in political and trade union meetings, cultural festivals, singing in a chorus and certainly drinking 4 Roses whiskey in the bar.

Elizabeth Kracht was instrumental in a major developmental edit and Elizabeth Risberg and Jan Rylewicz made sure my errant commas found correct homes and my dyslexic word combinations were untangled.

Final thanks go to Sven Davidson and the rest of the crew at Rebel Satori Press. Without them, you would not be reading this book.

Printed in the USA
CPSIA information can be obtained
at www.ICGtesting.com
JSHW081750251023
50808JS00004B/112

DAS BEETHOVEN
Papagenogasse 6, 1060 Wien
T: +43 (0)1/587 44 820

www.hotelbeethoven.at
info@hotelbeethoven.at

April 28
April 19
A 13

	1,022.76
	47.64
Target	
cameron Cafe	16.65
	187.82
Safeway	
	815.00
Unitree	
	1.67
transaction fee	
	.27
"	
	.54
"	
Dunkin Donuts	
Naked	9.16
	10.92
starbucks	11.44
taxi	17.29